MW00464494

# MY RULES

# ALSO BY T L SWAN

*My Temptation*
*The Bonus*
*Stanton Adore*
*Stanton Unconditional*
*Stanton Completely*
*Stanton Bliss*
*Marx Girl*
*Gym Junkie*
*Dr. Stanton*
*Dr. Stantons: The Epilogue*
*Mr. Masters*
*Mr. Spencer*
*Mr. Garcia*
*The Italian*
*Ferrara*
*Our Way*
*Play Along*
*Find Me Alastar*
*The Stopover*
*The Takeover*
*The Casanova*
*The Do-Over*
*Miles Ever After*
*Mr. Prescott* (coming 2025)

# MY RULES

## KINGSTON LANE

### T L SWAN

 Montlake

Text copyright © 2024 by T L Swan
All rights reserved.

Published by Montlake, Seattle

www.apub.com

Amazon, the Amazon logo, and Montlake are trademarks of Amazon.com, Inc., or its affiliates.

ISBN-13: 9781662512759
eISBN-13: 9781662512766

Cover design by @blacksheep-uk.com
Cover photography by Michelle Lancaster

Printed in the United States of America

# GRATITUDE

*The quality of being thankful;*
*readiness to show appreciation for and to return*
*kindness.*

*I would like to dedicate this book to the alphabet, for those twenty-six letters have changed my life. Within those twenty-six letters, I found myself and live my dream.*
*Next time you say the alphabet, remember its power.*

Number 14

Number 13

Number 12

Number 11

THE GREEN

Number 10

Number 9

Number 8

Number 7

Number 6

TO THE CITY

KINGSTON
LANE

# Map Key:

Number 6 - The Navy House

Number 7 - Winston Brown's House

Number 8 - Ethel Davidson's House

Number 9 - Antony Deluca's House

Number 10 - Rebecca & John Dalton's House

Number 11 - Juliet Drinkwater's House

Number 12 - Carol Higginbottom's House

Number 13 - Henley James' House

Number 14- Blake Grayson's House

# Chapter 1

*Blake*

"I'm going to book the flights tonight," I say as I push through the heavy glass door leading into the suit shop.

"No." Henley sighs. "Do you even listen to me at all?"

"Not if I can help it."

Antony smirks as he listens.

In a world full of chaos, there's only one thing that I know for certain.

Family matters, and I'll do everything in my power to take care of them, even if they don't want me to.

I walk up the aisle of suits and begin to flick through them, annoyed. "You're having a bachelor weekend whether you like it or not," I tell him.

Henley is getting married, and it's up to us to make sure we go all out to celebrate the occasion, because if Antony and I don't make this happen . . . who will?

"I don't need a bachelor weekend," Henley replies. "I just want a quiet poker night at home."

"Ugh." I roll my eyes. "This is why we are never getting married, Ant; damn woman has his balls in her purse. He's that unbalanced; it's a wonder he can fucking walk."

Antony keeps looking through the suits. "What look are we going for here?"

"I don't know, something weddingish," Henley mutters, distracted.

"Well, what look do you want?" I snap, annoyed. "White jacket, black jacket, fucking green pants. Fairy. What?"

"What *is* up your *ass* today?" Henley fires back.

"You and your ridiculous notion of no bachelor weekend. It's a rite of passage to go to Vegas to be wild, watch strippers, smoke cigars, and drink all the alcohol."

Henley curls his lip in disgust. "Strippers could not be further from my mind."

I exhale heavily and pinch the bridge of my nose. "Are you hearing this bullshit, Antony?"

"Unfortunately," Ant replies as he keeps looking.

Henley answers his phone. "Hey." He smiles as he listens. "Yeah, okay." He glances up. "You two want to go to Marconi's with the girls tonight?"

"Yeah." Ant nods as he continues to flick through the suits.

"Nothing better to do, I guess," I say with a shrug. I'm not interested in dinner; all I really want to do is lock in Vegas.

"Uh-huh," Henley replies. "Just looking now." He listens again. "I don't know, send me a picture." He twists his lips as he looks around the shop. "I can't see any."

"Is that Juliet?" I ask.

He nods, and I snatch the phone from his hand. "Jules."

"Blake," she replies. I can hear that she's smiling.

"You need to talk to your pussy-whipped boyfriend; he thinks he isn't having a bachelor weekend in Vegas."

"Good," she replies. "I'm good with that plan."

"What is wrong with you people?" I roll my eyes. "I guess you're having a knitting party for your bachelorette party, are you? Could you two be any more fucking boring?"

"Probably not. Listen, Henley is a big boy. If he wants to go to Vegas, he can go to Vegas; it has nothing to do with me."

"Ahh." My mouth falls open, and I put the phone on speaker. "Can you repeat that, Jules?" I point to the phone as I hold it out for the boys to hear.

"Henley is a big boy, and if he wants to go to Vegas, he can go to Vegas," Juliet repeats.

"Thank you." I smile. "This is why we are marrying you, sweet Juliet."

"I'm not marrying you, Blake," she replies dryly.

"So you think." Antony smirks as he goes back to flicking through the suits.

Henley holds his hand out for the phone.

"Goodbye." I end the call and pass him back his phone.

"I wanted to speak to her," Henley replies.

"Tough, she's gone and we have things to do." I walk over to the rack of suits. "I think you need a white jacket and a black bow tie, and we'll wear black dinner suits."

"Why black dinner suits?" Ant asks.

"Because I look good in a black dinner suit."

Henley rolls his eyes, unimpressed.

The salesman comes out of the back. "Can I help you?" he asks us.

"Yes, please," Antony replies. "Henley here is getting married, and we want him to look as pretty as a picture for his big special day."

Henley gives Ant the side-eye, and I smirk. "And we're going to need a white jacket."

3

The cool, crisp flavor cleanses my palate; there's nothing better than a cold beer after a hard, long day.

The restaurant is loud with chatter, and a tantric beat sounds through the oversize speakers. Marconi's is the hippest bar in town—luckily, because we come here way too often.

My eyes linger on the opposite end of the table, and as Rebecca licks the salt from her margarita glass, I feel it all the way to the tip of my cock.

Her dark hair is up in a high ponytail, her rounded, full breasts peek out of the V-neck in her dress, and as she smiles I'm quite sure that somewhere in the distance I hear a choir of angels break into song.

Ugh. I sip my beer, unimpressed with where my mind is going . . . again.

*This woman . . .*

She's my neighbor, my friend's ex-wife . . . my best friend, a member of my own group of friends, a quite close one, actually, and frankly, she's impossible to avoid.

Rebecca.

Beautiful, smart, and funny. She's the whole package.

We're in the friend zone.

So deeply that she thinks of me as a big brother, but behind closed doors, I carry a sordid secret: I'm the big brother that fantasizes about doing unspeakable things to her body.

In my dreams she uses me just as hard as I use her.

"You seeing Cindy tonight?" Henley asks.

"Yeah." I sip my beer, my eyes lingering on the forbidden fruit.

"When's her expiry date?" Antony asks.

"Must be coming on soon, surely," Hen replies.

Rebecca laughs out loud at the other end of the table, and my stomach flutters.

4

*Cut. It. Out.*

Rebecca Dalton is as far from my type as physically possible, a good girl who's still in the trenches as she gets over her marriage breakdown. Her husband cheated on her with his secretary.

*What a fucking idiot.*

"Well?" Henley asks, interrupting my thoughts once more.

"What?" I glance over to him.

He raises his eyebrow in question. "Cindy's expiry date?"

"Oh . . ." I sip my beer. "I don't know. She's not Mrs. Grayson, that's for sure."

"Nobody will ever be Mrs. Grayson," Ant chips in.

"What makes you say that?" I ask.

"The kind of women you like." Antony widens his eyes, and Henley chuckles.

"Fuck off." I sigh, unimpressed. "We can't all be fucking boring like you two."

He's nailed it in one . . . there probably won't be a Mrs. Grayson. I can't help that I have a definitive type, and if I could change it, I would.

I like the bad girls, the ones with sexual stamina who can fuck as well as I can.

As much as I want them to, innocent women do nothing for me.

If I do end up on a date with one, I find myself glancing at my watch all night, wishing for it to be over.

Rebecca stands, and my eyes drop to her defined quad muscles in her minidress. I sip my beer as I imagine them around my ears.

"You're drooling," Henley mutters under his breath.

I snap my eyes away, rattled at being caught. "Fuck off."

"You need to make a move already," Antony whispers.

"I'm not making a move." I sip my beer again as I watch her walk to the bar. "We're not like that."

"Well, while you're not being like that, she's going to fuck her ex out of her system with every Tom, Dick, and Harry," Henley replies. He taps his bottle with mine and winks sarcastically. "It's going to be fun to watch you watch her."

"Fuck you."

I clench my jaw. I hate the thought of her sleeping around, but there's no way around it; I know she needs to do it. She's only ever slept with one man before, and as her friend I want her to have fun and experience the world.

"You're an idiot," Antony mutters under his breath. "Someone's going to steal her right out from under you."

"Only she isn't under him." Henley winks.

"You know what this is?" Antony replies.

"Karma."

"Shut. Up. Don't you two have anything better to do than stalk me and my love life? It's fucking creepy."

"Not really." Hen smirks.

"Anyway . . . karma has nothing to do with this. Rebecca and I are just friends."

"You wish."

We fall silent as she comes back to the table and sits down; she glances up, and our eyes lock. She smiles softly as she pushes her chair in, and my dick throbs in appreciation.

Yeah . . . this has to stop.


*Rebecca*

"Everything all right over here, ladies?" Ronald smiles as he bends down and kisses Taryn's cheek.

"Perfect, Ronny." She beams up at him.

"Let me know if anyone gives you any trouble, okay?" Ronald calls to the table.

"Thanks, man." The boys all politely smile and nod.

Life is weird. If someone told me five years ago that my group of friends would be the people who live in my cul-de-sac, neighbors, I would have thought they were crazy.

But here I am, surrounded by the best friends a girl could ever ask for. Moving to Kingston Lane was the best thing I ever did. There's Henley, Blake, and Antony. Henley is an engineer, Blake is a doctor, and Antony is a lawyer. Then there's Juliet—she's a nurse and engaged to Henley; they met when Juliet moved next door. Chloe is Juliet's friend who I've also become close to; she's a nurse. And then there's Taryn. Taryn moved in with her mother when her marriage broke down. At the beginning she drove us all mad, but her weirdness and wild ways are infectious, and she's become a friend.

Taryn is sleeping with the manager of the club and gets us the best table and half-price drinks every time we come here.

"I'll swing by on my way home?" Ronny asks Taryn. He gives her a sexy wink, and his eyes drop down to her large breasts.

"I'll be waiting," she gushes.

Eww . . . Taryn has the worst taste in men. Ronald gives me the ick . . .

Total sleazebag vibes, but somehow she thinks he's the hottest man on the planet.

I don't know much about men, but I do know that Taryn's boobs attract a hell of a lot of them. They're like a Venus flytrap . . . for sleazebags.

"Here he is now." Chloe stands and waves.

A handsome man with honey-brown curls walks through the restaurant, looks over, and smiles broadly before waving and heading toward us. Chloe has a new boyfriend; his name is Oliver, and he's so adorable that I can't stand it.

He's got this playful boyish charm, and she's totally smitten; I don't blame her.

She met him at the movies at a daytime showing. She was there alone, and he was there alone, the only two in the cinema. They made a joke of it and bonded over their popcorn and ice cream choices and ended up sitting together.

That was three months ago, and the rest, as they say, is history. I've never seen her so happy; she floats around on air.

"Look who's with him!" Chloe bounces excitedly in her chair as she elbows me. "Here we go, Bec."

Oliver has a friend, a very cute friend.

"Ahhh," I giggle, glancing down at my drink. Whoa, these margaritas have some punch. I'm feeling tipsy.

"Ladies." Oliver bends and kisses Chloe's cheek. "Look how beautiful you are." He smiles as he tilts her chin.

*Swoon . . .*

He turns to his friend. "You remember my friend Michael?"

"Of course." I smile up at him. "Hi."

"Hello." Michael's eyes light up. "I was hoping you'd be here."

"Hey," Henley calls from the other end of the table, and the boys wave.

"Hi."

There aren't any spare seats. "Let's go over to the bar to talk," Chloe suggests. She grabs my arm and drags me out of my chair. "You're coming."

Chloe leads me to the bar by the hand while my heart sits in my throat.

*Bang, bang, bang* go the nerves.

Stop.

I need to get over myself, and letting myself like someone is a step in the right direction.

So my husband cheated . . . so what?

Am I really going to let him ruin the rest of my life and never go on another date again?

No.

No, I am not.

Are all men sleazebags?

Probably.

*Stop!*

Logically, I know that's not true. I keep thinking I'm ready to date, and then when it gets closer, I panic and freeze, then decide that I'm not ready.

Enough!

I'm better than this wallowing-in-self-pity crap. I *am* stronger now, and I've got this.

I'm in my prime, and at thirty-two I have so much to look forward to. It's been twelve months, and I really do need to get over this and move on with my life.

"So." Michael leans in closer so only I can hear. "I've been thinking about you."

"You have?"

"Nonstop." He widens his eyes to accentuate his point.

"Nonstop?" I smirk into my drink. "That's a lot."

"Have you been thinking about me?"

"Maybe." I play it cool.

"Maybe yes?" He raises a playful eyebrow.

"Maybe yes." I laugh.

He glances at his watch.

"Are you working tonight?" I ask.

"Yeah." He shrugs. "I hate working Saturday nights. It's the only time I hate shift work."

"What time do you start?"

"Eleven."

Michael's a security guard; his jobs are varied, and he works a lot of night shifts.

I glance at my watch. "It's nine thirty; why did you come out if you have to leave so soon?"

"To see you. I knew if I didn't come to see you tonight that I wouldn't get a chance to ask for your number for another whole week."

"Really?"

"Yes, really."

"So?" I bite my bottom lip to hide my smile.

"Can I have your number?" He takes out his phone.

"That depends."

"On what?"

"What are you going to do with it?"

"Call you and ask you out on a date."

"Or . . ." I can't believe I'm saying this out loud. "You could just ask me now."

"Rebecca." He gives me a beautiful broad smile. "Will you go out on a date with me?"

*Ahhhh!*

"Okay."

"Next . . . Saturday night?"

"Uh-huh."

"It's a date then."

"I guess it is." Nerves flutter around in my stomach; this is the first guy I've felt any kind of spark from in so long. My eyes roam over the fine specimen.

Michael is tall and built like a Mack truck, huge and muscular. The kind of man I imagine could fuck you through a wall.

10

The thought makes me weak in the knees. Damn . . . it's been a long drought.

I've been as dry as the Sahara and am in desperate need of a good weekend of hot and heavy rain.

"I'm going, Bec." A voice snaps me out of my dirty daydream, and I glance up to see Blake standing beside us. "Do you want a lift home?" he asks.

"Oh." I frown.

"I can take you home," Michael interrupts.

"Okay." I smile.

"Who are you?" Blake asks.

"Oh, sorry." I shake my head, embarrassed by my rudeness. "Blake, this is Michael. Michael, this is Blake, my friend."

They both force a smile and shake hands. "Hello."

Blake looks Michael up and down as if sizing him up. "And what do you do, Michael?" he asks.

"Security."

Blake sips his beer. "It's Saturday night; shouldn't you be off . . . securing something?"

A frown flashes across Michael's face.

Oh my god, Blake can be such a rude prick when he wants to be. I widen my eyes at him.

*Stop it.*

"Just secured a date with this lovely lady, actually," Michael fires back.

"Really?" Blake's eyes flick to meet mine before giving him a sarcastic smile. "Good luck with that."

*What?*

"Excuse us for a moment, Michael. Just walking Blake out." I fake a smile as I pull Blake away by the arm. "See you." Michael nods.

"Bye," Blake replies without making eye contact.

"What the hell are you doing?" I whisper as I drag Blake toward the door.

"What the hell are *you* doing?" he fires back.

"I'm enjoying talking to a very nice man, and you're being very rude."

"Him." He huffs. "He's as far from a nice man as I've ever met."

"You don't even know him," I scoff.

"Come on, Rebecca." He rolls his eyes as we arrive at the front doors. "Your douchedar *cannot* be that way off."

"Douchedar?" I frown. "What the hell is douchedar?"

"A douchebag radar."

"Ha," I snap. "He is not a douchebag."

"And you know this how?" He puts his hands on his hips.

"I know him . . . very well, actually," I lie.

"Yeah, well, I can spot them a mile off, and he's a king."

"It takes one to know one."

"Having fun does not make me a douchebag." He fakes a smile. "Although dating one *does* make you stupid." He kisses my cheek. "Good night, Rebecca." He turns and walks out through the front doors, and I watch him disappear down the road.

Ugh . . . he's so annoying.

I walk back to my place at the bar with Michael. "Who's he?" he asks.

"Ahh." This is awkward. "He's my neighbor." I force an embarrassed smile. "A friend."

Michael's eyebrows shoot up as if he's unimpressed.

"He's a little overprotective—ignore him. I do." I tap my drink with his. "Let's talk about something interesting."

"Like what?" He smiles, mollified for the moment.

"Like where we're going on our date next week."

He slides his hand around my waist. "Where do you want to go?"

An hour later, the car pulls to a stop in front of my house, and Michael looks over at me in the darkness. "Damn, you make me want to call in sick tonight."

I smile over at him. "Next week."

"Next week."

Hope blooms in my chest. There really is something here between us.

I feel giddy.

He leans over and takes my face in his hands. His lips brush over mine as he kisses me softly.

*Oh* . . .

His tongue slides against mine, and my eyes close at the perfection between us.

He kisses me again and again, and good lord . . .

I pull away from him, overwrought with arousal.

"Wow," he pants as he looks at me.

"Wow." I smile.

Wow is right . . . ahhhhhh!

"Have fun at work." I open the door and lean in through the window. "Call me." I bat my eyelashes playfully to be cute, and he winks and revs the engine on the car.

I practically float inside and close the door, leaning up against the back of it as excitement runs through me.

Can it be next Saturday night already?

I put the plug in, turn the hot water on, and let it run. I'm in the bath, and it's after midnight. The room is steamy, and I've lit candles to add to the ambience. It's funny—I never used to take baths; I always saw them as a waste of time.

But lately they've become part of my self-care routine.

A deep, hot bath is cathartic and a simple pleasure that I've become addicted to.

After my dreamy first kiss with Michael tonight, I'm floating on air. My mind keeps going over and over it, the way he kissed me . . . the way it made me feel.

I have this simmering excitement deep inside.

My phone beeps a text. I lean out, dry my hand on the towel, and pick it up.

It's a text from Michael. Ahh . . . I swipe it open.

**Can't stop thinking about you.**

I smile broadly and reply.

**Me too.**

Another text bounces in.

**Send me a teaser.**

Huh? I frown. What does that mean?
Another text bounces in.

**I need something to get me through to next week.**

What's he talking about?
Another text arrives.

**I'll go first.**

My phone dings again, and I open the message.
It's a cock shot.

14

*Huh?*

I stare at it in confusion. "What the fuck?" The photo is taken in a bathroom, and I can see a reflection of the window in the mirror. This photo was taken in the daytime.

This erection was for someone else, and he's sending me sleazy photographs of the evidence.

Eww . . .

My phone beeps again.

**Now it's your turn.**

Is he for real?
I reply.

**You want me to send a nude?**

He texts back immediately.

**Fuck yeah.**

What is he, fourteen years old?
I exhale heavily and drop my phone onto the floor.
Yuck.

Ugh . . . I slide down into the water. Why are men such fucking idiots?

Do I have the sign *sleazebag target* on my forehead?
Another text bounces in, and unable to stop myself, I open it.

**I'm ready and waiting**
**??**

I roll my eyes and reply.

## It was nice knowing you.
## Not really.

I hit send, then swipe through and block his number.

I get out of the bath in a rush and turn the shower on. Even just receiving that text makes me feel dirty. He's probably sent that exact cock shot to at least three hundred women. Recycled, used dick.

Ugh . . . gross.

I soap up my hands and begin to scrub my skin.

It's official: I hate men.


*Blake*


*Knock, knock, knock* sounds at the door.

"Who is knocking at this hour of the morning?"

I put my bread in the toaster and walk out to answer the front door. I open it to find Rebecca standing there.

"Bec."

"Can I come in?" She's still in her pajamas, and I frown as I look her up and down.

"What's wrong?"

"Nothing. Can I come in or not?" she snaps impatiently.

"Sure."

"So, I was thinking about what you said last night," she says as she follows me into the kitchen.

"Yeah." My toast pops, and I hold a piece up. "Want some?"

"No thanks."

I go to the fridge and open it. I peer in.

Rebecca pulls out the stool to sit at the kitchen counter and frowns. "What is this?" She holds up a mauve lace bra on her fingertip.

Yeesh . . . What's that doing there? I snatch it out of her hand. "It's Antony's," I lie.

"Why would Antony be wearing a mauve bra?"

"Because it matches his mauve panties, that's why," I snap. "What do you want?"

She sits down on the stool. "What is a douchedar, and how do I use it?"

# Chapter 2

*Rebecca*

"What do you mean?" Blake frowns.

"Well, you said last night that Michael showed up on your douchedar."

"Yes." He continues to butter his toast.

"So . . . how did you know he was a douchebag?"

He takes a bite of his toast and smirks. "Don't tell me the idiot fucked up already?"

I let out a deflated breath. "He asked me for nudes and then sent me a recycled cock shot."

He smirks.

"This is not the least bit funny, Blake."

"Little bit." He leans his behind on the kitchen counter and crosses his legs at the ankle. It's only then that I notice he's in boxer shorts, and his broad, tanned chest is on display. Damn it, even Blake is looking good lately. I snap my eyes away.

I really need to get laid. Maybe I should have sent the nudes.

"So?" I ask hopefully.

"So what?" He keeps casually chewing his toast.

"Can you explain the whole douche-radar thing. Like . . . how did you know? What were the signs?"

"Bec . . ." He stares at me for a bit, as if thinking. "I just don't think you're ready yet."

"I am. I know I am."

"What makes you so sure?"

"Because I get turned on by the wind changing."

"Really?" He smirks as his eyes hold mine.

"Yes, really."

"I know someone who could help you out with that."

"Will you be serious for just one minute?"

"Only too happy to donate my penis for your wind changes." He gives me a playful wink.

"Blake." I widen my eyes. "Are you listening to me at all?"

"Not if I can help it." He grabs my hand and pulls me off the stool. "We'll talk about it through the week."

"I want to talk about it now."

"Not a good time, Bec."

"Why not?"

"Blake," a female voice calls from upstairs. "Are you coming back up?"

*Oh my god.*

"Who's that?" I mouth, horrified.

He holds his two hands up, as if he's just as surprised as I am. "I have no idea," he mouths back. "Maybe the tooth fairy."

I roll my eyes. "Can you ever be serious for one minute?"

"No." He grabs me by my two shoulders and turns me toward the front door. "Go home and go for a run or something."

"I don't want to go for a run." I sigh as I walk out onto his porch.

"Then take a nap."

"It's first thing in the morning." I throw my hands up. "What am I supposed to do now?"

"Forget about men."

"Why?"

"Because we are no fucking good, that's why."

My shoulders slump in disappointment. Even he openly admits it.

"Look." He sighs as he pulls me into a hug. "I'll come over later."

I stand rigid in his arms.

"Okay?" he mumbles into my hair.

"Fine . . ."

"Are you cooking me dinner?" he asks.

"Ugh . . . Why don't you get the tooth fairy to cook you dinner?"

"No." He scrunches up his nose as he steps back from me. "She can't cook for shit."

"How do you know?"

"I just do. Lasagna?"

I really do want to find out about this douche radar.

"Ugh . . . fine."

"Got to go." He closes the door in my face, and I stare at it for a beat.

The tooth fairy can't cook, which can only mean one thing . . .

She gives good head.


### 12:30 p.m.

I refold the napkin in my lap and look around the restaurant as I wait.

Where is he?

Typical of John, the prick, to make a grand entrance.

I glance at my watch and roll my fingers on the table as my impatience grows.

Fifteen minutes late.

If I didn't know him, I would assume he isn't coming, but unfortunately I do, and I know that this is his way of trying to assert dominance. He'll swan in and pretend he was tied up at work when really, he is just too self-centered to worry about making anyone wait for him.

"There you are." He smiles calmly before bending to kiss my cheek in greeting.

I turn my head. "Don't kiss me, and you're late."

"Apologies." He sits down in the chair opposite me. His eyes hold mine. "You look good, Rebecca."

*Don't even . . .*

"Why haven't you replied to my lawyer?" I ask.

He casually pours himself a glass of water from the jug. "Because my relationship isn't with your lawyer."

"It is now."

"No." He takes a sip. "It isn't." He opens the menu and peruses the choices. "What are you having?"

"I'm not eating."

"Aren't we meeting for lunch?"

"No. We're meeting because you won't answer my lawyer's calls."

"The answer is no," he snaps.

"You cannot stop me from divorcing you," I whisper angrily.

"We're not getting divorced; we *are* going to get through this." He casually sips his water. "All couples go through a rough patch. When we come out the other side of this, we are going to be more in love with each other than ever."

"You were sleeping with another woman for eighteen months. This is a little more than a rough patch, John."

"I was having a midlife crisis," he whispers. "I made a mistake."

"That I will never get over. I want a divorce."

"No."

"We've been separated for over twelve months, and we are not coming back from this. Ever."

His eyes hold mine, and he circles his pointer finger over the tablecloth. "Why do you want a divorce so badly?"

"I just do."

"Why?"

"I don't like living in a house that you pay for. I want this finalized so I can pay my own way and look after myself. While I live in a house that you pay for, I'm in limbo."

"Oh please," he scoffs. "What the hell can you afford?"

I open my mouth to say something nasty but close it again before I do.

*Stay civil until he agrees to my terms.*

"I want the house in the settlement, and you can keep everything else."

His eyes hold mine. "No. You can have the ski lodge in Aspen."

"I don't want the ski lodge. I don't even ski."

"You can have the Manhattan apartment."

"No, you like the city; you keep it. I want to stay on Kingston Lane."

"How are you going to maintain a house of that size?"

"I think I'm capable of mowing lawns."

"We still have a mortgage on it. You can't afford to pay that."

"I'll find a way."

"Why would you want to stay there?"

"Because my friends are there?"

His jaw ticks in fury. "Blake Grayson isn't your friend, Rebecca; he wants to fuck you."

"Oh please." I roll my eyes. "Blake is my friend."

"Blake was *my* friend, and he just chose to be a traitor and go to your side." He fakes a smile. "You don't have to be a rocket scientist to know why."

"Shut up," I whisper angrily. "Leave Blake out of this. Not everyone is a sex maniac. I want the house in the settlement, and I want a divorce. And you're going to give it to me."

"No."

"This isn't up to you."

"Actually . . ." He narrows his eyes. "I think I'll move back into *my* house."

Panic sets in.

"No. You won't."

"You can't stop me."

"I wonder what your mom and dad would say if they found out what you've done," I fume. This is below the belt, but damn it, he cannot, under any circumstance, move back in with me.

"Don't threaten me, Rebecca."

"Here's the deal . . . I want the house *and* a divorce, or . . . I'm going to your dad, and we both know that little family trust of Grandma's will be ripped out from under you if they learn what kind of sleazebag their only grandson really is."

"We're going to get through this." He sits forward and takes my hand in his. "I love you. You're my wife; we are meant to be together forever."

I snatch my hand out of his. "Don't touch me."

"I made a mistake; I'm human. So kill me. Do you honestly think that ninety-nine percent of the male population hasn't made a simple mistake before?"

"You put your dick inside another woman's ass," I spit angrily.

The people at the tables around us glance over, and I cringe. That came out a lot louder than it was meant to.

23

"Keep your voice down," he whispers angrily. "Fine . . . you can have the house." He shrugs as he thinks out loud. "I'll sign it over, but I won't agree to a divorce. I love you, and I won't give up on us."

"You'll sign it over?" I frown, surprised.

"On the condition that we don't divorce."

"What?" I screw up my face. "That's ridiculous."

He shrugs.

"For how long?"

"Forever."

"No, I want a set time." I think of a counteroffer. "If we haven't gotten back together in two years, then we get a divorce."

"Eight years."

"No way," I scoff. "Three years."

"Six."

"Four."

"Five." He sits back, annoyed. "Final offer: I'll sign the house over to you, but we don't divorce for at least five years."

I stare at him as the idea rolls around in my head.

*I really want the house.*

"Take it or leave it, Rebecca."

Five years . . . is a long time.

Not that it matters, I guess. I have no intention of ever marrying again.

"Why do you want such a long time?" I ask him.

"Because I can't lose you, Rebecca, and I need you to forgive me. We need time to heal. I can't imagine a life without you in it."

"But you could very easily imagine yourself in a bed without me in it . . . couldn't you?"

"I made a mistake," he says softly. "How long are you going to throw that in my face?"

"Forever."

"Five years."

24

"I need to get some advice from my lawyer."

"I'll send you a schedule of the repayments and monthly costs. I'm telling you that you can't afford it. You don't need to do it alone; you have me."

*I never had you.*

"I'll be the judge of what I can afford." Annoyed, I stand to cut our meeting short. "Send me the details, and I'll let you know."

"I love you." He smiles hopefully up at me.

My heart sinks. I hate that he still says it to me every time we speak. I hate that the man I thought was my soulmate is nothing more than a huge disappointment.

I hate that I'm single and lonely, and damn it, I . . . I hate that he ruined the perfect life I had.

"Goodbye, John." I walk out of the restaurant and push out through the heavy glass doors into the cool air.

I put my sunglasses on and look up the street toward my car. Well, that was a disaster . . .

Five years . . . *fuck.*

I stare at the computer screen and screw up my face. "What?"

John's financial estimate email has come through, and I'm spending the afternoon going through the expenses.

"Surely this can't be right?"

I bring up the calculator on my phone and begin to add up the yearly figures.

Loan repayment.

Maintenance.

Property tax.

Utilities.

Insurance.

I add them all together and then divide them by twelve. "This should be the monthly amount of costs." I hit enter on the calculator.

$3,312.00

My eyes widen in horror. "Three thousand three hundred and twelve dollars?" I gasp. "Per month?"

Shit. I quickly divide that by four.

$828.00

"What the hell . . . a week?"

I slump back into my chair. "That's going to be all my income, and I didn't even pay for food or gas and car costs yet."

*Damn it.*

I see John's smug face when he told me that I wouldn't be able to afford to keep the house.

He was right . . .

That selfish bastard infuriates me. He thinks that I'm going to go back to him because I have no other choice.

I slam my computer shut and stare at the wall.

What the hell do I do now?

### Blake

I pull my front door closed and walk across the lawn to Rebecca's. It's just 7:00 p.m. I have a bottle of wine under my arm, and I've been looking forward to this lasagna all day.

Nobody can cook like Rebecca can. Best damn chef in the United States, if you ask me.

I walk up the stairs onto her porch.

*Knock, knock.*

I wait . . .

What's happening in there? I peer through the window; she's probably slaving away in the kitchen for me. I smile and knock again.

*Knock, knock.*

This is the perfect way to end my weekend: dinner with my favorite girl.

The door opens in a rush, and my eyes drop down to Rebecca's feet and rise back up to her face. She's wearing odd flannelette pajamas: canary yellow pants with huge red lips all over them and a pink top. Her hair is in a messy bun on the top of her head, and her face is covered in a green face mask. "I love it when you dress up for me," I mutter.

Rebecca rolls her eyes. "I'm not in the mood for your sarcasm tonight," she snaps impatiently. "What is it, Blake?"

"Lasagna, I'm hoping."

"Oh." Her face falls. "That's right, I invited you for dinner, didn't I?"

"You forgot?" My mouth falls open in horror. I've been looking forward to this all day, and she just *forgets.*

"Sorry." She sighs as she steps to the side to let me in. "I've had a . . . day. Come in."

I walk in through the foyer and into the living room to see the television is paused. There's a packet of chocolate cookies and the empty wrappers of two blocks of chocolate on the coffee table in front of the couch. My eyes rise to her and notice that she has a defeated demeanor. I know this look anywhere.

*She saw John today.*

"So . . ." I shrug. "I'm guessing there's no lasagna."

She shakes her head and flops onto the couch. "Sorry. I just . . ."

I wait for her reply.

"I can't seem to do anything right today." She shrugs sadly.

"Well, that's not true." I sit down next to her and pull her into a hug. "You are totally nailing the cute housewife look." I feel her smile against my shoulder. "I'll tell you what, I'll make us dinner."

"You will?"

"Not really." I stand. "We're getting takeout." I take my phone out of my pocket. "What do you feel like?"

"Carbohydrates," she says as she holds the remote up to the television and presses play.

"Romanes Italian?" I ask.

"I guess."

"Well, I can't order the lasagna because it will only highlight how bad it is in comparison to yours." I curl my lip. "You owe me lasagna, woman."

"Okay." She forces a smile. "I'll have garlic bread. A large size. Actually, make it a family serving of pasta carbonara with extra cream and fresh Parmesan, and then I'll have a Nutella pizza for dessert with a double serving of strawberries on the side. And I'll have a Coca-Cola, in a glass bottle if possible."

Eww . . .

"Sounds"—my eyebrows flick up in surprise—"healthy."

"Don't even . . . ," she growls.

I hold my two hands up in surrender. "I wouldn't dare." I dial the number of the restaurant.

"Hello, Romanes."

"Can I order some takeout, please?" I ask.

"What will it be?" the bored receptionist asks.

"Family serving of pasta carbonara with extra cream and fresh Parmesan, spaghetti marinara with extra chili, and a Nutella pizza with extra strawberries on the side."

"Is that it?"

"A Coke." My eyes float over to Rebecca as she watches me. "In a glass bottle."

I tell them the address and hang up; my eyes rise to the television. "What are you watching?"

"*The Notebook.*"

"Why are you watching sad love stories? Isn't it time you start watching *Breaking Bad* or something?"

"What's *Breaking Bad* about?" she asks, distracted.

"Well, there's this science teacher who's diagnosed with terminal cancer, so he thinks fuck it and begins to make methamphetamines in a lab."

"That sounds terrible." She screws up her face. "Why would I want to watch a show about someone dying and making drugs?"

"It's badass and a lot better than watching fuckwits in love."

She smirks as her eyes hold mine.

*Is she going to tell me what happened today?*

She stays silent.

"I'll tell you what we're going to do." I sit down beside her and tuck a piece of her hair behind her ear.

Her eyes hold mine.

"You're going to go take a shower and wash that green shit off your face." I tap her on her nose. "And I'm going to pull out the sofa bed from the couch and make you a pillow fort with the snuggliest blanket of all time."

She smiles softly.

"We'll eat dinner, and then we're going to have a *Breaking Bad* marathon," I continue.

"Thank you, Blake." Her eyes well with tears as she stares at me. "I've just had a bad day, you know?"

"I know." I smile. "It's okay, baby." I pull her into a hug. "I've got you."

She stays in my arms for a beat longer than usual, and damn it, I fucking hate that guy for how hard he broke her.

If I ever see him on a dark street, he may not survive.

"You want to talk about it?" I mumble into her hair.

"Not really."

Her inability to talk to me stings more than it should, and I pull out of her arms and stand. "Shower."


Rebecca's regulated breathing is quite possibly the most comforting sound in the world. We are on the trundle bed in her living room, wrapped up in our snuggly blanket. Lying flat on her back and wearing her flannelette pajamas, she is fast asleep. I lie on my side facing her. It's late, and I have to work tomorrow. I know I should tiptoe out of here and quietly leave, lock up her house and let her sleep in peace.

But how can I . . . when watching her sleep is like a dream come true?

*If only . . .*

# Chapter 3

*Rebecca*

"Well, what are you going to do?" Chloe flops onto the couch and rests her face on her hand.

"I don't know." I fill our glasses of wine. "Maybe I shouldn't even go for the house. I mean, what's the point if I can't afford it anyway."

"You can't let him have it out of principle," Chloe huffs. "Get it, and then if you have to, you can sell it, but no way in hell is that dickhead living here when you can't."

"He wouldn't even want to live here anymore," I reply. "He and Blake would kill each other."

"Exactly. The very first thing he would do is sell it. He only wants it because it means something to you."

"The bastard is weaponizing my house." I pass her the wine-glass and take a seat beside her, curling my legs up beneath me.

"He's trying to manipulate you; that's what he's doing. He thinks he can force you to go back to him." She sips her wine. "Five years with no divorce? Get fucked, asshole."

I smile. There's only one thing better than listening to myself rave on about John, and it's listening to my friends do it. I don't think there has ever been a more hated man on earth. He's Kingston Lane's public enemy number one.

"So he thinks he can move you here, away from all your family and friends, screw his secretary for eighteen months behind your back, get caught, and then bribe you to not divorce him."

My eyebrows flick up. "Sounds really bad when you say it out loud."

"That's because it is really bad. He's such a selfish asshole that I can't stand it."

I exhale heavily and sip my wine.

"What did Juliet say?"

"I haven't seen her yet. She's worked all weekend."

"Well, Blake is going to go postal."

"Do *not* tell Blake," I warn her. "He came over last night for dinner, and I didn't say a word. I am not in the mood for one of his lectures."

"He's just being a good friend."

"You know he's overbearing when it comes to John."

She gets up, goes to the window, and peers through the curtains at the boys playing golf. "Still fine as fuck, though."

I roll my eyes. "I thought you were all in love with Oliver?"

"I am." She keeps watching the boys. "I'm taken, not dead." She smiles. "There isn't a woman on earth who doesn't find Blake Grayson totally irresistible."

I raise my hand. "Me."

"Admittedly"—she raises her wineglass toward me—"you are the exception."

"Back to my lack of finances. What am I going to do?" I sigh, uninterested.

Chloe continues to peer through the curtains as she studies the boys some more. "The only thing you can do."

"Which is?"

"Open an OnlyFans."

Chloe and I carefully walk down my front steps with our trays of food. Chloe made chicken satay skewers, and I made a large potato bake and some fried rice. We each have a bottle of wine under our arms as well. The boys are on their putting green; I still can't believe we have a golf green in the middle of our cul-de-sac.

"Nooo," the boys collectively cry as Antony sinks a golf ball into the hole.

"Fluke," Henley yells.

"You guys coming over?" I call as we walk past them to Carol's.

"In a minute," Blake calls as he picks up the putter. "Just got to show these losers who's boss." He sticks his tongue out to concentrate as he lines up to the ball.

We walk down the road and up Carol's front steps.

"Come in, my loves," Carol calls.

We walk in to find her in her apron, bent over and peering into her oven. "This damn oven is acting up."

"Let's get the party started, people," Taryn laughs as she walks through the door. She's in a skintight hot-pink tube dress and carrying a huge-ass cooler.

How does she look so hot in everything she wears? "What the hell is in there?" I frown.

"Party punch. Here, help me," she replies.

I take one end of the cooler from her, and we struggle into the kitchen. "This thing weighs a ton."

"Put it down in here."

*Clunk.* We drop it with a thud, and she opens the lid to pull out a giant glass punch bowl and ladle. "I make the best party punch in the history of life." She pulls out a few two-liter bottles of an orange liquid and begins to fill the punch bowl.

"If you do say so yourself." I laugh.

"Exactly." Once the punch bowl is full, she pours in a container of chopped-up fruit. "Get a glass," she instructs me.

"In here, dear." Carol opens the top cupboard and retrieves some tall glasses. "A big punch bowl deserves big glasses." She passes me one, and Taryn fills it to the very top.

Yeesh . . . that's a lot of punch.

I take a slow sip. It's orangey and lemony, and wow, I'm pleasantly surprised. I lick my lips to really taste it. "This is delicious, Taryn. Doesn't even taste alcoholic."

"I told you so." She wiggles her eyebrows. "Who else wants one?" she calls.

"Me, please." Chloe holds out her glass. Taryn fills it and one for herself, then Carol too.

Loud, boisterous laughter comes bellowing through the front door as the boys arrive.

"Hello, my boys." Carol kisses their cheeks as they walk in.

"Here she is, my favorite." Blake smiles as he hugs her.

"Hello, sweetheart." She smiles and holds his two cheeks in her hands as she stares up at his face. Henley and Antony follow behind, along with Winston.

Antony and Winston are overly boisterous; their cheeks are rosy, and it's obvious they've already had a few too many beverages.

"I made us punch," Taryn announces proudly. "Do you want some?"

Henley picks up a glass. "Sure do."


*Three hours later*

34

We clap fast as we sing "Happy Birthday" at the top of our voices. Winston jumps up onto the couch and rips off his T-shirt, twirling it around like a lasso above his head as we all squeal in excitement.

My stomach is sore from laughing; this was just what I needed. Such a fun night.

Eating, dancing, good friends, laughter, and I've come to a conclusion: there's no way in hell that I can ever move out of this street.

I don't know how, but I'm going to find a way to afford it . . . I have to.

*Blake*

*Boom, boom, boom.*

The pounding of my head wakes me, and I bring my two hands to my forehead to try and get some relief.

"Oh . . ." I screw up my face. "Ow . . ."

I open one eye and then the other. Wait . . . Where am I? My eyes flick around to see I'm in the spare bedroom of my house.

Why did I sleep in here?

I lean up onto my elbows and look around, confused. Wait, what?

I lie back down as I troll my brain for a memory. I was dancing . . . then . . .

That's it.

What happened after that? I blink as I try my hardest to remember something.

*Boom, boom, boom* thumps my head.

Fuck, I need some Advil.

I drag myself out of bed and glance down at my naked body.

I see my jeans crumpled up on the floor and look around for my T-shirt or underwear; both are nowhere to be seen.

Huh?

I struggle to pull on my jeans and stumble down the hall to see that my bedroom door is closed.

Someone's sleeping in there.

I quietly knock on the door. No answer. I tentatively push it open to see my bed is empty and still made from yesterday.

I screw up my face in question. What?

Hmm . . . that doesn't make sense. Why would I sleep in the spare room if nobody was in my bed?

Weird.

I have no idea what's going on around here.

I make my way downstairs as I search for a semblance of a memory. How on earth did I get so messed up?

Hazy visions of dancing on Carol's couch float through my mind.

Wait . . .

I drag my hand down my face. Ugh . . . How was I so drunk? I fill a glass of water and go to the medicine cabinet. I pour some Advil into my hand and throw them into my mouth.

I wince as I feel them go all the way down.

Seriously, my headache is so bad. I'm probably having an aneurysm or some shit.

*Bzzzzz buzz . . . buzz bzzzzz.*

My phone vibrates on the kitchen counter, and the name *Henley* lights up the screen.

"Hey," I answer.

"Are you alive?" his croaky voice whispers.

"Barely." I close my eyes. "But I suspect the end is near."

"Hell . . ."

"How did . . ." I frown. "I don't even remember getting home."

"Me neither. Jules said she found me asleep in our front garden when she got back from work."

"What time was that?" I frown as I try to retrace our steps.

"I don't know, midnight."

"What were we drinking?"

"Taryn's punch."

"Hell." I drag my hand through my hair. "How's Deluca?"

"Not answering his phone."

"Go check on him. He's probably dead."

"Based on the way I feel, it wouldn't surprise me."

My stomach rolls, and I dry retch over the sink. "This is a fucking code-red hangover." I heave again. "What the hell was in that punch?"

"Who knows."

Holding my stomach, I lean my behind against the kitchen counter and feel something dig into me from the back pocket of my jeans. I reach my hand in and pull something out. It's a pale-blue flash drive.

I stare at it. "What the hell is this?"

"What are you talking about?" Henley replies.

"There's a flash drive in the pocket of my jeans."

"What's on it?"

"I don't know." I walk to the hall and glance in the mirror, and my eyes widen in horror when I see my reflection.

There's a giant love bite on my neck.

*What the fuck?*

I turn my head to the side as I stare at the dark-purple bruise. My mind begins to race. Who did this?

"What's on the flash drive?" Henley repeats.

"Who cares? I've got a bigger problem than a stupid fucking flash drive." I drag my hand down my face in disgust. "Who the hell did I hook up with last night?"

"What?"

"I have a giant-ass hickey on my neck."

"From who?"

"That's what I would like to fucking know," I snap.

"Well, nobody else was there, and you didn't leave to go anywhere . . . so that can only mean one thing."

"Which is?"

"You hooked up with someone from Kingston Lane."

My eyes widen in horror.

"Surely not."

The sun beams red through my closed eyelids.

"Pass me another bottle of water, will you?" Ant says from the deck chair beside me.

"Another?"

"Yes. Another," he grunts.

I reach into the cooler, rattle around in the ice, dig out a bottle of water, and pass it over.

We're dying a slow and painful death by the pool, in the depths of hangover hell.

My phone beeps a text.

**Can someone set my house on fire?**

I read it and chuckle.

"What?" Ant looks over at me as he squints into the sun.

"Hen wants us to set his house on fire so that he doesn't need a couch."

Ant smirks as he sips his water. Juliet's on a mission to buy a new couch, and much to Henley's disdain, she's dragged him around the shops for hours.

Ant closes his eyes and puts his hands up beneath his head. "Any memory of who you railed yet?"

"No, but . . ." I sip my water. "I've come to the conclusion that it couldn't have been anyone exciting if I've forgotten it."

"Fair point." His eyebrows rise. "And what were they doing with a flash drive?"

I glance over at him. "You think the flash drive was from the person who gave me the hickey?"

"Obviously." He shrugs. "Why else would you have it?"

"True." I think this over for a moment. "So theoretically, all I have to do is look on the flash drive and it should tell me."

"Uh-huh." Ant's eyes are closed as he worships the sun. "The question is, though, do you really want to know?"

I let out a deep sigh. "Probably not."

"It has to be Taryn."

I scrunch my eyes shut and pinch the bridge of my nose. "It better not be."

"I hope it's Carol." He smiles into the sun. "That would make my life complete if you gave the sausage to Carol."

I roll my eyes.

"Maybe you screwed Winston."

"Fuck off." I throw my bottle of water at him, disgusted by the thought. "When we get back to my house, we're looking on that stupid flash drive."

"Fifty bucks it's Taryn." He glances over to me. "Who you betting?"

I wince as I go over the choices. "If it's Taryn, I'm moving houses."

"Yeah, because it's not going to be awkward seeing her every day."

"Just shut the fuck up."

A message bounces in from Henley.

**S. O. S.**

The thought of him being dragged around the shops brings a smile to my face. "This is why we are never getting married. Can't even have a hangover in peace."

"Amen to that."

*Four hours later*

"Okay." I plug the flash drive into my desktop computer. "Let's go."

Henley and Antony are lying on my couch.

**Rocket Cock**

I sit back in my chair, shocked. "Rocket Cock—what the hell is Rocket Cock?"

"What?" Henley calls from the other room.

"Something on here about a Rocket Cock?" I call.

They both dive off the couch and come to look over my shoulder at the computer screen.

> When Brodie McAlister investigates a noise
> in her garage, the last thing she expects to find
> is a seven-foot-tall green alien.
>
> Huge and muscular, he towers over her.

"Huh?" I screw up my face. "The hell is this?"

Two huge green cocks hang between his
legs.

My eyes widen as the boys burst out laughing. "What the
fuck is this shit?" I cry.

His balls are the size of baseballs, and as
he stares at me with hunger, his weeping cocks
begin to grow.

"Who the hell wrote this?" I cry in outrage.

"Looks like you slept with an alien last night, bro." Antony
slaps me on the back.

"How were his two cocks?" Henley replies. "So convenient,
one for your asshole and one for your mouth."

The boys chuckle.

"You're hilarious," I huff. "I have no idea about any of
this crap."

"Sure you don't. Why was it in your back door . . . I mean,
pocket?" Henley corrects himself.

"Bit sore today, bud?" Antony replies. "I did notice you
were walking odd."

Henley laughs and steps backward, tripping and stumbling,
making Antony laugh harder.

"Very funny," I mutter as I scroll down in search of a clue.
"Who wrote this shit?"

*Knock, knock.*

"Someone's at the door," I snap, annoyed. Now is *not* the
time. "Go. Away."

"Might be him."

"Shut. Up."

*Knock, knock.*

41

"Fuck it." I run into the bathroom, grab a towel, and wrap it around my neck.

Nobody can see this.

*Rebecca*

I stand and wait at Blake's front door. I know he's home; I saw him come over from Antony's earlier. I knock again.

The door opens in a rush, and Blake comes into view. He seems surprised to see me. "Rebecca." He smiles; he has a towel around his neck.

"Are you going swimming?" I ask.

"What?" He wraps the towel tighter around his neck. *What is he doing with that towel?*

"The towel."

"Oh . . . yes."

I hear Henley and Antony's loud laughter coming from inside. "Am I interrupting something?" I ask.

"Not at all." Blake glances inside to where the laughter is coming from, then steps out onto the front porch and closes the door behind him. "What's up?"

"I just wanted to talk about last night." I twist my hands in front of me nervously.

"What about last night?" he replies quickly.

"I just wanted to thank you for being so honest. I've been thinking about it ever since."

His eyes widen. "Honest . . ."

"Yeah." I smile. "When you told me about your old girlfriend and what she did."

Blake's eyes narrow as he stares at me. "Go on . . ."

"And . . ." *Ugh, he's not making this easy for me.* "I just . . . I think I want to do it."

"Right . . ." He frowns as his eyes hold mine.

"Well, not that I want to, but I feel that I need to."

"Oh . . . kay."

"But I don't want anyone to know. You have to promise to keep it a secret."

He opens his mouth to say something and then closes it again before he does.

Loud laughter erupts from inside his house.

"What's so funny in there?" I frown.

"Um . . ." He drags his hand down his face. "You wouldn't believe me even if I told you, anyway . . . so, this secret."

"Yeah, if you could help me, I would really appreciate it. I mean, I know how busy you are, and to fit this in every day is a big ask."

He blinks as if processing my words.

"Aren't you hot in that towel?"

"Nope, I'm cold." He grips it harder.

"So . . ." I pause. "Do you think we could start tonight? I just want to stop overthinking this and get started before I can chicken out."

"Um . . ." He pauses.

Laughter erupts again from inside.

"Are they still drunk?"

"No doubt," he stammers. "Listen, Bec." He twists his lips as if thinking. "We had so many conversations last night. Remind me what we are talking about again?"

"Foot Finder."

He screws up his face. "What about it?"

"Remember you told me that your girlfriend from college used to upload pictures of her feet to Foot Finder and get a few hundred dollars every week from it, and nobody ever knew?"

His mouth falls open. "Oh . . ."

"I know this is extreme, but I'm going to have to move if I don't find an extra eight hundred dollars a week."

"Right. Okay, now I'm on board." He nods. "You can definitely upload pictures of your feet. Weirdos pay big money for hot little feet like yours."

"But they can never find out it's me, can they? Like, I'm not going to have some serial killer come and find me and chop my feet off, am I?"

"I sincerely hope not."

"You said last night that you can take the daily photos for me. Will that be a hassle for you, though?"

"Looking at your feet and hot legs could never be a hassle."

I smile, relieved. "So we can start tonight?"

"Yes." He thinks for a moment. "Where did you sleep last night?"

"Very funny." I smirk.

"Is it?"

"Oh my god, I bet Taryn is feeling it."

Confusion flashes across his face. "Feeling what, exactly?"

"Oh my god, Blake, stop." I smile. "You're such a tease."

Laughter erupts inside again. "Listen, I have to go," he stammers in a fluster. "I'll be over later."

"Remember, nobody can ever know about this," I remind him.

"Of course not."

He disappears inside, and I smile in relief. That wasn't half as embarrassing as I thought it was going to be. Blake is the only one I would trust to help me with this. He's the most unjudgy person I know, and besides . . . he knows what images will sell. If anyone knows porn, it's him.

We start this tonight, and tomorrow, I tell John to stop paying my bills.

He can go to hell.

I've cleaned my house until you could eat off the floor, and suddenly I'm feeling reinvigorated. This is it; this is the answer I've been searching for.

Sell a few anonymous foot pictures, and voilà, the house is saved.

I smile as I buzz around with a spring in my step. Things are looking up.

Right at eight, *knock, knock*.

I open the door to see Blake standing on my porch with his big fancy camera.

"Hello." I smile.

"Hi."

"Why are you wearing a scarf?"

"I've got a stiff neck and need to keep it warm."

"Oh . . ." I frown. "When did you do that?"

"Last night."

"Are you okay?"

"Fine. Professional Foot Finder at your service." He dips his head as he walks past me, and I giggle.

"Is this crazy?"

"Totally." He looks around my house. "Listen, I was thinking you should be naked for these photos."

"I knew you were going to say that." I smirk. "Upstairs, pervert." I head to the stairs, and he follows me up. "So, how does this work?"

"I was googling it before I came over. I think we set up a profile, pick a name for you, and upload a few shots. Then people subscribe or something, and they get access. And if you want, you can charge for specials or whatever."

I walk into my bedroom. "Specials—what does that mean?"

"People can request things and pay extra for it."

"Like what?" I frown.

"I don't know, fucking ice cream on your toes or some shit." He flops onto my bed and lies across it.

"Why would anyone want to see ice cream on my toes?" I frown, horrified.

"Why would anyone jerk off to a photo of a foot is the question," he mutters dryly.

"You think they're jerking off to this?"

"One hundred percent."

"Eeewww." I screw up my face in disgust.

"Who fucking cares? Just show us the cash is what I say." He begins to scroll on his phone. "I'm going to join."

"What? Why?"

"Because then I can spy on our competitors and see what kind of photos they're uploading. Who's the highest-grossing model and stuff like that."

"What kind of photos they're uploading—what does that even mean?"

"I don't know, but if you need a cock in your photos, I volunteer mine," he replies, distracted by his phone.

I roll my eyes as I begin to get my stilettos out of my closet. "I will not need a cock in my photos. Didn't you learn anything from Michael's demise?"

"Apparently not." He reads on his phone. "And besides, he's a loser. It says here you need a profile name."

"Hmm." I keep retrieving all my shoes. "Like what?"

"I don't know, something sexy, I guess." He thinks for a moment. "What about Pinkie Hoe?"

46

"What?" I screw up my face.

"You know, instead of Pinkie Toe—Pinkie Hoe."

"Oh my god," I scoff. "That is the worst name of all time."

"Sole Sucker?" He shrugs.

"Sole Sucker?"

"You know, the sole of your foot, and it sucks."

"If you think a foot should suck, you're perverted."

"The evidence does suggest that."

"Can we add the name bit later?"

"Yeah, I guess. It has to be good. We really need to nail the name."

"Hmm." I put my hands on my hips. "Okay, so what do we do now?"

"Ahh." He sits up and looks around. "Let's start with some naked foot photos, I guess."

"You mean just feet photos?"

"Naked sounds better." He smiles.

"How do you want me?"

"I've been waiting for you to say that to me for years now."

"Will you behave?" I smirk. "Are you ever serious?"

"Not if I can help it." He gets down onto the floor and lies on his back as he holds his big, chunky camera toward me. "Walk toward me."

I slowly walk toward him, and he begins to snap away.

"Turn back around and walk the other way." He keeps taking photos. "Now step over me."

"You're not taking photos of my vagina, Blake."

"That plan worked perfectly in my head." He keeps snapping away. "Curl your toes up as if they are wrapped around a cock."

"What?"

He chuckles as he keeps taking photos while lying on his back. "I think I'm going to love this job."

# Chapter 4

My hands are curled through his hair; his head bobs up and down between my legs, and I moan as a deep shudder runs through me.

"Fuck yes," I whisper into the darkness as my toes curl.

Big hands are on my thighs, holding my legs back as he loses control, and his face thrashes from side to side as he completely devours me. His stubble burns my skin with a familiar sting.

*Fuck . . . so good.*

Hell, I needed this.

He slides three thick fingers into my sex, and my body ripples around him as my back arches off the bed.

"Ahhh . . . ," I cry.

The sound of my voice jolts me awake . . .

Gasping for breath, I look around my dark and quiet room.

Nobody is here.

*Oh.*

I pant as my brain catches up with reality . . . it wasn't real; it was just a dream.

Disappointment fills me.

I close my eyes and throw the back of my arm over my forehead.

"Fuck."

I'm alone . . . always alone.

I throw my legs over the side of the bed and drag myself up to a seated position. My skin is wet with perspiration; the orgasm was so close, I could taste it.

What the hell is going on with me lately?

That's three nights in a row I've dreamed about sex.

I know we had a wild party—hell, I can't even remember what happened—but whatever Taryn put into that punch must have awoken a monster in me.

A fuck monster who's craving it hard.

I don't know where I am in my cycle. I must be ovulating or something; this is so unlike me. I let out a dejected sigh and drag myself out of bed and into the bathroom. I flick on the light and stare at my reflection.

I'm disheveled and flushed; my hair is wild, but the only thing I can see is a primal hunger. There's a glow radiating out of my body and bouncing around the room.

A tangible force that not even I can control.

My body needs a good working over from a strong man.

For so long, sex has been the last thing on my mind; after all, it is the one sin that stole my perfect life from me.

But it's not a want anymore—it's a need, and if I have to screw my vibrator one more time, I'm going to go crazy.

I wash my face and amble back to bed. I lie there and stare at the ceiling while I go over the last three days. Why do I feel so different?

There are a lot of things that I don't know in this world, but there is one thing I am 100 percent sure of: I'm not going to be able to sleep until I come.

I reach over to my bedside drawer and take out Bob, my trusty partner. The one man who never lets me down. He gets the job done every single time.

I part myself and bring him down to the lips of my sex. My eyes close as I feel the tip of his cock.

*Hmmm . . .*

Now . . . where were we?


### Monday, 1:00 p.m.

I walk into the café and see the girls sitting in the back corner. I give them a wave and make my way over. "Hi." I fall into my seat.

"This is a nice surprise." Chloe sips her coffee. "How did you get the afternoon off?"

"Staff development day." I pick up the menu. "However, there is no staff developing going on today for me." I look around for the waitress. "Have you guys ordered food?"

"Not yet," Juliet replies. She picks up the menu to look over the choices. "I'm going to have the salad and grilled chicken."

"How's the wedding dress fitting now?" I ask.

"Tight." She widens her eyes. "Why the hell would I buy a dress that was already fricking tight? What was I thinking?"

"Like everyone, you were under the assumption that we are all going to lose weight?" Chloe replies for her. "You look great in it anyway; it's not too tight at all."

"Lose weight, ha! If anything, I've bulked up." Juliet slams the menu shut in disgust. "I'm eating everything there is to eat on this honeymoon."

"Including a lot of dick, I imagine," Chloe replies as she studies the menu.

"This time in two weeks, you'll be a married woman." I smile.

"I can't wait." Juliet hunches up her shoulders in excitement. "Oh, did you hear the boys are going to Vegas this weekend for the bachelor party?"

"They are?" I wince.

"One guess whose idea it was?" She looks at me deadpan.

"Dr. Grayson?" I smirk.

"Why is he so out of control?" Juliet adds. "If he thinks this is going to be a reenactment of the *Hangover* movie, I'm going to kill him with my bare hands."

"Oh no." Chloe holds her temple. "I'm having bad flashbacks."

"Of what?" I sip my water.

"I have hazy memories that we had the talk the other night at the party."

"The talk?" I frown, confused. "With who?"

"I don't know, I remember . . ." She frowns as if concentrating. "Why were we so drunk that night, anyway?"

"I don't know what Taryn put into that punch, but it was lethal," I reply.

"For real."

"Oh hell. I hope Blake doesn't remember."

"Remember what?" I ask her.

"I vaguely remember that I told him I had a crush on him before I met Oliver, and he . . ." She shrugs before cutting herself off.

"He what?" I ask.

"He said something, but I don't know what. The conversation is hazy."

"I don't even think I saw you talking to him." I frown.

"Oh, that's right," she gasps, wide eyed. "I forgot about that."

"Forgot what?"

"I walked in on him and Taryn," she says.

"He was with Taryn?" Juliet gasps.

"I don't know." She shrugs. "They were in the laundry room together with the door closed."

*What?*

"Were they . . ."

"Wouldn't surprise me." Juliet sips her coffee. "He's the world's biggest fuckboy."

I sit back, annoyed. He's always told me he doesn't find Taryn in the least bit attractive.

Ugh . . . men are all such liars.

"So what did he say when you told him you had a crush on him?" I ask.

"I don't remember, and I sure as hell hope he doesn't."

"I don't think he does. He was blind drunk . . . we all were," I reply. "When did you have this conversation, anyway?"

"When we were playing golf."

"When were we playing golf?" I frown. "I seriously have no recollection of this at all."

"At one a.m. at the top of your voices," Juliet snaps. "Honestly, what happened to you guys that night? I came home from work to find Henley asleep in our front garden."

I bubble up a giggle. "He was?"

"Oh yes." Chloe nods as she remembers. "He was sitting there watching us play."

"Who was there?" I ask.

"Carol, Ethel, Winston, Hen, Ant, and Blake, and then Heath and Levi from the Navy House came over too." Juliet shrugs. "I could hear their voices when you were playing golf, but it was late by then."

"What the hell were Carol and Ethel and Winston doing playing golf at one in the morning?" I screw up my face in question. "I don't remember this at all!"

"Being very loud, apparently."

"I think Blake took you home by then," Chloe says.

"Why did Blake take me home?"

"You know how he is with you." Juliet rolls her eyes. "He thinks you're his little sister that he has to look after all the time."

52

I'm still reeling about him hooking up with Taryn. "Why does he think that?" I huff. "It's so annoying."

"Be grateful you got home without being gangbanged by the Navy House."

There's a house at the end of the street where six Navy SEALs live, and they have a reputation for sharing their women.

"Is that supposed to be a good thing?" I widen my eyes. "That actually sounds like exactly what I need right now."

"What's wrong, Bec?" Juliet smirks. "Hungry, kitty?"

"Starving." I sigh. "Why does Taryn get all the dick around here, anyway?"

For fuck's sake, I'm annoyed if Blake hooked up with her. I turn my attention to Chloe to change the subject. "How's Oliver?"

"Dreamy." Chloe smiles. "He's taking me somewhere special tonight for our three-month anniversary."

I smile and take her hand in mine. "Good for you."

## Blake

I pull into my driveway just after 8:00 p.m. It's been a hell of a day.

Back-to-back appointments with two interns in tow, and then to top it off, just as I was leaving, one of my patients who has an infection took a turn for the worse. I rushed to the hospital and ended up staying for the last two hours until we could stabilize him.

I turn the car off and sit in the silence for a moment. This is the first minute of silence I have had to myself all day.

*Bang, bang, bang* sounds loudly on the window, scaring me. "What the hell?"

Antony is standing on my driveway in the dark. He opens my car door.

"What are you doing?" I huff.

"Did you find out anything about green cocks?"

"No." I climb out of my car and slam the door. "Why are you still obsessed?"

"Well, did you read the full story yet?" He begins to follow me up the path as I walk.

"I haven't had time to fart today." I unlock my front door.

"It's been a week. You haven't even looked at it again?"

"Get off my case already." I walk inside and put down my things.

"So Hen and I have been thinking about this." He continues to follow me.

I roll my eyes as I undo my belt. "*This* is what you thought about all day?" I pull my belt out of my pants. "Green aliens with two cocks."

"Hard cocks." He widens his eyes. "Weeping, hard cocks."

"I swear to god, you two are gay." I sigh as I go to the fridge.

"We think it must be Taryn."

I drink the milk from the carton. "Why?"

"Who else would have two-cocked green men on their brain?"

"Apart from you two, you mean?" I roll my eyes and take another swig.

"Yeah," he continues. "So basically . . . you fucked Taryn."

I frown at the thought. "That is not . . . great news."

My phone beeps a text, and I walk back out to the hall to read it. Rebecca.

**I made you lasagna.
Do you want me to bring it over?**

"Thank god." I sigh. "Finally, a useful friend."

I text back.

**Just got home.**
**I'll be over soon.**

"What does that mean?"

"It means I have something going on tonight, so you have to leave." I walk toward my stairs.

"What do you have going on?" He follows me.

"Stuff."

"Can I have the flash drive for the night if you're not going to look at it?"

"No."

"Why not?"

"Finders keepers."

"I want to read it."

I stop halfway up the stairs. "You're really into Mr. Green Cocks, aren't you?"

"His name is Ezra." He smirks. "And no . . . I'm not into it. I'm just intrigued as to who wrote it."

"Go. Home."

"Well, what am I going to tell Henley?" he calls. "We've been waiting for you to get home; he's going to come over."

"Henley is waiting to read it too?"

He breaks into a guilty smile, and I smirk. "You two are like old women. Go watch some porn like normal men." I walk into my bedroom.

"You're fucked," he calls. I hear the front door close as he leaves.

I look in the mirror at the huge love bite that's still on my neck. It's not fading fast enough. "Literally."

Half an hour later, I'm showered and wearing tracksuit pants and a T-shirt as I make my way over to Rebecca's. "Hello," I call in through her screen door.

"Come in."

I walk in and inhale the heavenly scent. "Something smells delicious," I say as I turn the corner into the kitchen. Rebecca is in flannelette pajamas, makeup-free, and her hair is in a high ponytail. Just the sight of her brings a smile to my face.

"Hello." She smiles. "Somebody told me you wanted lasagna." She frowns when she sees my scarf. "Your neck is still stiff?"

"Yep." I take a seat at her kitchen counter. "Something smells good." I try to change the subject.

"It's the least I can do when you're helping me." She begins to dish our dinner into bowls.

"About that."

She keeps serving.

"You know you don't need to do this photo thing?" I tell her. "I can loan you some money."

She stops what she's doing, as if annoyed.

"What?" I reply.

"I'm sick of relying on men. I want to be financially independent. Why is that so hard for everyone to understand?"

I knew she was going to say that.

"If you don't have the time to help me with Foot Finder, that's fine. I get it." She puts the bowl down in front of me with a thud. "Trust me, uploading pictures to a pervert website is the last thing I ever imagined doing." She slumps onto the kitchen stool beside me. "I feel like such a failure. I think I've hit rock bottom. If anyone ever found out about this, I would die a thousand deaths."

Shit.

*I need to be a better friend.*

I take a bite. "You're the best Italian cook I know."

"Except that I'm not Italian." She keeps eating.

I go over her choices. "Look, I don't necessarily think Foot Finder is a bad thing; it's a different thing, but not a bad thing."

Her eyes search mine.

"Well, why don't we put it this way . . . if you always do what you've always done, you will always be where you always were."

"Yeah . . ." She stares at me for a beat. "That's a good way of thinking about it."

"And who cares what anyone thinks anyway." I keep eating. "I don't give a damn what people think of me, and you should be the same. Being financially independent is a good goal to have and something to be proud of."

She gives me a lopsided smile. "Thank you."

"For what?"

"You always have a way of making me feel better."

"Yeah, well . . ." I shrug. "Don't thank me yet. We haven't even set up your profile properly. We need to come up with a name before we can go any further."

We eat in silence for a while.

"What name do you think?" she asks.

"Well, I've been thinking about this, and if you want my honest opinion—"

She cuts me off. "I do."

"Maybe we make it more like a porn name, something super sexy that would appeal to a mass market."

"Not foot related?" She frowns.

"I don't know; it doesn't allure me."

"But you're not into feet."

"True, although I have to admit that yours are pretty cute."

She smiles softly, and I feel it in the pit of my stomach.

*Stop it.*

"Okay, so what's my stage name?" she replies with renewed excitement.

I stare at her for a moment. "Bambi."

"Bambi?" She scrunches up her nose. "Why Bambi?"

"Because when they see you, they are going to be deer in the headlights."

She rolls her eyes. "Dear god."

"Trust me." I smile. "They don't stand a chance."

She goes back to eating. "So we have enough photos for the week?"

"Yep, you just have to finish making your profile, and as soon as it's approved, we can get started."

"So how much did your friend make when she did this?" she asks.

"She was getting up to sixty dollars an image, and that was ten years ago."

"If I could just make one hundred dollars a day, then my life would be set."

"Well, at least until we work something else out," I reply.

"Right."

We finish dinner, and she gets out her computer and sits at the table while I lie on the couch and flick through the channels. "I swear this is the best couch of all time."

"Pretty comfy," she agrees. She keeps typing. "I heard you hooked up with Taryn the other night," she says without looking up.

I sit up, horrified. "Who told you that?"

"So . . ." Her eyes stay on her computer screen. "Did you?"

"I . . ."

*Fuck.*

"Well?"

"Not that I . . ."

"What?" she snaps.

"Know of." I wince.

Her eyes rise to meet mine. "What the hell does that mean?"

"It means Taryn's stupid punch totally screwed me over, and I can't remember a damn thing."

She goes back to typing.

"I don't like her," I stammer.

"Whatever, Blake." Her eyes stay on her computer. "I don't care who you sleep with anyway. It's none of my business."

Disappointment fills me, and I lie back down.

She stays silent as she types, and I continue pretending to watch the movie.

Great.

*Now she hates me.*

"Are you angry?" I ask.

"Nope." She hits the keys with force.

"You're acting angry."

"I just . . ." She shrugs before cutting herself off.

"You just what?"

"I just find it fascinating how you always say that Taryn isn't your type, and then the first time you have too many drinks around her . . . you just . . ."

"I just what?"

"You act like a typical horny dickhead of a man."

Nailed it.

I drag my hand down my face.

Taryn . . . good god, not Taryn. Anyone but Taryn. What the hell was I thinking?

Seriously . . .

*Why can't I keep it in my fucking pants?*

I stare down at Blake. He's fast asleep on my couch. His hands are up above his head, and his bulging biceps are peeking out of his T-shirt. My eyes linger over his strong body.

No matter how much of a fuckboy Blake is . . . there's no denying he's a beautiful man.

My eyes drop lower . . . to the bulge in his crotch.

*Virile.*

My eyebrows flick up in disgust at myself. It's official.

I need a man.

If I'm even perving on my friend, who I have absolutely no intent to ever like that way . . . I need a man.

Blake's words from earlier come back to me. *If you always do what you've always done, you will always be where you always were.*

I blow out a defeated breath. He's right. I know he's right.

And yet . . . how do I change what I've always done when I've only ever been myself?

I pull a blanket over Blake and tuck a pillow under his head. He rolls onto his side and snuggles in as he gets comfortable. I go into the kitchen and take out a notepad and a pen. I need to make sense of all this.

I walk upstairs, lie on my bed on my stomach, and flick the pen around while I think.

Okay . . . so . . .

I think for a while. I can't work out what I want until I really know who I am.

What am I now?

I begin to list my attributes.

> Intelligent
> Kind

Soft
Not flirty
Mommish
Sensible

I twist my lips as I think some more.

Predictable
Boring

Yep . . .
The last one's the killer.
Boring . . .
How the hell did I end up boring?
I was never like this. *I* was the fun one. *I* was the spontaneous
one. The girl that John wasn't good enough for. He chased me for
years in college before I caved and went out with him.
*John* was the sensible, boring one, and somehow, as we got
older, we switched places. He blossomed into a successful surgeon,
and I became the dutiful doctor's wife who always put his needs
before my own.
I stare at my list for a while as the words sink in, and as much
as it pains me, I know that every word is true.
I drag myself out of bed and get into the shower. I lean on the
tiles under the hot water as a tidal wave of regret washes over me.
Why did I let him change who I was? I guess it was so gradual
that I didn't even realize it was happening.
Always doing the right thing, always putting others' needs
before mine, worrying what people think of me.
I don't even know who I am anymore.
*Little Miss Perfect.*

The truth is, I wish I could be more like Blake. He sees something that he wants, and he just goes for it without hesitation.

I finish up in the shower, put on my pajamas, and climb into bed. I stare up at the ceiling in the darkness.

They say that everything comes into your life for a season or a reason.

Maybe the reason is that I have to find the girl I once was.

To feel whole again.

So what . . . my marriage failed. Millions of marriages fail every year.

I didn't fail. He did.

This is on him; I don't know why I'm feeling guilty and beating myself up about it when he sure isn't.

Honestly . . . I'm done with this crap.

Tomorrow I start working on trying to get back to the real me.

The old me . . . the fun me, the girl I was before I met him.

*If you always do what you've always done, you will always be where you always were.*

Blake's right.

I need to be more calculated with my choices going forward. I need to learn how to use my douchedar and see the red flags. I mean . . . this is need-to-know information.

I flick my pen as I think, and I write down the heading of a new list.

A better-way-to-do-things list.

### The dos and don'ts of dating

Hmm, where do I start?

### Attributes I want in a man

He must be:
>
> Hot
>
> Honest
>
> Kind
>
> Sensitive
>
> Caring
>
> Funny
>
> Romantic
>
> Family-oriented

**Red flags—Men to avoid**
>
> He can't be:
>
> A liar
>
> A player
>
> A cheater
>
> Cold
>
> Selfish
>
> Controlling
>
> Mean
>
> Nasty
>
> Heartless

If there's a god out there, please hear my prayer.

Please let me meet a man who is worthy of my love.

I'm losing faith that he exists.

*Blake*

**My phone alarm vibrates on the coffee table, and I drag my sleepy eyes open.**

Where am I?

Rebecca's couch. Damn, I must have been tired last night.

I've got to get moving. I drag myself up and walk out into the kitchen. Rebecca must still be upstairs; I'll take her up a cup of coffee before I go.

I'm still feeling guilty about Taryn . . . who could blame Bec if she hates me. I kind of hate myself right now. I make her coffee, wrap my neck in my stupid scarf, and head up the stairs. I walk into her bedroom to see that she's on her side and still sleeping. I carefully put her coffee down on her side table and sit on the edge of her bed. Her dark hair is splayed across her pillow, and her chest rises and falls as she breathes.

Her long eyelashes flutter across her cheeks, and I smile as I watch her.

So angelic.

I could watch her all day, but I've got to get to the hospital. I stand, and as I walk out of her room, I notice a notepad and a pen on the end of her bed. I pick it up and read it.

Attributes I want in a man

He must be:
Hot
Honest
Kind
Sensitive
Caring
Funny
Romantic
Family-oriented

Red flags—Men to avoid
He can't be:
A liar
A player
A cheater
Cold
Selfish
Controlling
Mean
Nasty
Heartless
If there's a god out there, please hear my prayer.
Please let me meet a man who is worthy of my love.
I'm losing faith that he exists.

I read and reread the last two lines.

Please let me meet a man who is worthy of my love.
I'm losing faith that he exists.

Sadness fills me.

Her list of attributes she wants in a man . . . I've never met anyone who . . .

I sit back down on the side of her bed and watch her for an extended time. My mind is racing with a million thoughts. None of them good.

She doesn't deserve any of this. She never did.

I want her to be happy. I want her to find the man of her dreams. I want someone to love her as much as she loves them.

I tuck a piece of her hair behind her ear, and I know what I need to do.

I'm going to find her a good man . . . even if it kills me.

# Chapter 5

*Rebecca*

"Pack away your pencils, and then we're going to do some recorder practice," I call from my place on the stepladder. I hold the painting up to where I want to hang it, take the thumbtack out of my mouth, and push it into the corner.

Decorating my classroom is my favorite hobby and most definitely an extreme sport.

"Miss Dalton . . . ," a little voice calls. "Lucy took my pencil sharpener."

"Lucy," I call. "Did you accidentally take Carter's pencil sharpener?"

"No," Lucy calls.

"Do you want me to check your pencil case for you, just in case?" I ask.

Lucy's eyes dart around guiltily. "Um . . ."

"Sometimes things accidentally get mixed up," I say softly. "Don't they?"

"Yes." Lucy nods in an overexaggerated way. "I'll look now."

I smile and go back to my picture hanging. Kindergarten, the home of cuteness overload and mini kleptomaniacs . . . all accidental, of course.

I love my job; I love every single second of every single day . . . but only in the mornings, of course. Ask me again in the afternoon when I've had a day from hell, and I will tell you I'm resigning tomorrow. Five-year-olds and I have a lot in common: our moods change hard and quickly. Good times turn bad in the bat of an eye.

"Oh look, here it is." Lucy holds the sharpener up as if she's just won the gold medal.

Carter scowls and snatches it from her. "I knew you had it."

"Carter . . . what are our classroom values?" I ask him.

Carter rolls his eyes, and his little shoulders slump. "Be kind and understanding," he mumbles.

"Yes," I call as I push in the last thumbtack. "That's right." I climb down the ladder. "Everyone, grab your recorder and take a seat on the mat, please." I pull out my desk drawer to grab my music book just as my phone flashes a text. I glance around and then sneakily read the message. It's from Blake.

**We are live, Bambi!**
**It's go time.**

A surprised giggle escapes me before I quickly hide it. I quickly text back.

**OMFG!!!!**

I cannot believe we are actually doing this; I throw my phone back into the drawer and take out my music book.

"Let's go, little people," I call as I clap my hands. "Everybody sit on the mat."

Casual as casual can be.

Lunchtime and I'm acting like a spy.

I sit in the lunchroom and discreetly peer at my phone under the table.

**Sales: 0**

Hmm. I click out of the app.

What if I don't get any clicks? What if my feet are considered ugly in the world of foot porn?

I mean . . . I am only listening to Blake, and maybe he's biased. Shit.

I glance down at my feet. Maybe I should have gotten a pedicure. I text Blake.

**No sales yet.**
**Maybe I should have painted my toenails red?**

I wait for Blake's reply, but it doesn't come, which isn't surprising. He doesn't have his phone on him through the day at work.

Damn it, why does he have to be so diligent?

I check my phone again.

**Sales: 0**

Hurry up and call me back, Blake.

Gah . . . I can hardly wait to speak to him. What if I've done the profile wrong or something? I glance back at my feet once more. Tonight I'm going to up my game, get really inventive.

These perverted sick fucks want to get nasty . . . so will I.

Maybe I should do some research on Google to see what kind of fetish pictures people actually want. My eyes float to the other people at the lunch table. Not here, though.

Tonight . . .

I can't mess this up. I need extra income . . . and fast. I refuse to touch the joint bank account ever again, and the bills are beginning to pile up.

Damn it, what if I never sell a single photo?

No, I can't think like that. I have to be optimistic.

Blake will know what to do. I feel like driving to the children's hospital and paging him to the front counter for an emergency consultation.

Of course, I have a stupid staff development meeting tonight, and I won't be home until late.

I check again.

### Sales: 0

I stuff my phone into my handbag and bite into my apple.

Turns out that living a double life as a camgirl isn't as glamorous or profitable as one would think.

### Blake

It's 7:00 p.m. I pour myself a beer, take a seat at my computer, and plug in the flash drive. I have to admit that I, too, have been thinking about this all day, since Ant reminded me. I'm truly fascinated as to who could have written the stuff on this flash drive.

The screen lights up, and I scroll down as I read the contents. There are lists and stories. I frown as I keep going through it; this appears to be some kind of backup.

I scroll much farther down this time as I look for some kind of clue.

**Author Nooky Nights**

I frown. Nooky? Who would give themselves a pen name of Nooky Nights . . . whoever wrote this is a confirmed fucking weirdo.

The door opens, and Henley and Antony appear. "Are we on?" Hen asks.

"Yeah." I keep scrolling down.

They both pull up a chair and sit behind me as I scroll through the screens.

"Any idea who yet?" Henley asks as he grabs him and Ant a beer from my fridge.

"Their author name is Nooky Nights," I tell them.

"Nooky Nights?" Henley frowns.

"I like it." Antony opens his can of beer. "Catchy."

"So do you think the person who lost this is freaking out?" Henley asks.

"About what?"

"Losing all their work."

"I think it would just be a backup, right?" I shrug. "They maybe don't even know it's lost."

We read on.

Titles releasing:

*Fisting Frenzy*

My eyes widen.

"*Fisting Frenzy!*" Henley chokes on his beer.

"What the fuck?" Antony leans in to take a closer look. "What the fuck is a fisting frenzy?"

"Something that is one hundred percent never happening to me." I wince as I get a bad visual.

### Creamy and Wet

"Although . . ." My eyebrow rises. "I do like the sound of this one. Creamy and wet is my favorite two-word combination."

I hear a car, and I glance out through the curtains to see Rebecca arriving home. She's home late tonight. I keep scrolling.

### The Daddy Swap

"*The Daddy Swap* . . . what the actual . . ." Henley erupts into laughter.

"So it's a woman," I think out loud.

"What makes you say that?" Antony asks.

"*Daddy* is a term females use; no man is thinking hot things about daddies."

"Facts," Henley agrees.

"Unless he's gay, and then I'm thinking that daddy swapping would be goals."

I screw up my face in disgust as a new, more disturbing visual comes through. "If you ever think about my father, I'll murder you."

"I'll murder myself first, don't worry," Henley utters dryly. "Nobody is that desperate."

"My father is way above average," I scoff. "You'd be lucky to look half as good as him at his age."

"If you say so." Henley widens his eyes, and Ant chuckles.

"*Count Lazarus*, what's this one about?"
We read on.

> *Bang, bang, bang.* The knock is desperate, a haunting sound. Filled with terror and fear.
>
> I can hear them coming. Their war cry echoes from the surrounding buildings.
>
> "Witch. Witch. Witch," they yell.
>
> Carrying flaming torches, they march through the town in search of their next victim.
>
> "Freya." The door bangs again. "Run, Freya. Run. They're coming for you."
>
> "Run, Constance," I yell through the door. "Save yourself."
>
> Constance is my younger sister; she needs to get out of here, or they will kill her too.
>
> "I'm not leaving you here," she yells through the door.
>
> "Witch. Witch. Witch." The cries are closer as they turn the corner.
>
> "Run," I scream. "Run while you can."
>
> I hear her panicked footsteps, and I peer through the curtains to see her just make it across the field and into the forest before they come around the corner.
>
> I run to the back door and out into the field. "There she is," they scream.
>
> And I run.
>
> I run as hard and as fast as I can.

Hands grab my hair and pull me back. I struggle. I fight. I scream and kick.

They capture me anyway.

Hours later, bruised and battered, fear is running through my blood like a wildfire.

Like a prized possession, the townspeople gather around for the show. I stand with my hands tied behind my back within a giant pile of wood.

Tonight, I will be burned at the stake.

Dirty, bloodied, and broken, I don't have any fight left in me.

"What kind of fucking book is this?" Henley snaps. "I don't want to read depressing shit."

"Who wrote this?" Antony frowns. "This story does not go with daddy kink."

Fascinated, we read on.

The guard holds up the torch of fire, and I close my eyes in preparation.

I always knew they'd come; the writing was written on the wall. They killed my grandmother and great-aunt before me.

Both had the curse.

Tainted with the same brush as I.

The wind picks up. Dirt flies through the village, a mini tornado that begins to tear apart everything in its path. The skies go black as people scream; the thatching flies from a nearby roof.

I look around at the destruction. What the hell is happening?

Then among the chaos, I see him.

Walking toward me in slow motion, his dark eyes hold mine. Standing at over six foot five with black hair and olive skin, his jaw is square. His body is large, but it's his presence that overwhelms me.

A darkness that can be felt from afar.

The crowd sees him and begins to scream as they run, scattering in all directions.

No . . . it can't be.

My heart begins to race as fear runs through me.

I've heard whispers, of course, but I never knew if they were true.

He holds his hand up in a silent command, and the ropes that tie my hands fall to the ground.

Dear god.

No.

Please, no. I would rather be burned at the stake.

It's Lazarus.

The most powerful vampire on earth.

And he's here . . . for me.

"What the fuck?" I whisper, wide eyed. "Vampire porn." I scroll down the page in a panic. "Where's the rest of it?" I keep scrolling.

"Oh, get fucked." Henley pushes me out of the way and begins to use the mouse to scroll down. "What does he do?"

"I don't know." I snatch the mouse back.

"Please tell me he rails her." Antony hovers over my shoulder, peering at the computer screen.

"Well, obviously . . . he must."

"You reckon he's got two cocks?" Ant asks.

"Hopefully."

"Henley," Juliet's voice calls as she comes through the front door. "Where are you guys?"

I immediately flick the computer off, and we all stare at each other, rattled but intrigued, just wanting to read on.

Juliet walks into my office. "Hi." She smiles all casually.

"Hi, Jules."

"What are you guys doing?" She looks between us.

"Wedding stuff," Henley lies.

"Oh, you guys are writing speeches?" she says hopefully.

Henley's eyes flick to me, and I bite my bottom lip to hide my smile. "Something like that."

*Rebecca*

## OVERNIGHT MIRACLE SERUM

I read the label before I dip my finger into the jar and rub some onto my face. I'm freshly showered with a towel around my head. I'm in my pajamas and feeling very sorry for myself.

No sales. Not even one.

I mean, I don't know what I expected, but the way Blake talked about it made it sound like it was easy.

Maybe my feet looked dry and old . . . hmm.

I put my foot up onto my bathroom cabinet and rub in the overnight miracle serum. Then I rub it into the other one too.

I check my phone again.

Ugh.

This stupid fucking Foot Finder dashboard . . . is it even working?

I hear a *knock, knock* from downstairs.

*Blake.*

I bounce down the steps to see him standing at my front door, and I open it in a rush. "Hello." He bows his head as he walks past me into my house.

"Hello, Dr. Grayson." I slam the door closed. "You didn't text me back today."

"I was busy." He looks around. "Where are your bookshelves?"

"In the hall."

"I want to read a book; can I borrow one of yours?" He walks out into the hallway into my kitchen and begins to run his finger over the spines of my books on the shelf as he goes through them.

"I don't think I have anything you'd like." I cross my arms as I lean up against the wall. "We didn't sell one picture today."

"Do you like vampires?" he asks, distracted.

"Are you listening? I didn't sell one picture today. My feet must be a turnoff."

"How many cocks do the people in your books have?"

"What?" I scoff. I throw my hands up. "I don't know what goes through that mind of yours sometimes. Focus." I turn and march out to the living room.

I hear him pull a book off the shelf. "Can I take more than one?"

"Since when do you like romance books?" I call back.

"I'm trying to learn how to be romantic."

"You are?" I screw up my face. "Since when?"

"Since now."

"Why would you want to be romantic?" I call.

"Ahhh . . ." He hesitates. "I'm thinking of settling down."

*What?*

"With who?"

"Ahh . . . I don't know yet." He walks out into the living room with a huge stack of books. "I'm borrowing these."

I stare at him, my mind a clusterfuck of confusion. "Since when do you want to settle down?"

"It's just a thought." He shrugs. "So . . . your feet?"

"Are obviously ugly."

He rolls his eyes. "That's a load of crap, and you know it."

"Well, why haven't we sold one? Not a single hit."

"It's early days." He puts his pile of books down and flops onto my couch. "Relax."

I let out a deep, deflated breath. "Maybe we need to do better photos?"

"Possibly." He rubs the backs of his fingers over his stubble as he thinks. "Is there fisting in your books?"

"What?" I screw up my face in horror. "No."

"What about fisting frenzies—any fisting frenzies?"

"I thought you wanted to learn how to be romantic?" I gasp.

"I do. I do."

I widen my eyes. "A fisting frenzy is how you want to be romantic?"

"Yeah." He widens his eyes back. "It is, actually."

"Eww."

"You don't like fisting?" He raises an eyebrow in question.

"No. I do not."

He sits forward, as if interested. "Ever tried it?"

"Never have. Never will."

"Ha," he huffs as he sits back. "Famous last words. You all say that."

*Did he fist Taryn?*

The thought turns my stomach. "You're repulsive."

"Many women find me irresistible."

"Yeah, well, they have giant, stretched-out vaginas, so they don't count."

He tilts his head to the side in silent agreement.

*Knock, knock* sounds at the front door.

"Who's that?"

Blake rolls his eyes. "It will be Antony."

"What does he want?" I begin to walk to the door.

"Probably some books."

"He's trying to learn how to be romantic too?" I squeak. What the hell is going on with these guys?

I open the door, and my face falls as I see John, my ex-husband; my hackles instantly rise. "What are you doing here?" I snap.

"Hi." He gives me a lopsided smile as he brushes past me into the house, then stops suddenly when he sees Blake lying back on my couch.

"What the hell are you doing here with my wife?" John growls.

"She's not your wife." Blake stands and walks to John and pushes him hard in the chest. "Get the fuck out."

# Chapter 6

They grab each other by the shirt as they get in each other's faces.

What the hell?

That escalated at a million miles per minute.

"Stop it," I yell. Blake throws John toward the front door. Damn it. "Blake, stop it."

"Get the fuck out, and don't come back," Blake growls.

"Blake," I yell as I begin to get angry with him too. I need to speak to John. "Will you listen to me? Go home."

"No." Blake wrestles with John.

"Oh, it's all making sense now, Rebecca," John fumes. "This is why you want a divorce."

"I want a divorce because *you* are an idiot," I spit. "Blake. Will you stop pushing him?"

"Nope." He pushes John down the stairs, and he goes flying across the lawn. "When I tell you I want a reason to kick your ass, I mean it."

"You touch me again and I'm calling the police." John stands and dusts himself off. "And to think . . . while I thought you were my friend"—he sneers—"you had your eye on my wife the entire time."

"Because you were too busy looking at other women," Blake screams as his anger hits a crescendo.

I see Antony's front door open, and he walks out onto his porch to see what's happening. Antony begins to make his way over. "Blake," he calls.

"Go home. Both of you." I look up to see Juliet and Henley have come out front too.

"What's going on?" Henley calls as he crosses the road toward us.

"You think you have it all figured out, Rebecca," John yells. "What a pathetic downgrade. Blake Grayson is the biggest womanizer I've ever met. He will throw you to the curb as soon as someone new comes along, and everyone fucking knows it. I love you; I made a mistake. You mean *nothing* to him."

"You lying prick." Blake throws a punch, and it connects with John's jaw. He staggers back. John loses control and runs full speed at Blake, and they both crash to the ground.

This situation is completely out of control.

"Stop it," I cry. "Somebody, do something."

Blake punches John in the face, hard.

"Blake," I yell.

He punches him again and again, and oh my god, he's actually going to kill him.

"Enough." Henley and Antony wrestle Blake off John, holding him back by the arms. Blake is panting and red; adrenaline is surging through his system. "You come around here again, and I'll fucking kill you."

"Not if I kill you first," John pants. He's on his hands and knees as he tries to collect himself. He spits blood onto the grass.

My eyes go to Blake as he struggles to get free, and that's when I see the fading red love bite on his neck. My stomach rolls in disgust. A hickey from a woman who he claims to have no attraction to.

An outright lie.

John's right; they *are* tarred with the same brush.

Twins, both trying to control my situation. Neither of them giving me an inch of respect.

I ask John to go home; he refuses. I ask Blake to go home; he refuses. Everything is all about what they want.

That's it.

"Don't come near me again. You both make me sick." I turn and march inside, slam my front door shut, and lock it. Having an ex-husband and a friend who act exactly the same is fucking toxic and not something I need in my life.

That's it; I'm done.

I storm upstairs and get into the shower; I stand under the hot water as I try to calm myself down.

I hear more screaming coming from outside, and I put my hands over my ears.

Hopefully they kill each other.


I sit in the café and sip my coffee as I watch the sun set. As the sunlight fades, my mind wanders off into something really depressing.

I don't want to go home.

It's been three days since the front yard boxing match, three days since I've spoken to Blake.

It's one thing to be disrespected by my ex-husband. It's another thing to be disrespected by a friend. Blake had no right to order John to leave; it *is* still legally John's house, after all. Here I am, trying my best to keep it civil so that I have at least a chance of a good outcome in the divorce courts, and my supposed friend is doing all he can to sabotage my mission. When I asked Blake to leave and go home so that I could talk to John, he point-blank refused and then proceeded to beat him to a pulp.

It's not okay.

John came around to our house to have a conversation with me about financial matters and our impending divorce. What gives Blake the right to react that way?

He acted like a jealous child. I understand that he hates John. I do, too, but that doesn't excuse violent behavior.

I didn't leave a controlling, toxic marriage to enter into a controlling, toxic friendship.

I feel so deflated and flat, and my rose-colored glasses have been well and truly smashed.

To make matters worse, I haven't sold a single image on Foot Finder. I guess my toes don't have what it takes, and I feel like a fool that I ever imagined they would.

This time last week, I was excited and had hope that I was going to be able to afford to keep my house. This week, I'm just not so sure.

I glance at my watch. It's 6:30 p.m. The boys leave for Vegas tonight, and I didn't want to see Blake before he left. He's called me at least twenty times over the last few days, and I just . . . I don't even want to talk to him. I mean, what is there to say.

*You're a disappointment* is all I've got.

The door opens, and a little old man and woman walk in. They must be at least eighty years old. I smile sadly as I watch them. They're holding hands and chatting away to each other; they look so in love.

*How long have they been together?*

I feel a deep, overwhelming sadness. Lost dreams and a sad statistic are all my marriage amounted to, and an unexpected wave of emotion fills me.

I was a good wife; I swear I was.

The worst part is, I know that the part of my heart that loved so deeply and unencumbered has died. Never to be resurrected, and there's not a damn thing I can do about it.

I'm not the same girl I once was.

Quite sure I'll never trust a man again, let alone be able to love one.

The vision of the old couple blurs as my eyes fill with tears, and I discreetly wipe them away. I drag myself off the stool and stumble out to my car, and then once safely alone, I let myself cry.

**8:30 p.m.**

My phone vibrates on the coffee table as a text comes in from Juliet.

**Hi Bec,**
**Where are you?**

I close my eyes. Ugh. I am not good company right now; I've fallen into a self-pity hole, and I just need to sleep it off.

I reply.

**I'm at home but I'm beat.**
**Breakfast in the morning?**

I feel a twinge of guilt as I see her dots bouncing. I hope she didn't want to do something tonight with Henley being away.

**No worries,**
**I'm tired too.**
**Saving myself for tomorrow night.**
**Love you, good night.**

**Xox**

I'm looking forward to tomorrow night too. I smile in relief and reply.

**Good night,**
**Love you too.**
**Xox**

I turn off the television and head upstairs for a long, hot bath and bed.

Tomorrow is a new day.


*Blake*

"This is the captain speaking; welcome to Las Vegas." The voice sounds through the intercom. "The current local time is nine forty p.m. We trust you had an enjoyable flight and look forward to seeing you again soon. Safe travels, everyone."

The plane drives down the tarmac toward the airport. I turn my phone off flight mode and discreetly look at the screen.

"Did she call?" Antony asks from beside me.

"Who?" I raise my eyebrow in question.

"You know who."

"No," I reply. "I don't." I stuff my phone back into my pocket.

"What did you expect?" Henley mumbles. "You beat her ex to a pulp, and you aren't even with her."

"Imagine if he was." Antony laughs. "A for-real fucking psycho."

I roll my lips as I glare out the window, not in the mood for these fuckers tonight.

I messed up.

Bad.

But in my defense, his face is a major fucking trigger for me, and I had no control over myself.

"She'll calm down," Henley says as he scrolls through his phone. "Give her some time."

"I don't know who you're talking about," I reply, uninterested.

"Liar." Henley smirks.

I fake a smile and then immediately drop my face. "We are in Vegas. I don't want to think about my annoying neighbor."

"Right." Antony nods.

"And if she thinks that when she finally decides to call me back that I'm going to pick up her call, she's going to be sadly mistaken."

"Right." Henley nods.

"If anything, she should be thanking me."

"For . . . ?"

"Defending her honor," I huff.

"Because violence is always the way you do that," Antony agrees with an eye roll.

"Maybe I should defend your honor right here, right now?" I stand and grab my bag from the overhead.

"Come at me."

We stand as the line slowly trickles out of the plane.

"Come on, guys, perk up. We're in Vegas," Henley reminds us.

He's right; snap out of it. This is Henley's bachelor party; we need to give him the time of his life. I feel a little of my mojo return.

"For the record, my name this weekend is Lazarus," I casually tell them as we exit the plane.

"Why is that?"

"'Cause I'll be fucking those witches." I wink.

They both laugh out loud, and in that moment, I know the weekend is saved.

I will *not* think of her again.


*Rebecca*


"Delivery for Juliet Drinkwater," the man at the door says as he holds up the roses.

Juliet bounces on the spot as she signs for them, and Chloe and I gush with excitement for her. She closes the door and passes me the beautiful bunch of red roses. "Hold these while I read the card." I take them from her and inhale the heavenly scent. "Jules, these are gorgeous." She reads the card and holds it to her chest. "Oh, I love him."

"What does it say?"

She passes me the card.


**Seven days until you walk down the aisle to me.**
**I can't wait to marry you.**

**xox**


"Ahhhhhh." We all swoon.

"Who could ever have imagined that Henley James would end up being so perfect?" Chloe smiles dreamily.

"I did." Juliet beams with happiness. "I knew all along that he had it in him." She carries her roses into the kitchen. "He's going to be the best husband that ever lived. Better put these in some water."

Chloe and I walk into the kitchen, and while she sits down on the stool, I get to making us a cup of coffee.

Juliet dials a number and holds her phone with her chin as she fills the vase with water. "Hello, Mr. James." She smiles. "I just got a beautiful delivery." She laughs and then listens as she begins to undo the ribbon around the bunch of roses. "Seven."

"She's walking on air," Chloe mouths.

"I know." I smile. Juliet's happiness is contagious. "I can't wait for the wedding next weekend."

"My god, me too."

"She's going to be the most beautiful bride."

"Definitely the happiest."

"Thank you." She smiles. "I love you." Her eyes float over to us as we listen in. "Oh, he does?" She laughs out loud. "Yes, put him on." She keeps rearranging her roses. "Hello, Antony." She smiles. "Well, you behave yourselves." She laughs out loud, as if surprised by something he said. "No. I will not bail you out of jail."

"She totally would," Chloe whispers.

"Well, you look after him." Her eyebrows rise. "Blake's what?" Her mouth falls open. "That can't be good. Send me video updates of this, please." She laughs. "I mean it, Deluca. You are in charge."

Chloe and I exchange looks. What's going on?

"Goodbye." She hangs up the phone. "Blake is out of control already."

"Why?"

Juliet's phone beeps a text, and she opens it. It's a video, and we all lean in to watch it.

It's Blake. I frown as I try to get my bearings. "What is he doing?"

He's shirtless and in his swimming trunks. His body is glistening with tanning oil.

88

"What the hell is he doing?" Chloe frowns.

Then the sound comes through, and we giggle as we hear the song. He's in a sombrero hat and doing the Macarena by the pool to a band with a group of old ladies.

His carefree, boyish charm is infectious, and I give a lopsided smile, my eyes lingering on his glistening, oiled-up body. His muscles are flexing as he dances, and he's laughing out loud. "Those grannies are going to think all their Christmases have come at once."

"Right?" Juliet agrees. "This will be the highlight of their lives."

"He sure knows how to have a good time," Chloe replies.

The girls go back to chatting while my mind stays by the pool in Vegas with Blake.

I wish I knew how to be carefree and fun like him.

Doing the Macarena with grannies—the thought brings a smile to my face.

He's one of a kind.


Onstage, we sing at the top of our voices; Juliet is wearing the customary short white veil, with glitter on her face and a very tipsy demeanor.

Twenty-five of us girls are singing our hearts out and having the best night of all time to an ABBA tribute.

We are at the bachelorette party.

Next weekend, Juliet Drinkwater is getting married to Henley James, and it's the most monumental and exciting thing in forever.

Juliet points into the audience as she sings along to "Dancing Queen."

She's totally lost in the moment, and we all laugh out loud. "She thinks she's really in ABBA."

"She's better than ABBA."

They pulled her onstage to sing the last song, and she's absolutely crushing it.

"Are we still going out after this?" Chloe calls.

"I don't know." We both watch Juliet onstage, and as she sidesteps, she's so tipsy that she nearly trips. "Maybe not."

"I think we should get her home."

"Yeah, me too."

The song ends, and the crowd cheers. Juliet does an overexaggerated bow and blows kisses into the crowd as if she's a rock star. Who are we kidding—tonight, she is.

I hold my hands up in the air and clap loudly. "Go, baby."


"Goodbye," Juliet calls from the cab window. "Thanks for the best night of my life." It's taken us forty minutes to bundle her into the cab. I think she said goodbye to every single person in the club.

"Hello, Mr. Driver," she slurs from the back seat.

"Hello." He smiles.

I'm sitting in the front, and Chloe is in the back with her.

"Did you know I'm getting married next week?" she tells him.

"The veil did give me a clue." He smirks.

"Oh." She smiles. "Did it?" She hiccups, and Chloe and I get the giggles. She would be mortified if she could see herself right now. Someone's pink lipstick is smeared across her cheek, her hair is standing on end, and the short, cropped veil is all ruffled up and strongly resembles a bird's nest.

*Ding . . .*

"Oh, I got a message," she slurs. She digs through her bag and pulls out her phone and swipes across. "Oh, it's Antony." She narrows her eyes to concentrate on the screen. "I have *lots* of video messages from him." She scrolls back and clicks on the screen and holds it up for us to watch too. There are at least fifty men in what appears to be a foyer of some sort, and they are all in position for a photo to be taken. The men in the front row are sitting; the ones in the next row are kneeling. And the guys behind them are cheering.

"Is that how many guys are away in Vegas with them?" I ask in horror.

"Yep," she hiccups.

"When was this sent?" Chloe asks.

Juliet looks and frowns. "Two this afternoon. I must not have seen it."

We watch as two guys strategically strap a ball and chain onto Henley's ankle as all the boys cheer.

Juliet's face screws up. "Do we even want to watch this?"

"Probably not." I wince.

She clicks on the next video. "Chug, chug, chug," chants the crowd. Henley, Blake, and Antony are onstage somewhere chugging beers. Blake finishes first and turns his glass upside down on top of his head as the crowd goes wild.

"Ugh." I screw up my nose. "It's like a bad frat house situation."

"What the hell are they doing?" Juliet asks.

"Drinking." Chloe shrugs.

She clicks on the next video, and Henley is at a blackjack table. "Antony is taking his keeping-you-updated promise very seriously." I smile.

"Right?" She giggles. Henley appears to win, and everyone screams and picks him up and throws him around as if he's as light as a feather while he laughs out loud.

"Okay, this is ridiculous." Juliet winces. "They are completely out of control."

I turn back to the front and stare out the window as we drive around for a while.

"Oh god, look at Blake," she says as she watches the video again.

I turn back around. "What's he doing?" She hits play again and passes me the phone.

Antony has filmed Henley playing cards, but in the background, you can see Blake talking to two beautiful, scantily dressed women. He has his hand on one's behind, and he leans in and kisses the other on the lips. He says something, and they both giggle on cue.

"What the hell?" I whisper. "Two?"

Henley wins the game, and Blake jumps in the air and joins in the celebrations, leaving the two women alone while he carries on like a lunatic.

"Ugh, I don't even want to know what they're doing." I hand back the phone in disgust. I hear another video play from the back seat, and I can hear them all laughing out loud. "Are they in an elevator?" Chloe asks.

"I don't know what's happening, but it must be hilarious. Blake and Antony's laughter is hysterical." Juliet hiccups. "What could possibly be so funny?"

Ugh, good-time Blake Grayson . . . always the life of the party.

She clicks on another video, and Antony's voice comes on as he's filming. "Jules, Miss Juliet Drinkwater," he announces as if he's a television presenter. "Henley is getting your wedding present."

"Oh no," Juliet gasps. "They're in a tattoo parlor."

"*What?*" I spin around. "Seriously, they are out of control right now. He is never going to Vegas again." I lean in to watch the footage.

Once again, the sound of uncontrollable laughter is echoing. The footage flicks to Henley getting a tattoo on his chest over his heart.

## JULIET

"Oh my god," we all gasp.

"He's going to regret that tomorrow." Juliet laughs. "I wish he got it on his forehead."

"Ahhhhhh," we hear in the background. The camera flicks to Blake lying on a bed.

"What's he doing?" I lean in to see closer. "Don't tell me he's getting a tattoo too."

"Beat it," we hear someone call.

"Yeah, that's it," someone else cries.

A woman comes out with a surgical tray, and everyone erupts into hysterical laughter. An out-of-control man cheers.

"What *is* happening?"

Antony is laughing so hard that the camera is flicking all over the place, and we can't tell what's going on.

"Got to go." Antony laughs. "Grayson's about to beat the meat."

"What's happening?" I frown.

"I have no idea."

"He's getting his cock pierced." Antony laughs hard.

The camera goes black, and we hear Blake's hysterical laughter as it fades into the distance.

"*What?*"

"Oh. My. God," Juliet gasps. "Blake is actually getting his dick pierced. Is he insane?"

"Obviously." I drag my hand down my face in disgust. "Why am I not surprised?"

"He's seriously out of control," Chloe replies.

Another video bounces in, and Juliet opens it. It's a photo of Henley asleep in the bathtub. He has a bucket and a pillow under his head.

"Oh, thank god, he's back home safe." Juliet sighs with relief.

"Why would they put him in the bathtub, the assholes?" I scoff.

I turn back to the front, and my mind flicks back to the two women that Blake was kissing earlier.

I don't know much about life, but I do know one thing: there will be no more videos sent through tonight.

Blake and Antony probably dropped Henley at home and then went back out.

What happens in Vegas stays in Vegas.


The sun is shining, and the birds are chirping. It's a beautiful day, and I'm late for work.

It wouldn't be a Monday if I wasn't.

I pour my coffee into my thermos cup and grab some fruit from the refrigerator.

Now that I'm on a budget, I have to pack my lunch all the time. Those little coffees and carryout snacks here and there add up. I grab an apple and an orange and the sandwich that I made last night from the refrigerator. I put my handbag over my shoulder, grab my coffee, and make my way out the front door.

From my peripheral vision, I can see that Blake's garage door is going up, but I refuse to look over.

*Refuse!*

I'm still angry with him, and to make matters worse, he hasn't bothered to try and call me in days.

So now I'm angrier.

I hope his new piercing makes his dick fall off.

I open my car door and sling my handbag in to sit on the front seat. I lean down and peer through the window of my car to see Blake walk out the front door of his house in a navy suit. His dark sandy hair has a wave to it, and he's standing tall. The way he carries himself screams confidence.

I narrow my eyes, infuriated by the mere sight of him.

He gets into his car and starts it. The Porsche roars like a kitten as she warms up.

Ugh . . .

I walk around to the driver's side, and as I'm climbing in, I fumble my orange and drop it. It rolls down the driveway and into the road just as Blake is driving out.

He pulls the car to a halt so that he doesn't run it over.

I stomp down the driveway, and he opens his window. "Can you keep your fruit under control?" he says dryly.

"Apparently not. If Tuesday night is anything to go by."

"What did you say?" he spits.

I snatch the orange from the road, and I hear his car door open.

*Here we go.*

"Did you just call me a piece of fruit?" He puts his hands on his hips, indignant.

"Yeah." I put my hands on my hips too. "I did, actually. Although I guess it really should have been meat."

"What the fuck is that supposed to mean?"

"It means you're a giant meathead, that's what it means."

"Oh, right." He leans in close and points to his chest. "I'm a meathead because I threw your loser ex-husband off your property."

"He was here to discuss our divorce," I whisper angrily.

"Oh please," he scoffs. "You cannot be this stupid. Divorces are discussed over email. The only thing that warrants a visit to your ex's house late at night is the scent of reconciliation."

"What?" I scoff. "You're an idiot."

"And you're an ungrateful wench."

"Me?!" I explode. "How am I ungrateful?"

"I escorted someone who has caused you nothing but heart-break from your property before he had the chance to lie to you again . . . and yet . . . *I* am the asshole."

"When I asked you to leave, you should have just left, not beat him up."

His eyes hold mine for an extended beat. "Fine." He throws his hands up in defeat. "You'll never have to ask me to leave again." He gets back into his car and slams the door. "You and your red flags have a nice life." His Porsche roars as he takes off up the road.

*Asshole.*

# Chapter 7

*Blake*

I drive onto Kingston Lane just at 7:00 p.m. It's been a long, hard week. I've suffered the crippling effects of alcohol poisoning for all of it, and the worst thing is that I'm about to do it all again. It's Thursday night, and tomorrow at lunchtime, we all leave to go and spend the weekend at the Fairmont Resort, the venue of the much-anticipated nuptials.

We have the wedding rehearsal tomorrow afternoon and then the prewedding dinner. The wedding is on Saturday, where thankfully, I'm not allowed to have one sip of alcohol. I would love to tell you it was Juliet's idea, but in truth, it was Henley's. Apparently, I can't be trusted with my speech if I'm inebriated, and my first drink of the night will be as I make a toast.

With the way I feel right now, that suits me just fine. I don't want to drink again for the rest of my life anyway. I pull into my driveway, and as my garage door goes up, I can see that the lights are on in my house.

Ugh . . .

I park my car and head into my house through the internal garage door.

Henley and Antony are in my kitchen, sitting at the counter with a pen and paper.

"What are you morons doing here?" I sigh as I open my fridge and peer in.

"Writing speeches," Antony replies. "You need to help."

"I . . ." I shake my head as I pull out a carton of orange juice. "I'm incapable of writing anything remotely interesting." I open the carton and begin to drink from it. "I'm tired."

"Tired?" Henley frowns. "How can you still be tired? It's Thursday."

"Vegas fucked me up the ass, okay? I'm flatlining. I've had a hangover that's lasted four days, I'm busy as all hell at work, my voice is hoarse, my dick is fucking sore, and to top it off, I'm now having hot flashes."

"Your dick is sore because you dry humped a mannequin twenty minutes after you had it pierced, you fucking idiot," Henley snaps.

I pinch the bridge of my nose as the memory swings back around. "Honestly, I don't know what goes through my pea brain at times."

"We need to do these speeches."

"Tomorrow." I keep drinking the orange juice as I peer into the depressingly empty refrigerator. "I keep hoping that the food fairy is going to miraculously deliver me groceries every day while I'm at work, but the bitch never shows."

"Pull it together, man. Who gives a crap about groceries?" Antony sighs. "We have speeches to write." He picks up his pen. "And why the hell would you be having hot flashes?"

"He's in menopause now." Henley rolls his eyes. "Nothing would surprise me anymore."

I slam the fridge shut. "Why are you at *my* house doing this?"

"Because Juliet's cousins are all at my place, and they've taken over everything, and I'm about to jump out the window to put myself out of my misery," he says in a creepily calm voice as he fakes a smile. "That's why."

"And my brother is fighting with his wife in my kitchen while his children sleep on my living room floor," Antony adds.

*Huh?*

I hold both my hands up in question but am too tired to even open my mouth to ask it. "Whatever." I slide my shoes off and walk into the living room and lie on the couch. I kick off the cushions and raise my legs to rest on the back of the couch. "Someone at least order takeout or something. I'm fucking starving." I put the back of my forearm over my eyes. "I really need to go to bed. Actually . . ." I get up and get a packet of frozen peas, lie back down, and put them over my crotch. My cock is throbbing like a motherfucker.

"Better?" Antony asks.

"Better."

"What do you want to eat?"

"I don't care." I sigh.

"Lasagna?" They have a chuckle between themselves.

"Very funny," I snap. "Antony, we are swapping partners at the wedding."

"No, you're not," Henley snaps.

"I am *not* talking to Rebecca, let alone dancing with her."

"Yes. You. *Are.*"

"And don't you dare go on with your jealous ape act and beat up anyone who looks at her at the wedding," Antony warns.

"I am not jealous of Rebecca." I screw up my face. "As if."

"Yeah right," Antony scoffs.

"I escorted John from the property because he deserved it." I point to the front door. "Now . . . get out of my house before I escort you both out in the same manner."

I load the car with our bags, and Antony climbs in. "We have to pick up Chloe after we get Rebecca."

I pull up out front and beep my horn, and the front door opens. "I'm coming." Bec holds up her finger. "Two minutes."

I stop the car and get out as I wait. Eventually I walk through the open front door and into Rebecca's house. The best way to get through this weekend is to just pretend everything is normal. "Can I take this suitcase out to the car?" I call.

Rebecca comes around the corner. "Yes, please."

"You know we're only going for two nights, right?" I look over her giant suitcase.

"Yes." She turns the television off and switches her alarm on.

"I hope this huge suitcase fits in my car."

"Oh. I hadn't thought of that. Should I drive my car?"

"No, it'll be fine. I'll give my bag to Henley to take in his car." I wheel her suitcase down the driveway and then open the trunk. I pull out my bag and begin to rearrange.

"Hi, Bec." Antony gets out of the car.

"Hello." She smiles and gives him a peck on the cheek. "I'm so excited."

"Me too."

"Hi, guys," a voice says from across the street. We glance up to see Taryn; she's in short denim shorts and a hot-pink bikini top, and she's wearing roller skates. Her huge boobs are hanging out everywhere.

"Whoa. What's happening with the girls today, Taz?" I say before I put my mouth-to-brain filter on.

"Oh." She laughs and shimmies her shoulders, and they wobble around. "They're hard to hide, so I don't even bother trying anymore."

Antony and I exchange glances.

"Yeah, well." I dig out Antony's bag from the trunk. "Don't give yourself two black eyes."

"Ha ha, I'll try." She twirls her hair around her finger. "You guys leaving for the wedding?"

"Yep," I reply as I continue to rearrange the trunk.

"I'll see you there tomorrow."

"Okay."

"I have some great footage from the other night, boys."

"What night?" I ask. I pull one bag out and put it down onto the road.

"Carol's party night."

*What?*

My eyes meet Antony's again, and a frown furrows his brow.

"Okay then, see you tomorrow, Taryn," I say. "We have to get going."

*Go away. Go away right now.*

Taryn shimmies her boobs again. Seriously . . . those things need their own zip code.

I glance into the back seat at Rebecca to see the subtle roll of her eyes.

*Fuck it.*

"Help me take the bags over to Hen's." I widen my eyes at Antony as I throw my bag into his arms. I grab his bag and power walk over to Henley's as Antony runs to keep up.

"What footage does she have of us?" I whisper under my breath.

"Who knows."

"Did we fucking tag team her or something?"

"No," he scoffs.

"Are you sure?"

"Yes." He shrugs and then shakes his head. "Pretty sure."

"Pretty sure?" My eyes widen in horror. "Pretty sure is not good enough."

"Well . . . what were *you* doing at the time, dickhead? Why is it only up to me to remember your misdemeanors? Because trust me, there's a lot of them. I can't keep up."

"I'm never touching alcohol again," I huff as I stomp up Henley's front steps. "This is it; I have reached my limits."

Henley casually walks out the front door. "What are you doing?"

"Taryn has footage of us from the night of Carol's party," I whisper.

Henley's eyes rise across the road to see Taryn in her roller skates talking to Rebecca through the car window. "That can't be good."

"Oh . . . you think?" I spit.

"Did you ask Rebecca if she wrote the book?" Henley asks.

"No," I snap. "She didn't write the fucking book."

"And we know this how?"

"Because I asked her about a fisting frenzy and she was completely horrified. Thank you for throwing me under the bus on that, by the way."

We all look back across the street to the two of them talking.

"I don't think Taryn wrote it," Henley replies.

"Why not? A fisting frenzy is right up her alley," Antony quips.

"Listen, we've got bigger fucking problems than a stupid flash drive," I whisper. "Taryn—"

"Boys." We are interrupted by Winston coming around the corner.

"Hello, Winston." We all step back from each other.

"Listen, Blake. Can I have a quick word in private?" he asks as he gestures around the corner.

Huh?

I don't have time for this shit right now.

"Sure."

I look up to see Taryn is now doing spins on her roller skates.

*Fuck me.*

I walk around the corner with Winston. "What is it?"

"Look, Doc," he says as his eyes dart around guiltily. "I need your help."

"With?" My eyes rise back across the street to Roller Boob Barbie. If she says something to Rebecca, I swear I'm going to run her over with my car.

"Well . . . with the wedding and all . . ." He shrugs.

"What is it?" I snap impatiently as my eyes stay across the street.

"I'm staying at the hotel tomorrow night, and with all the new ladies in town . . ."

My eyes come back to him, confused.

"I need some blue pills."

"Oh." Fuck me dead. "Right." I finally understand. "Winston, you know I can't prescribe Viagra to you without a full medical, and I don't have time to do that right now."

His shoulders slump in disappointment.

"Why don't you go and see your PCP this afternoon? He has your medical records, so he can give you a script."

"He won't give me anymore."

"Why not?"

"Because he said I'm using too many."

"How many are you using?" I frown.

"A couple of packets this month."

"A couple of packets?" I gasp. "Who the hell are you fucking all the time, Winston?"

"I'm in the prime of my life," he scoffs. "What do you expect?"

I pinch the bridge of my nose. "Not this."

*Good god.*

This man is eighty in the shade, and he's getting more action than anyone I know.

"I can't help you. I'm sorry, I have to get going. Please, go and see your doctor."

I march back around the corner in time to see that Roller Boob Barbie has fallen over, and Rebecca is out of the car helping her. This is all I need. If she's broken something, we are *not* taking her to the hospital.

"Can we just fucking go already?" I snap to Antony. "This street is getting on my last nerve."

"Ready when you are."


*Rebecca*


I stare out the window and watch the scenery go by. The car is filled with excited chatter between Chloe and the boys, and every now and then I smile and add to the conversation. But on the inside, all I can concentrate on is the eerie feeling of déjà vu that's creeping in.

I remember driving to my wedding venue as if it was yesterday.

Just like this wedding, we had ours at a resort, and all the guests stayed for two days of celebrations. Feels so recent . . . and yet so far back in time.

A lifetime ago.

"Here she is," Blake says as we turn into the fancy driveway. The resort comes into view, and we all gasp. It's a huge country estate with a four-story old mansion and the most beautiful gardens you have ever seen. "Oh wow, check this place out." Blake smiles. The car drives around a large lake that has ducks swimming in it.

"I hope one of those ducks walks through the wedding when it's going on." Chloe smiles as she looks out the window.

"I hope a duck attacks someone," Blake agrees. "Causes complete chaos."

"Henley, I hope it attacks Henley." Antony smiles. We all chuckle as we imagine it.

"I'm hoping the wedding cake crumbles when the waiters bring it out," Blake says as he parks the car. "Can we have just one chaotic incident, please?"

"Be nice," I gasp. "I can't believe you are hoping for things to go wrong."

"Not wrong," he replies. "The times you remember the most are the times when crazy shit goes down."

"True," Antony replies.

Be careful what you wish for, Dr. Grayson. The crazy shit you dream of is probably going to be me and you fighting to the death.

We get out of the car and make our way into the reception area; our mouths drop open as we look around in wonder. It has black-and-white marble tiles and huge chandeliers and lamps everywhere. The furnishings are all velvet and fancy upmarket antiques.

"Wow," I whisper. "Will you look at this place."

"Incredible," Blake agrees.

"It has a real French feel," I whisper. "I mean, not that I've been to France, but from what I've seen in books and magazines."

"It *is* very French." Antony nods as he looks around.

"You've never been to France?" Blake frowns.

"No." I shake my head. "I've never been to Europe at all."

"Oh, you have to go," he says as he steps up to the reception desk. "It's a must for everyone."

"One day." I give a halfhearted smile. Not that I'll ever be able to afford it.

"Hello, we are here for the James and Drinkwater wedding," Antony says to the girl at reception.

"Yes." She types into her computer. "You are the bridal party."

"Yes."

Chloe and I smile in excitement. *It's happening.*

"We have you booked in the executive suites on the third and fourth floors."

Blake pulls out his credit card. "I'll take care of all the rooms, please."

"No, no." I cut him off. I've been saving for this.

"The rooms have already been taken care of by the groom," the receptionist tells us.

"Oh."

"Idiot," Blake grumbles. "I told him not to pay," he thinks out loud. "Okay, thank you."

The receptionist hands over the keys to the rooms. "I have Blake Grayson and Rebecca Dalton on level three. Take the elevator over on the right to level three, and your rooms are down the end of the corridor."

"Thank you."

"Then Antony Deluca and Chloe Willcox are on level four. Your elevator is on the left, and your rooms are halfway down the corridor."

"Thank you."

We make our way through the foyer. "What time is the wedding rehearsal?"

"Three o'clock."

I glance at my watch. "Meet back down here in an hour?"

"Okay."

Blake and I walk to the elevator and push the button. We wait in awkward silence.

The doors open, and we walk in and turn to face them. They close, and we begin to ride up to our floor.

"You know—"

"Don't talk to me," he cuts me off.

My mouth falls open. Of all the nerve. "Don't talk to you?"

"That's right." He keeps his eyes facing forward to the doors.

"Don't you dare gaslight me, Blake Grayson."

"Ha." He rolls his eyes. "That's a joke. *You're* gaslighting *me*. Telling me I'm gaslighting you is typical gaslighting behavior. Can you even hear yourself?"

"How am *I* gaslighting *you*?" I snap, outraged.

"You tell me that you hate this man; you tell me that you don't want him anywhere near you. You tell me that he isn't allowed on your property. Then he shows up, and I set a clear boundary for him to leave you alone. He refuses, so I step in, and suddenly I'm the *bad* guy."

I glare at him.

"I'm not a pushover like some people." He raises his chin defiantly.

The doors open, and he strides out.

"You think I'm a pushover?" I fume as I follow him down the corridor.

"Don't think it, I know it."

"We are trying to come to an agreement on the divorce settlement."

"Oh please," he scoffs. "There is no agreement. He is going to railroad you into getting exactly what he wants."

"How do you know that?" I put my hands on my hips.

"Because unlike you . . . I can see through him. I can see through all these fucking idiots that you think are good guys."

I begin to hear my angry heartbeat in my ears. "You know what? Coming from a walking red flag like you, that's a joke."

"How am I a walking red flag?" he whispers angrily.

"Oh please." I throw up my hands in disgust. "You cannot be this obtuse."

"Obtuse." His eyes bulge in their sockets.

"That's right," I spit. "You know as well as I do that you party way too hard every weekend. You sleep with every hot woman you meet. Even our neighbor, who you have constantly told me is not your type . . . which is repulsive, by the way. You keep talking about all these kids you want to have, and yet at the age of thirty-five, you can't even hold down a girlfriend. When are you planning on settling down and having these children, when you're eighty? And to top it all off, you get holes punctured through your dick in Vegas and probably have syphilis now." I grab the key to my room. "If that isn't out of control, I don't know what is. So excuse me if I refuse to take relationship advice from a fucking train wreck."

"How do you know about my dick? I'll tell you what's a fucking train wreck," he spits. "A woman who has a friend who would literally do anything for her, and she treats him like shit." He grabs his key and holds it to his door.

"I do not treat you like shit, Blake."

"Want to bet?"

"How?"

"I've had the worst ten days feeling like absolute shit because you won't speak to me, and I've missed you, and yet all you're worried about are the feelings of your toxic ex."

My heart sinks.

"You can go to hell, Rebecca."

He walks into his room and slams the door shut in my face.

Damn it.

I walk into my room and flop onto the bed. I stare up at the ceiling as his words roll around in my head.

He's right. I am a train wreck.

# Chapter 8

The sun is shining, and there isn't a cloud in the sky, only a dark storm brewing in my heart.

"You stand here." The wedding celebrant grabs Blake by the shoulders and puts him into position. "And you are here." She moves Antony into place under the arch. He smiles broadly and goes up onto his toes in excitement.

We are in the garden beside the lake. The scent of freshly mowed grass is pungent, and gardeners are pruning hedges in preparation for tomorrow's ceremony.

Bees buzz around the canopy of white flowers, and anticipation fills the air.

She turns toward me and Chloe. "You stand here." She moves me into position. "And you, darling, are here."

The four of us stand in place with our hands clasped in front of us.

"Henley," she calls. "You come down now."

Henley smiles broadly and walks down toward us. He proudly takes his place in the center. He turns back to the boys, and Blake slaps him on the back as they chuckle.

*My heart.*

I don't know if I've ever seen a groom so excited to get married, or maybe it's just that I've never paid close attention. The celebrant begins to explain the proceedings, but somehow, I'm lost. I can't explain it, but have you ever been involved in an event and felt as though you're sitting up in a tree and watching it from afar?

As if there is a piece of glass . . . or, in this case, ice, between you and the happenings. Tomorrow is a happy day, the best day, and yet all I can feel is a deep, overwhelming sense of sadness.

Two of my very best friends in the entire world are diving headfirst into a lifetime of love, and I want to go into this wedding with an open heart.

But alas, how can I when I'm reliving the nightmare of handing yourself over to someone forever?

They keep chatting around me, and a vision comes through my mind, only it isn't a vision. It's a memory, crystal clear and cutting like a knife.

*Me, walking down the aisle . . . to him. The look in his eyes, the love in my heart.*

Was he cheating even then?

I was so naive.

My eyes fill with caustic tears at the thought.

"Rebecca, Rebecca . . . Rebecca," the marriage celebrant says sternly, and I glance up. "I need you to listen, dear."

"Sorry," I stammer as I'm brought back to the present. I blink to try and hide my tears. "I'm sorry, I beg your pardon?"

"You need to go with Chloe." She gestures in front of us.

"What?" I look around in confusion to see that Chloe is now down at the end of the aisle with Juliet. "Sorry, sorry," I say in a fluster as I take off down to them.

"Now, pretend to hold your flowers, and walk up the aisle to the music." The music begins. She holds her hand up. "And now." I take the large steps up the aisle. "Now you, Chloe," she calls. "And finally, our beautiful bride, Juliet."

We get to the front and take our places like we practiced. Then Juliet joins us, and Henley takes her hands in his. Unable to help it, he kisses her softly, and as everyone chuckles, my eyes fill with tears anew.

*Stop.*

This is not about you, Rebecca. Get ahold of yourself.

In a detached state, trapped somewhere between the past and the present, I watch as we go through the logistics of tomorrow's ceremony.

"Well done, everyone," the marriage celebrant tells us. "Let's celebrate with a glass of champagne." She gestures to the restaurant. "We have canapés and champagne ready and waiting for us."

Everyone chatters excitedly as we walk toward the event center, and the closer we get, the higher my need to be alone grows.

I feel unstable.

Once inside, I fake a smile and take off in search of the ladies' room. I take the stairs; I'm going to go to the upstairs one. I need some distance.

I burst in the door and sit on the toilet and put my head into my hands.

I'm hot and clammy and . . . fuck.

My breath is ragged, my heart is thumping hard in my chest, and I sit for a long time as I try to pull myself together.

I hear the door open and shut. "Bec," Blake's voice says softly.

I close my eyes . . .

"You okay?"

"I'll be out in a minute," I say in as happy a voice as I can.

My heart beats harder. Damn it.

*Leave me alone.*

"Okay, see you outside," he says. The door opens and closes, and I put my hand over my mouth and sob out loud.

I don't want to be this person.

"Open the door," Blake's voice snaps.

Shit.

"I'm fine, Blake."

"Open it, or I'm climbing over the top."

Damn it. I open the door, and the minute I see his face, I burst into tears.

"Hey." He wraps me in his arms. "What's wrong?"

"Nothing." I snuggle into his chest as he holds me. The lump in my throat hurts so bad as I try to hold my tears in.

"Bec. What's wrong?" he whispers into my hair. "Talk to me."

"Nothing, I'm being stupid."

"No, you're not."

"It's just . . . it's just . . . failure is running through my veins like poison."

"Babe." He holds me tighter.

"This isn't what I thought my life would be," I whisper. "It wasn't supposed to go like this. I don't want to be a divorcée."

"I know," he says softly.

"And you're completely right. I am a train wreck."

He smiles against me. "I may have exaggerated the train wreck part, but in my defense, you did call me one first."

I look up at him.

"Here's what we're going to do," he says softly as he wipes my tears away with his thumbs. "We're going to forget that we had a fight, and we're going to forget that you ever got married, and we're going to go out there and celebrate with our friends, and you're going to start again."

"But . . ."

"No buts; no more living in the past." He kisses my forehead. "That's it. Those are the last tears you will ever cry over him."

"It's not even him I'm crying about." I sniff, feeling stupid. "He's an idiot. This isn't about him."

"What's it about, then?"

"I don't know." I shrug. "Lost dreams, I guess."

He gives a subtle shake of his head.

"What?" I look up at him.

"We're a fucking mess, you and me."

"How so?"

"You only like players; I only like party girls. Neither of which can give us the desired outcome we want."

"Train wrecks," I reply.

"Total fucking train wrecks. Come on." He pulls me out of the stall and turns on the tap. "Dry your eyes, crybaby, and snap out of it."

I give a halfhearted smile.

"Because today is the last day that you and I are going to live like this."

"Like what?"

"In the past."

I blink, confused. "I know I do . . . but . . . how do you live in the past?"

He shrugs casually, as if he doesn't have a care in the world. "I think I'm twenty-one."

"Feeling twenty-one is not a bad thing, Blake."

"It is if you act it, and you were right—everything you said to me is true. I am a walking red flag."

I smile sadly.

"And for the record, I probably do have syphilis in my dick; it wouldn't surprise me."

I bite my lip to hide my smile. "I can't believe you got your dick pierced."

He cocks his leg and rearranges his crotch. "I actually have an ice pack in my underpants right now." I laugh out loud, and he does too. "Oh," he says, "I've been dying to ask—are you a foot millionaire by now?"

"No," I scoff with a roll of my eyes.

"No?"

"I haven't sold one single picture."

"Not one?"

"Nope."

"Meh." He shrugs. "Those weirdos don't know hot feet when they see them."

He bumps me with his shoulder, and I bump him back.

I think our fight is over.


The violins sound, and I hunch my shoulders up in excitement. "This is it, Jules."

We are at the top of the garden, about to walk down the aisle. We can see the boys in their black suits down below, waiting for us under the arch.

She bounces around on the spot. "I can't believe this is actually happening."

She's wearing a fitted white lace dress and the most beautiful antique veil; it was her great-grandmother's. Her hair is up, and I've never seen a more beautiful bride. She is literally glowing.

I kiss her cheek. "Go marry your man."

She laughs again. Her excitement is palpable. Chloe pulls her into a hug and then begins to walk down the aisle in slow double steps. I take off next and make my way down. Chloe and I are wearing ice-blue strapless dresses. I feel like a glamorous Grace Kelly; the dresses have a real old-Hollywood vibe.

As I get closer, I see that Henley is watching his beloved Juliet walk down the aisle to him through tears.

*Oh . . .*

I look around to see that both Blake and Antony are choked up too.

*My heart.*

We take our places and turn to watch Juliet on her father's arm walk the last of the aisle. As Henley wipes his tears with the backs of his hands, Juliet is giggling like a schoolgirl. She's practically running to get to him.

She turns and passes me her bouquet, and then her father kisses both her cheeks and passes her to Henley.

"Hi." He smiles.

"Hi," she gushes.

"You look so beautiful," he mouths.

"So do you," she mouths back.

He leans in and kisses her softly, his lips lingering over hers, and from my peripheral vision, I see Blake wipe his eyes too.

Who knew these boys were so emotional?

"We're getting married," Juliet whispers, as if this is a surprise.

"I did notice that," Henley whispers back, and we all laugh.

This is such a happy day.

The best.

The waitress carries out a huge tray of cupcakes and puts them down on the table. "Oh." From across the room, my eyes widen in excitement, and I drag Blake over toward the table. "Let's go get some."

There must be fifty cupcakes laid out in the shape of a giant heart. "Look how pretty." I smile as I look over the choices. "Take a photo of this for me."

Blake takes out his phone and snaps a photo. "Hold a cupcake up," he instructs me.

I pick up a cupcake. "They're still hot," I gush. "And the icing is oozing." I take a big bite. "Oh . . ." I go cross-eyed in pleasure. "You have to have one of these. The icing is lemon."

"You all right there?" Blake frowns as he looks at the ground.

I glance down to see the hot icing has drizzled down my shin and all over my foot. I giggle. "Eww."

"Hold that thought." Blake gets down on his knee and begins to snap photos of my foot in my strappy stiletto.

"What are you doing?" I glance at the people surrounding us. "You look like a weirdo."

"Yeah, well, you look like you've got come all over your foot, and if it's turning me on, imagine what those sick fuckers would do."

"What?" I whisper.

Blake stands and grabs my hand and drags me outside. "Sit down and take your shoe off. I'm going to video it."

"Huh?" I frown in confusion. "What do you mean?"

"Just fucking do it."

I sit down on the edge of the garden. "Don't get my face in this."

"I'm not." He begins to video and puts his finger up to his lips for me to be quiet.

I slowly untie the strap and slide my foot out of my shoe. The white icing is now dripping between my toes.

He stops filming for a second. "Now, swipe your finger through it, and bring it up to your mouth," Blake says.

"What?" I whisper as I look around guiltily. "I don't want my face in anything."

"I'll edit it out; just do it." He holds the camera up and then drops it again as he has another thought. "Don't put your finger in your mouth; smear it across your lips instead."

"*What?*"

"Just fucking do it," he whispers.

I do as he tells me, and he smiles and holds his thumb up. "Do it again."

I do it again.

"Now, smear your fingers through the icing on your foot, and then rub it into your toes."

"You're perverted, you know that?"

"I do know that." He keeps filming, and after a good ten minutes, he says, "Okay, I think I've got it." He scrolls back through his photos and smiles. "This is hot."

"How is this hot?" I frown as I lean over his shoulder to look at the photos.

"I'm going to upload this one," he tells me.

The photo is of my foot when we were inside by the cake table. It's the one with the icing drizzled down my leg. "Yeah, okay."

He passes me his phone. "Log me in to your dashboard from my phone so I can upload it." I log in to Foot Finder and pass him his phone back. "No faces."

"I know, I know." He concentrates and goes through the process. "I'm going to add a teaser for more content and put a ridiculous price on it."

"What do you mean, a ridiculous price?"

"I don't know." He shrugs. "We're faking it till we make it here."

I bite my lip to hide my smile. Faking it till I make it has literally been my life motto lately.

He keeps concentrating on his phone.

"I'm going to the bathroom to wash this icing off. I'm sticky as all hell."

"Okay." He keeps typing in his phone. "See you inside."


Blake swings me out and then rolls me back in as I laugh out loud. We've had the best time dancing and laughing—so much laughing.

We are on the terrace dance floor; the fairy lights twinkle above, and the magical night is coming to an end.

Blake holds me in his arms as we sway to the music. "I have a confession to make."

"Uh-oh." I look up at him. "Do I want to hear it?"

He chuckles. "Maybe not."

"Hit me."

"I read your list." We keep moving to the music.

I frown, confused. "What list?"

"The dos and don'ts of dating that you wrote."

Huh?

I try to remember when he would have seen that.

"I came in to say goodbye to you in the morning, and it was on the end of your bed. I hate to tell you, but the list was a complete hit and miss."

"Oh."

*What did I write?*

"You know, I've been thinking about it, and I've got an idea."

I roll my eyes as we dance. "Whatever it is, the answer is no."

"Hear me out." He smiles down at me. "What if I helped you?"

"Helped me?"

"You want to have fun and new experiences, don't you?"

"Yes."

"But you don't want to get hurt."

"True."

"What if I showed you the ropes?"

"What do you mean?"

"What if . . ." He gives a halfhearted shrug. "What if I coached you through your first few dates?"

We sway to the music. "How would you coach me?"

"I don't know." He thinks for a second. "Maybe we could go on a few double dates, and I could . . . observe."

I frown. "Observe?"

"You know, just watch over you and keep you safe, and you could"—he shrugs again—"have the fun you wanted. The next day, we could go through my observations and tweak certain aspects of your"—he tries to articulate himself—"delivery."

"Who would you bring to our double date?" I ask.

"I don't know." He shrugs again. "I'm sure I can find someone."

I think this over as we dance. "And what happens at the end of the date?"

"What do you mean?"

"What happens at the end of the night when I want to go home and have sex with my date?" I ask.

"Then you go home and have sex with your date," he replies. "Hopefully he's got a good dick and gets the job done well."

The idea rolls around in my head. "So let me get this straight—you want to coach me on how to be a player?"

He smiles wistfully. "I wouldn't put it like that, but . . . in a nutshell, I guess that's a good analogy."

I think on it for a moment. I do want to play the field, and maybe . . . I mean, if Blake did finally meet someone, I wouldn't rely on him so much either. "Okay, on one condition."

"What's that?" He looks down at me.

"I get to coach you on how to be boyfriend material."

"Ahhh." He smiles as he looks out over the crowd. "But there lies the problem. You see, I don't want to be a boyfriend."

"So just take the few dating lessons and then don't be a boyfriend, but you will have the knowledge in your tool kit for later on when you do."

His eyes hold mine as we continue dancing. "I just want to help you; I don't need help. When it comes to women, I have my ducks in a row."

"I beg to differ. Your ducks are completely out of control. Do we have a deal?"

"No. I just coach you."

"Not happening. It's a two-way street. It's both of us or nothing."

His eyes hold mine, and I can see his brain ticking as he thinks it over.

"Do we have a deal?" I ask hopefully. "You are the only one who I trust to help me with this." I shrug. "And besides, who else can show me how to be a player better than the best player himself?" I smile up at him. "You were literally made for this job, Blake."

"Because I'm a red flag?"

"You are the *king* of red flags."

He rolls his eyes, unimpressed, and I know I'm wearing him down.

"Come on." I smile up at him. "Even you know that this is a good idea."

"Fine." He sighs.

"Fine what?"

"We have a deal."

# Chapter 9

*Blake*

I drag my heavy eyelids open and inhale deeply. I glance around my hotel room.

Ahh, a morning without a hangover.

*Nice . . .*

I lie for a moment in the silence, and then I remember something from last night. I reach over and grab my phone and log in to Foot Finder.

STICKY SITUATION IMAGE
IMAGES SOLD: 32 $22.00
VIDEO REQUESTS: 16 $250.00

I blink and try to focus my eyes. Huh?

What does that mean?

I rub my eyes. Wait a minute—am I seeing this right?

I sit up and really focus.

STICKY SITUATION IMAGE
IMAGES SOLD: 32 $22.00

Wait, what?

I'm reading this right, aren't I? I open the calculator on my phone. Seven hundred and four dollars. My eyes widen. What the fuck? And if I edit the video to make sure no faces are in it and let those sick fucks buy it, that's . . . I do the math again. Four thousand dollars.

I spring out of bed. What the . . .

I immediately dial Rebecca's number.

*The number you have called is unavailable.*

Damn it. Why doesn't she ever charge her stupid phone? I glance at my suit pants. I still have her key in my pocket from yesterday, when she had nowhere to carry it. I'm going to surprise her.

I grab my phone and both keys and walk out into the corridor. I swipe the key on her door and walk in. The room is freezing cold, and she's sleeping like a baby.

Why is it so cold in here?

I sit on the side of the bed and watch her for a moment. Her long dark hair is splayed across her pillow, and her angelic face is clear of makeup.

*So beautiful.*

"Bec," I whisper.

She keeps sleeping.

"Bec," I say a little louder.

She jumps awake with a start and screws up her face at me. "What?" she snaps.

"I have good news."

She rolls over and puts her back to me as she pulls the blankets up around her face. "Go back to sleep, Blake."

"It's fucking freezing in here."

"I don't know how to work the air conditioning," she grumbles.

"Well, I'm freezing."

"Get under the blankets," she snaps. "You big baby."

I get into bed beside her, and she continues to sleep with her back to me while I scroll through my phone.

I didn't imagine this, did I?

I log back in to Foot Finder and do the math again.

Nope, I was right.

"You made forty-seven hundred dollars yesterday," I say out loud.

She's quiet for a moment as she registers what I said. "What?"

"On Foot Finder. Our icing pic went off."

"What?" she scoffs as she rolls over in a rush. "What do you mean?"

I show her the dashboard screen, and she squints to read it.

"Do you need glasses?" I ask.

"One hundred percent." She keeps squinting.

"Are you fucking blind or something?"

"Oh my god." She sits up in a rush as she stares at my phone, and it's then that I see she's wearing a see-through nightdress.

It's pale pink and sheer, and I can see the coloring of her nipples on her full breasts. My eyes drop down to linger on her cleavage and then lower to her breasts.

*Thump . . . thump . . . thump . . .* goes my cock.

Pain radiates through me.

"Ahh." I wince.

This fucking piercing has got to go. I can't even get an erection without having a near-death experience.

The pain begins to spiral up to my balls . . . *Oh, fuck me dead.*

"Wait a minute, is this for real?" she gasps.

"Yep." I wince as I try to will my cock to go down. "Ahhh." I lie back in pain. Sweat covers my brow.

"What's wrong with you?" She frowns as her eyes stay fixed on the screen.

"Ahh, this piercing." I lean back on the bed as my cock nearly tears in half.

"What?" She stops what she's doing. "Is it really that bad?"

I nod.

"Can I see?"

"You don't want to." I shake my head. "*I* can't even look at it."

"Show me."

I pull the tip of my cock up and over the waistband of my boxer shorts.

Her eyes widen in horror. "You pierced through the entire head?"

I nod as my face screws up.

"Oh my god, Blake." She jumps out of bed. "You need to take that out. What the fuck were you thinking?"

"It's supposed to be incredible during sex." I screw up my face in pain. "Once you get through this healing part."

It's then that I look up, and I can see her entire body through her nightdress.

Curves and voluptuous breasts and a small patch of dark pubic hair. My loins begin to tingle.

*Thump, thump, thump* goes my cock.

Arousal screams through my blood, and this time, it does nearly tear the tip of my dick clean off.

"Ahhh." I lie back.

"Why is it hurting so bad?" she cries.

"Because your nightdress is making me fucking hard."

She glances down at herself and then sees what I see. She screams and runs into the bathroom.

I lie in pain. "Can you get me some ice, please?"

Silence.

"Bec," I call. "I'm dying here."

"Hang on, you idiot," she calls. She comes out in her bathrobe and begins to riffle through her suitcase. "I cannot believe you came in here when I was practically naked and then started packing heat." She storms back into the bathroom.

"Don't take it personal." I wince as I lie back. "All boobs make me hard."

"Oh my god," she calls. "I'm going to reception to get ice. Stay there."

"Where else am I going to go like this?"

"To the fucking hospital."

She marches out and slams the door as perspiration wets my skin.

I've got to take this out; I can't hack it. But . . . the deep fucking I could give a woman with this. Surely I'm nearly past the worst of it.

I screw up my face in pain. I'll give it three more days.


"Good morning, Nigella," I say as I walk into the nurses' station.

"Good morning, Dr. Grayson."

Nigella is the friendliest, loveliest nurse on staff. She's sixty in the shade and probably knows my job better than I do.

"How's my favorite nurse today?" I ask her.

"She is well." She smiles. "How is my favorite doctor today?"

"He is well," I reply as I drop into a chair. I open the computer and begin to go through the notes sent through from pathology. She sits down at the desk beside me and writes up some notes. Another nurse walks in. "Hey, Aria."

"Oh my god, Nigella. I'm reading the best book on my Kindle."

I keep reading my notes as I eavesdrop.

"Honestly, BookTok has shown me a whole new world. I can't get enough."

"Like what?" I reply, uninterested.

"I'm currently reading a fae book," she continues to tell Nigella.

"Oh man, the hottest recs have been coming up in my feed lately."

"Me too."

I frown. "Speak English. What's hot on your feed?"

"She's a fairy and he's a werewolf, and she's just become a part of their pack to be shared among the alphas."

"Oh, reverse harem. My favorite," Nigella replies.

"Huh?" I glance up, my interest piqued. "What's this?"

"A book I'm reading."

"There are books like this out in the real world?" I frown, fascinated.

"A million. They're seriously hot too. All men should be reading this stuff. It would make them a million times better in bed."

"Where do I read these?"

"On Kindle."

"Hmm."

They keep talking, and I discreetly text the boys.

**I have intel.**
**We need to buy a Kindle.**

Aria and Nigella finish up their conversation, and Aria finally wanders off.

"Tell me, Nigella, if you were going to find your daughter a nice man, where would you look?"

"A fun man or a nice man?" she asks.

"Nice and honorable." I think for a moment. "And fun."

"Hmm." She twists her lips as she thinks. "Maybe church."

"Apart from church." I swing on my chair as I hold my pen in my hand. "Like a nice, wholesome . . . good guy."

"The marrying type?"

"Yeah, I guess."

"Hmm." She thinks again. "Who is this for?"

"A close friend of mine has a nightmare of an ex, and I want to set her up with someone . . . but he has to be good."

"Hmm, well . . . in my experience, I wouldn't set her up with a doctor."

"Absolutely not," I reply. "That is *out* of the question."

"And I wouldn't set her up with a policeman or a security guard. They always seem to be on the prowl for extra action."

"This is true."

"And I wouldn't set her up with an unavailable man."

"Well, obviously." I roll my eyes. "If he's with someone else . . ."

"I mean emotionally unavailable."

"Emotionally unavailable?" I frown. "Meaning what?"

"Well, lots of men think they want to settle down, but the reality is that they like playing the field, so they end up sabotaging every relationship they get into so that they can go back to being single."

I stare at her for a moment as my mind processes this information.

*Hmm . . .*

"Sound familiar, Dr. Grayson?" She smirks.

"Not in the least," I lie as I stand. "Anyway, if you know of any good guys, send them my way."

"Uh-huh."

"But he has to be financially independent, good looking, tall, and straight as fuck."

"Straight?" She frowns.

"I mean, like a good guy. No funny business."

Neil walks into the nurses' station.

"Here comes a straight guy right now." Nigella smiles.

"Yeah, right." Neil smiles. "Dream on, baby."

"Dr. Grayson is looking for a straight guy," she tells him.

"Ohhh," he teases. "I could be straight for you, Doctor."

I roll my eyes. "You are an incorrigible flirt, Neil."

"That's what makes me so loveable." He winks before picking up a chart and disappearing down the hall.

### *Rebecca*

The bus pulls out into the traffic, and I turn toward the next line. I'm on bus duty, and afternoons are hectic. "Rebecca," a voice calls from behind me.

I turn to see the father of one of my students from last year. He was always cute and quiet.

"Hi." I smile.

*Shit, what is his name?*

"Long time, no see." He smiles broadly.

"Yes. I know." The next bus pulls up, and I gesture for the line to start getting on. "How is Greg doing?" I ask.

"He's great." His eyes hold mine as if he has something to say. "Listen . . . I . . ." He puts his weight onto his back foot. "I couldn't ask you last year because it wasn't really appropriate."

I raise my eyebrow in question.

"Would you like to go out sometime?"

"Oh . . ." I'm taken aback. I was not expecting this. "What happened to your wife?"

"We haven't been together for years." He gives me a lopsided smile.

"Right." Shit, I should have known that. "You want to go out on a . . . date?"

"If I'm overstepping, I apologize."

"No, no. I'm just . . ." Actually . . . this could be perfect. "This is going to sound weird, but would you be opposed to going on a double date?"

"Oh . . ."

"It's just, I haven't dated since my marriage broke up, and . . ."

"You're feeling nervous?"

"Apprehensive, and my brother is in the same boat. So we decided for our first few dates, we would try and go out together, if possible."

"Oh." He nods as he thinks it through. "Your brother?"

"He's a nice guy, and it's just a thought . . . it doesn't matter if . . ."

"No, sure. Why not?"

"Really?" I smile.

"Saturday night?"

"Sounds great."

He gets out his phone. "What's your number?" I tell him my number, and he types it into his phone. "I'll call you Thursday, and we'll make the arrangements," he says.

"Sounds . . . perfect."

We stare at each other for a beat, and he gives me a broad smile. "Speak to you on Thursday?"

"Okay."

He turns and walks off, and I watch him disappear into the distance.

Oh my god, I have a date.

Ahhh. I have to call Blake and let him know all about . . . I frown as a new thought flashes through my mind. A horrifying thought at that.

*What is his name?*


*Ring, ring . . . ring, ring . . . ring, ring.* I sit in my car in the parking lot, and I smile goofily as I wait for him to answer.

"Blake Grayson."

"Guess who has a date for Saturday night?" I beam.

"Really?"

"Uh-huh."

"With who?"

"He's a dad of a student I used to teach."

"The old single-dad trick, huh?"

I giggle. "Yep. So Saturday night for our double date, is that okay?"

"Sure is."

"But how do you know if you'll be able to get a date for this weekend at such short notice?" I ask.

"Trust me, I know."

"Oh." I frown. Ugh, what must it be like to have every woman in the world fall at your feet? "So, he's going to call me on Thursday night, and we will tee something up."

"Right."

"Who are you going to ask out?" I ask him.

"I'll find someone."

"No time-wasters; girlfriend material, right?" I remind him.

"Bec." I can almost hear his eyes roll. "I'll have a date. That's all you need to worry about."

"Okay." I smile as I hang on the phone. "So, what do we do now?"

"What do you mean?"

"Do we strategize or make a plan or something?"

"Oh my god, no."

"No?"

"We let it happen."

I frown, confused. "But how do we know what's going to happen if we don't plan it?"

"That's the point—we just go with it and see what happens. I can't observe you if I don't see you in your natural dating habitat."

"Oh." I nod, feeling stupid. "Right."

"All right." He tries to wind up the conversation.

I hang on the line. "Are you coming over tonight to take pictures?"

"I can't tonight. I have something going on."

"Oh." I bite my lip as I listen. "A date?"

"Yes, a date."

*With who?*

"Like a . . . just-fucking date?"

"Rebecca."

"Right." I shake my head. Why did I say that? "Sorry."

"Goodbye."

"Have a good night."

"I intend to." The phone goes dead as he hangs up.

I look out over the parking lot as I think . . . hmm, turning him into boyfriend material is going to be a lot harder than it seems.

I pace back and forth in my bedroom. It's official: I am an idiot.

This is the stupidest idea of all time.

It's bad enough that I'm going on a date, but to have Blake there judging me for the entire night?

What was I thinking?

And to top it all off, I don't even know my date's name. I've tried to find it out. I looked in the files in the office and everything, and all I got was his surname, which I already knew.

Oh god, this is a disaster waiting to happen.

I call Blake. *Ring, ring . . .*

"Hi," he answers.

"Hi, everything still okay for tonight?"

"Yeah, why?"

"So you're meeting us at the restaurant at seven o'clock, right?"

"Uh-huh."

"Okay." I nod. "Are you ready?"

"Just getting in the shower now."

I glance at my watch. "You're going to be late."

"No, I'm not."

I put my hand over my stomach. "I'm so nervous, I feel sick."

"Relax, it's fine."

"Is it? Because it really doesn't feel fine."

"I'll see you there."

"Okay." Then I remember. "Oh, Blake."

"Yes, Rebecca." He sighs in exasperation.

"When you get there, can you introduce yourself before I have to?"

"Why is that?"

I screw up my face because I know how lame this sounds. "I don't remember his first name."

"Ha ha, classic rookie error. Look at you. You're nailing this player thing already."

"Not funny." I roll my eyes. "Goodbye."


I see the headlights swing into my driveway, and I take one last look in the mirror.

I'm wearing a cream fitted dress, and my hair is down and curled. I'm rocking a fake tan and high heels, and I haven't made this much effort in years.

I feel utterly ridiculous.

*Knock, knock, knock* echoes from downstairs, and I close my eyes in horror.

I've changed my mind; I don't want to go anymore.

*You have to.*

I slowly make my way downstairs and open the door.

"Hi." His friendly face smiles.

"Hello."

"Are you ready to be wined and dined?" He's wearing jeans and a shirt, and he looks nice.

"Uh-huh."

He holds his hand up in the air.

*Huh?*

I frown, and he holds his hand up higher. "High-five it, baby. Hit me."

I fake a laugh as I give him a high five.

"Touchdown." He smiles broadly.

*What?*

Well, if that isn't the most awkward thing I've ever done.

"Let's go paint the town red." He wiggles his eyebrows.

*Or not.*

As we walk out the front door, I catch sight of myself in the mirror. I look like I'm about to throw up . . . that's probably because I feel like I am. We walk to the driveway, and the blood drains from my face.

All of it.

Every last drop.

His car is florescent green and has a big wing on the back, as if it's a race car, and it has a huge antenna, as if he's intending to talk to space.

Only it isn't a race car or a spaceship—it's a family car pimped out to look like a race car.

*Fuck me . . .*

"Isn't she great?"

"Yes." I smile awkwardly. "Great."

"I love my cars like I like my women. Fast and hot." He laughs out loud, and I'm so embarrassed for him that I laugh too. He holds up his hand for another high five.

I awkwardly slap it.

*Help.*

I glance up to see Blake walk out his front door. He's in dress pants and a sport coat and looks like he just stepped out of a magazine.

This can't be happening.

I practically run and dive into the Kermit the Frog car and slam the door behind me.

Mr. No Name gets in behind the wheel, and Blake casually drives past in his brand-new silver Porsche.

*Vroom, vroom, vroom.* Mr. No Name revs the engine.

I look over at him. "What are you doing?"

"Showing you what she's capable of."

"Wow," I whisper. "Powerful."

"You know it, baby."

Beads of sweat begin to drip down my back. This *cannot* be happening.

He revs the engine a few more times for added effect as I stare out the window, feeling like I'm in a bad episode of *Pimp My Ride*. I consider jumping out of the car and lying on the road so that he can run over me. I'll do anything I can to get out of this date.

Mr. No Name happily chats all the way to the restaurant while I continue to sweat like a pig. We park the car and get out, and then it dawns on me: I want to be in there first, before Blake arrives, so he and his date don't have to watch us walk in.

This is awkward enough.

"Come on, we can't be late." I begin to power walk in front.

"Hold up, old girl."

My eyes flicker red. *Old girl* isn't something I want to hear on a date, you dickhead.

We push through the doors, and I march straight up to reception. "Hi, we have a booking under the name Dalton, for four."

She looks through her booking sheet. "Ah, yes, this way." She walks through the restaurant, and we follow her to a nice table in the back. Kind of hidden—good. At least something is going right.

"Can I get you a drink while you wait?" the waitress asks.

"Yes," I fire back without hesitation. "I'll have a margarita, please."

"Oh," Mr. No Name gushes, "onto the hard stuff, huh?" He holds his hand up for a high five, and I awkwardly slap it.

"Make it a double." I fake a smile.

The waitress smirks as she writes down my order. She knows exactly what's going on here.

"I'll have . . ." He looks through the drinks menu and begins to read every single line of every single page. He keeps reading and reading.

We wait.

We wait some more.

The waitress and I make eye contact, and I try to send her a telepathic message. *Poison my drink so I can get the hell out of here, bitch.*

She smirks again, as if reading my mind.

He keeps reading and reading, and this is just unbelievable.

*Just order something, fucker!*

"I'll have a draft beer," he finally says.

I stare at him deadpan. Ten minutes of reading, and all you came up with was a tap beer?

Dear lord . . . hurry up, Blake.

"Your drinks will be out soon," the waitress says before disappearing into the back.

"I've been looking forward to seeing you all week," he tells me.

Oh no . . .

Now I'm a bitch. He's trying to be nice, and I'm just being a bitch.

"Me too," I reply. It's not a lie. I was looking forward to it before he showed up.

Now, not so much.

"Here you go." The waitress puts our drinks down in front of us and gives me a wink.

*Fast.*

"Thank you."

"Thanks, love," he says.

I glance up to see Blake standing at the reception desk with his date. She's a beautiful blonde with a figure to die for. He's holding her hand, and they are laughing at something as they talk.

They look like Barbie and Ken on crack.

Oh hell, just when I thought this night couldn't get any worse.

I pick up my margarita and take a huge gulp as I glance around for the nearest exit.

He leads her through the restaurant and over to the table by her hand. "Hello," he says. "I'm Blake, and this is Ruby."

Mr. No Name stands up and shakes their hands. "Hello. Nice to meet you both."

He doesn't say his name.

Fuck. Me. Dead.

"Hi." I stand, and Blake kisses my cheek. I shake hands with his date. "I'm Rebecca. Lovely to meet you."

Blake pulls out Ruby's chair, and she sits down. Her long blond hair is so shiny, thick, and healthy. I don't remember the last time I saw a natural blonde.

Blake sits down opposite me while my eyes linger on Ruby.

She looks like Grace Kelly, absolutely stunning; *this* is the date he scrambles to get days before.

"Isn't this fun." Mr. No Name smiles. He holds his hand up to me for another high five. "Hit me, baby."

*I want to die.*

I weakly slap his hand.

"Wow, you guys are on high-fiving terms. I'm jealous," Blake says. He holds his hand up to Ruby. "Hit me, baby."

Ruby goes to give him a high five, but then he grabs her hand and kisses it. "Only joking. Just wanted an excuse to touch you."

Ruby giggles on cue. "Oh, Blake," she gushes. "You're so funny."

I glare at Blake across the table as mischief dances in his eyes.

*Fucker.*

I give him a swift kick under the table, and he rolls his lips to hide his smile.

The waitress walks over. "Can I get you two a drink?"

Blake gestures to Ruby. "Ladies first."

"I'll have a cosmopolitan, please." She smiles.

"Hmm, that sounds good. Make that two," Blake replies. He casually picks up Ruby's hand and puts it on his thigh.

She swoons into her chair while I want to vomit in my own mouth.

I try to make conversation. "So, how did you two meet?" I ask.

Blake smiles. He's so self-assured, and he gestures to Ruby to answer. "You go."

Ruby giggles on cue.

I take another huge gulp of my drink.

"I'm a neurosurgeon." Ruby smiles. "We met in the children's ward about two years ago when we shared a patient. We've been friends ever since."

*A neurosurgeon?*

What the fuck?

How do you get those looks *and* brains?

"Oh. How great." I fake another smile and tip my head back and drain my glass.

"How did you two meet?" Ruby asks.

"Well, Rebecca was my son's teacher last year," Mr. No Name replies. "And she's the most perfect teacher of all time. The children all adore her." He smiles proudly over at me.

I smile in surprise. Oh . . . that was nice.

"What do you do?" Blake replies flatly. "I didn't catch your name, sorry."

"Herman. My name is Herman."

Amusement flashes in Blake's eyes.

*Don't do the Pee-wee Herman joke, or I will end you.*

I squish Blake's foot into the ground, and he kicks me back. I jump as his kick connects harder than he meant, and he drops his head to hide his smile.

"So, Ruby," I say. "Wow, a neurosurgeon, so impressive. I've never met a neurosurgeon before."

"Oh, thanks," she replies. "What grade do you teach?"

"Kindergarten."

She's not so bad, actually pretty nice.

"What do you do?" Blake asks again as their drinks arrive. "Thank you," he replies to the waitress.

"I'm a firefighter," Herman says. "I was special ops but retired from the army three years ago."

*Oh . . .*

Ruby and I smile like giddy schoolgirls over at Herman while Blake raises an unimpressed eyebrow.

Oh, the night just got interesting.

# Chapter 10

"What?" Herman says. "You don't believe me?"

"I never said that." Blake sits back in his chair. "Why wouldn't I believe you?"

"You just . . ." He shrugs. "I don't know what that look is on your face."

"What look?" Blake smirks over at Herman, as if issuing a silent dare.

*What is he doing?*

I tread on Blake's foot so hard, I swear his toes must break in ten places.

They stare at each other in a silent standoff.

"These drinks are good." I hold mine up to Ruby. She gives a weak smile and gulps hers down.

*Awkward.*

"Looking out for your own. I respect that. You're all right. Give me five, brother," Herman says as he holds his hand up for a high five.

Blake fakes a smile and slaps his hand.

"You know," Herman continues as he sips his beer, "I've always had a thing for your sister."

"My sister?" Blake frowns.

Oh no . . . I forgot to tell Blake that Herman thinks we are siblings.

*Ahhhhhh . . . abort mission.*

"How the hell do you know my sister?" Blake asks.

"We met at school," I stammer. "Remember, Blake?" I widen my eyes. "I taught his son."

"Oh . . ." Blake nods as he catches on. "That's right." He runs his hands through his hair as if flustered.

"What was it like growing up with her?" Herman asks.

"Surprising." Blake's unimpressed eyes flick to me.

*Shit.*

"I do love surprises." Herman smiles broadly. "How so?"

"Well, I guess it's expected if you live with a champion pole vaulter."

What?

"You're a pole vaulter?" Herman gasps.

"Best in the land." Blake smirks as his equilibrium returns. "She nearly made the Olympic team, but then . . . she didn't." He shrugs.

I tip my head back and drain my margarita glass as I try to think on my feet.

"Ruby, did you know that Blake's first job was in a piercing parlor?" I ask.

"It was?" Ruby gasps as she looks between me and Blake.

"Yes, he did his training in Vegas," I reply.

"Vegas?" She frowns.

"Yes, they practice on all the drunk men."

"What did you pierce?" Ruby asks.

"Penises," I blurt out. "Shriveled-up, drunk penises."

A swift kick connects with my shin, and I drop my head to hide my smile.

"That's where I got the idea of being a doctor," Blake says.

"Because putting holes in things that shouldn't have holes in them is so similar to being a doctor." I nod seriously. "Your thought process is truly fascinating."

Blake glares at me across the table, and I smirk.

"Let's go to the bar and get a round of drinks, Rebecca." Blake pushes his chair out.

"Now?" I frown.

"Now," he snaps as he pulls me up by the hand. "Back in a minute." He smiles to our dates. He drags me around the corner to the bar. "What the fuck are you doing?"

"What the fuck am *I* doing? What the fuck are *you* doing?" I whisper angrily. "Pole vaulter? You couldn't think of anything better than a fucking pole vaulter?"

"Two cosmos and a margarita and a draft beer, please," he tells the waiter.

"Sure thing."

"It would have been nice to know that I'm your brother."

"I forgot to tell you."

"And if that dweeb tries to high-five me one more time, I'm breaking his hand."

"Oh please," I scoff with a roll of my eyes. "You're always so dramatic."

"He is not ex-army. He's ex–fucking weirdo, that's what he is."

My mouth falls open in horror. "What a horrible thing to say. What the hell is with your date, anyway?"

"What about my date?" he scoffs.

"A brain surgeon who looks like Barbie." I narrow my eyes. "You don't think that's a little bit over the top . . . even for you?"

"Are you jealous?"

"Ha," I spit. "Jealous of her?" I put my hands on my hips in outrage and wobble my head around. "No."

"Well, you should be," he whispers angrily. "She's perfect for me."

"Good. Go marry her, then."

"Maybe I will."

"Ha." I turn toward the bar. "Wait until she sees your pig-on-a-spit cock. She's going to run for the hills."

"What?" His eyes nearly pop from his head.

I throw my head back and laugh. "That's the best comeback of all time."

Unable to help it, he bursts out laughing too. "Agreed."

"Listen, I'm eating dinner, and then I'm getting the hell out of here because I do not like Herman."

"Good idea." He nods. "Neither do I."

"You liked him until he was ex-army." I put my hands on my hips. "Maybe it's you who's jealous."

"Jealous," he scoffs. "Of him?"

"Yeah." I nod. "I think you are."

"I think you're on crack."

"Listen." I look around guiltily. "When we get back to the table, go to the bathroom and text Chloe and ask her to call me at the table with a fake excuse to leave."

"Okay." He nods. "Good plan."

An hour and a half and a million high fives later, the plan comes into play.

My phone rings on the table, and Blake snatches it up before I can answer it. "Hello."

He listens. "Hi, Dad."

I frown. What's he doing?

"Oh, really? Shit." He listens. "Yeah, okay." He nods, all serious. "No, it's okay. We can do that. We're on our way."

He puts his hand over the phone as he plays along. "It's Nana."

"Nana?" I frown.

144

"She's fallen down a flight of stairs."

"Oh no," Ruby gasps.

"See you soon, Dad. We're on our way."

He hangs up the phone. "Well, this is a real downer." He shrugs sadly. "I'm so disappointed."

I roll my lips to hide my smile. He is the worst liar in the history of all liars.

How have I never seen this before?

"Herman, do you think you could possibly drop Ruby at home?" he asks.

"Sure thing."

"You two should go for a drink or something," I suggest.

"Yeah." Herman's eyes light up in excitement. "We should."

Ruby's eyes flick between Blake and him. "Ahh."

"Yes, do that." Blake nods. "It's only fair. Don't let us spoil your fun."

"Oh." She shrugs. "I guess so."

Ha ha, sucked in, Ruby.

You arrive in a Porsche with a hot date, and you go home in a pimped-out Kermit the Frog with a serial high-fiver.

"We should get going," Blake tells me as he stands. "My apologies, guys. Have a fun night."

Herman stands, and I give him an awkward hug. Ruby stands, and Blake kisses her quickly on the lips. "I'll call you."

"Okay." She swoons. "I look forward to it."

Blake grabs my elbow and escorts me out of the restaurant and onto the street. "Are you ever calling her?" I whisper.

"Not on your life." He scrunches up his nose. "You were right. A neurosurgeon who looks like Barbie is overkill . . . even for me."

As if running from a crime scene, we rush to his car. He opens the door for me, and I climb in. He dives into the driver's

145

seat. "Now . . ." He starts the car. "Where are we going for dessert?"

Twenty minutes later, on the other side of the city, Blake pulls into a covered parking lot.

"What is this place?" I frown.

"The best-kept secret in town," he replies.

"What if we run into them?" I look around guiltily.

"Then we run into them. Who gives a fuck?"

"I do."

"Look." He turns the car off. "We both know they're going to be too busy high-fiving all night to look for us."

I get the giggles as I imagine the scenario. "Poor Ruby." I open the car door.

"Yep." He winces as he gets out of the car. "I do kind of feel bad leaving her with that dweeb."

"Oh." Disappointment fills me as I realize how selfish I've been. "I'm sorry. I ruined your date, didn't I?"

"It's okay." He shrugs. "The fact that as soon as I had an out, I took it is a good indication of where the date was going anyway." He picks up my hand and links it through his arm as we walk along. We are on a busy street full of restaurants and bars.

"How come you don't like her? She's, like . . ." I try to search for the right analogy. "Perfect."

He twists his lips as if unimpressed. "I don't know. On paper, she's perfect. I just don't feel it."

"Feel what?" I stare up at him.

"Anything." He shrugs again. "Baffles me, too, don't worry."

"Oh." I have an epiphany. "You don't like her because she's a woman who you could actually fall for."

He thinks on it.

146

"That's it, isn't it?" I ask.

"I honestly don't know." He pushes through heavy dark wooden doors, and we arrive in the coolest place I have ever been. It's dark and moody with a mix of big velvet couches and cute little tables for two. It has huge pendant lights and a marble bar. Music is playing, and the crowd is eclectic.

"What is this place?" I gasp in wonder.

"Bruno's, my favorite dessert bar."

"*This* is a dessert bar?" My eyes widen in astonishment as I look around.

"Only the best for my champion pole vaulter." He throws me a playful wink.

I get the giggles. "Where the hell do you come up with this shit?"

"Can I help you, sir?" the waiter interrupts us.

"Table for two, please."

"This way, sir." We follow him through the restaurant, and he holds his hand out to a low table in a bay window that faces the street. "How is this?"

"That's great." Blake smiles. He pulls out my chair, and I sit down. There are colorful pansy flowers in window boxes on the outside of the bay window, and two long white candles are in silver candlesticks in the center of the table. The waiter hands us two menus. "Can I get you any drinks to start?"

"I'll have an Irish coffee," Blake says.

My eyes flick up to him. "What's that?"

"Coffee with a nip of alcohol. Trust me, it's good."

"Make that two, please." I smile. The waiter leaves us alone, and I open the menu to see rows and rows of dessert. I begin to read down the list.

Chocolate fondant
Raspberry cheesecake

Caramel ganache
Hummingbird cake
Tiramisu

"Oh my god." I begin to salivate at the choices. "This place is so cool."

"A personal favorite."

I glance up at him. "How many times have you been here?"

"A lot."

"Is this where you bring your dates at the end of the night to seal the deal?"

He gives me a slow, sexy smile but doesn't answer.

"So that's a yes?"

"That's a"—he gestures to the menu—"make a choice."

The waiter arrives with our drinks. They are in huge glass steins and have froth on the top, and the coffee is layered in colors in the glass. "Oh wow," I gush. "Thank you."

"Would you like some dessert tonight?" the waiter asks.

"Um . . ." I quickly peruse the choices. "There's just so much to choose from. I'll have the white chocolate cheesecake, please."

Blake smiles as he watches me.

"And for you, sir?"

"I'll have the chocolate fondue and strawberries for two."

The waiter smiles. "Excellent choice, sir." He disappears out the back.

"I still can't believe tonight happened." I sip my hot drink. "Oh, yum, this *is* delicious."

"Told you." He sips his too. "I don't trust that Herman."

"Why?"

"Don't you think it's odd that he said *Don't you believe me?*"

"What do you mean?" I blow on my drink to try and cool it down.

"Think about it. If you're telling someone a story about where you work, the last thing you would ask is if they believe you. It wouldn't even cross your mind to say that unless you were lying about it."

I frown as I think back. "Come to think of it, that *is* odd."

"I think he makes up the ex-army story to get chicks."

"Surely not?" I scoff. "Nobody would outright lie about a job."

He raises an eyebrow as his eyes hold mine.

My heart sinks. "I'm so gullible, aren't I?"

"No." He smiles over at me. "You are trusting. Trusting and gullible are two different things."

I sit back, dejected. "I don't know if I'll ever get the hang of this dating thing."

"Well . . ." He sips his drink. "You won't be dating long."

"Why do you say that?"

"Because the first man who gets a chance with you is going to snap you up and keep you forever."

I smile as I go over his words. "What about you?"

He snorts and chokes on his coffee. "What?" He coughs. "I mean . . ."

"Oh . . . crap." I cringe in embarrassment. "I didn't mean *you* snap *me* up. As if you would ever snap me up," I stammer. "I mean . . . a girlfriend for you. I mean Ruby."

He rolls his eyes as if knowing what I'm going to say next.

"What are you actually looking for in a woman?"

He rolls his lips, as if contemplating his answer before saying it out loud. "I don't actually know." He gives a subtle shrug. "Someone kind and honest. A fun best friend to do life with."

"You've never met a woman like that before?"

"Well, I know I haven't spent a night with her yet." His sandy-brown hair hangs in curls over his forehead.

"What does that mean, exactly?"

"Well . . . I think I like them, and then I spend the night with them, and I want to chew my arm off to get out of there and run for the hills."

I smile over at him. "How many women have you slept with?"

"Too many to answer that question."

We stare at each other as the air changes between us. I can't put my finger on what the change is. All I know is that it's there.

"You look beautiful tonight," he says softly.

I feel my face blush as his eyes linger on me. "Thanks."

"And now that you're a famous foot model . . ." He gives me a slow, sexy smile.

"Ha ha," I laugh. "What about that? Can you believe it?"

"Absolutely."

"I cannot believe I made fifty-two hundred dollars in one week." I get the giggles. "I just can't . . . my mind is blown."

He chuckles and leans his face onto his hand; his pointer finger steeples up to his temple. His eyes are dark, and his lips are big, and it suddenly dawns on me that Blake Grayson is probably the most handsome man I have ever met.

"How can I ever pay you back for this Foot Finder thing?" I say to curb my wayward thoughts.

"Well . . . there *is* something."

"Name it."

He scrunches up his nose as if knowing this is a huge ask. "Can you come to my cousin's wedding with me? I cannot handle another wedding with my aunts all trying to set me up with every woman in attendance."

I smile. I can so imagine that. "Sure."

"But there's a catch."

"A catch?"

"It's in Mexico. So it means a whole weekend away."

"That's okay. I have never been, so it will be fun. When is it?"

"Six weeks."

"Okay."

"You'll probably be all in love by then, so . . ."

"You'll still come first, Blake, no matter who I am dating."

He reaches over and takes my hand in his. "Promise."

I stare at him as the air swirls between us. The feeling of his large hand wrapped around mine makes butterflies swirl in my stomach.

"I promise."

*What the hell is going on here?*

*This is Blake.*

*Blake Grayson, player extraordinaire and one of your best friends.*

*Cut it out.*

I snatch my hand from his grip. "Here you are." The waiter puts my cheesecake in front of me and a huge chocolate fountain in front of Blake.

I get the giggles when I see it.

"And your strawberries." He lays down long, skinny forks and leaves us alone.

I take out my phone and take a photo. "Here, pose."

Blake smiles, and I snap photos of him and his giant chocolate fountain.

"You get in the shot too. Take a selfie," he says.

I try to lean over.

"Come over this side."

I get up and walk around to his side of the table, and he pulls me down onto his lap and holds me close as he wraps his arms around me.

*Oh . . .*

His large, hard body underneath mine sends a surge of adrenaline screaming through my body.

With a shaky hand, I hold up the camera and take a photo of the two of us.

"What about now?" He pretends to bite my shoulder, and I giggle as I continue to take the photos. He nibbles up my arm as I try to escape him. "That's enough." I scramble to get off his lap, and I go back around and sit in my chair.

He winces and leans back.

"What's wrong?"

"Having you on my lap made my dick hurt."

I giggle in surprise. "Is that thing ever not hard?"

"Not when I'm around you, it's not." He smiles.

*Oh . . .*

"Can I ask a serious question?"

"Not a fan of serious questions." He widens his eyes as he picks up a strawberry and dips it into chocolate.

"I know, but . . ." I smirk. "I can't believe I'm even asking this, but what on earth would make you pierce your dick?"

He chuckles as he puts the whole strawberry into his mouth and chews it. "Well, the truth is, it wasn't *completely* spontaneous."

"It wasn't?"

"I've wanted to do it for a long time, and when the boys and I were in Bali a couple of years ago, I was going to do it then, but when they brought out the needle, I chickened out and got the hell out of there."

"Why do you want an earring in your dick?"

"It's not an earring, it's a bar, and it's not for me."

I frown in confusion.

"Sex for a woman is apparently ten times better with an apadravya piercing, and the concept fascinates me."

I blink in surprise.

152

"Because"—he pops another strawberry into his mouth and chews it—"why not enhance the pleasure of my favorite pastime?"

"What?" I frown. "You would put yourself through all this pain just so you're better in bed?"

He smirks as his eyes darken. "Well . . . if you're going to do something, why not be the best at it?"

I watch as he picks up a strawberry and dips it into the chocolate. In slow motion, he licks it off. His tongue is long and thick, and a throb of arousal pumps through my sex.

*The best at it.*

I guiltily snap my eyes away. Okay . . . fuck. I need to get laid. This. Is. Blake.

Just Blake . . . friend Blake, not a *best at it* fuck buddy.

"Would you ever . . . ?" he whispers.

"Truthfully?" I ask.

He nods.

"I'd be scared that the condom would break and I'd end up pregnant."

His face falls in horror.

"You hadn't thought of that?" I laugh. "Oh my god, aren't you a doctor?"

He chuckles and drags his hand down his face. "Maybe I didn't thoroughly think this through."

"Look, if you want a baby, that is none of my business." I hold my hands up with a laugh. "I'm just saying, I like it rough, so . . . the condom *would* be breaking."

His eyes darken and then drop to my lips as if imagining something. I feel it all the way to my bones.

Oh no . . . Did I just say that out loud?

"I mean . . . ," I murmur, embarrassed.

"I know what you meant," he cuts me off.

I take a nervous sip of my alcoholic coffee. "This stuff is making me very . . ."

"Hot?" he murmurs.

"Verbose." I sip my coffee again, feeling awkward; I really need to stop drinking.

For a moment, we eat our desserts in silence. I'm worrying that I came across flirty, and he's probably thinking I'm a horny ho.

*He could be onto something.*

"You know what we should do?" he says to change the subject.

"What?"

"We should drizzle this chocolate all over those money-making feet of yours. Chocolate *and* feet." He taps his temple. "Sure to be a winner."

I laugh out loud and feel my equilibrium return.

"So, when are we going on our next double date?" he asks.

"Really?" I wince. "After tonight's disaster?"

"Tonight was just a . . ." He shrugs. "Speed bump."

I lean on my hand as I smile over at him.

"You want to date without strings," he says.

"You want to settle down but don't want to admit it," I add.

"Just . . ." He smirks, and I know that I'm onto something. "Happy to explore my options."

"Where am I going to find another date?"

"Ahh . . ." He smiles as he pulls out his phone. "We have two options."

"Such as." I keep eating my cake.

"Elite Singles. Or Bumble."

"Are you on those apps?" I ask in surprise.

"I'm on Elite Singles."

"Why that one?"

"It's for professionals over thirty."

*Oh . . .*

"What's that look for?" He frowns.

"I just . . ." I shrug.

"You what?"

"I didn't realize you were after a professional."

He frowns. "What do you think a professional is?"

"Someone like Ruby."

"Not at all. I mean . . ." He breaks into a smile. "Someone like you."

I roll my eyes. "I'm not a professional, Blake."

"It's for people who are looking for intelligence in a partner." He reaches over and picks up my hand in his. "Or are you looking for a boxer who's been knocked out two hundred times?"

I snatch my hand out of his, annoyed. "Maybe if he's got a good dick, I am."

"I guess," he chuckles. "That could work."

"Well, what's the other one?"

"Bumble."

"Hmm."

"It's a different demographic."

"Okay."

"And no more picking you up from your house. From now on, we meet them there. I hate that Herman Munster knows where you live now."

"Herman Munster?" I giggle.

"That's right." He points to my phone. "Choose an app. We're going through the candidates."

"What, now?"

"Next weekend." His eyes dance with mischief. "I'm choosing your date, and you're choosing mine."

155

*One date from hell for you coming right up.*

I pick up my phone. "Sounds good to me."

### Two hours later

Blake bursts out laughing as he reads my phone.

"What?" I laugh before I even know what he's going to say. We've been in hysterics all night. Who knew going through a dating site for someone else could be so funny?

"Listen to this . . ." He laughs again before he composes himself to read the blurb.

**Cuckhold wanted.**

He tips his head back and laughs again as he slaps the table.

"What?" I laugh. The thing is, I think we may be delirious by this point and are laughing at literally everything. He tries to straighten his face so that he can spit it out.

**Looking for a jockey to ride my friends.**

I laugh out loud. "What?" I put my hands over my mouth. "Surely not."

Blake is laughing so hard, he's not making any noise.

I have tears streaming down my face from laughing. This has been the funniest night of all time.

**If you like being watched enjoying men, by your man.
I'm your guy.**

"I don't understand." I frown. "He wants someone to bang his friends?"

"I think so."

"Why would he want that?"

"I don't know." He shrugs. "I think he wants to watch his friends get their cocks out, but he can't let them know he's into them, so he throws a decoy into the picture."

I laugh again.

"Excuse me," the waitress says as she interrupts our hilarity.

"Yes." I continue to wipe my tears.

"We're closed, so I'm going to have to ask you to leave."

Blake and I look around the restaurant to see that it's empty. "Oh, sorry."

We instantly get up and make our way to the reception area, where we pay.

I'm teetering in my heels after a few of those lethal coffees, but Blake's barely sipped at his drinks all night because he is driving.

We push out of the doors, and I go to walk to the left, and Blake grabs my hand and pulls me to the right. "This way." He throws his arm around me, and we walk to the car.

"If you make my date with Mr. Cuckhold, I'll never forgive you."

"Yeah, well, if you make my date with Miss Instagram Famous, I would rather die."

We laugh again as we arrive at the car, and Blake turns me toward him.

"You know, sometimes I wish I didn't live on Kingston Lane," he says softly.

"You do?" I frown. "How come?"

"Because then . . . we wouldn't be friends."

My eyes search his.

"And . . ."

He pulls my spaghetti strap back up onto my shoulder. "And what?" I whisper.

"And . . . we could have just met as strangers."

Everyone else in the street disappears as we stare at each other.

"And I would have asked for your number."

# Chapter 11

My face falls. *Oh no.*

Why on earth would he want to risk our friendship for something that we both know would never work out?

"Blake—"

"I know," he cuts me off.

"It's just—"

"I know." He opens the car door for me, and unsure of what to say, I slide into the car.

He gets into the driver's seat, pulls out of the parking lot, and we begin to drive in silence.

Gone is the laughter that's been between us, replaced by . . . I don't even know what feeling this is.

*And I would have asked for your number.*

Horror, this is horror.

I stare straight ahead through the windshield as I try to make sense of what just happened.

Did he mean what it sounded like he meant, or have I totally misread this situation?

I glance over to Blake as he drives. He's silent and somber. His jaw is ticking, as if he's thinking, or perhaps something else . . . *Is he angry?*

"Um . . ." I try to think of something to say that will rectify this situation. "What have you got going on tomorrow?" I ask.

"Not much." His fingers tighten around the steering wheel.

I stare over at him as I wait for him to say something . . . he doesn't.

"I had a great time tonight." I smile awkwardly.

He nods and keeps his eyes on the road. "Same."

He can't even look at me.

*Fuck.*

I twist my fingers together on my lap. Why would he say that . . . he knows we're not like that. This is a disaster.

"Are you going to call Ruby?" I smile hopefully.

He shrugs.

"I'm not going to call Herman." I shrug. "But I guess that was pretty obvious already."

More silence, more staring through the windshield.

"So . . ." I shrug. I scramble for conversation, anything to restore how we were just ten minutes ago. "I'm going to set you up for your date next week with someone insanely hot."

"Good," he fires back as his fingers tighten around the steering wheel. "Blond."

My stomach dips as if I'm on a roller coaster. "Okay . . . blond."

"Any requests for your date?" he says in an almost sarcastic tone.

"No," I reply softly.

We round the corner onto Kingston Lane, and he pulls the car up to the front of my house. "Thanks." I smile over at him. "I had a fun night."

He nods. "Night."

I stare over at him. No kiss on the cheek, no hug. Not even a smile.

I get out of the car and slam the door shut, and without even a wave, he drives to his house. I watch as his garage door slowly goes up.

*What is his problem?*

He drives into his garage, and the door shuts. I roll my eyes and storm into my house. He had to go ruin a good night, didn't he?

Ugh . . . men.


Second after second, minute after minute, hour after hour. I stare at the ceiling as the words roll around in my head.

*I would have asked for your number.*

Why did he say that?

Was he playing around, or was he serious?

I would have been sure he was playing, but then he went quiet afterward, as if he was annoyed . . . hurt, even.

But it's Blake, and he doesn't feel like that about me.

Does he?

No. I'm sure he doesn't.

I go over our dessert date tonight and how much fun we had together, and sadness falls over me.

*Please don't ruin this.*


### Blake

I hear my front door open and close. "Hey," Henley calls.

"In the kitchen." I flick the dish towel over my shoulder as I flip my eggs. "Want some breakfast?"

"No thanks, we're getting going soon." He slouches onto the stool at the counter.

"Coffee?"

"Yeah, okay."

"I'll have one too." I dish my breakfast onto my plate. "Thanks."

The front door opens, and Antony walks in. "Hey."

"Hi," I grumble.

Henley drags himself off the stool and begins to make our coffee. "How was last night?"

"Okay." I give a subtle shrug. "I guess."

He glances over at me as he makes the coffee. "Not fun?"

"Not really."

"How come?"

"Just . . . boring night."

Henley smirks as he passes me my cup of coffee. "Rebecca on a date with another dude a bit too much to handle?"

"Fuck off with this Rebecca shit." I sit down and begin to cut through my toast. "We're just friends." I take a big bite.

"According to her." He chuckles as he sips his coffee.

"According to me, actually," I snap, annoyed.

"All right, so you have the details?"

"Yes." I widen my eyes. "Why are you being such a fucking nag about this?"

"Well, we're away for a week, and you need to know what to do."

"I'm well and truly capable of looking after Barry the dog." I sip my coffee. "Just fuck off to your honeymoon already."

"So he's going to sleep at Rebecca's."

"Yes." I roll my eyes.

"And you are going to walk him each morning, and Antony is going to walk him each afternoon."

"How many fucking walks does one dog need a day?"

"If you don't walk him, he turns into a prick and ruins shit."

"If he ruins any of my shit, he's a dead dog."

"What's wrong with you today?"

"Nothing," I snap. "It's eight o'clock on a Sunday morning. Stop busting my balls about your dog."

"Rebecca's walking him now, and when they get home, she's going to put him back in our yard."

"Isn't he staying at Rebecca's?" I frown. "Why isn't he going to her house?"

"Yes, but through the day, he has to go back to our yard, because if he's left in anyone else's yard while nobody is home, he will try to escape."

I drag my hand down my face. "Got it."

"And you'll call me if anything happens."

"Yes."

"Did you speak to Taryn about the flash drive?"

"No."

"Why not?"

"Because I'm avoiding Taryn like the plague."

"I've been thinking about this." He goes to the window and peers through the curtains into the cul-de-sac. "I don't think anything happened with Taryn."

"I'm sure it didn't." I keep eating. "Why do you say that?"

"You have zero attraction to her."

"I know."

"And you never hit on girls you don't want."

"Exactly." I keep eating. "I'm telling you, I did not hook up with Taryn. But then she said she had footage of me and Antony."

"Yeah." Antony winces. "I'd find out what that is . . . stat."

"Who did I get the love bite from, then?" I continue thinking out loud.

"I don't know." Henley keeps peering through the curtains. "Logan's making his move."

I keep eating, uninterested.

"He's just waiting to sink his teeth into her and share her with his housemates."

"Pretty sure Taz has already tasted everyone in that house."

"Not Taryn. Rebecca."

"What?" I snap.

"Every day Logan is out on the street, tuning her."

I get up and march to the window and peer through the curtains. Rebecca is standing in front of her house talking to Logan. He's wearing a barely there singlet with his muscles hanging out, and she's wearing her gym clothes, with Barry on his lead. "Good," I snap. "He can have her." I march back to the table and go back to my breakfast.

"Am I sensing a little animosity with Rebecca today?"

"Nope." I shovel a forkful of food into my mouth.

"I downloaded this Kindle app," Antony says as he sips his coffee.

"And?" Henley asks.

"Well . . ." He shrugs. "There's a plethora of porn on there."

My eyes flick up from the newspaper I'm reading. "Vampire porn?"

"Yep." He nods.

"Alien porn?" Henley replies.

"Uh-huh."

"How many cocks do these dudes have?" I ask.

"I don't know. I didn't get the books . . . obviously."

"Well, get to it, man. We need all the fucking tips we can get."

"I'm not sure about you . . . but my one cock will never be two." Antony rolls his eyes. "Which isn't ideal."

"No wonder women have ridiculously high expectations these days. How are we supposed to compete with this shit?" Henley scoffs.

"It's all right for you. You've already got your girl, and she thinks you've got a golden cock," Antony fires back.

"Because I do." Henley widens his eyes. "Everybody knows that."

"I seriously doubt that." I go back to reading my paper. "I'm going to download this app myself. I'm actually digging this vampire shit."

"Okay, you read a vampire one, I'll read an alien one, and Henley, you read a kink one."

"What kind of kink?" He frowns.

"I don't know, like . . ." Antony shrugs as he tries to think. "I can't even think of a kink that women would want."

"Dildo?"

"That's not a kink, that's normal," Henley replies.

I smirk as I keep reading the paper.

"What?"

"No woman's ever pulled a dildo out on me. My cock is more than enough."

They roll their eyes. "In your dreams."

Antony looks around as if remembering something. "Oh, I almost forgot why I came over. Is my duffel bag here?" he asks.

"Why would it be here?" I frown.

"Last year you borrowed it for something."

"I don't remember." I think for a moment. "Oh, there is a random bag underneath the bed in the second spare bedroom upstairs."

"You didn't think to return it?"

"I didn't know whose it was!"

He takes off up the stairs.

"Did Rebecca sleep with her date last night?" Henley asks.

"No. She did not."

"How do you know?"

"Because I dropped her at home."

His eyes light up. "Did you sleep with her?"

"This isn't a fucking porno. She's not sleeping with everyone, you know."

"Did you fight?"

"Will you just shut up about Rebecca Dalton?" I keep eating. "I give zero fucks about her."

He smiles into his coffee cup as he watches me.

"Stop."

Antony walks back into the room with the duffel bag under his arm.

"You found it?" I ask.

"Yeah, who've you been boning in the spare room?"

"What?"

He holds up a pair of pink pajama pants. They have big red love hearts all over them. "Found these under the bed."

"What?" I screw up my face. "Where under the bed?"

"At the top, in between the wall and bed."

I take them off him and stare at them in confusion. "I have no idea whose these are."

"Bec's about to get it on with Logan," Henley calls from the window.

"Yeah, I guessed that." Antony goes to the coffee machine. "He's putting in the work. Every day he's out at the front of her house, small talking."

"Small talk from the small dick." I go to the bin and scrape my leftovers into it. "We need to bomb that Navy House as soon as possible."

"Knock, knock," Rebecca's voice calls from the front door.

*Great.*

"Speak of the devil," Henley mouths.

"Fuck. Off," I mouth back. I snatch the pajama pants off him and stuff them into the cutlery drawer. "Come in," I call.

Rebecca comes into view; her dark hair is up in a high ponytail, and her skin has a just-exercised glow to it. Her big brown eyes find mine across the room. "Hi." She smiles.

"Hi." I keep washing my plate and cutlery.

"Hello." She and the boys begin to chat while I take my time washing the last few coffee cups.

I don't even want to talk to her.

*Go home.*

"Are you all packed?" Rebecca asks Henley.

"Yep. Juliet is just dropping her parents at the airport, and then we're leaving. I've been briefing the boys."

"Right." She looks between us.

"Blake is walking him in the morning and Ant in the afternoon."

"Uh-huh." She smiles. "And sleepovers at my house."

"Blake is going to give him breakfast every morning back at our house."

"He isn't a fucking baby," I snap. "Relax, I think we can look after a stupid dog for a week." I pick up the dish towel. "Go . . . screw your new wife, stupid."

"What's *wrong* with you today?" Ant curls his lip.

"Nothing is wrong with me." I widen my eyes. "Apart from the fact that it's eight o'clock in the morning, and I have a lot of annoying people in my kitchen."

"Blake, do you want to come over for dinner tonight?" Rebecca asks.

"No, thank you." I keep wiping down my kitchen counter with vigor.

"I'm making your favorite. Lasagna," she says sweetly to try and coax me into it.

"I have plans."

"Oh . . . okay." Disappointment sounds through her voice.

"What are you doing?" Antony asks.

"I have a date."

"With who?" Antony asks.

*Shut. Up.*

"With whom," I correct him. "And that is *none* of your business. I'm taking a shower." I walk upstairs as I hear them continue to chat. I take my time and shower. I make my bed, and I can still hear them downstairs.

*Go home already.*

Eventually, I can't dawdle anymore, and I make my way back downstairs. Now they're all on my front porch, sitting on the steps, and I walk out and sit in the chair.

"So, Bec . . . ," Antony says. "What's going on with Logan?"

Her eyes immediately flick to me and then back to Antony. "Nothing."

"He seems interested."

"Ah . . . not at all." She shrugs casually as she tries to blow it off. "He's just being friendly."

"Are you going out with Ruby tonight, Blake?" She turns her attention to me.

"No."

Her eyes search mine. "So someone new, then?"

"Yes."

She nods, as if thinking over my answer.

"Anyway, I'm going to get going," Henley says. He gives Antony a slap on the back and then hugs me. "Don't get into any trouble while I'm gone."

"Ha. How can I when the troublemaker will be away?"

"I'm coming over to see Juliet in a minute," Rebecca tells him.

"Okay, bye, guys." Antony and Henley disappear, and Rebecca lingers.

*Go home.*

"I'll see you later." I force a smile as I go to walk inside.

"Blake . . ."

I turn back to her.

"Are we okay?"

"Why wouldn't we be?"

"You just seem . . . off."

"I'm fine." I point inside my house with my thumb. "I've got a lot to do. I'll catch you later, okay?" I walk into my house, and I hear the screen go as she walks in behind me.

"You said last night that you sometimes wish you didn't live on Kingston Lane."

I roll my eyes as I walk into my kitchen.

*Here we go.*

I go to the fridge.

"Blake." I pour myself a glass of water. "Can you look at me?"

I exhale heavily and drag my eyes to meet hers. "What?"

"And I cut you off, and I didn't say what I wanted to say."

My eyes hold hers.

"What I wanted to say was that I would never wish for you not to live here or for us not to be friends."

I nod. "Is that it?"

"And . . ." She cuts herself off.

"What?"

"And I know we don't talk about anything important."

I raise my eyebrow.

"But my conversations with you about nothing important . . . are my most important conversations."

Her eyes search mine.

"And I wouldn't trade those conversations for anything, not even your number."

I nod once. "Got it."

"Because when you give someone your number, they come and go. And . . . I don't want you to ever go anywhere."

We stare at each other.

"Blake . . ." She hesitates, as if she's trying to articulate herself. "We're in this super-short window of time where we can be close friends. Because as soon as you meet your future wife, we won't be able to hang out on weeknights, and you won't be able to sleep on my couch whenever you feel like it."

"Why not?"

"Because she's always going to think there's something going on, and it's weird to sleep on another woman's couch when you have a girlfriend."

*Hmm . . .*

"And the thought of that makes me sad."

"Me too," I say softly.

"But not as sad as the thought of not being your friend and never seeing you again." She takes my hand in hers. "Me and you are meant to be friends forever, Blake."

"I know."

"I just want to make sure we're okay."

"You're being overdramatic. We're more than okay. Relax, I just wanted to have sex with you."

"Ha!" She explodes. "How can you have sex with a sore dick?"

"Because I knew it would be the only time you could handle my power." I grab my crotch. "My thirty percent capacity is equal to a normal man's two hundred percent. I wanted to give you a fair chance of survival."

She laughs out loud. "So you're a superhuman lover now?"

"That's right."

"Why are you such an idiot?"

I smirk. "Just stick to your end of the bargain and get me a blonde with great tits for Saturday night."

She smiles. "And if I don't?"

"Then we're not friends anymore . . . I'm done with you," I tease. "Then we *can* have sex."

She laughs and pulls me into a hug and squeezes me, and eventually I put my arms around her waist and hug her back. I nuzzle my head into her neck and close my eyes. She's warm and soft and . . . strangely comforting.

"Do you really have a date tonight?" she asks.

"I made it up when I didn't know lasagna was on the table." I sigh. "Kind of regretting it now, to be honest."

"Meh . . . I lied. I'm not cooking," she mutters dryly. "I was going to buy a frozen one."

I smile into her hair. "Good thing I'm going out, then."


*Rebecca*


I stare at the figures on the screen.

## IMAGES SOLD: 0

"Oh, for god's sake," I huff. How can you sell so many images one week and then this week sell nothing?

The images I uploaded this week were good . . . or so I thought.

How can the income go from $5,000 to nothing? I thought I'd cracked the code and hit the jackpot.

This online marketing business is so damn unpredictable.

So infuriating.

I get into the shower while I think.

What worked last week . . . well, apart from the fake-jizz part? I troll my brain as I think.

Spontaneity.

Maybe my photos are too staged . . . hmm, that's probably it. What if I took some photos in a different location?

Yes.

I wash my hair while my mind runs away with the possibilities of shoot locations.

Maybe the beach. That could work. Sand and oil: those perverts are sure to get off with anything oily.

Damn it, I should have gotten some more in the hotel room last weekend.

Ugh, I was hoping to have some kind of idea of how this was going to go financially moving forward. I'm meeting with John tomorrow afternoon to discuss his non-divorce proposal.

Ugh . . . I need to up my foot game . . . and stat.

# Chapter 12

*Blake*

"Good morning, Beryl." I turn the corner into the nurses' station just to see Ruby disappear into a room.

I duck behind the wall.

Fuck.

"What's wrong, Doctor?" Beryl the nurse says as she continues filing. "You look like you just saw a ghost."

"What is Dr. Mansfield doing here?" I frown as I peer around the corner.

"She has a patient in room six."

"Since when?"

"Since last night."

I peer around the corner again to see where she is. I do *not* want to run into her today. She called me on Saturday night to see if I wanted to come over after I sorted out Nana, and I never replied.

*Fuck.*

"How long has she been here?" I ask as I continue my spying.

"Not long." Beryl looks over the top of her glasses at me. "Why would you be hiding from Dr. Mansfield?"

"Long story." I keep peering.

"Sounds like the story was too short for her," she mutters.

I fake a smile and drop it immediately. "Less judging, more filing, Beryl." I glance at my watch. Damn it. I can't delay; I need to do my rounds. "I'm starting at the other end today."

Beryl smirks as she types.

I keep peering around the corner.

"Dr. Grayson." Ruby's sarcastic voice sounds from behind me. "Who are you looking for?" I turn toward her.

"Oh, hello, Ruby." I smile. "I had no idea you were here."

Beryl spins her chair toward me and looks over her glasses with a raised eyebrow.

*Not now, Beryl.*

Ruby folds her arms, unimpressed, and also raises an eyebrow. Beryl smirks as she looks between us.

Christ on a cracker.

"Can I have a word?" I ask her.

Beryl keeps watching attentively.

"In private."

"If we must," Ruby snaps. She walks around the corner, and I follow her like a dog with my tail between my legs.

"So." I smile as I widen my eyes. Fucking hell . . . How do I get myself into these situations? "I must apologize for Saturday night."

Her eyes hold mine, but she shows no emotion.

"Nana fell down the stairs, and it's been very hectic." I'm talking fast to try and brush past the lying. "And then I had to look after my neighbor's dog, and he chewed up all the socks, and I haven't been able to find any pairs. So . . . therefore, I couldn't possibly leave the house."

"Let me get this straight." Her eyebrow rises. "You didn't call me because you couldn't find a pair of socks?"

"Precisely. What I'm trying to say is that . . ."

She raises an eyebrow as she waits. *Don't make this any easier, bitch.*

"I perhaps shouldn't have asked you on a date because . . ." I troll my mind for an intelligent reply. Because why? . . . Fuck it!

"I'm waiting," she snaps impatiently.

"I know you're not the kind of woman who just . . ." I widen my eyes as I search for a word . . . any fucking word will do. "And I thought I was ready for something more, but it turns out that I'm not, and I'm sorry."

Her eyes hold mine as she processes what I've just said.

"Does she know?" she eventually asks.

"Huh?" I frown.

"Rebecca."

"What about Rebecca?"

"Oh please," she scoffs. "You spent all night staring at her with love hearts in your eyes."

My mouth drops open in fake horror. "Are you insinuating that I'm lusting after my sister? Dr. Mansfield, I take offense."

"I'm not insinuating anything; I *know* you're lying."

"Why would you even suggest such a thing?"

"Because I googled your sister, and she isn't her." She pokes me hard in the chest. "*You.* Blake Grayson. Are a loser."

I wince. "The evidence does support that."

"Don't ever call me again." She disappears around the corner, and I drag my hand down my face.

*Don't worry. I wasn't planning on it.*

\*\*\*

"Let's get into the spa." Sara smiles. She gets off the chaise longue and leans over me, putting her two hands on my knees. "You're quiet tonight, baby." She kisses me softly.

"I'll be in a minute."

"He *is* quiet today, isn't he?" Michelle replies. She runs her hand through my hair. "A spa with your two favorite girls will help." She leans over and kisses me, her lips lingering over mine. "Come on." She gets up and grabs my hand.

"I've just got to make a call. Be there in a sec," I tell her.

She takes off into the bedroom, and I sit alone on the couch. I hear the tap turn on as they fill the bath, and I can hear them talking with excitement in their voices.

This is nothing new. I've been fucking around with these two naughty girls for years.

Roommates, friends, hot, sexy, *and* willing to share my cock. Not a common combination at all.

So why the fuck am I just not into it tonight?

"Grayson," Michelle calls. "Hope you're warming yourself up out there."

I puff air into my cheeks. What the hell is wrong with me lately?

I thought that if anyone could pull me out of my funk, it would be these two.

*Snap out of it.*

I haven't had sex in four weeks, and sure, a piercing has had some hand in that, but deep down I know who's had a bigger one.

And I can't even like her.

176

Because she doesn't feel the same.

The tap turns off, and I hear the girls giggling and chatting as they slip into the water. We've had hundreds of baths together, the three of us.

Some nights we spend hours in there. Talking, fucking, taking turns—you name it, and it happens.

Lately, though . . . something's missing.

And I would love to blame the girls, or the situation, or anything really, but the truth is . . .

It's me.

Something's changing in my DNA, and like a train barreling toward a broken track, I can feel myself unraveling with no idea how to put the brakes on.

I need to sort my shit out.

Fast.

I drag myself up off the couch and walk into the bathroom. The girls are naked and in the water. Big, beautiful breasts and bare skin. Normally I'd be rock hard and in there.

Tonight . . . nothing.

Michelle gets up on her knees and curls her finger in a come-here signal. "Grayson," she whispers darkly. "Get over here. I've missed you."

*I can't do this.*

"Bad news." I walk over and lean down and kiss Michelle first and then Sara. "I've got to go."

"What?" They both flinch.

"I've got an emergency at work," I lie.

"We'll be quick." Sara stands, and water sloshes over the sides. "Get in here."

"Ten minutes." Michelle grabs for me. "Seriously, I'll make you come in three pumps."

I step back, out of her reach. "Sorry, guys, rain check." I turn, and to the sound of their protests, I hotfoot it out of there. I march to my car, get in, and take off at top speed, as if I'm being chased by a wild animal.

In essence, I am; a horny woman is not to be messed with. Two of them is a disaster.

I grip the steering wheel with white-knuckle force. *I cannot believe I just did that.*

What the actual fuck is wrong with me?

I drive and drive, and I don't even know where to go because that has never happened to me before, and what now?

Where's the fun guy who loves to punish naughty girls?

Partying is my entire identity.

It's who I am. It's what I love to do.

So why does it feel wrong all of a sudden?

Perspiration dusts my skin as a new fear unlocks, and I pull my car over to the side of the road.

*What's happening?*


An hour later, I pull into my driveway and wait as the garage door slowly goes up.

I drive in, grab the tub of ice cream from the passenger seat, and walk back out front and hit the remote. The door slowly goes down. Before I can stop myself, I walk over to Rebecca's.

*What* are *you doing?*

I don't even try to stop myself.

I walk up her front steps. "Barry, no," I hear Rebecca's voice call from inside.

*Knock, knock.*

The door opens, and there she stands, pajamas, green face mask, and her hair in crooked pigtails. "Hi." She smiles.

I hold out the tub of Ben & Jerry's ice cream. "I brought you a present."

"Oh, chocolate crunch. I love you." She goes up onto her tippy-toes and hugs me, and I snap my arm around her waist to hold her closer.

*If only she really did.*

"That shit on your face smells toxic," I whisper into her hair.

She giggles. "Don't I know it. You should smell it from the inside; I'm about to pass out." She grabs my hand and pulls me into her house. It's then that I see Barry the dog pacing in the kitchen.

"What's he doing?" I frown.

"Walking around like a lunatic." She flops onto the couch. "He won't listen to me at all."

"Barry." I point to his bed. "In your bed."

He ignores me and keeps walking around.

"He's stressed because Hen and Juliet are away."

"Maybe we should take him back to his house?" I reply.

"He can't stay there by himself. He'll calm down." She gets two bowls out of the cupboard. "I thought you had a date tonight?"

"I rushed out of there to bring you ice cream." I wink.

"Very funny." She smiles.

It wasn't a joke . . . actual facts, and yes, it's confirmed. I'm a loser.

She dishes out two bowls of ice cream and passes me one.

"I'll pull the fold-up out; my back is hurting," I tell her.

My back isn't sore. That's a deplorable lie.

I just like lying next to her, and sometimes, if I'm lucky, we even fall asleep this way.

I pull out the couch, and she dives onto it and sits cross-legged as she eats her ice cream. As I watch her for a moment, bright-green face, uneven pigtails in her hair, and flannelette pajamas, I have an out-of-body experience.

Did that really just happen?

Let me get this straight—I pulled out of sex with two of the hottest women on earth to eat ice cream with someone who doesn't give a shit about how she looks in front of me.

The thought is utterly ridiculous, and I smile over at her.

"What?" She smiles back.

"What is that green stuff supposed to do, anyway?"

"Make me irresistible."

"To who . . . aliens?"

"Let's hope." She puts a huge spoonful of ice cream into her mouth. "So good," she mumbles with her mouth full.

I take a taste. "Hmmm . . ."

"Don't forget about the school visit this week," she reminds me.

"How could I forget? You've told me ten million times."

"Yeah, well. It's important."

"Since when is a five-year-old interested in what a doctor has to say?" I reply.

"Since now." She watches me for a minute and then smiles. "So . . . tell me about your date."

"Well, the whole time I was there, I was dreaming of ice cream and you, so . . ." I shrug.

"You idiot," she laughs. "Are you ever serious for one minute?"

*More than you know.*

"What happened?" she repeats.

"I don't know." I sigh. "I'm over dating. I'm over women in general, actually."

"Since when?"

I shrug, unsure how to answer.

"You know what I think? I think you're just over playing the field, and you're getting ready to settle down."

I twist my lips; the thought is depressing.

"It's fine. This is a transition period, and you know what transition periods signify?"

"Boredom."

She gives me a broad, beautiful smile. "New beginnings."

"Yeah, well." I keep shoveling in my ice cream. "I kind of liked my life how it was."

We eat in silence for a while, both lost in our own thoughts.

"You want to watch a movie?" she asks.

"Yeah, I guess."

"What do you want to watch?" She looks over at Barry. "Barry, in your bed."

I point to the bed, and somehow, he listens and goes and lies in it.

"See how authoritarian I am?" I reply. "When I speak, he listens. He knows who's boss around here."

"Right." She widens her eyes.

"About time you realize I'm the boss too." I nudge her with my foot.

"Really?" She nudges me back with her foot. "We both know who's boss around here."

I roll my eyes at the irony. The only place I want to be the boss is the one place I'm not.

What a joke.

Two hours later, I lie on my side propped up on my elbow as I watch Rebecca sleep. The movie is on in the background, but I won't turn it off because then she may wake up and go upstairs to her bed instead of sleeping beside me.

Her dark hair is out and splayed across the pillow. Her olive skin is flawless against the cream linen. My eyes roam over her shoulders, then down to linger on her cleavage.

*What is it about this woman?*

She's not a supermodel or a rocket scientist, and hell, she doesn't even like me that way.

But for the life of me . . . I cannot stop thinking about her.

It's like I've had a spell cast on me, a magical one of infatuation and wonder. If I'm out, all I want to do is rush home to see what she's doing.

But I don't know why.

We aren't like that. We have never been like that. We're just friends, and she's right. I know she's right.

Having her in my life forever means a lot more than a flash-in-the-pan, hot-and-heavy romance.

*Hot and heavy.*

My eyes drop lower to her bare thigh as it hangs out of the blanket. The definition in her quad muscle calls to me like never before.

I swallow the lump in my throat. What I wouldn't give for one night.

How would she taste . . .

A wave of arousal washes over me, and I close my eyes to try and will it away . . . just like I've done a million times before.

No matter what, I can't let it win.

Nothing good will ever come from me acting on this stupid, childish crush.

All it would achieve would be to push her away.

I roll onto my back and stare at the ceiling. Her regulated breathing sounds through the room as I fight every primal urge to slide under the covers, spread her legs, and taste her.

Bury myself so deep inside her body that . . . my cock throbs at the thought.

*Fuck . . . stop it.*

I point the remote toward the television. I hope she wakes up. It's actually a good thing if she goes upstairs to bed.

She's not safe here with me, and maybe she's right—maybe I'm just craving a connection with one woman. Maybe it's not her at all; maybe I'm just . . . I don't know, maybe I *am* ready to have a relationship of my own.

With one woman.

She rolls over in her sleep and snuggles into my chest. Her head rests on my arm, her top leg leaning over mine. The warmth from her body begins to liquefy mine.

Fuck . . .

I put my lips to her forehead as I hold her. She's warm and sensual and feels perfect in my arms. Like a luxury that I could never afford.

With my lips resting against her skin, I close my eyes and pretend that she's mine.

*Rebecca*

*Bzzz, bzzz, bzzz . . .*

A quiet vibration breaks the silence.

*Bzzz, bzzz, bzzz.*

I feel movement as Blake reaches over and turns off his alarm.

Hmm. I smile with my eyes closed. What a great night's sleep. I'm warm and toasty and . . . I relax and doze some more.

"Mind removing your knee from my balls?" a husky voice asks. "They're sitting in my neck."

Huh?

My eyes spring open as I realize I'm sprawled all over Blake. My head is on his chest, and my top leg is over the top of his. I scramble back from him. "Sorry," I stammer, embarrassed. "I was asleep." I look around as I try and get my bearings. "We must have fallen asleep last night."

"Hmm," Blake grumbles with his eyes still closed. He raises his arm to wipe his face, and it's then that I see he's no longer wearing his T-shirt. His biceps are bulging with muscle, and his broad chest is on display.

My eyes linger over his muscles . . . *damn.*

Suddenly this feels too intimate, too . . . in my space. "Well, aren't you going?" I snap impatiently. "Why set your alarm if you're not getting out of bed?"

"I have to walk the fucking dog." He sits up on his elbow and looks around. "Where is the mutt, anyway?"

"What?"

"Where's Barry?"

I sit up and look around. There's no sign of him. "Um . . . that's weird."

Blake gets out of bed, and I'm hit in the face with his huge erection tenting his boxer shorts. "Blake?" I snap.

"It's morning," he growls. "I can't help it. If you don't like it, then stop looking."

I flop down onto my back and put my hands over my eyes. "Of course I don't like it." I fake disgust.

That's some big tentage action.

Jeez . . .

Unable to help it, I glance back. That's not a two-man, no sirree—that's a family tent . . . maybe even a gazebo.

He could really do some damage . . . yeesh.

*The mind boggles.*

Blake stands at the end of the bed as he looks around. "Barry," he calls.

Silence . . .

I sit up too. "Barry," I call. He barks from upstairs. "Come down here for walkies."

He barks again in excitement, and I can hear his tail hitting the wall as he wags it.

I drag myself out of bed and walk into the bathroom as I hear Barry clomping down the stairs.

"Oh shit . . . ," I hear Blake say. "What did you *do*?"

Huh?

I try to hurry up.

"What happened?" I call.

"We've got a problem out here." I hear Blake walking up the stairs. "What the fuck?" he yells. "No, Barry. No. Oh my fuck . . ." I hear Barry happily bouncing around, as if this is the best game of all time.

"What happened?" I call.

Silence . . .

"What happened?" I call louder.

For fuck's sake, can someone answer me already? I quickly finish and wash my hands; I open the door to see Barry standing there, looking up at me all innocent-like.

Only he isn't innocent at all. His snout is covered in all different kinds of bright colors . . . What? I frown as I lean down to look closer at him. "Lipstick!" I cry. I take the stairs two at a time and notice red smears on the carpet on every step. "Oh my god."

"I wouldn't come up here if I were you," Blake calls. "It's a crime scene."

I come flying around the corner to see Blake down on his hands and knees, and my eyes widen in horror at the carnage. My ripped makeup bag is on the floor, and every single piece of makeup that I own is chewed up, destroyed, and smeared all over the floor. The lipstick canisters are squished with teeth marks all through them, and the eyeshadows are shattered into a million pieces. I pick up my brand-new mascara that I haven't even used yet; it's so chewed up that you can't even open it.

"Barry!" I cry.

Barry looks up at me and wags his tail and smiles, and it's then that I see his teeth are all covered in lipstick. A dog with lipstick on his teeth isn't something I see every day, and I burst out laughing.

"I fail to see the humor," Blake mumbles as he tries to pick up the mess.

Barry barks and leans back onto his hind legs in excitement for his walk.

"No walking today," Blake huffs. "You're grounded, mutt."


"Everybody sit on the mat, please," I call to my class. "Our very special visitor will be here any moment." I look around at all the excited little faces. "Let's see how straight we can sit up." I straighten my back as I sit cross-legged on the mat with them. "I win." I smile. "Am I sitting up the straightest?"

Everybody sits so straight that they are nearly doing a backbend. "Look at me, Miss Dalton," Wendy calls.

"Oh yes, very impressive."

"I'm winning now," Brandon tells us.

"Wow," I agree. "You are *so* straight."

"Hello, everyone," comes a calm voice from the doorway. "My oh my, look how fabulous you are all sitting."

The children all smile proudly.

"Good morning, K2." The principal smiles.

"Good morning, Mrs. Murphy," my class sings. It's then that I notice all the girls from the front office are standing in a pack behind her.

"We have a wonderful visitor today," she tells the class. "Dr. Grayson has come to talk to us." She calls him over, and Blake appears. He's carrying a black bag and wearing a navy suit and a crisp white shirt. He's tall and handsome. His sandy-brown hair has a wave to it, and he looks like McDreamy . . . only better.

"Hello, Dr. Grayson." I smile enthusiastically. "Welcome to K2."

His eyes find mine across the room, and he gives me a slow, sexy smile and a subtle nod. "Hello, everyone." He walks in and up to the front of the class.

I glance back to the office girls, and they are now all standing at the back of my classroom, smiling goofily as they watch him.

*This isn't a strip show, girls.*

"Oh my god," Veronica mouths as she fans her face with her hands.

I drop my head to hide my smile. Could they be any more obvious? This is the last day in career week, and so far, nobody from the office has bothered to come and see any of the parents talk about their jobs.

Only today . . . coincidence? I think not.

I can guarantee not one of them gives a damn about what a doctor does at work . . . they are only interested in this particular doctor's activities.

Blake stands at the front of the class and looks around. "Wow." He smiles. "I've never seen a class sitting up so straight."

"Really?" I play along. "How wonderful. Did you hear that, K2?"

They all nod as they smile broadly.

"Dr. Grayson, thank you so much for coming to talk to us today."

"You're most welcome, Miss Dalton." His eyes have a mischievous glow to them. "I like to be helpful."

I get up off the mat and stand to the side. "Why don't you tell us a little about what you do in a day?"

"All right, then. I'll just bring my assistant out to help us."

Huh?

He puts his black duffel bag on my desk and digs around in it as we all watch in wonder.

What is he doing?

He pulls out a white coat and flicks it in the air for a dramatic effect. He puts it on over his suit, then pulls out his stethoscope and puts it around his neck. "This is my uniform." He looks down at himself and then holds his hands up at the girls in the back. "How do I look, ladies?" he teases.

"Great." They all smile and give him a thumbs-up.

I giggle. He's such a performer. He really should have been an actor.

"Now, K2, may I have the privilege of introducing my best friend and assistant doctor, Dr. Cecil." He reaches into his black bag and pulls out a huge soft penguin toy. It's wearing a white coat and has a stethoscope around its neck.

Everyone squeals and laughs in excitement, me and the office girls included.

"Dr. Cecil and I work at the children's hospital," he tells us as he looks around.

"Every day, we look after children who are unwell until they get better."

We sit in silence as we hang on his every word.

"Now, may I have a volunteer to help me and Dr. Cecil?"

Everyone's hands fly up as they desperately try to be his volunteer.

He looks around the class, and I can see him doing an internal assessment. "You look like an excellent assistant." He points at the little boy sitting alone on the end. "Come up here, please."

The boy bounces up and stands beside him. Blake bends and shakes his hand. "My name is Blake, and this is Cecil. What is your name?"

"Aaron."

"Hello, Aaron." Blake shakes Aaron's hand and then holds out the penguin's little wing to shake hands too.

Everyone laughs as Aaron shakes hands with the penguin.

"Now, you are going to be our student doctor and look over Cecil as I show you what to do. How does that sound, Aaron?"

Aaron gives an overexaggerated smile and nods. Blake hands him the play stethoscope. "Now, do as I do and look over Dr. Cecil."

He puts the earpiece in his ear and holds his stethoscope to Aaron's chest. "Just like this."

Aaron holds the stethoscope to Cecil's chest and listens.

"Very good." Blake smiles. "You're a natural at this."

Aaron beams with pride as he looks around the classroom.

*Oh, my heart.*

This is his spiel that he does with the children every day at the hospital.

"Now we are going to take Cecil's temperature." Blake hands Aaron a digital thermometer. "Hold it to his forehead and be very still."

Aaron concentrates on doing his job as Blake takes Aaron's temperature.

"You are an excellent doctor," Blake tells him.

I get a lump in my throat as I watch him. He's so tender and sweet. Instructing Aaron on how to be the doctor while sneakily checking Aaron for the same things.

I mean, I always knew he was special, and I know he's a doctor, and I know he's a pediatrician. None of this is new information, but this is the first time I've actually seen him in action.

I'm in awe . . .

I watch on as Aaron is instructed on how to give Cecil a full check-up: ears, eyes, and bones. Reflexes and ligaments. They check Cecil's blood pressure.

Blake pulls out a fake syringe and helps Aaron draw blood from Cecil as I blink away tears.

Over the next half hour, I stand to the side of the classroom, transfixed by Dr. Blake Grayson. I don't hear much of what he's saying; it's what he's not saying that means so much.

His empathy and giant heart are shining through.

"Thank you, Aaron," he says. "Everybody, give Aaron a big clap for a job well done."

Aaron dances back to his spot as the class cheers.

Blakes smiles. "Now, who would like me to listen to their heartbeat?"

The hands shoot up. "Me!" "Me!" "Me!"

"Line up," he tells them.

One by one, they step to the front, and he listens to their heartbeats. "Wow," he gushes. "Sounds like magic in there." He listens again. "I think you can actually make magic."

"Maybe."

Veronica smiles proudly. Every single child has a new comment about their heartbeat, and honestly, I don't ever think I've heard something so beautiful.

I blink back tears for the tenth time today.

"Miss Dalton." Blake turns to me.

"Yes."

"I would like to listen to your heartbeat."

*Don't—I guarantee it's fluttering right now.* "Okay." I step forward. He puts the stethoscope to my chest and gives me a sexy wink.

I smirk as I try to act casual.

"Ahh." He smiles as he listens. "This heart is very special." He listens intently again. "It's big and . . . loving." He listens again. "K2," he calls. "I think this is the sweetest heart that I've ever listened to."

*Oh . . .*

The class cheers, and I unexpectedly tear up again. His eyes hold mine for a moment before he turns away and holds up Cecil. "Everybody thank Dr. Cecil."

The class goes wild, and I stare at the stranger in front of me.

The best friend and neighbor that I know has suddenly turned into something much more appealing.

I swallow the lump in my throat as I watch him continue to work the room.

This is a disaster.


Hands slide down my thighs and hold my legs open. His thick tongue swipes through my flesh as I quiver on the brink of orgasm.

Two fingers slowly slide inside my body . . .

My back arches off the bed, and I moan in ecstasy. My hand roams over his shoulder muscles, and I smile into his neck as he climbs over me.

"Rebecca," a voice whispers in my ear.

My eyes spring open, and I sit up in a start. My heart is racing. Perspiration wets my skin. I glance at the clock: 4:00 a.m. It's okay, it's not real. It never happened.

I pant as I go over the dream—or was it a nightmare?

I know that voice. I'd know it anywhere.

*Blake.*


I sit on the back steps as the sun comes up. Barry is out doing his morning potty, but I haven't slept a wink.

Spending the entire night having sexually explicit dreams of your platonic friend will do that to you. I was living in a nightmare . . . a very hot one, at that.

This is . . . bad. Bad, bad, bad.

"Hey." I hear Blake coming down the side through the gate. "You ready for a walk?"

"Oh," he says in surprise as he sees me sitting on the steps. "You're up early."

"Yep." I force a smile. *Not going to tell you why, though.*

"Actually, this is good timing," he says.

"It is?" I frown. Oh no . . . he knows.

He sits down beside me on the steps. "I've been thinking about what you said."

"You have?"

*Oh no . . . what did I say?*

"You're right. I can't keep going on as I am. It's time for a change. I'm tired of playing the field, and I think I am ready to settle down."

Where's he going with this?

"You are?" I frown. That's not what I was expecting to come out of his mouth.

"Yes. So I've been thinking. Don't get me a date for Saturday night."

"Why not?"

"I know who I'm going to ask out."

"You do?"

"I've liked her for a long time, and I could never ask her out, but it's time to just . . . do it."

"Oh . . ." I think for a moment. "Do I know her?"

"No. Her name is Kayla. She's a nurse I used to work with. I've had a crush on her for years."

# Chapter 13

I sit at the table and wait, and as always, he's going to be late.

This is John.

I'm over his power plays. I'm over the way he does things, and more than anything, I'm over this marriage.

I sip my coffee as I go over my options. I know I have to do this, and even though I don't want to, I know it's for the right reasons.

If this Foot Finder thing has taught me anything, it's that I can look after the house by myself, even if I don't sell pictures every day or even every week. When I do have something go well, I just need to bank it for a rainy day.

He was wrong. I *can* do this alone.

So today I'm making a deal with the devil, literally.

I'm going to agree to not divorce John for five years. Of course, I'm going to try and get it down to three years, but regardless of the terms and situation, I need him to sign the house over to me.

The café doors open, and John walks in like the rock star that he thinks he is. He smiles and waves and makes his way over to me. "Hello, my beautiful wife," he sings.

I look at his lying face and arrogant persona and wonder what I ever saw in this man. In fact, I want to vomit in my own mouth. He makes me sick.

He sits back, all powerful-like. "You wanted to see me."

*No, I didn't. I want my house, fucker, and you're going to give it to me.*

"I've been thinking about your offer of signing the house over to me," I say.

"I thought you may have."

"And . . ." I can't believe I'm about to say this. "I'm willing to agree to no divorce in exchange for you signing the house fully into my name."

He smiles and takes my hand over the table. "This is for the best, babe."

*I'm not your babe.*

I want to rip my hand from his grip. I want to throw my drink in his face. I want to turn the table over and scream to the demons from hell to come and drag him back down.

But I won't. Why? Because just like him, maybe I've turned into the darker version of myself, and I'll do anything that I can to get that house in my name, even be nice to this prick.

"Okay, so let's get this straight. I say you will sign the house over to me if I agree not to divorce you for three years."

"Five years."

"Five years is too long, John."

"That's the deal. Do you want the house or not?"

My eyes hold his, and damn it, how did I ever love this monster? "I do."

"Great. I'll get the paperwork signed and the house over to you."

"Thank you."

He squeezes my hand in his. "We're going to get through this, baby."

"How long do you think the contract will take to do?" I ask.

"I've already had a lawyer working on it, so it won't be long. A week, tops."

Ugh . . . he knew I was going to sign it.

*Keep calm.*

"Okay, that's great." I contemplate saying the next thing because it goes against everything I agree with, but it is true. "Thank you, John. I appreciate it." He doesn't have to sign the house over to me, but I know that deep down, he knows I could never afford to buy him out and that this is the right thing to do.

"Can we have dinner on Saturday night?" he asks.

"I can't, I'm sorry."

His eyes search mine. "Do you know how much I miss you?"

"John, don't."

"Some nights, I wake up in the middle of the night and feel like I can't breathe because I miss you so much."

I know that feeling well. I've suffered the same affliction. The lump in my throat begins to hurt.

Now those feelings of dependency on John have been replaced by another man.

As much as I hate to admit it, I think I have feelings for Blake Grayson, and I don't know what to do with them. I'm completely bewildered by the entire thing. It sneaked up on me, and I don't even know if it's real or a crush or what the hell it is.

I swore to never make the same mistake again, to never go for the same kind of man. And as much as I hate to admit it, if there's any man in the world that bears a resemblance to the type of man John is, it's Blake.

Anyway, that's a different horror story for another day. I'll worry about this horror story first.

"Okay, I'll wait to hear from you with the contract?" I ask.

"Yes."

"Can we try and maybe meet back here next week for lunch?" I smile hopefully. "We will have lunch just to celebrate signing."

He smiles, mistaking my kindness for a weakness. "That sounds great. I'll bring the paperwork with me then."

"Thank you."

He stands and kisses my cheek, and for the first time since our separation, I think that one day I'll be able to look back on this divorce as a blessing. A lesson that I needed to be taught, and who knows, maybe it was written in the stars all along.

I walk out of the restaurant with my head held high. The house is going to be mine and mine alone.

I push out of the doors and into the cool air of the street. I want to jump in the air and punch it. But I won't, because this is John, and until I get that contract signed in front of me and the house completely signed over to me . . . I can't actually trust a word he says.

I walk up the front steps and knock on the door. Taryn's smiling face comes into view. "You ready?" I ask.

"Just a minute; let me get my shoes." She darts off, and Barry and I walk out and sit on the front steps. It's a beautiful afternoon, and I have to admit that having the job of walking Barry every afternoon has made me exercise more. He's been so naughty that he's getting three walks a day now. I've walked more this week since I've had him than I have in the last twelve months.

Maybe I *should* get a dog of my own?

Taryn bounces down the stairs. "Let's go." She's wearing gray tights and a matching sports bra; her stomach is cut, and her boobs are perfect. She looks incredible. I'm wearing a baggy T-shirt that has paint all over it and my old pants.

"I really need to make more of an effort. Look how gorgeous you look," I tell her. "No wonder all the men look you up and down, Taryn. You've really got all your shit together."

"You've got to be kidding." She sighs. "If I didn't have my tits out all the time, no one would even look at me."

"That's not true, and you know it. You could wear a potato sack and still be killing it," I tell her. We make our way down the road, and I have to ask a question that's been burning a hole in my tongue. "Have you heard from Blake?" I ask.

"Why would I hear from Blake?" She takes Barry's lead off me. "Let me hold him. I want to pretend I have a dog for a day."

"You know, I thought that after you and Blake hooked up a couple weeks ago, he would have called you or something."

"What are you talking about? I never hooked up with Blake."

"I thought that night after Carol's, you two got it on."

"No." She screws up her face in question. "Why on earth would you think that I hooked up with Blake?"

"Well, he had a huge hickey on his neck, and I thought you were the only one capable of doing it." I smirk.

"Oh my god." She rolls her eyes in disgust. "Trust me, I do not give men hickeys. I don't want to remember it myself. Why would I leave evidence for the world to see?"

I laugh. "That makes sense, I guess." I frown as a new thought comes through. "But if you didn't hook up with Blake, who gave him the love bite?"

"No idea." She thinks for a moment. "There was no one there that night but us."

"Yeah, I know, very interesting," I think out loud.

"Maybe it was Carol."

"What the hell." I laugh. "Why would it be Carol?"

"I saw Carol sneaking back into her house that night at about four a.m."

I frown as I stare at her. "Sneaking back in from where?"

"I don't fucking know." She sighs. "Our street is getting out of control."

I laugh in surprise. "I mean, if Carol is getting some action and I'm not, there is a serious problem around here."

"You could have action if you wanted to have action."

"As if. With who?"

"Open your eyes, you weirdo. Mr. Dr. Grayson is madly in love with you."

"No, he's not. He just told me that he wants to have a relationship with some fucking Kayla woman."

"You're an idiot if you let him go," she huffs as we walk.

"What do you mean, let him go? I don't have him in the first place to let him go."

"Have you seen the way he looks at you? All he does whenever he's around you is look after you, look out for you, run after you."

I stare at her in confusion. "Do you think he likes me . . . as more than a friend?"

"I don't think it, I know it."

"Has he ever said anything to you?"

"He doesn't have to; everybody just knows."

I think on this for a moment as we walk. "Does anyone else think this or just you?"

"Everybody knows it. Blake Grayson has been madly in love with you since before your marriage even broke up. That's why John hates him. John knows exactly how he feels."

"I don't know about that. We're just friends."

"Correction, Blake is *your* friend, but you're Blake's dream girl, and you're being pretty fucking stupid if you ask me."

"What do you mean?" I snap, offended.

"Because he's gorgeous, and he's rich, and he hangs on every word you say, and if you don't open your eyes and see what's

199

right in front of you, some stupid bimbo is going to come in and sweep him off his feet and steal him right from underneath your nose."

Her words hit a nerve, and I stop walking. "He's never said anything to me."

That's a white lie; he did insinuate something that night he said he would ask for my number. But then he said he just wanted to have sex and to not get carried away.

"Have you ever asked him?" she says as we walk.

"No." I shrug. "What if he doesn't and I ask him? Then it will be super awkward between us, and I don't want that to happen."

"Okay, I'm going to do it."

"Do what?"

"Ask him if he likes you."

"What? Just come out with it like that?"

"Why not?"

"Just be more, I don't know . . . subtle." I think for a moment. "Somehow casually work it into the conversation. Something like, 'If you ever had a chance with Rebecca, would you take it?'"

"I'll go over tonight and ask him."

"No, not tonight. That's too obvious. Just next time you see him."

Taryn smirks as her eyes hold mine. "Why, do *you* like him?"

"No," I scoff.

"Are you sure?"

"I'm interested to see what he says, that's all." I shrug. "I told you, he said that he likes some Kayla girl. He's bringing her on the double date this weekend."

"I call bullshit."

"What do you mean?"

"He doesn't like her, no way."

"You think?"

"Okay, tomorrow night I'm going to go to his house. I'm going to ask him, and then I'm going to come straight over to yours after and tell you what he said."

"You don't mind?" I wince.

"Are you kidding? Matchmaking two of my neighbors is like a dream come true."

"What's going on with you and Ronald, anyway?"

"I don't know." She sighs. "Not really in a relationship with Ronny. I'm in a relationship with his dick."

"Is it good?"

"It's the best, which is becoming a real problem."

"Why is that?"

"Because Ronny the man is annoying. Ronny's donkey dick, however, is on point. And unfortunately, I can't have one without the other. It's like a double-edged sword. Great sex or great guy: it's one or the fucking other. When am I ever going to find a man who has it all?"

I smile. "I love you. You are so refreshingly honest."

We walk in silence for a while.

"What are you going to do if he says that he does like you in that way?"

"That's the million-dollar question." My eyes search hers. "I actually have no idea, but I do want to know who gave him that hickey."

Taryn rattles on about Ronny while I troll my mind for an answer . . . Maybe my security camera picked something up from that night?

Hmm, I'm going to watch it back.

### Blake

**I look at the ball, and then I look at the hole and line up the two. I gently tap it in. "So who is this guy Bec's going out with, anyway?" Antony asks.**

"I don't know, some loser. His name is Gregory."

"I always think the name Gregory sounds like a cat."

I give him the side-eye. "I never met a cat called Gregory." I hit the next ball into the hole.

"I think if I ever had a cat, I would call it Gregory."

I roll my eyes. "And you think about this how often?"

We continue taking turns putting.

"I've been doing some research, and I think I've narrowed it down to who Nooky Nights is."

"Go on." I pull the ball back with my putter and hit it again.

"One hundred percent Taryn."

"What makes you say that?" I ask as I sip my beer.

"Well, who else is tapped enough to be talking about aliens with two cocks and double penetration?"

"This is true." I think on this for a minute. "Although I imagine all women fantasize about getting fucked with two green cocks in both holes. I mean, what's more forbidden than alien cock?"

"True. I mean, I would if I was them."

"Same."

"I'm going to ask her," he says.

"Here's your chance. She's coming over now."

"Taryn." I smile. "Coming over to get your butt kicked in golf?"

"Ha, highly unlikely." She picks up a putter that's leaning against the chair.

"What's been happening?" I ask her.

"Not much. I've been working and hanging out with Ronny."

"How's it going? You seem to be spending a lot of time together lately."

"It's good." She shrugs. "Better than dating my vibrator, put it that way."

I smirk as I hit my next ball into the hole.

"So, are you going on your double date this weekend with Rebecca?"

"Uh-huh." I keep putting.

Antony takes the stick off me and has his shot.

"Who's Rebecca taking on her date this week?" Taryn asks.

"I don't know, some loser."

"What about you . . . Who are you taking?"

"Girl I used to work with. Her name is Kayla."

"Right." She widens her eyes at me. "I think you're crazy."

Antony hits his next shot.

"Why is that?" I ask.

"Well, I always thought if you had a shot with Rebecca, you would take it."

"Didn't we all," Antony replies.

"Firstly, I don't have a shot with Rebecca. And secondly, she has made it abundantly clear that we're just friends."

"But if she wanted more, what would you say?"

"I would say that we're just friends."

"Figuratively speaking, let's just play pretend for a minute. If Rebecca wanted more from you . . . would you be willing?"

"Any man on earth would be willing." I take another shot.

Taryn smirks like the cat that got the cream.

"What's that look?" I ask.

"Nothing." She watches us for another few minutes. "You want to know what I think?"

I roll my eyes. "Not really."

"I think you like Rebecca."

"I think that you're off your tree and perhaps still high after too much dick." I take the golf putter off Antony. "That reminds me, I've got your pajama bottoms at my house."

"Why would you have my pajama bottoms?"

"I don't know." I shrug. "I found them under my bed the night after Carol's party."

"Are you high? I didn't sleep in your bed after Carol's party." Taryn frowns. "Show me these pajama pants."

"All right." I walk into my house with her and Ant hot on my heels, and I open the second drawer in my kitchen and pull out the pajama pants.

Taryn holds them in her hand and looks them over. "These aren't mine, and besides . . ." She frowns as she tries to articulate her thoughts. "Why would my pajama pants be under your bed?"

"Well, I was going to ask the same question. Did we hook up that night?"

"No." She frowns. "What on earth would make you think that we hooked up that night?"

"Well, I woke up with a huge hickey on my neck, and I remember dancing with you, and then I found these pajama pants under my bed."

"Fuck no, Blake. Rebecca asked me the same thing," Taryn scoffs. "Ronny came over and stayed at my house that night, and as far as those pajama pants go, I've never seen them before in my life."

"Maybe someone else came over that night?" Antony chimes in. "Maybe it was Carol."

"Carol did hook up that night."

"What?" Antony and I both snap at the same time.

"I saw her sneaking into her house at four a.m."

"Where had she been?" Antony gasps. His eyes come to me, and he begins to chuckle.

"It wasn't fucking Carol," I snap, disgusted. "Look . . . all I know is never give me that punch again. I've never, ever blacked out in my life. I have no idea what happened or how I woke up with a giant hickey and pajama pants under my bed."

"I have no idea either." She shrugs. "Anyway, I've got to go."

"Where are you going?" I ask as we all head back out to the putting green.

"I'm having dinner at Rebecca's."

"Oh." My eyes rise over to Rebecca's house. "I didn't get an invite."

"Probably because you're too gutless to tell her that you like her."

"I *don't* like her." I widen my eyes to accentuate my point.

"Are you sure about that?" Antony chimes in.

"Fuck off," I snap.

My eyes rise to meet hers, and I know that she knows.

"Don't say anything to Rebecca," I warn her.

She smirks. "I wouldn't dare." She wanders around the cul-de-sac and disappears into Rebecca's house.

"You trust her?"

I hit the ball. "Not one bit."


*Rebecca*


"Hey," Taryn calls as she walks in my front door. "Told you so."

"Told me what?"

"Blake likes you."

"He said that?" I frown as I stop stirring dinner.

"Not . . . exactly."

I roll my eyes. "So he didn't say it at all?"

"He didn't need to. It was what he wasn't saying that gave it away."

"Like what?"

"I asked him if he liked you, and he said no."

I hold my hand up. "And there it is, in black and white."

"Then I gave him the look, and he gave me the look back and said, *Don't tell Rebecca.*"

I stare at her as her words roll around in my head. "He said that?"

"Uh-huh." She picks up a cookie and takes a bite. "He also said he wants to show you his dick."

"What?" I gasp.

"Nah." She smiles. "He didn't say that. Just checking if you're listening."

I roll my eyes, and I actually have no idea whether to believe her story or not.

Maybe she's just in matchmaking mode?

"So, what's for dinner, anyway?" Taryn asks.

"You are literally looking into the saucepan as we speak."

"Oh, spaghetti?"

"Yeah." I smile at my ditzy friend. "Spaghetti."


### Saturday night

I wind the hair up around the curling wand and wait for it to set.

Blake's words from our first double date come back to haunt me: *I like your hair like that.*

It's been the weirdest week; I've barely seen Blake since he came to my classroom. I have, however, dreamed of him every night and thought about him all day, every day.

206

To be honest, I don't even know if this is real or if this is just me realizing that he's a good catch . . . for someone else.

It's like this beacon of light has gone off in my brain, and no matter how many times I try to go back to the way I was thinking and feeling about Blake, I can't seem to manage it.

My biggest fear is that I will ruin what we have, because I know he's a lot like John. Everything that I said I would never fall for again.

Charismatic, funny, sexy, and a doctor. Not to mention that every woman who meets him falls madly in love with him.

This is not the kind of guy that I need to be involved with.

So I won't be.

Tonight, I'm going to give it my best chance with Gregory.

Blake said that he was going to help me date, and to be honest, he hasn't given me much feedback so far. I mean, with the first date, we both bailed and went and had dessert, and then . . . we had that moment when he told me that he would have liked to have asked for my number if we met in different circumstances.

Does that still stand?

The thing is, as much as I know how Blake plays around and jokes about everything being about sex, I don't feel it's like that for the two of us.

We do have a deeper friendship. *One that I don't want to ruin.*

It's fine—it's just me realizing he's a good man. It doesn't mean I like him, just the opposite. This is me appreciating my good friend.

I finish my hair, and I step back and look at myself in the mirror. I'm wearing my favorite cream fitted dress, with my hair down and curled. And tonight I'm catching an Uber there because I want to drink, and Blake is right—I don't want any more weirdos knowing where I live, so I'm not getting anyone to pick me up anymore. Blake is picking his date up in an Uber too. He said he doesn't want to meet Kayla at the restaurant because it seems impersonal. Forever the gentleman.

Ugh . . .

I keep going over his friendship with Kayla. I wonder if it's the same as his friendship with me. He's so caring and thoughtful when it comes to us. Is he like that with her too?

Deep down, I hate that thought. I hate that someone else has his friendship like I do. I thought it was something special just between us. Maybe not.

But I guess I'll be able to tell.

He's drinking tonight, not driving, and I've never seen Blake have a few drinks on a date with someone that he likes. Not that I've ever seen him with someone that he likes.

I'm not sure I want to either.

I take a deep, steadying breath, grab my purse, and head downstairs to call my Uber. Tonight will be very telling, and I will know once and for all if this Blake thing is all in my head. I really hope it is.

My life is complicated enough already.


I glance at my watch as I wait around the corner. Tonight I want to be strategically late. Well, at least five minutes, anyway. The last thing I want to do is watch Blake walk in with his date hand in hand.

I saw Gregory, my date, walk in about five minutes ago, and when he texted me to ask where I was, of course I lied and told him I was still in my Uber. I've lied already: not a great start.

Worst part about it is, I'm just about to go into a date with one man, when the other man at the table is all I can think about.

I'm going to like the other guy, even if it kills me.

Ugh . . .

What has my life turned into? It's like a fucking soap opera.

With one last steadying breath, I drop my shoulders. *You can do this.*

I walk in through the restaurant and see them sitting at a table by the window. Blake is talking to his date, and Gregory looks up and sees me. He stands and smiles.

Oh, he's cute. This is a pleasant surprise.

"Hello." I smile. "I'm Rebecca." I hold out my hand to shake his, and he leans in and kisses me on the cheek.

"I'm Gregory. Nice to meet you."

Blake glances up. "Hi, Rebecca." He smiles. "This is Kayla."

"Hello." I smile awkwardly as I sit down.

"Hello, so nice to meet you," she replies. My eyes linger on her for a moment.

*Oh no.*

Kayla is pretty and attractive, with the girl-next-door vibe. Nothing like the supermodels that Blake normally dates.

Great.

This is it. She's the one.

They've been friends for years, and he said he's always liked her. Oh my god, how did I get myself into this situation? I feel myself begin to sweat.

Gregory moves around so that he's closer to me. "I was worried you were going to bail on me."

*Me too.*

"No, no, I'm here." I smile awkwardly. My eyes roam over to Blake and Kayla. They've gone back to their conversation, and Blake is totally immersed in whatever she's saying. He's hardly noticed that I've arrived.

"What would you like to drink?" Gregory asks.

I open the drink menu and look over the choices. "What are you guys having?"

"Hmm, not sure yet," Kayla says as she opens her drink menu.

Gregory calls over the waiter and gestures for me to go first. "What can I get you?" the waiter asks.

I feel like the awkwardness of tonight is going to make it where if I drink something that I like, I could get way too tipsy, and fast. *No, stick to a drink that you don't like.*

Safer that way.

"I'll have a glass of white wine, thank you." I smile.

"And you, sir?" he asks Gregory.

"I'll have a scotch on the rocks, please." The waiter writes down our orders and turns his attention to Blake and Kayla.

"Really?" Kayla smiles all excitedly. "Oh my god," she whispers.

"I know, I couldn't believe it either." Blake laughs.

*What couldn't you believe?*

"I can't wait to tell you all about it," he says. "It's a funny story."

My stomach twists in jealousy. I hate that he has another girlfriend. Here I was thinking that what we had was special. Now he can't wait to tell her all about it, and I don't even know what it is.

"What can I get you, ma'am?" the waiter asks.

"I'll have a margarita, thanks." Kayla smiles.

*That's my drink, bitch.*

"Hmm, that sounds good." Blake smiles all sexy-like. "Make that two."

"So . . ." Gregory smiles over at me. "I've been looking forward to this night all week."

"Me too," I lie as I smile nervously back.

From my peripheral vision, I see Blake take Kayla's hand and put it on his leg.

Why does he always do that?

It's infuriating.

Here I am thinking that he's touching me because he wants to, when that's just his language; that's how he speaks to all women.

"So, what do you do, Gregory?" Blake asks.

"I'm in tech."

"What kind of tech?" Blake raises his eyebrow in interest.

"At the moment, I'm working on robots that defuse bombs."

"Bombs?" Kayla gasps. "Who employs you to defuse bombs?"

"The United States government," he tells us. "They're mostly used in international deployments."

"Wow." I smile.

"Impressive." Blake smiles. "How did you get into that?"

"I'm an engineer by trade, and I used to make robots for the army for testing, and they told me what they needed going forward, so I designed the technology. And I guess it went from there."

"Where do you work from?" Blake asks.

"I have a team. Our offices are downtown."

"A team?" Blake frowns. "How many in your team?"

"Thirty-seven."

"Impressive, man." He smiles.

Gregory turns his attention to me. "So . . . tell me about your class."

"Nothing much to tell." I smile, embarrassed. In my peripheral vision, I see that Blake and Kayla have gone back to their conversation. Her hand is still on his leg, and they are talking softly between themselves.

My stomach twists in jealousy. This is a living fucking nightmare.

The waiter arrives with our drinks, and he passes them out. "Thank you." Blake smiles as he gives them out to us and then holds his glass up. "I would like to propose a toast."

We hold our glasses to his.

Blake's eyes go to Kayla. "To new beginnings."

He taps his glass with hers, and they smile softly at each other as they take a sip.

I bite the inside of my cheek so hard that I taste blood.

"To new beginnings." Gregory smiles. I take a sip of my wine as his eyes hold mine.

His eye contact is getting a little bit intense, so I turn my attention back to Kayla and Blake.

"So, where did you two meet?" I ask.

"Where did we meet?" Blake smiles and narrows his eyes, as if trying to remember.

"Years ago," Kayla replies. "Funnily enough, it was on another double date. Blake was dating my roommate at the time."

I begin to hear my heartbeat in my ears. "And you had that instant thing when he was with your roommate?" I act casual, as if the answer doesn't matter.

"Funnily enough, I knew I liked Kayla right away, so I went home and broke up with her roommate with the intention of hopefully being able to ask her out one day."

"You said *funnily enough* before." I fake a smile.

*Nothing is funnily enough here, fucker.*

Blake's eyes hold mine with a mischievous glow. Wait a minute . . . Does he know that he's annoying me?

"And then we worked together for a couple of years." Kayla smiles.

"Where do you work, Kayla?"

"I used to work at the children's hospital with Blake, but now I work at the children's cancer hospital."

"You work with children with cancer?"

"Yes." She smiles. "It's hard some days, but bringing happiness to the children has really been life changing for me."

I smile sadly. Kayla is a good person.

I sip my wine and decide that I will not say anything more. If Blake likes this woman, it's for a reason.

The night goes reasonably smooth. Gregory is kind and funny and very interested in everything I say. But I really don't pay much attention to him at all because I am too busy eavesdropping on what Blake is saying to Kayla.

They've laughed and whispered, and at one stage, he even kissed her cheek. We've had dinner and dessert and a few more drinks, and the four-piece band is starting up. "Let's dance." Blake stands and holds his hand out for Kayla. "I want to spin you around the floor a little bit."

Kayla smiles up at him as if he's a rock god.

My heart sinks into a puddle on the floor.

He really likes her, I can tell.

"That's a great idea," says Gregory. "Let's dance too."

Really, Gregory? I am not in the mood for dancing right now.

He leads me to the dance floor regardless.

It's a band, and they're playing an older song. I've heard it before but can't remember where or who sings it. Gregory looks down at me. "You look beautiful tonight."

"Thanks."

I glance over to see Blake smiling down at Kayla. She says something, and he laughs out loud.

*Ouch.*

"You know, when you accepted my message request, I never envisioned that you would be so beautiful."

I feel my cheeks go red with embarrassment. "Well . . . you're not so bad yourself."

Gregory is tall, and he looks down at me as we sway to the music. "How do you think tonight's gone?" he asks.

"Honestly, it's been great." I smile. Not a lie; it has gone really well.

We turn as we dance, and I peek over Gregory's shoulder just in time to see Blake softly kiss Kayla. His lips linger over hers.

213

My heart sinks.

I can feel the electricity between them from here.

They kiss softly again and again, and she says something, and Blake smiles as he leans with his cheek to hers.

*This is it; she's the one.*

I'm not doing this to myself. I don't want to sit around here all night and watch Blake make out with his dream girl.

I snap my gaze away from them and drag it back to Gregory's handsome face. "Do you want to get out of here?"

"Really?" His eyes dance with delight. "Where do you want to go?"

"I know this really great little dessert bar on the other side of town."

"Shall we ask the others to come?"

"No, I want you all to myself." I take Gregory's hand in mine and lead him from the dance floor and back to our table. "Let's just pay our half of the bill and leave them to it."

"We are going to say goodbye, though?" Gregory asks.

I glance up to the dance floor just in time to see Blake kiss Kayla, not a peck but a full-on tongue kiss, and I watch in horror as his eyes close, as if he's totally lost in the moment.

"We'll give them a wave on our way out," I force out as I smile.

I feel like crying howl-to-the-moon sobs.

I'm too late. I finally realized how perfect Blake is, and he's on a date with his dream girl.

They're probably going to get married and have babies and live happily ever after in a house two doors down from mine.

Fuck. My. Life.

We pay our half of the bill while I try desperately not to look at the dance floor, although it's kind of hard when they're just about making a porno in the corner.

Gregory waves goodbye, and Blake hardly even looks up. He waves and goes back to kissing Kayla.

My heart sinks lower than it has in a very long time.

This night can't be over soon enough.

Three hours later, I stand in the cab line with Gregory.

"I'm going to call you tomorrow." He smiles down at me.

"Sounds good."

"This is the part of the night I've been looking forward to the most," he whispers.

Oh no.

"Why is that?" I force a smile. *Please don't kiss me.*

"Because I'm hoping I get to kiss the girl."

"Oh." I smile nervously. He steps forward and his lips take mine and he kisses me, and it's sweet and warm and nice.

Comfortable.

*Not bad, actually . . .*

I get a vision of Blake and Kayla kissing, and I step back from him, disappointed in myself. I desperately wanted the earth to move with that kiss.

But it didn't.

"I'll call you tomorrow."

"Okay." I get into the cab, and he closes my door and then waves as it drives away.

I feel hot and sweaty. I put my head in my hands in the back seat. Every time I think I'm ready, it turns out that I'm not. I don't know if I'll ever be ready to move on.

Gregory was nice. Gregory ticked every box. Gregory liked me . . . but all I can do is be sad about Blake.

What the hell is wrong with me?

### 4:00 a.m.

I sit by the window and watch the street. Blake still hasn't come home. I don't know why I'm doing this to myself.

I mean, it's obvious where he is.

But I needed to know, and now I do.

Right now, somewhere out there, he's having sex with Kayla.

# Chapter 14

Barry paces back and forth in front of the door as I sip my coffee and plot Blake's murder. It's Barry's walk time, but of course Blake isn't home from his date last night yet, so we all know that's not happening.

I imagine myself ripping him limb from limb.

Barry paces and paces as he looks up at me all excited. Like, ugh . . . "Fine," I snap. "I'll take you for your walk." I grab his lead and open the back door, and Barry races outside and runs around with the zoomies. He runs full speed one way and then the other, then he circles the entire garden. I roll my eyes. I usually think it's cute when he does this, but today, not so much.

I'm tired and I'm cranky and I'm well aware of why . . . I hate men.

On Monday morning, I'm going to buy myself eight cats to grow old with.

"This way." I hold up the lead, and he comes trotting over. I attach him and open the side gate, and right on cue, he takes off and nearly pulls my arm out of the socket, and I go flying forward.

"Barry!" I yell. I try to rein him in with all my might. "Don't pull."

"That dog is a menace in the mornings," Carol calls as she waters her garden.

"Sure is." I fake a smile. "Morning, Carol." I wave.

"Hello, dear." She keeps watering.

If there's one thing I can always depend on, it's seeing Carol in her pink dressing gown watering her garden every morning at six.

After a few houses, Barry calms down, and we get into our normal routine, and he begins to behave.

The silver Porsche comes around the corner, and my blood boils. He winds down the window and pulls up beside me. "I was going to walk him."

"You're too late," I spit.

*Act cool.*

"Wait for me. I'll come with you," Blake says.

"I'm good." I roll my lips to try and hold my snarky tongue.

"Did you have a good night?" He smiles through the car window.

*Not as good as yours.*

"Great night."

"You like him?" He smiles.

"Gregory could be the one." I'm lying through my teeth. Not even close. There is zero chemistry between us, not that I'll ever let on. "And your night was . . . ?"

"It was okay."

I stare at him, deadpan. "Just okay?"

"Maybe . . ." He breaks into a slow, sexy smile. "More than okay."

I clench my jaw so hard, I'm surprised that my teeth don't crack in half. "Great." I can't even push a single word past my lips.

"When are you seeing him again?" he asks.

"Ahh." I'm so flustered that I can't even think straight. "We're going bowling on Tuesday night."

"Bowling?" He smiles. "Nice . . ."

Fuck . . . Why did I say that? Bowling was never discussed. I couldn't even commit to a date. I told him to call me during the week.

"I love bowling," Blake replies. "I haven't been in ages."

*Fuck.*

I begin to sweat. I'm the worst liar in history. Why couldn't I think of a hotter second date than stupid bowling?

I try to cut the conversation short. "Anyway, have a good day."

"We might come," he says as he rests his arm over the steering wheel.

"Wha . . . where?"

"Bowling."

"What do you mean?" I frown.

"Well . . . can Kayla and I come to bowling?"

"Didn't you come enough last night?" I fume.

His eyes dance with mischief. "A gentleman never tells." He taps the side of his nose. "You know that."

"She's not even your type." I put my hands on my hips.

"Are you kidding?" He frowns. "Kayla is everyone's type."

And there it is . . . the answer I was looking for. He thinks she's as wonderful as I do.

This is all going to hell on a broomstick.

"Okay, bye." I begin to walk, and he drives the car beside me.

"So, what time on Tuesday?"

"Blake," I snap in exasperation, "you and Kayla do your own thing."

"I thought we were double dating for a while?"

"That was until—" I cut myself off.

"Until what?" His eyes hold mine intently.

*Until you bonked her brains out on the first night . . .*

"I just don't . . ."

219

"I know."

"You know what?" I cut him off.

"I know it's hard for you to start dating. But I want you to know that I'm here for you."

Is he kidding?

"Oh no, that's not it at all. I just want Gregory all to myself, and no offense, but you and Kayla are kind of cramping our style." I keep walking.

"Right." He smirks as he drives along beside me. "Hot night planned, huh?"

"Yep."

"All right, just one bowling match, and then Kayla and I will get going," he calls as he drives off. He waves out the window.

I watch his Porsche disappear down the road and pull up at his house. His garage door slowly goes up, and then he drives inside.

Ugh . . . Why do I say such dumb crap?

### Blake

"The honeymoon was good?"

"It was fucking great."

"So get this." Henley puts the ball into the hole. "I was on the app while I was away."

"Yeah." We look around guiltily and move in closer.

"There's a book trope called hucow," he leans in and whispers.

"What's that?" I whisper.

"Breastfeeding during sex."

My eyes widen in horror as my cock twinges with excitement.

"What?" Antony whispers. "That's fucking disgusting . . . and extremely hot."

"I know, right," Henley agrees.

"So, like . . ." I frown as I try to picture it. "Is the baby there?"

"No." He looks left and right in guilt. "It's these hot women who are taking drugs to make them lactate to satiate men's kinks," he whispers. "Hot women with huge, voluptuous tits."

My mouth falls open in horror as my cock begins to thump. I rearrange my erection in my pants. "That is . . . gross."

"Yeah, that's why you've got a semi."

"There's no semi; it's a raging boner."

"I started reading one story, and it was so fucking hot that I had to stop and make Juliet have sex with me."

"I've got a date with my right hand after even hearing about it," I murmur. "What did she say about you reading that stuff?"

"She thinks I was reading a crime story, commended me on winding down properly."

I chuckle.

Antony grabs the golf putter off him and lines up his shot. "Send me the name of this book. Might even be worth having kids for."

I chuckle. "I'm pretty sure if you have a baby and your wife is feeding it, and you come at her naked with a hard-on and say *My turn* . . . it isn't going to end well for you."

The boys both laugh as we imagine the scenario.

"A man can dream, though, right?" Ant smiles.

"Look, all I'm saying is, this Kindle . . . is the fucking mother ship of sex tips for deviants," Henley tells us. "I'm going to have a doctorate in this shit by the time I've finished reading all these books."

"Excellent." Antony putts the ball. "Same."

"Knock, knock, anybody home?" a familiar voice calls.

"Juliet!" I cry in excitement. "How was the honeymoon?" I open the door in a rush and give her a big hug. "Oh, I missed you. Feels like you've been gone for a month."

"Oh my god, me too. Barry was so excited when we got home."

"I bet he was. Come in, come in. Tell me all about it."

"We had the best time." She smiles dreamily. "We lay in the sun and slept and ate and went to the most beautiful restaurants."

"How does it feel to be a married woman?" I smile.

Juliet holds her hand up to show me her wedding rings. "Amazing." She looks around my house. "What have I missed? Was Barry well behaved?"

"He was a perfect angel," I lie.

I'm not going to tell her about all my makeup being ruined, that he chewed up four pairs of my lace underpants, killed all my potted plants, and the small fact that he ate Blake's two-thousand-dollar rug.

"I'm even thinking of getting a dog myself." Not a lie—I actually am, but I want a well-behaved one. "Let me put the kettle on. I want to hear every detail." I smile. "You have no idea how much I missed you."

"Same." Juliet walks in and flops down on my couch. "It's great to be home."

"What about this one?" Chloe holds out the dress into the change room.

"Hmm." I twist my lips as I eye it over. "I was trying to go sexier."

"So what's this guy like that you're going bowling with, anyway?"

"He seems nice. We've been chatting online for a couple weeks. We went out once and had a pretty good time."

"What does Blake say about this?"

I frown as I pull the next dress up over my hips. "Why would Blake have anything to say about this?"

"Because you know how he is with you. He'll be jealous as all hell."

"Oh please," I scoff. "Blake and I are just friends." There's no hope of anything more, not with Kayla in the picture.

"Keep telling yourself that. Trust me, I'm a Blake Grayson expert. I have been watching that man for eighteen months, and there's something that I know with one hundred percent certainty."

"What's that?"

"Whenever you're in the room, nobody else exists for Blake. I've learned to live with it by now."

I open the curtain and look at Chloe. "Are you serious?"

She nods.

"That makes me feel like shit, Chloe, knowing that you've liked him all along. I'm sorry. Is that really what you think?"

"Yeah, I do, and that's not a bad thing. You don't need to apologize. I just had a crush on Blake because he's gorgeous. We didn't really know each other, and I knew pretty early on that he was smitten with you."

"You know, it's the weirdest thing. Taryn said the same thing to me the other day."

"Because it's true."

"I hate to think that if you liked him, and you thought he liked me, that you wouldn't have said something." My eyes search hers.

"Blake and I never had chemistry. I just thought he was gorgeous, and now that I have Oliver, I'm actually glad that nothing ever happened."

I shrug, unsure what to say to that, so I go back to trying on another dress. "Try this one on." She holds another dress through the curtain.

I think out loud. "Anyway, he's got a new girl, Kayla, and I think she might be the one for him. It's probably a good thing. If something did happen with me and Blake and it didn't work out, I worry that we would lose our friendship."

"But what if it did work out."

I stick my head out of the curtain, and my eyes hold hers for a moment.

Her eyes widen. "Wait a minute . . . you *do* like him? You do, don't you?"

"No. I'm confused; there's a big difference. Blake has always been like a big brother to me, but recently I've just had a few weird moments where the lines have been blurred, that's all." I'm trying to convince myself it's true, but the words sound hollow to my own ears.

"If I was you, do you know what I would do?"

My eyes search hers. "Please tell me, because I would love some insight from someone who knows the both of us."

"I would grab hold of Blake Grayson with two hands, and I would make him fall madly in love with me. And I wouldn't let him go . . . ever."

"What if he doesn't like me that way?"

"Trust me, he does." She goes back to looking at the racks. "I'm going to find you something sexy for bowling and not for stupid Gregory. I'm finding you something sexy for Blake."

I roll my eyes. "Why?"

"You two belong together."

"Hey," I call as I walk through Rebecca's front door. "Photog is here."

"Hi." Bec bounces down the stairs. She's wearing gym clothes, and I have to concentrate on keeping my eyes on her face.

"I bought some oil." I pull it out of my pocket and hold it up.

"What for?"

"I thought we could oil up your feet tonight."

She blinks. "You want to rub oil into my feet."

*I want to rub oil all over you.*

"It will sell pictures."

"You think?"

"I know."

*I'll buy the fuckers myself.*

"Okay." She shrugs. "Where will we do this?"

"Probably on your bed."

"You can't oil me up on my bed. I'll get horny."

"That's the point."

She smirks. "Will you behave for just one minute?"

"Fine." I roll my eyes. "Kitchen counter it is."

I follow her into the kitchen, and she sits up on the kitchen counter. I slide her leggings up to her knees. Her muscular calves feel good under my hands.

She sits silent as she watches me.

*Thump.*

*Thump.*

*Thump* goes my cock . . .

I drizzle oil onto her feet and slowly begin to massage it in.

"You look like you're enjoying that a little too much." She smiles.

"Yeah, well, for the record, I'm totally jerking off with this oil when I get home."

She bubbles up a surprised giggle. "Sure you are."

Ha!

She thinks I'm joking . . .


Laughter rings out through Kingston Lane. We're having a street get-together tonight to celebrate Henley and Juliet coming back from their honeymoon.

We're all playing golf on our Kingston Lane green, and Winston is lingering around like a bad smell, which can only mean one thing.

"So, Doc," he whispers under his breath as Henley takes a shot.

"Yes."

"I've been thinking."

"And . . ."

"What are the chances of you accidentally losing a prescription pad?"

Fuck me, not this again. Who the hell is this eighty-year-old man screwing all the time?

"Zero to none."

He twists his lips as he looks at me. "Come on, it makes no difference to you. But it will make a huge difference to me."

"Firstly, having no job *will* make a huge difference to me, Winston, and I'm not sure if you're aware of this, but having a constant erection does not improve the quality of your life."

He throws up his hands. "You really have no idea, do you?"

I smirk over at him because we both know I'm telling ridiculous lies.

An orgasm is life and one that I can't imagine living without. When I get to his age, I probably will be doing the same, overdosing on Viagra on the daily.

On that note, my dick is about to fall off with gangrene.

Henley interrupts us. "So, what happened while I was away?"

"Nothing much."

He gestures over to the end of the street, where Rebecca is talking to the boys from the Navy House.

"Looks like a lot is happening over there."

My eyes linger on the boys all gathered around Rebecca. She's laughing and carefree as she talks, and they are hanging on her every word. I begin to hear my jealous heart beating in my ears.

"I kind of thought you and Rebecca might have hooked up by now," Henley says casually.

"Why are you always rattling on about Rebecca?" I snap in frustration. "When are you getting it through your thick head? We are just friends."

I would love to tell them all about what's going on between me and Rebecca, but the thing is that we all live on the same street, which is already rife with gossip. There's also the small fact that Henley is married to Rebecca's best friend. If I tell him, he tells Juliet. Juliet tells Rebecca, and my world blows up. It's all a bit too close for comfort, and I just need to keep everything to myself until I figure this mess out.

I'm not denying that it would be great to talk to someone about this right about now, though. The boys have been teasing me for years about my crush on Rebecca. I can't imagine what it would be like if they knew that I actually did have feelings for her.

Are they feelings, or is it just a crush?

My eyes linger once more on her talking to the other guys, and honestly, it's like sticking a knife in my stomach. I can't bear the thought of her with someone else, and I drag my hand through my hair in frustration. I've never felt so out of control in my life.

Rebecca laughs out loud.

*What's so fucking funny?*

I begin to feel unstable. Everything feels like it's coming to a head all of a sudden, and I have no idea why.

The only thing I do know is that this is a living nightmare.

"So, Henley," Winston says. "Do you have any spare prescriptions from Blake?"

"What?" I screw up my face. "Give it a rest already, you sex maniac."

Henley frowns over at Winston. "Why would I have a prescription?"

"Well, you just got back from your honeymoon. Surely he wrote you a script for Viagra."

"I still have all my senses, Winston, and an insanely hot wife. Viagra is hopefully a good twenty years away for me yet," Henley mutters dryly.

I tap the top of my beer bottle with his and take a sip.

He leans in close so only I can hear. "For the record, I *will* be stealing those prescriptions when it gets to that stage," Henley adds.

"Trust me." I sip my beer. "I'll already be on it."


I pull up to the curb at Kayla's, and before I can get out of the car, she jumps down her front steps. "Hello." She smiles happily.

"Hi," I grumble.

"What's wrong with you?" she asks.

"This is not working."

"It is, trust me."

"I don't know how I let you talk me into this harebrained idea. Rebecca is not jealous one single bit. In fact, she said that he's the one."

"Oh please," Kayla scoffs. "She spent all night watching you. Trust me, he is *not* the one."

I pull out into traffic, and we drive for a little while.

"What's the plan of attack tonight?" I ask.

"Okay, so I've been thinking about this, and I think the best way to go is for you to be all over me."

"Do you know how hard it is for me to be all over you when she's right in front of me?" I snap angrily. "Nothing has been harder than kissing you in front of her. It fucking kills me."

"You are so sweetly pathetic." She rolls her eyes. "Where's my Blake the fuckboy prick that I've always loved?"

"Listen, don't get fucking smart. Are you going to help me or not?"

"I'm here, aren't I?"

"I guess. For some reason, I get the sinking feeling that tonight's going to go to shit." I sigh as I turn the corner.

"Stop thinking like that. It's easy. We walk in there, and you're all over me. I'm telling you, she's jealous. One more night and you're going to have her in the palm of your hand."

"And if I don't?"

"Then our plan backfired, and you probably pushed her into *his* arms."

"Oh, just great." I drag my hand down my face in disgust.

Kayla and I used to fuck, for a long time actually. But we were never romantically involved. She was a friend with benefits. Funnily enough, she used me a couple of years ago to make her crush jealous, and they ended up falling madly in love. It wasn't forever, though, and they just recently broke up, so I thought I would return the favor.

She isn't even a nurse; she works in a pharmacy as a dispensary assistant, and yes, she's an excellent catch, but she's definitely not the woman I want to settle down with.

Great in bed, though.

Right. I try to steel myself as we pull into the parking lot of the bowling alley.

"Of all things, why this? I fucking hate bowling."

Kayla laughs. "This is so off brand for you."

"Bowling is, I have to agree."

"No. The whole freaking-out-over-a-woman thing."

"Right?" I widen my eyes as I pull the car to a stop and put the hand brake on. "I don't even know why she's got me so crazy."

"I do. She's beautiful."

"It's not even her outside that I like . . . I mean, that's good, too, of course."

"Look at you." Kayla smiles over at me. "Totally smitten. What I wouldn't have given to have you fall in love with me a couple of years ago."

I roll my eyes at her. "Don't be ridiculous." She laughs.

I get out of the car and take Kayla's hand in mine. We walk through the parking lot as a million scenarios of why this is a bad idea run through my mind. My heart is hammering hard in my chest. "If she finds out that I did this on purpose to make her jealous, shit is going to hit the fan," I whisper as we walk in through the front doors.

"She's never going to find out," Kayla whispers as she brushes my shirt. "You look hot tonight, by the way."

"Thanks. Not as hot as you." I peck her on the lips as I begin the charade.

"And who knows, if it turns out that she doesn't like you, then maybe when you drop me home tonight, I can have my payment in dick." She throws me a sexy wink.

I spot Rebecca across the room, and I smile softly. "Shut up," I whisper with my eyes locked on my girl. "We are not fucking tonight."

"Where *did* you sleep the other night, anyway?" she asks.

"In a hotel."

"Wow, you are really going balls to the wall with this one."

"Well, the plan isn't going to work if she doesn't believe it, and the good thing is, she *did* notice that I didn't come home, so that looks promising."

"I'm telling you, she's totally into you. A woman knows these things."

"If she likes me, then she'll be jealous of you. If she's not jealous of you, then I am giving up on this for the last time."

"Why don't you just act like a normal person and have a conversation and ask her?"

"Because if she doesn't like me like that, I'm going to ruin our friendship, and I will not risk that for anything."

"Surely you know if she likes you or not. You can't be this stupid?" she whispers as we walk toward Rebecca and Gregory.

"She gives me mixed signals. Some days I'm sure that she does, and other days I'm positive that she doesn't."

I smile sweetly over at Kayla, my fake date. "It's showtime, bitch. Let's do this."

Blake and Kayla walk hand in hand over to us. "Hi." Kayla smiles.

"Hello," Blake says as he looks between us.

"Hi," Gregory replies with his hands on his hips.

"Nice shoes," Blake says.

"Thanks."

"They go with your pants." Blake smirks. "Stylin', brother."

I glance down to see that Gregory has his brown pants tucked into long white socks.

Ugh . . . he looks ridiculous.

Gregory looks down all innocently. "That's what you do at bowling."

Blake's eyes dance with mischief. "Okay."

I widen my eyes at Blake. *Don't you dare be in this mood tonight. Be nice, fucker.*

"Blakey, can you put my shoes on me?" Kayla says in a baby voice as she sits down.

"Sure I can." He kneels in front of her and takes her shoe off and kisses her foot.

My blood boils.

He pulls one sock on and then the other as she puts her hands in his hair. "I love it when you're on your knees for me," she whispers loudly.

"Me too." He nips her knee with his teeth.

Ugh . . .

"You two should probably get a room." I pick up a bowling ball and imagine hurling it at their heads.

"Wait for us," Blake says. He puts Kayla's shoes on and then takes a seat, and Kayla gets down and takes his shoes off.

"Oh please," I scoff. "Don't touch his feet; he has terrible tinea."

"We share our germs, don't we, baby?" Kayla giggles.

Her head has somehow turned into a red bull's-eye target, and I glare at her as I imagine knocking her clean out.

"While you're down there . . . ," Blake jokes.

"I wish," Kayla purrs.

"You two are making me jealous." Gregory smiles. He puts his arm around me. "Lay one on me." He kisses me.

*Lay one on me?*

What does he think, that he's Kenny Rogers and this is a country song?

He goes in for a tongue kiss, and I pull out of his grip . . . awkward. Public tongue kissing is not my thing.

Especially with Kenny Rogers.

Enough.

"Let's get bowling," I snap. I pick up the bowling ball, run, and hurl it down the alley. It knocks over every pin.

Ha, anger makes me bowl better.

"Nice shot." Gregory smiles. He comes in for a kiss.

*What?*

He grabs my head and holds me in. His tongue takes no prisoners.

Ahhhh.

I pull out of it to see Blake stand. He glares at Gregory and picks up a bowling ball.

"I'm going to wipe you off the planet, Gregory." He fakes a smile.

Huh?

Kayla giggles, thinking this is the best fun in forever.

Blake runs and hurls the bowling ball. It bounces nearly three feet high and runs into the gutter before it even gets to the end.

"Unlucky," Gregory calls. "Watch this, baby," he says to me. He calmly picks up the ball and bends his knees and acts all professional-like. He stands there and waits, as if he's mentally psyching himself up to take the shot.

"This isn't the Olympics," Blake mutters under his breath.

Kayla giggles again . . . *What is so funny, bitch?*

Gregory takes his shot, and then he does some weird crossing-his-leg-behind thing as he waits for his ball to go down the alley.

"Yes!" he yells as he gets a strike. "Boom! That's how it's done." He claps his hands together. "Oh yeah, wiping the table with you, Grayson."

Blake's eyes flicker red, and Kayla laughs again.

Honestly . . . if she keeps laughing, I cannot be held responsible for dropping a bowling ball on her toe.

"Your turn, baby," Gregory tells me. He slaps me on the behind, and Blake inhales sharply as he sits on the chair.

"Just think of the reward you're going to get tonight if you win, babe." Kayla smiles.

I stuff my fingers into the holes on the bowling ball. *This bitch is going down.*

"Do you mind not talking dirty while I'm trying to bowl?" I snap.

"Not at all." Blake smiles.

"You're balking me," I growl.

"Well, his legs in those socks are balking me," Blake hits back.

Gregory looks down at his legs. "What's wrong with my legs?"

"Nothing, baby." I smile. "Those legs are hot." I grab Gregory and kiss him just to spite these two assholes.

"Yes . . . baby, hit me," Gregory says as he grabs my behind again.

Ahhh . . . too far. *You had to ruin it, didn't you?*

*Hit me?*

Good lord, this man is ridiculous.

"Gregory . . ." Blake stands. "Don't touch her again."

"I'll do what I want with her," Gregory fires back. "She is *my* date."

"Yeah, well." Blake glares at him. "You should probably back the fuck up."

"Leave it," Kayla whispers under her breath.

What the hell is going on here with these idiots?

My angry pulse begins to sound in my ears, and I run up and take my shot. It bounces into the gutter, and I don't knock even one pin down.

Blake slow claps. "Well done."

*Fuck you.*

I storm back and take a seat.

Kayla takes her shot, and of course, she gets a strike, and then it's Gregory's turn again.

He takes the ball out of the thing and puts his fingers in the holes.

"Show us what you've got," Blake says.

They glare at each other, and some kind of hidden message passes between these two idiots.

Why do they suddenly hate each other? Did I miss part of the conversation?

"What are you fucking looking at?" Blake sneers.

"Your ugly face," Gregory snaps back.

*Uh-oh, shit's turning south here.*

"Yeah, well, don't bother."

Kayla drops her head to hide her smile . . . *I swear to god, stop laughing, stupid.*

"What *is* your problem?" Gregory spits.

Blake stands, and he and Gregory come face to face. "You're my fucking problem."

"You don't like the fact that"—Gregory smiles darkly—"I'm just about to kick your ass at bowling."

*What the hell?*

"Yeah, well . . . maybe I'm just about to kick your ass in the parking lot." Blake pushes Gregory in the chest, and Gregory pushes him back.

"Stop it," I snap.

Blake pushes Gregory again, and Gregory steps back. His huge, goofy bowling shoes get caught, and he stumbles back and trips over onto the floor.

"Blake," I stammer. "What are you doing?"

"Get out."

We all look up to see the manager of the bowling alley standing over us. She points at Blake, then at the door. "You have one minute to leave the premises, or I'm calling the police."

Blake looks between us.

"Now!" she yells.

Blake gasps. "I didn't do anything."

"I've been watching you two the entire time," the manager says. "Both of you, get out."

"Sorry," Kayla whispers.

Blake collects his things, and he and Kayla storm out as I stare after them.

"Are you going to help me up?" Gregory calls from the floor.

I look down to the giant dork in the long socks being all dramatic on the ground.

Ugh . . . Do I have to?


Fury—has there ever been a more toxic emotion?

I sit on my front steps with my coffee and watch as the sun comes up over the houses. But today, the sun isn't golden. It doesn't have a warm glow, and I most definitely am not basking in it.

Today, the sky is red.

Blake purposely upset me last night. It wasn't an accident; it was a planned attack.

He was all over Kayla, which is whatever; he can do whatever he wants to do. But to blatantly be mean to Gregory and bait him into fighting?

What the hell?

This isn't even the first time that he's crossed the boundary. What about when he punched out John just for daring to knock on my door? I don't know what's going on with him lately, but it's not good enough.

I'm so off him.

I wouldn't put up with this from one of my other friends, so why am I putting up with it from Blake?

I hear his door, and I glance up to see him walk out the front of his house. He's wearing his gray suit and tie and looks all handsome and professional for work. He's holding his coffee cup in his hand and seems totally unaffected by the theatrics of last night.

Something comes over me, and before I can stop myself, I'm striding over to his house.

He glances up and gives me a slow, sexy smile, and I just want to slap it from his smart-aleck face.

"How dare you?" I growl.

He puts his weight onto his back foot, as if shocked by my venom. "Good morning, Rebecca," he says casually as he puts his briefcase into the back seat.

"Do not *good morning* me," I growl.

It's then that I notice there is a small suitcase in his back seat.

"Where are you going?" I snap.

"A business conference, not that it's any of your business." He puts his hands on his hips. "What's wrong with you?"

"Don't dare act as if you don't know what's wrong with me."

He raises an eyebrow. "Nope, can't say that I do."

Steam shoots from my ears. "Then let me spell it out for you, dumbo. You are a rude pig who has absolutely no boundaries."

"No boundaries?"

"That's right."

"I think I would know if I had no boundaries."

"You were too busy falling all over your date in a ridiculously over-the-top public display of affection to notice anything."

"Are you jealous?" He raises an eyebrow.

"No. I'm not jealous of you and her. What I am is fed up."

"I don't like him. He's not the man for you," he snaps angrily.

"I don't like him either," I spit. "And I'm beginning to realize that perhaps there isn't a man for me at all, because I thought I could count on you, but obviously now you're proving that I can't even do that."

His eyes hold mine, but he remains silent.

"Well?" I put my hands on my hips. "What's your excuse for being such an arrogant asshole last night?"

"I don't need an excuse," he replies calmly.

"Poor Kayla. She was so embarrassed by your behavior last night."

"Ha." He rolls his eyes. "I don't care what Kayla thinks."

"Well, you should. I thought she was your dream girl that you wanted to settle down with."

From the very back of my psyche, a little voice starts screaming in the background.

*Stop talking.*

"There you go again, throwing Kayla in my face. I'm going to ask you one more time. Are you jealous of her?"

"I'm jealous that you're nice to her. I'm jealous that you respect her enough to accept her opinion. And more than that, I'm jealous that she hasn't seen your horrible side yet. Because I have, and let

238

me tell you, Blake, it's not nice. Quite frankly, I don't think we should be friends anymore."

His jaw ticks as his eyes hold mine. I know that I've just hit a nerve.

"I won't be seeing Kayla again."

It's me who steps back this time, shocked. "Why not?"

"Because she's not the girl I want." He gets into his car and slams the door.

*Who is?*

"Move," he growls, and I step back out of the way. He reverses the car out at high speed and takes off down the road in first gear. The car revs loudly as he disappears into the distance.

The street falls silent again.

Damn it.

Why are we fighting so much lately?

I blow out a defeated breath and turn to go back to my house. It's then that I see Carol is standing there in her dressing gown and holding her garden hose.

As usual, she's pretending to water her stupid garden. She doesn't fool me. She comes out here every morning to find out what's going on in the street.

"Morning, Carol." I wave and fake a smile as I stomp back toward my house.

"Morning." She smiles. "Don't worry about him, dear," she calls. "Lovers' quarrels make all men crazy."

What the hell is she going on about now? I frown.

*What is wrong with everybody?*

"Of course, it's no secret—when Blake said she's not the girl he wants, it's obvious to all who know him which one he does," she calls.

"Who?"

"Oh, Rebecca." She laughs. "Are you really this clueless?"

I stare at her as I begin to hear my heartbeat in my ears. "Obviously, yes, because I don't know who his dream girl is."

"It's you, dear. I'm not sure if he even knows it yet, but it's definitely you."

Poor deluded Carol, the woman who thinks she knows everything but actually knows fucking nothing.

She's a bona fide idiot.

"Have a nice day, Carol." I wave, then walk back into my house and flop on the couch.

This is just great.

The day is a disaster, and it's not even 7:00 a.m. yet.

The problem with anger is that it never lasts for long. It comes in like a tsunami, crashing and smashing everything in its way. But as the tide leaves and washes back out to sea, all that is left is a lot of debris and regret.

*I don't think we should be friends anymore.*

What a horrible thing to say to somebody, even somebody you just want to be friends with. Let alone somebody that you have feelings for.

I sit in my classroom, and as the class plays freely, I stare out the window. I'm sad today. It's like this big deadweight is sitting on my shoulders. I'm not here with my class; I'm miles away.

Blake is at a conference, and I can't even go over and tell him I still want to be friends, because I do.

He's a great friend. Things have just gotten a little out of hand lately, and I need to rein it in. But we obviously can't double-date together anymore.

Carol's words from this morning—about me being his dream girl—keep coming back to me.

Is she right?

Honestly, it feels like everybody these last two weeks has just been telling me how Blake and I are meant to be together, and I'm even feeling it myself.

But Blake was never in my plan.

And unfortunately, he has shown me a side of himself that scares the living crap out of me. He says mean things. He's spontaneously crazy. Why the hell would I know that about a person and purposefully go back into that zone?

I wouldn't; it's stupid.

I'm just confused.

I wish I could talk this out with my friend, because that's what I would normally do. The problem is that the friend I would normally talk this out with is the person I want to talk about.

"Miss Dalton," Toby calls, pulling me out of my daydream.

"Yes, Toby."

"Can we color now?"

*You can do whatever you like, Toby. Hell . . . set the classroom on fire, for all I care.*

"Sure, why not." I fake a smile because, let's be honest, I'm not teaching this class anything today.

They're on their own.


I lie on my couch and stare at the television. It's late. Past 9:00 p.m., and I should be getting ready for bed to try and get a good night's sleep. Lord knows I haven't slept in the three days since I told Blake I didn't want to be friends anymore.

I'm flat.

Flatter than I've been in a long time.

And it's weird because I had a very successful week. John called, and the documents are here. Tomorrow I'm meeting him, and he's signing the house over to me. Another one of my images went viral.

Of course, it's from the same lot that Blake took at the wedding with the icing, but anyway, I made an extra $3,000.

This is a time for celebration. I'm getting everything I ever wanted.

I'm financially stable, the house is being signed over into my name, and yet all I feel is empty. All because I told Blake I don't want to be his friend anymore.

I miss him already.

I get a lump in my throat as I think about life without him in it. It's not something that I can even comprehend. Until this happened, I didn't realize how much I depend on him. He was there to pick me up after John. In fact, he has been there to pick me up every day for the last year. He's been such a supportive, wonderful friend, and the first little hiccup we have on a double date, I tell him I don't want to be friends at all.

What kind of ungrateful, selfish witch does that?

I need to make this right.

I'm just going to text him and say sorry. I know that I probably broke something between us, but I feel like he broke it first.

At least texting will clear my conscience, and we can hopefully move past this and carry on as friends.

I take out my phone and think about what I should text him. Hmm, do I apologize, or do I just act like normal?

No, I just have to apologize. I text him.

**Hi Blake.**
**I'm sorry for our fight.**
**I didn't mean what I said.**

My phone instantly rings, and the name *Blake* lights up the screen. Shit.

"Hello," I answer.

"Hi, Bec." His voice is soft and cajoling.

"Sorry to text so late," I say.

"It's okay. I was lying here in bed thinking about texting you anyway." I get a vision of him lying in the dark in his hotel room.

We both hang on the line. The silence between us is deafening. A million words that I want to say but just never seem appropriate.

"Blake?"

"Yeah," he replies softly.

"What would have happened if I gave you my number?"

He thinks for a moment. "You mean when I said before that if we met under different circumstances, I would have asked for your number?"

"Yes. If you asked for my number and I gave it to you, what would have happened?"

"Then I would have called you that very day, and I would have asked you out on a date that night . . . because I couldn't have waited one more hour to see you. I would have been nervous before I picked you up, and you would have worn my favorite red dress, and I would have worn your favorite pair of blue jeans."

My heart swells as I listen.

"And we would have gone to our favorite restaurant, Little Italy. You would have ordered the beef ragù, and I would have ordered the fettuccine," he says softly.

I smile as I listen.

"And we would have drunk a bottle of red wine and ordered dessert, and then by the end of the tiramisu . . . I would have known that you were the one."

# Chapter 15

Confusion runs through my body . . . then panic . . . then, like an avalanche, an overwhelming sense of relief.

"That sounds . . ." What's the word I'm looking for? "Perfect."

*Silence.*

I close my eyes, unsure what that silence means.

"Bec," he says softly.

My heart is beating so hard in my chest that I can hear it in my ears.

"Yes."

"Can I have your number?"

I smile softly. "It's 555-7289."

"Okay."

More silence.

"I have to go. Good night, Rebecca."

"Good night, Blake." I hang up. Did that really just happen?

My phone begins to ring, and the name *Blake* lights up the screen. I laugh out loud. That idiot.

"Hello," I answer.

"Hi, Rebecca, it's Blake Grayson. We met the other day. I'm not sure if you remember me."

"Ah, yes, Blake." I smile as I play along. "I do remember you."

"I was wondering if you'd like to go on a date with me?"

My stomach flutters. "I'd like that. Where do you want to go?"

"I know this fabulous Italian restaurant."

"You do?" I smile. "What's it called?"

"Little Italy. Shall I meet you there, or . . . ?"

"Why don't you pick me up?"

"I can do that."

"Actually, let's keep Carol on her toes, and I'll meet you there."

"Good idea."

I can tell that he's smiling, because I'm smiling too.

We both hang on the line, and there's this weird, serendipitous feeling floating between us. Like a tangible force. I can feel it.

*Can he feel it too?*

"I'll be home on Monday," he says softly.

"Good. I don't like you being away."

"Me neither."

"Good night, Blake." I smile.

"Good night, Rebecca." The line goes dead as he hangs up.

I stare at the phone in my hand, giddy as a schoolgirl.

Holy shit.


### Sunday

"You need to sign here." John points to the line. "And here." He turns the page. "And then on this page."

He slides the paperwork over, and my eyes skim the lines as I read.

"Here's a pen." He holds the pen up for me and taps it on the table, as if to hurry me up.

"I'm reading exactly what I'm signing, thank you." I take the pen from him and keep reading; I might have been stupid enough to trust him before . . . but not now.

That girl is long gone.

I slowly read through everything, and surprisingly, it's exactly as he promised. The house is mine as long as I don't legally divorce him for five years. After that time, this contract is void, and the house will remain mine. If I try to break this contract earlier and demand a divorce, then the house will go back to joint ownership between us, and the usual divorce settlement laws will come into place. The other properties we own cannot be sold or moved out of his or my name until this contract term is over.

The thing is, I know that if it ever comes to that, the house is as good as gone. I can't afford to buy his half out, and there is no way he would just sign it over. He'll sell it out of spite; he knows this is the only weapon he has left to hurt me.

I haven't told anyone I'm signing this, because deep down I know they will all tell me it's a mistake. But it's the only way I can guarantee the outcome. If we do go to court, there's a big risk that I'll lose it.

Not that I would expect anyone to understand this, but my home is the only thing I have left from what I thought was my happily ever after . . . and I'm keeping it as a souvenir. It's not just bricks and mortar; this is personal. A big *fuck you* to my pathetic excuse of a marriage.

I hold the pen to the paper and hesitate. *Should I do this?*

Yes.

Yes, I should.

I sign on the dotted line. I turn the page and sign again, and then again on the last page. I exhale heavily when I'm done, as if a huge weight has been lifted from my shoulders, and I look up into John's satisfied smile.

"I knew you didn't want to divorce me." He takes my hand over the table.

I snatch it from his grip. "Oh, but I will."

He smiles, as if knowing a secret. "We're going to get through this. You and me . . . we are meant to be."

I stare at this evil, deluded man . . . he has no grip on reality at all.

"You know what?" I push out my chair. "I don't feel like lunch anymore."

"But you promised."

"Promises can be broken, John." My eyes hold his. "I learned that from the best." I turn and walk out of the restaurant and smile as I hit the fresh air.

I did it.

I don't have to live in fear anymore . . . the house will always be mine.

I win.

*Blake*
*Monday night*

I sit on the plane and smile out the window. I'm finally going home.

It's been a long week.

And tomorrow . . . I get to see her.

I don't get nervous.

But this date has me jumpy. The ramifications of the outcome are important and involve something that I very much want.

In fact, I don't think I've ever been this nervous about anything. I rub the backs of my fingers through my stubble as I think about how things could go right or what could go wrong.

There's only one thing I know for certain: I get one chance, and one chance only, with her.

I can't fuck this up.

## Rebecca
### Tuesday night

I pull tissues out of the box and put them under my arms.

I can't stop sweating.

My nerves are at an all-time high.

I'm in my underwear and putting on my makeup, and damn it, if this keeps going, I'll have to take another shower before I even leave the house.

I dab my forehead with a tissue and then fan my face as I pace back and forth in the bathroom. I glance at the requested red dress that is laid out on my bed, and I feel my stomach drop.

*Jeez . . .*

In the words of Taylor Swift, I need to calm down.

This is just ridiculous. It's only Blake.

He sees me in a face mask every other day, and never once has he flinched. Why am I so worried?

*Because tonight is important.*

I know damn well that we are probably only going to get one shot at this date, and if it doesn't go well and we don't click romantically . . . then I don't know where that lands us.

The only thing I am sure of is that it won't be the same between us ever again.

But in saying that . . . I do think it's worth the risk.

At least, I hope it is.

Perspiration beads on my top lip, and I reach in and turn on the tap. Time for a second cold shower.

The Uber pulls up outside of Little Italy, and I close my eyes.

This is it.

"Thank you." I smile.

"Have a good night." The driver nods.

"You too." I get out of the car, and with shaky feet, I walk into the restaurant.

It's dark and moody, and candles flicker on every table. There is someone being checked in in front of me.

*Thump.*

*Thump.*

*Thump* goes my heart.

I look around and see Blake stand and wave. He's by a table at the back, and he's wearing my favorite blue jeans.

I nervously make my way over. He stands and watches me as he waits, and . . . oh man.

What was I thinking?

"Hello." I smile.

"Hi." He leans down and kisses my cheek. The familiar heavenly scent of his aftershave tickles my senses. "You look lovely." He smiles.

"Thanks."

He pulls my chair out, and I sit down.

Adrenaline is screaming through my body, and I honestly don't think I've ever been so nervous.

He sits down opposite me and smiles softly as his eyes hold mine. "Hi."

"Hi," I whisper.

"Are you okay?" he asks, as if sensing my inner turmoil.

"I'm nervous."

He reaches over and takes my hand in his. "Me too." He lifts it and kisses my fingertips, and goose bumps scatter up my arms as I stare at him.

"We should drink . . . alcohol," I stammer.

He laughs out loud, and it's a beautiful, calming sound. "All of it."

"I actually can't believe we're doing this," I whisper.

"I can." In slow motion, he lifts my hand and kisses my fingertips again. This time, I feel it all the way to my toes. "I've been waiting a long time for this."

"You have?" I frown.

He nods.

"That's not creepy at all." I smirk.

He smiles bashfully as he rearranges the napkin on his lap. "Maybe a little."

"So . . ." I shrug as I look around. "What happens now?"

"You drink red wine while I try my hardest to charm you."

"What if I'm already charmed?"

"It's not nearly enough." His eyes search mine, and I smile over at the beautiful man opposite me. He's just as nervous as I am.

A waitress arrives with a bottle of red, and she begins to uncork it.

"Thank you." He smiles.

She fills our glasses and brings out her notepad. "Are you ready to order?"

"I'll have the beef ragù," I tell her.

Blake smiles softly over at me as the air crackles between us.

"I'll have the fettucine," he replies, his eyes not leaving mine. "Thank you."

The waitress disappears, and Blake reaches around and grabs the side of my chair and pulls it toward him so that we are sitting together. "That's better." His eyes hold mine, and there's an intensity to them that I haven't seen before.

"Is this where I get to experience the Blake Grayson A-game date?" I ask.

"No." He rolls his lips, as if unsure what to say next, and an awkward silence falls between us.

"Can I?"

"What do you mean?"

"I think the best way to not let nerves get the better of us is to . . ." I shrug. "Pretend that we don't know each other."

He smirks over at me.

"Maybe we could pretend that we just met on Bumble?"

"You know we were matched last weekend," he replies.

"What?" I frown. "How do you know?"

"Because I swiped on you."

"You did?"

"Uh-huh." He smiles. "Don't pretend you didn't see it."

"I honestly didn't. I haven't been on the app at all."

"Swipe on me." He sips his wine, and he has that mischief in his eyes that he gets.

"What, now?" I smile.

"Why not?" He shrugs.

"Okay." I open the app and go through my matches.

"How many do you have?" He frowns as he looks down at my phone. "Did everyone on the app swipe on you?"

I shrug. "I'm a woman, and men are pretty easy to . . ." I widen my eyes. "Hook."

I scroll and scroll. "This is me," he says.

"Which one?"

"Go back."

I scroll back up, and there's a picture taken from behind of a man with a surfboard.

"This isn't you." I frown.

"Well, it is. About ten years ago." He sips his wine again. "In Spain, I think."

"Okay." I smile as I swipe on him. "Let's see what you've got."

I read the bio.

**Looking for Andie Anderson.**

"Oh my god." I put my hand to my mouth in surprise. "*That* is your heading?"

He chuckles and throws me a sexy wink. "Works every time."

"You are the living end." I laugh out loud.

"Andie Anderson is the quintessential dream girl . . . even for me."

I laugh harder. Andie Anderson is the lead character in the movie *How to Lose a Guy in 10 Days*.

"That is good, I have to admit. Every woman on earth knows who Andie Anderson is . . . and wants to be her. They also want a Benjamin."

He gives me a slow, sexy smile.

I keep reading.

### Qualities: Fun loving.
### Interested in: Margarita-loving people.

"Wait a minute, is this aimed at . . ."

"Who doesn't love a good margarita?"

I smile and keep reading.

### Favorite Pastime: Ripping the nets off those slutty
### oranges.

Huh? I get a vision of how you have to tear the oranges out of their bag, and I throw my head back and laugh out loud. "Are you serious?"

"Deadly." He laughs too. "You got to admit, they're begging for it. Tearing off those net bags is the highlight of my life."

This is the funniest thing I've ever read, and I can't stop laughing. It's so true. Tearing the nets off oranges is just like tearing off fishnet stockings.

"Those slutty oranges . . ."

"Right." He widens his eyes. "Begging for it."

No wonder every woman wants to meet him. He has no profile picture, he's not loving himself, and his answers are all intelligent, witty, and funny. And then when he walks into the date . . . their jaws must fall to the floor because they realize they've hit the jackpot.

He pulls out his phone. "Let me read yours."

"No." I try to grab his phone from him. "Mine seems so lame now."

"You could never be lame." He swipes on me and frowns when he reads my heading.

**Looking for someone to stay young with.**

His eyes rise to meet mine. "Why that answer?"

"Well . . ." I shrug. "Everyone always says they are looking for someone to grow old with."

His eyes hold mine. "But not you?"

"I want someone to stay young with."

He goes back to reading.

**Interested in: Honesty.**
**Favorite pastime: Laughing.**

He smiles as he reads and casually reaches over and picks up my hand and puts it on his thigh.

I feel his thick quad muscle beneath my hand, and I hold my breath as I watch him read my profile.

**Hoping for: A fairy tale.**

His brow furrows as he reads the last line, and he puts his phone down. His eyes rise to meet mine. "We have something in common."

"What's that?"

"I'm looking for a fairy tale too."

We stare at each other as the air crackles between us, and this is probably premature, but I get the feeling that this is going to be the best date of my life.

"I don't need to wait for the tiramisu," he whispers.

My eyes search his as my heart free-falls from my chest.

In slow motion, he leans over and kisses me, his lips barely brushing over mine, and huge butterflies swirl deep in my stomach.

*Oh . . .*

"Why not?" I whisper against his lips.

"Because . . . I already know."


### Five hours later

The cab pulls onto Kingston Lane. "Just the white house on the left," Blake directs the driver. The street is dark and deserted, unlike my heart. For I am bright and full.

What a magical night. We laughed until my sides hurt.

He kissed me once at dinner, but not again since, and to be honest, I feel like I've been waiting for his next kiss all night.

But maybe that's his game. Maybe this is all part of his grand plan.

Give me a taste . . . and then take it away.

And now that we're here, arriving at home, I'm suddenly nervous again. What happens now? Does he kiss me goodbye?

Do I invite him in for *coffee*?

What is expected in this situation? I'm just not sure . . .

God, I hate dating. I hate not knowing what's going to hap-pen next.

The car pulls up at my house, and I gingerly climb out. Blake pays the driver and walks with me up onto my porch.

"So . . ."

He turns to face me. "So . . ."

We stare at each other, and it's there again, the electricity bouncing between us.

A force so strong and foreign to me.

I've never felt it before.

I smile softly. "I had a great time."

"Me too."

I get the feeling that he's as nervous as I am.

"Um . . ." I frown as I try to articulate my feelings. "I was wondering."

"What?" His eyes search mine, and I know that he wants me to invite him in.

"I . . ." I swallow the lump of sand in my throat. "Can we . . . take things a little slow?"

He nods. "Okay." He steps back from me as if I'm rejecting him.

I take his two hands in mine. "I just want to . . ." I shrug as I look out into the street. "I really want this to work out."

"Me too."

"And I haven't . . ."

"I know."

My eyes search his. "I've been waiting for you to kiss me again all night."

He gives me a slow, sexy smile and takes my face in his hands. "It nearly killed me not to." His lips take mine, and he kisses me softly. He towers over me, and his large stature emits power.

My eyes close as my feet feel like they rise from the floor.

His kiss deepens, and I feel a little tongue, just a whisper. A hint of what it could be.

*Oh . . . the way he kisses.*

Just when I'm beginning to relax into it, he steps back from me. "I'll let you go."

"Oh." I nod, embarrassed. "Okay." My eyes search his.

"So . . ." He points to his house with his thumb. "Blake Grayson, your date, is going to go home now."

"Right." I nod again.

"And Blake, your friend . . . was wondering if you wanted to watch a movie on your fold-out."

I smirk.

He holds up his two hands, as if surrendering. "Completely platonic movie-watching only . . . don't get any ideas."

"On one condition," I reply.

"What's that?"

"We wear face masks while we watch," I tell him as I put my key into the door.

"Deal." We walk inside. "But I'm telling you, if an alien with two cocks arrives, you're taking one for the team."

"What the hell does that mean?" I frown.

His eyes flick up, as if he's surprised. "Ignore me, I'm drunk."

# Chapter 16

*Rebecca*

I put my keys down on the bench. Blake is behind me, and he sits on the lounge.

It's suddenly awkward, as if we both know this is a bad idea.

What was I thinking?

In my defense, he did say that he wanted to be here as my friend. But now that he's inside, it feels decidedly like the end of a date.

"Do you want a cup of tea or something?" I ask as I walk around the corner into the kitchen.

"Sure." He holds the remote up to the television. "What do you feel like watching?" he calls.

"A movie sounds good."

"Any requests?"

"No, not really," I call back.

Suddenly I'm panicked.

I take out my phone and go into my group chat. I text Juliet and Chloe. They think I went out with a new date. I left out the Blake part.

**I have a situation.**

I watch the dots bounce as a text comes back.

**Such as?**

**I asked my date in for coffee after our date, what do I
do now?**

I wait for the reply, and I can see them both typing furiously.

**You jump his bones, that's what you do.**

I begin to sweat, and I type my reply.

**I don't think I'm ready.**

I wait for the answer.

**Well, do you like him?**

**I think I do.**

**Then stop overthinking it.
You will never feel ready.
Only one way to get over this.**

I begin to pace in the kitchen as I wait for the kettle to boil.
The thing is, I know they're right; I've always got an excuse . . . but
this one means more.

Another text comes in.

**Nobody is more ready than you.**
**Rip the band aid off and do it.**

They're right. I know they're right.

I begin to slowly make our cups of tea, and as I peer into the living room, I see Blake is also on his phone messaging someone. I go back into the kitchen and keep messaging the girls.

**Okay give me some pointers, and quick.**

*Blake*

My eyes roam up to the kitchen to check that the coast is clear, and I text my group chat with Henley and Antony.

**I'm at a girls house and she told me she wants to take it slow.**
**Define slow.**

Antony is the first to reply.

**Slow in my mind means making out with no sex.**

Henley chimes in with his answer.

**Slow for me means that she gets to come and you don't.**

I screw up my face in question, and I text back.

**What do you mean she gets to come and I don't?**

259

**So what . . . you go to third base with her and do every-
thing except pull your cock out?**

A laughing emoji comes in from Antony, and I can see the
dots as Henley writes.

**Basically . . . yes.**

I text back.

**So you think she wants to go to third base?**

Antony replies.

**She did invite you in after the date didn't she?**

**True.**

I think for a moment. Does that mean that she does want
to make out?

Fuck me. I thought that I had this under control, but now it
has come to my attention that I know absolutely nothing about
how to act around a nice girl. I should have gone straight home
after the kiss. What was I thinking?

Antony texts.

**I think if she invited you in???**

I think for a minute. Okay . . . let me get this straight. I can
go to third base, and she can come, and I can't. I frown. Why
would anyone do that? And more importantly, why would they
want to?

I text my reply.

**What do you guys classify as third base?**

My eyes roam to the kitchen as I wait for their reply.

**I would think kissing and fucking her with your hand,
maybe a bit of dry humping?**

Fuck me, this is all too confusing. I reply.

**If I have my hand down her pants and we're making
out and she orgasms.
We are fucking.**

Another laughing emoji comes in from Antony.

Rebecca walks out into the living room with a cup of tea, and I guiltily put my phone to the side.

"Here we go." She puts it down onto the coffee table in front of me.

My eyes linger on the beautiful woman standing in front of me, and honestly, I have no idea what to do next.

I glance down and notice that there's only one cup of tea. "You're not having one with me?"

"I thought I might have a quick shower and take my makeup off." She shrugs, as if not knowing what to say. "Get into my pajamas."

"Good idea." My eyes drop to her toes and back up to her face in that dress.

*Or just stay naked.*

She disappears up the stairs, and I quickly text again.

**She's gone upstairs to have a shower and slip into
something more comfortable.**

Antony replies.

**You're in.**

Henley then sends fire emojis.

**Get up there and sort her out.**

I stand and begin to pace back and forth. I run my two
hands through my hair as panic runs through me.

Do I go upstairs, or do I sit here like a fucking dweeb and
wait for her to come back down?

I should go upstairs; surely I should go upstairs.

Taking a shower is code for *Come fuck me* . . . everyone
knows that.

*But does Rebecca?*

It's now becoming clearly apparent why I like bad girls.
There are no mind games, no innuendos about what I should
and should not be doing.

I know what to do. I know exactly what to fucking do.

Every damn time.

Before I can stop myself, I slowly go up the stairs, and as I
walk down the hallway, I can hear the shower running in the
bathroom.

I imagine Rebecca standing naked under the hot water. I
get a vision of myself holding her up against the tiles, her legs
around my waist.

My body buried deep inside hers.

She'd be wet and tight, and fuck me . . . I feel my cock throb just thinking about it.

I put my hand on the bathroom doorknob to go in . . . but then I hesitate.

*I want to take it slow.* Her words come back to me.

She always says that I push the boundaries and that I don't listen to her. Perhaps this is one of those times that I really should use the brain in my head instead of the one in my dick.

Maybe it's a test?

I imagine me opening the door and seeing her naked and then her going postal and screaming and shouting and ordering me out of the house . . . I mean, it's no secret that she can be overdramatic when she wants to be.

If I get this wrong, it could be catastrophic.

No, I can't go in.

I sneak down the hallway, quietly tiptoe back down the stairs, and slink onto the couch; I lean back and rearrange the erection in my pants. I'm so hard, it's becoming painful. Adrenaline is screaming through my veins.

This is an actual nightmare.


Fifteen minutes later, I hear the stairs creak and look up to see Rebecca walking down in a cream silk nightdress. It's fitted with spaghetti straps, and I can see every curve on that sweet body. Her hair is wet, and she smells of soap and shampoo and every sin known to man.

I let out a low whistle as my eyes drop hungrily down her body.

*Now we're talking.*
*Thump.*
*Thump.*

*Thump* . . . goes my cock.

I stand before I can stop myself, and as she gets to the bottom step, her eyes search mine.

"Wow," I whisper. "You look . . ." My eyebrows shoot up in surprise.

"Overdressed?" she whispers, as if worried.

"Perfect." I readjust the spaghetti strap on her shoulder as she looks up at me. "Bec . . ."

"Yeah."

"I don't know what *take it slow* means."

Her eyes hold mine.

"You're going to have to spell it out for me because . . ." I widen my eyes. "I'm hanging on to my control by a thread here."

"I . . ." She looks around, as if for divine guidance. "I don't actually know either."

"What *do* you know?"

"That I didn't want to say good night yet."

I dust my thumb over her bottom lip as I stare into her big, beautiful eyes. "Am I"—I lean down and kiss her; my lips gently brush over hers—"allowed to do this?"

Her eyes close as the heat from our kiss steals my breath.

*Holy fuck, she's on fire.*

She nods softly.

"Yes?" I ask for clarification. "This is okay?"

I kiss her again, and she smiles. "Yes," she breathes.

Our breath is ragged and echoing around the room. A million thoughts are screaming around me, but as her lips touch mine, they evaporate into nothing.

A peaceful abyss.

We kiss again, this time deeper, and I begin to lose control as I grab her behind and drag her onto me.

She whimpers against my lips, and the feel of her satin nightdress up against me starts a fire that I have no hope of controlling.

I fall back onto the couch and drag her down to straddle me. Our kiss turns frantic, and with my hands on her hip bones, I drag her over my hard cock.

*Ring, ring.*

*Ring, ring.*

Her phone rings and pulls us out of the moment, and she scrambles off my lap.

She walks backward from me as if she's seen a ghost.

*Ring, ring . . . ring, ring . . .* She picks up her phone and fumbles to decline the call. Her haunted eyes come back to mine.

"What's wrong?" I whisper.

"Nothing." She begins to pace as she drags her hand through her hair. "I just . . ."

She gestures down to my dick that's tenting my jeans.

"This is a problem for you?" I frown.

"I just . . ." Her eyes dart around the room.

*She's scared.*

"I'm sorry." I shake my head; this is not how this was supposed to go. "I'll go."

"No," she stammers. "I don't want you to go."

I stare at her in confusion.

"Can we watch a movie?" she whispers in a panic.

"Babe." I gesture to my crotch. "I'm in no state to lie beside you and watch a movie. I don't have that kind of control. It's okay, I'll see you tomorrow." I get up and step toward the door.

She swallows the lump in her throat, and the look on her face nearly breaks my heart.

*She's scared of me leaving in this state.*

*I fucking hate him.*

265

"What if . . ." I shrug. This is insanity. "What if . . . I had a shower upstairs . . . alone." I hold my hands up in surrender. "And I took care of business."

Her eyes search mine.

"And then I could come down and we could watch a movie . . . together." I try to think of the right thing to say. "Without"—I gesture to my crotch again—"any of this getting in the way."

"I just . . ." Her eyes well with tears.

"It's okay, Bec."

"It's not."

"Yeah." I pull her into a hug and kiss her forehead. "It is."

She stands in my arms for an extended time, and I can feel the regret oozing out of her. "It's not your fault that you're too sexy for your own good," I whisper into her hair.

I feel her smile into my neck.

"I'm going to take a shower."

She nods and steps back from me, and I slowly walk up the stairs and into the bathroom. I close the door and stare into the mirror at my reflection, wondering if I'm man enough to handle this crap.

Her cuts are deep.

She's got the baggage of a 747.

How must it feel to have your heart broken so bad that it still affects you physically over twelve months later?

I can't imagine ever having a love so deep. Maybe I'm in way over my head here? Maybe I should just run for the hills?

But we all know I won't.

Because it's her . . . and because she's the only one who makes me feel like this.

And whether that's a good or bad thing, I just don't know.

I take my time and turn the shower on, undress, and step in under the hot water.

My cock's still throbbing, begging to be milked . . . but the shine has gone from the apple. It's not as tempting as it was twenty minutes ago.

I don't want to jerk off alone in the shower. I want to be with her.

I stand under the water for a long time, my body excited. The rest of me, not so much . . . I begin to soap up, and the door slowly opens. I look up and frown as Rebecca walks in.

Her eyes drop down my body and linger on my erection before rising up to meet mine.

"Can I watch?"

# Chapter 17

*Rebecca*

"Of course you can," he whispers darkly. "Even better if you participate."

I swallow the lump in my throat as my eyes drop down his body. He's large and rippled with muscles. His skin is tanned, and with the water beading all over him . . . the vision nearly steals my breath.

Good lord . . . the finest specimen of man I have ever laid eyes on.

With his eyes locked on mine, he gives himself a long, slow stroke, and my sex instinctively clenches in appreciation.

He strokes himself again. "You want to touch me, Rebecca?"

I nod before my brain kicks into gear, and he gives me a slow, sexy smile.

"Come here," he breathes as he works himself again. The room is filling with steam, and I feel a rush of arousal throb down below.

*Dear lord.*

He steps out of the water and toward me. My heart hammers in my chest, and it takes all my strength not to step back from him in fear.

Stop it.

I anchor myself to the floor as my eyes hold his.

Seeing Blake like this is new and exciting, and if I'm being completely honest, a little terrifying. I always knew he would be something; I mean, the way women fall to their knees and worship the ground he walks on has been a hint.

But this . . .

Seeing him naked and in the flesh is a new level of enlightenment.

He's dominant and confident and not at all what I envisioned . . . although thinking back, I don't even know what I actually envisioned.

Because nothing could have prepared me for this visual sensation.

"Come." He takes my hand and pulls me in under the water with him as his lips take mine. He puts his hand down and strokes himself again. My eyes close at the feel of his lips against mine, of being so close to him that I can feel his arousal as it seeps through his skin, as if it's a tangible force.

We kiss, slow and tender.

A mile away from the vigor, his hand is stroking his cock as it hangs heavily between us.

*Oh god . . .*

I begin to lose control of myself, a need deep inside of me wanting to take over.

Primal instinct to mate.

My body wants what he has . . . *and she wants it hard.*

I reach down and wrap my hand around his cock and give him a slow, long stroke, and his eyes flutter closed. "Yes," he moans into my mouth.

Urged on by his reaction, I stroke him again, harder this time, and our kiss intensifies.

It deepens, along with the connection.

His hands begin to roam over my wet nightdress that is now totally see-through.

He kneads my breasts with aggression, and it nearly drives me to my breaking point.

I whimper into his mouth.

His lips drop to my neck as his hand slides up my thigh and down the front of my panties. Teeth graze my skin as he slides his fingers through my dripping-wet lips.

"*Fuck . . . ,*" he moans. "So wet, baby."

My strokes get harder, almost violent, as a means to try and put out this fire.

He slides one finger deep into my sex, and I flutter.

*Don't come.*

We keep kissing, and he adds another and another. Pumping me hard, working my flesh as he fucks me with his hand.

*Oh . . .*

I tip my head back, teetering on the edge.

"There's one thing you need to know about me," he whispers darkly.

"What's that?"

He jerks his hand aggressively. "I never come first." He lifts one of my legs and wraps it around his waist and begins to fuck me with his hand, so deep and so fucking well. Massaging my G-spot like nobody ever has.

Oh god . . . Is that where it is?

I see stars.

All the beautiful, blinding stars in the galaxy.

I can't even kiss him; my mouth is hanging open as he overtakes my body with his. It's never been like this before, so animalistic and raw and real.

The echo of the water sloshing sounds throughout my bathroom, and he almost growls as he bites my neck.

We fall back and hit the wall, both of our hands claiming each other.

Demanding the orgasms we want.

He puts his mouth to my ear and slows his fingers. I feel his breath up against my skin as he slowly and softly rubs his thumb over my clitoris.

The change in tempo has me about to explode, and I whimper.

I feel him smile up against my cheek, knowing that in this moment, I'm his puppet.

He rubs again, soft and barely there, before plunging hard and deep inside my sex.

"Oh fuck," I moan.

He repeats the delicious combination. Barely there over my clit and then hitting me hard deep inside. My legs begin to open by themselves, and I am lost.

*This man is the master.*

His thumb flutters over my clitoris, and then he adds another finger and fucks me deep. "Now," he growls. "You come now."

My body hears his command, and I shudder hard as an orgasm rips through me.

My sight nearly blacks out, and I tip my head back and moan out loud.

He puts his hand over mine on his cock and begins to fuck my hand hard.

Violent.

"Like that," he growls.

I feel him swell as his grip gets tighter. His girth is huge, and I can feel the thick vein that courses down the full length of him. The head so engorged and dripping with want.

Ahhhhhh.

It's all I can do to hold on, to stay up on my feet. My body is here, but I am floating way up above, watching us from the heavens as I have an out-of-body experience.

"Say when," he whispers darkly in my ear.

What . . . when . . .

*Who has this kind of control?*

I jerk him harder; his face contorts, and goddamn, I thought I liked Blake Grayson before.

Now I'm addicted.

"When." I grip him tighter, and his hips take over, and he pushes forward and lifts my nightdress as he pins me to the wall. Our teeth clash as he comes hard up against my stomach.

Hearts race between us as we pant into each other's kiss.

A high . . . so high.

He rubs his semen into my skin as he kisses me; there's a tangible feeling between us. Or maybe it's just my heart free-falling from my chest.

"Let's get you cleaned up." He grabs the bottom of my nightdress. "Arms up." I raise my arms, and he slowly lifts my wet nightdress up and over my head and throws it to the side.

Suddenly I'm standing before him completely naked. My eyes search his, and he gives me a soft smile and kisses me. "You're more beautiful than I could have ever imagined." Without another word, he drops to his knees in front of me and picks up one of my legs and puts it over his shoulder. I grab his shoulders to steady myself as his tongue swipes through my wet, swollen flesh.

"I've just . . ." I shudder at the feeling of his tongue on me. "Come."

"I know," he whispers into me. His eyes close in pleasure. "I told you I'm cleaning you up."

*What the fuck?*

He spreads me apart with his fingers and licks me deeper. My eyes roll back in my head.

"Hmm," he moans into me. "You taste so fucking good."

The blood begins to drain from my face as arousal thumps through me.

How is he so . . . hot?

He licks me deeper and deeper, and I cling to his shoulders as I lose all coherent thought. My body begins to take on her own agenda to move against him.

"Hmm," he whispers. "That's it, baby; ride my face."

His thumbs part me wider as his teeth graze my clitoris, and I shudder as another orgasm screams through me. He smiles into me as his eyes hold mine.

Is this a dream? Am I going to wake up any moment and realize this is all a figment of my imagination?

He kisses the inside of my thigh and stands. "That's all for today." He gives me a slow, sexy smile as he begins to wash me with the body wash. "Wouldn't want to rush things."

I stare up at him in awe . . .

Okay, what the hell is this hocus-pocus?

If he's trying to seduce me, he needn't bother; I'm already seduced. He can fuck me any way he wants to.

He turns me away from him and washes my shoulders and down my back, my arms, and then down lower, to my back entrance.

I close my eyes as he explores my body . . . *That feels good.*

"Where's your piercing?" I ask.

"I took it out today." His hands come around to the front to wash my sex. "I didn't want to scare you."

I smile softly at the tiles. "Well, seeing it is the only thing I've been able to think about since you had it done."

"What?" He turns me to face him. "You've been thinking about my cock, Rebecca?"

"Maybe." I smirk.

"You bad, bad girl." He bends and nips my ear, and I jump in surprise as goose bumps scatter up my arms. "You'll be punished for that."

*Yes . . .*

He goes back to washing me, and then he washes himself. I stand with my hands on his hips, frozen with arousal, or is it fear . . . or am I just fangirling so hard that I've lost the ability to function?

He's confident. I've never . . . I mean, I know I've only ever been with one man before.

But Blake Grayson is an entirely new species.

He turns the taps off, and I frown in question. *Wait, are we . . .*

He smiles down at me, as if reading my mind. "No."

"No?"

"No." He gets a towel and wraps it around my shoulders and begins to dry me. "We are not rushing this."

"Blake . . ." I screw up my face. "You just cleaned me up with your tongue; it's a little bit late for that."

He chuckles as he keeps drying me. "Baby . . . I haven't even started with the things I'm going to do with you."

Suddenly I'm feeling way out of control, and alarm bells scream in the distance.

His dark eyes hold mine. "When and *if* we have sex . . . you'll fucking beg for it."

I swallow the fear in my throat . . . because I want to get on my knees and beg right now.

*Help.*

Two orgasms in and I'm ruined.

He dries me and wraps us both in white towels, and we walk down the hallway. I go to walk down the stairs and he stops still, causing me to look back at him. "We're not sleeping on your couch forever, Rebecca."

"I know."

He raises an eyebrow with a silent dare, and I know he's right; I need to get over myself.

Sleeping in my bed with a new man seems so foreign, but after what just happened in the bathroom, the couch will no longer cut it as a sleeping arrangement.

"Okay." I nod, feeling stupid.

Damn it, why do I always revert back to my old habits?

John is never coming back, and I don't even want him to, so why would I still think of my bedroom as half his?

The house is all mine now, remember?

Determined to do better, I walk in and pull the blankets back. *You want to sleep in my bed . . . fine, let's do this.*

"Do you want a drink or anything?" he asks.

"Maybe a glass of water?"

"Sure." He picks up the remote and flicks the television on. "We can watch our movie up here."

I give him a stifled smile; I think he's trying to kill the awkwardness before it arrives.

And it will; it has to. We've been friends for years.

Five minutes later, he walks back into the bedroom looking like a supermodel. White towel around his waist and rippled muscles. He has a tray with two glasses of water and a tub of ice cream and two spoons.

"Nightcap?" He throws me a playful wink as he puts the tray down on my bedside table.

I smile up at the sleepover god. "I suppose some sugar would counteract the boredom of tonight."

He widens his eyes and launches over and play wrestles me as he throws me onto my back. He bites my shoulder, and I laugh out loud.

"Wrong answer, Rebecca."

## Blake

Sunlight peeks through the crack of the drapes, and the birds sing loudly outside. The serene sound of Rebecca's regulated breathing is all I can hear.

I lie on my side, staring at her like the creep that I am.

*She's perfect.*

And I knew it; I knew she would be. I knew from the first moment I laid eyes on her that this is where we were going to end up.

I hate that she didn't.

I frown at the wayward thought. Stop it.

I can't think like that. She was married. Of course she didn't think of me like that.

So why did I?

How did I know on first sight?

She rolls toward me and lies on her side, and I smile in appreciation. I don't care how we got here; I'm just glad that we did. Her long dark hair is splayed across the pillow, and her eyelashes flutter as she dreams. Her skin is creamy and alluring, and my eyes drop lower to her bare breast, then down over her hips.

The throb in my dick notifies me of his intentions.

*No.*

Not this morning. We are not having a quickie in the morning as our first time.

We're waiting.

She rolls over onto her back, and her legs fall open, and my cock instantly becomes painfully hard.

The carnal need to fuck begins to take me over.

*Stop.*

I close my eyes to try and will away my arousal. I want to wake up with her and make her breakfast and . . .

*Throb . . . throb . . . throb . . .*

Yeah, that's not going to happen.

If I stay here, we are 100 percent fucking.

With one last long look at the goddess, I quietly climb out of bed. I sneak out of the bedroom and close the door behind me. I find my clothes in the bathroom and gingerly put them on.

I don't want to sneak out, but I literally have no choice.

I got away with last night, but I'm pretty sure if I come in hard and heavy this morning, it isn't going to end well for me.

This is for the best.

I walk down the stairs and put my shoes on and then peer out the front window through the crack in the curtains. Where's Carol? That busybody is just waiting to catch me sneaking out of here. I mean, I do sleep over all the time.

So why am I worried about it today? *Because last night was different.*

A broad smile crosses my face. I can hardly contain my excitement.

*It happened.*

I get a vision of us in the shower last night and glance back at the stairs . . . a rematch?

No.

I keep looking through the curtains for Carol. Why am I even worried about her, anyway? Just go out there and act normal.

I go to the front door and drop my shoulders to psych myself up. Lying isn't my strong point; it never has been. In fact, I'm completely useless at it.

I open the door in a rush and quietly close it behind me. I look left and I look right, and the coast seems clear. I hotfoot it across the grass toward my house.

"Good morning, Blake," Carol's voice calls out.

*Damn it.*

I glance over to see her talking to Henley and Juliet on their driveway.

"Morning, Carol."

Henley's eyes widen as he connects the dots, and he points at me. Juliet's eyes widen farther.

*Fuck.*

Code red. I'm caught.

"Have a nice night, dear?" Carol asks all-knowingly.

*Fuck you, Carol.*

"Yes. Called in and watched a movie with Rebecca on the way home from my date. Slept on her couch as usual."

"Oh, I see." Carol smiles. Henley rolls his eyes, and Juliet continues to stare at me wide eyed.

I throw them a wave and march to my house.

"Wait up," Henley calls as he runs to catch up with me.

*Not now, fucker.*

He falls into step beside me. "Why you . . . old dog."

"What are you talking about?" I open my front door, march into the kitchen, and turn my coffee machine on.

"Rebecca is the woman in the shower?"

"No," I scoff.

He gestures to my hard dick in my pants. "Sure about that?"

"Oh my god," I whisper in a rush. "You are un-*fucking*-believable."

"So . . . ?" He smiles broadly and holds his hands up. "*How* was it?"

I stare at him blankly for a moment before I break and smile right back. "Incredible."

He slaps me on the back hard in excitement. "Ha, good man."

I can't wipe the smile from my face, and I turn my back to him to make the coffee.

"So . . ." He rocks up onto his toes as he waits for the details.

"So what?"

"How did things go? What happened?"

"I'm not discussing Rebecca with you."

"Why not? You discuss everyone with me."

"This is Rebecca . . . our mutual friend, and I'm going to respect her privacy."

"Oh . . ." He stares at me for a beat and then puts his weight onto his back foot. "Fuck me, you've done your nuts already."

"What?" I scoff. "Don't be ridiculous." I keep making the coffee.

"Be careful, man."

I hand him his coffee. "What does that mean?"

"Hurt people hurt people."

"Huh?" I sip my coffee.

"Just that. Hurt people hurt people."

I roll my eyes. "You're so fucking dramatic."

"No. I'm not. When I was seeing my psychologist, he told me that hurt people hurt people . . . without even meaning to, they just do. And I have to agree. You asked for my opinion, and I'm giving it to you."

"Well. Firstly, I didn't ask for your stupid opinion, and secondly, Rebecca is long over her divorce."

He lets out a deep sigh, as if this is the worst thing in the world that could have happened. "You always said you were never going to be the rebound guy."

"I'm *not* the rebound guy."

"Are you sure about that?"

"Oh my god." I point to the door. "Fuck off and go home already."

"All I'm saying is be careful, that's all."

"We kissed. You have nothing to worry about."

"You didn't have sex?" He frowns.

"We didn't have sex," I huff. "Not that it's any of your business."

"Good." He sips his coffee. "Just . . . stay cool, okay?"

I screw up my face and hold my hand up. "When am I ever not cool?"

"When it's Rebecca." He widens his eyes.

The front door bangs, and Antony comes into view. "Hey," he says as he walks to the coffee machine. "Carol told me you hooked up with Rebecca last night," he says matter-of-factly. He pushes the button and glances over at me for confirmation. "So, how'd you do?"

"What?" I snap. "How does she fucking know that? Was she spying through the windows or some shit?"

"Wouldn't surprise me." Henley shrugs. "It'll be on the national news tomorrow."

"This street is an invasion of my privacy," I huff as I open the fridge to try and find something to eat. "I have a good mind to move."

"You should," Antony agrees. Henley smiles and clinks his coffee cup with Ant's. "Best idea you've ever had."

"Please go home." I slam my sad refrigerator shut. "But first, you're taking me out for breakfast."

"Hello." I hear Juliet's voice as she comes through my front door.

"Hi."

"So . . . ?" She smiles.

"So." I hunch up my shoulders in excitement. "I . . . kind of got to second base."

"With Blake?"

My eyes widen. "What . . . what makes you say that?"

Oh crap, how the hell does she know?

"I saw him sneaking out of here." She puts her hands on her hips and raises her eyebrows. "So . . . yeah, Rebecca. Do you have something to tell me?"

"Um." I wince. "I was going to tell you, but I wasn't sure if I was right about it, and it turns out I was, and now I'm . . ."

"Relax." She laughs as she pulls me into a hug. "This is amazing."

"Is it, though?" I whisper. "He's a player and a smooth talker, and I don't know if . . ."

"Stop overthinking this. It's Blake. He's the best guy in the world, and if it doesn't work out, so what? At least you broke the drought with someone you can trust to look after you."

I wince. The thought is depressing.

"He's not a serial killer. At least we know that."

"I guess." I smile.

She jumps up and down on the spot. "How was it?"

"It was good." I try to act cool.

"Just good?"

I begin to jump alongside her. "It was fucking unbelievable."

I glance at my watch: 5:00 p.m.

Hmm, not a word from Blake . . .

281

Maybe last night didn't go as well as I thought it did.

I hold the remote to the television and change the channel. I'm in search of something to watch to take my mind off the whole situation.

Blake was gone when I woke up, and then . . . nothing.

I thought he would have called or come over or . . . I don't fucking know. More than this, anyway.

I hear my front step creak, and I sit up. *Knock, knock.*

*He's here.*

I fly off my couch and open the door, and there he stands. Six foot three of perfect male specimen.

"Hello, Miss Dalton." He smirks. He steps forward, forcing me to step back.

"Hello, Dr. Grayson." I smirk right back.

He keeps walking until I am backed up against the wall, and he bends and softly kisses me. "Good morning."

"Ha," I scoff. "You're ten hours late."

He kisses me quickly again. "Better late than never." He looks around my house. "I can't stay long."

*Oh . . .*

"On account of me taking things slow," he adds.

"Oh." I smile with relief. "Right."

"I just wanted to come over and talk about Cancún."

"Uh-huh." I act casual.

"I made some calls today and was able to reschedule some of my appointments, so . . ." He shrugs. "I can swindle a few extra days off."

Shit . . . I don't think I can. My face falls. "How many days?"

"Maybe we could stay until Wednesday. I mean, that's if you can take the time off. It's okay if you can't."

"No, no," I stammer as I try to think of a solution. "I'll take some annual leave or something. It's just if they can't get someone to cover my class, that's all."

"Okay." His eyes hold mine, and they have that look that he gets, the mischievous one that I love.

"Why do you want to stay longer in Cancún?" I act dumb.

"I have a few things in mind I would like to do."

"Such as?"

"Go to the gym, play golf. That sort of thing."

"Oh." I nod. "Right, well, maybe I can't get the time off, after all."

He grabs me aggressively and pins me to the wall. "Get the fucking time off." He bites my neck. "Or else."

I giggle up at the ceiling as his teeth ravage my neck. "Or else what?"

"Or else you won't be able to come to the gym or play golf." He steps back from me and gives me a broad smile.

My heart flutters in my chest at the sight of him.

"So . . ." He steps back again. "I'll see you later in the week."

*When?*

"Okay." I act casual.

*What time of what day will I see you?*

He takes me into his arms and hugs me as he holds me tight.

*Honestly . . .*

His lips take mine as he kisses me, and I feel my feet float from the floor. A little tongue, a little suction, and a whole lot of forbidden promise.

The way he kisses is just so . . .

"Goodbye." He steps back, but I'm not ready to say goodbye yet. I wrap my arms around his neck and pull him back down to kiss again.

"Did you put your piercing back in?" I ask.

His big hands wrap around my waist as he pulls me close. "You know, for someone taking things slow, you sure talk about my cock a lot."

I smile against his lips. "Well, it's a very interesting topic."

He chuckles and steps back, and I know he's making himself leave just as much as I'm making myself let him go.

"Try to get the extra time off," he reminds me as he walks through the front door and out onto my porch.

"Okay." I lean on the doorjamb and watch him walk down the front steps.

"Oh." He turns around and comes back. "By the way, Carol is onto us."

"I heard." I smirk.

"I thought we were keeping it a secret?"

"Why?"

He frowns. "You don't want to keep it a secret until your divorce is final?"

"I got the house signed over to me last week." I beam proudly.

"You did?" His eyes widen. "That's fantastic." He picks me up and spins me around, knocking me from my feet. "Why didn't you tell me?"

"I had so much going on, I must have forgotten."

"This is great." He kisses me again. "We'll celebrate in Cancún."

"Okay."

I watch him walk down the front steps and back over to his house as a dreamy sense of contentment washes over me. We are really doing this; it's actually happening.

Wait a minute . . . I just told him it's okay to tell people. What happened to my plan of taking this slow? Telling people is the opposite of slow.

Ugh, Rebecca.

You are officially hopeless.


"Okay, everyone." I smile at my class. "Grab your library bags. We are going up to visit Mrs. Jones for story time."

*Knock, knock.* I glance up to see Marlene from the front office standing at the door with a giant crystal vase filled with the biggest, most beautiful red roses that I have ever seen, and my eyes widen.

"Miss Dalton, you have a very special delivery." She smiles broadly.

I nearly skip over to her. "Thank you so much."

"Oh wow," my kids gush with excitement. "Who are they from, Miss Dalton?" someone calls.

*Ahhh, Blake sent me roses.*

Hot and romantic: this man is winning at everything. I set them on my desk and smile goofily as I open the card.

> *Fifteen years ago today, we went on our first date.*
> *Every happy memory I ever had is with you.*
> *Of you.*
> *You were my first love.*
> *My only love, my last love.*
> *Forever your husband,*
> *John*

# Chapter 18

My face falls as the fairy tale dissipates, and I stuff the card back into the envelope.

The kids all laugh and bounce around in excitement as they wait for some information from me, and I just want to scream. "There's been a mistake. These flowers aren't for me, Miss Marlene." I take them back to her. "These are for you."

The children all laugh, as if this is the funniest thing they have ever seen.

"What's wrong?" she whispers.

"You take them." I shove the vase into her arms. "I don't want them."

"Why not?"

"They're from my ex-husband."

"Oh." Her face falls.

"Do what you want with them," I murmur.

"Like what?"

"Throw them in the trash for all I care." I stuff the card into my handbag and clap my hands loudly as I march toward the door. "Let's go to the library. Mrs. Jones is waiting for us."

Marlene awkwardly toddles back to the front office with the huge bunch of roses as my eyes glow red. If he thinks he's going to ruin one more day for me, he has another thing coming. What a joke of a man he is.

How dare he send me flowers.


"So what are we looking for?" Chloe asks as we walk through the lingerie store.

"Something that doesn't say I haven't had sex in eighteen months, and my vagina is probably closed over by now, and I've totally forgotten what to do."

"Got it." She keeps looking through the racks. "Did Juliet tell you she's thinking of renting out her house?" she says.

"No." I stop what I'm doing and look up at her. "Since when?"

"Since Liam is looking for a new place to live."

"Liam, her brother?"

"Yeah."

"What happened to his house?"

"Juliet thinks that as long as he's living in the house he shared with his late girlfriend, he's never going to move on."

"That's a good point." I think about it for a bit as I keep looking through the underwear. "He's like the catch of the century; I don't understand how someone hasn't snatched him up. Gorgeous as hell too."

"I don't think he wants to be." She holds up a pink lacy bra-and-G-string set. "This is nice."

"It is." I flick through to find my size. "Hmm, probably true." I put it into my basket.

"I can't imagine what it's like losing someone you love to death."

"You know, as horrible and as selfish as this sounds, I think it would be easier than loving someone with your whole heart and finding out your entire relationship has been a lie," I say as I keep looking. "I mean, at least you know they loved you back."

"Yeah, but you get over assholes. Sure, it takes a while, but eventually you just do. But do you ever really recover from grief?"

"This is true." I throw another set of underwear into the basket.

"Oliver asked me to move in with him last night."

"He did?" I smile, but I notice her face is flat. "What's wrong? You don't want to?"

"I do . . ." She shrugs. "I don't know. I just kind of thought I wouldn't live with someone until we had some kind of commitment in place, you know?"

My eyes flick up to meet hers. "You want to get married?"

"No, but . . ." Her voice trails off.

"No, but what?"

"I just don't know if I want to live with him yet."

"So don't."

"But then I don't want him to think that I want to break up if I say no."

"Just tell him that you're not ready." I throw another bra into my basket. "Or say you don't want to live with your boyfriend until you get engaged."

"You don't think that sounds pushy, like I'm expecting a proposal or something? Because believe me, I'm not."

"No," I scoff. "Say it like it is. Chloe, if there's one thing I've learned over the last five years, it's that being Little Miss Nice Girl gets you nowhere."

"True."

Chloe glances at her watch. "Shit. We have to get moving. Our laser appointments are in half an hour across town."

"Crap." I begin to storm to the counter to pay. "I cannot miss that appointment."

The sun is just coming over the horizon, and I smile as I power walk along with a spring in my step.

It's just after 6:30 a.m. I'm out exercising, and I'm feeling very proud of myself. I've been eating well, sleeping great, and dreaming of a particular handsome man.

I feel good, so good that I can't wipe the dreamy smile from my face.

I turn the corner onto Kingston Lane as I plan my day. Once I get home, I'll go to school early and get some extra work done. Now that my weekend has turned into a six-day vacation, I want to get some extra lessons prepared for my substitute teacher.

Six days . . . with Blake.

I get a shiver of excitement. Honestly, things couldn't be going better between us.

He isn't being pushy or overbearing. In fact, I'm missing him. I usually see him a lot more than I have this week.

I glance up, and speak of the devil, Blake's garage door slowly goes up, his car pulls out, and he breaks out into a breathtaking smile when he sees me walking up the road.

His car slowly drives toward me, and I grab the bottom of my T-shirt to pretend I'm going to flash my boobs at him. He chuckles and pulls the car into my driveway and gets out. He's wearing a navy suit and a crisp white shirt. His heavenly cologne wafts through the air.

How didn't I notice all these dreamy things about him before now? The man is a bona fide walking orgasm.

"I'd like a word with you inside, young lady." He raises his eyebrow, as if acting angry.

"What about?"

"Street flashing."

A thrill of excitement runs through me, and trying as hard as I can to act casual, I walk into my house; he follows me in and closes the front door behind him.

As soon as we're in private, the mood changes between us. He stares down at me as I stare up at him, and the air crackles between us.

He steps forward and takes me into his arms and kisses me. His hands drop to my behind and grind me onto him.

Suddenly we're desperate for each other, and we fall back as arousal takes us over.

"You're all I can fucking think about," he breathes against my lips.

"Same." I push him to walk backward to the couch, and as his legs hit it, he falls down, and I climb over his lap. His hands go to my hip bones, and he begins to pull me down onto him as we kiss like animals.

He pulls out of the kiss to look up at me with dark eyes as my body rocks onto his erection. He's thick and swollen and . . . he'd feel so good deep inside me.

*Fuck.*

I don't want to play this waiting game anymore.

I want him now.

"Can you come over tonight?" I murmur against his lips.

He moans as his eyes flutter closed. "Cancún." He whispers the word out.

"I want our first time to be here, in my bed."

A frown crosses his face, and he pushes me off him and stands.

I try to sweeten the deal. "I'll make you lasagna."

"You don't have time to make me lasagna, and besides, what makes you think I'm a sure thing?"

"Don't do that to me." I pull a whiny face. "I'm counting on it that you are."

"We talked about this." He looks down at me and takes my face into his hands. "We are *waiting*."

"I know what I want, Blake." I push him back onto the couch and straddle him again. "I'm done with waiting. I need you now."

He smiles against my lips as his cock hits a new level of hard. "Be careful, Rebecca. I'm hanging on to my control by a thread here."

He has to go to work.

I peel myself off his lap and take a step back, and he gingerly climbs off the couch. He rearranges his hard length in his suit pants.

"Tonight," he breathes as he kisses me softly. This kiss is different. Soft and tender and filled with unspoken promise.

"Tonight." I smile against his lips.

"Do you want me to get dinner on my way home?" he asks.

"Uh-huh." I kiss him again and again and . . .

"Bec." He steps back from me. "Unless you are going to call into work sick today, you need to stop. Right now."

"Fine." I giggle and step back. "Goodbye, Dr. Grayson."

His dark eyes hold mine, and he rearranges himself in his suit pants again. "You're going to fucking get it."

"That's the plan."

He turns and without another word walks out of the house. With arousal screaming and thumping through my soul, I go to the window and watch him walk out to his car.

"Morning, Carol," he calls as he gives her a wave.

His silver Porsche purrs like a kitten as it pulls down the street, and I bounce up and down on the spot.

"Ahhhhhh."

Henley carries out a bottle of champagne and places it on the table in front of us.

"Wow, pulling out the big stuff." Blake smiles. "Must have been some honeymoon. Where are these photos?"

Juliet and Henley have called us over for celebratory afternoon drinks.

"Well . . ." Henley smiles proudly as he puts his arm around Juliet. "We have some exciting news."

Antony, Chloe, Blake, and I exchange looks . . . What's this about?

Henley gestures to Juliet. "You go."

"No, you go." She smiles shyly.

"All right, then . . . Juliet's pregnant." Henley rises onto his toes, unable to contain his excitement. "And we couldn't be happier. A little James is on the way."

*Oh . . .*

The room erupts into laughter, and everyone jumps from their seat to hug the two expectant parents.

"I can't believe this," I whisper to Juliet. "I didn't think you were even trying until later this year."

Juliet shrugs. "Neither did we, but somebody has stepped in and gifted us with a baby."

"Oh, I'm so excited." I smile. "What a beautiful wedding present." I put my hand down to her stomach. "So how far along are you?"

"Seven weeks. We were going to wait until the twelve-week mark to tell you all, but we just couldn't."

"And why should you? We want to celebrate this as well." Blake laughs as he pulls her into a hug. "I'm so happy for you. Congratulations."

"A little baby on Kingston Lane," I whisper in awe.

"Now the street really is perfect." Blake pulls Henley into a hug. "Well done, man. Well done."

"Hucow." Antony sneezes. "Hucow." He sneezes again.

Huh?

Blake and Henley burst out laughing at something.

"What's so funny?"

"The way he sneezes. He's a fucking idiot."


I walk into the staff room and take a seat at a table on my own. I don't feel like small talking today. I have bigger things on my mind. Blake Grayson in all his glory is coming over tonight, and I'd be lying if I said I wasn't nervous.

What happens if it isn't everything we both think it's going to be?

What if the sex doesn't live up to expectations?

I mean, it might not—just because our foreplay is off the hook doesn't mean the sex will be.

From deep down in my psyche, an insecurity is lurking in the darkness. Blake has slept with some of the most beautiful women in the world, and I'm . . . well, I'm just me.

Although I look after myself, I'm definitely no supermodel. I have stretch marks and a bit of cellulite and curves where they have no right being.

I know it's my personality Blake is in lust with, but what if my body lets down the party?

Realistically, moving forward, how long could he be with someone that he doesn't find attractive? I close my eyes in disgust with my wayward thoughts. *Stop it, you fool.*

*It's Blake.*

He knows my body better than anyone. He sleeps beside me all the time.

*Cut it out, you fool.*

If there's one thing I know about me beginning to date again, it's that I need to step up and be brave. I can't bring my baggage into this, or else we're doomed before we even begin.

I think back to the other night when I freaked out and how beautiful and patient Blake was. He was prepared to shower alone so that I could calm down. I mean, in the end, he didn't have to, and I joined him. But I know that if I didn't go into that bathroom, he would have done whatever it took to be able to stay.

And it means a lot.

The beauty of Blake is that he knows my history . . . the downside is that I know his.

I pull out my phone.

### Six missed calls.

John.

Fuck.

*Leave me alone already.*

Now that I have the house, I want nothing to do with him ever again. The phone rings in my hand. It's him. Of course it is. He knows I'm on break at this time of the day. I need to set him straight.

"Hello," I snap.

"Hi, Rebecca," he says all happy-like.

"Why are you calling me? Has your Barbie collection become boring?"

"Very funny."

"I think so." I smirk. Being a bitch to John really does give me pleasure.

"I'm calling to see if you got my flowers."

"They arrived." I roll my eyes. "Yes."

"Did you like them?"

"I threw them in the trash, John. I want nothing to do with you. Stop calling me."

"You don't mean that."

"Ahh . . . yes. I do."

"Can we go out on a date over the weekend? Like old times."

I screw up my face. This man is a fucking idiot. "Absolutely not. I don't even want to speak to you. I'm serious, John. Go back to Barbie town. Our ship has sailed."

"I know you don't mean that."

"Are you ignorant, dumb, or just plain stupid?" I whisper angrily. "We are over—forever." I look around to see if anyone can hear me.

"If we were over, you would have divorced me."

I frown.

"But you didn't, and you don't even realize it yet, but deep down, you didn't want to get a divorce either."

Honestly, this man is the living end. I'm selling pictures of my damn feet just to pay the fucking bills. How dare he think that he can even call me, let alone demand a date.

"The only reason I signed that contract is because I want the house." I hold the phone really close to my ear, hoping that nobody else can hear me. "That's it. Get the hell out of my life, and if you call me again, I'm blocking your number."

"You block my number, I'm coming over to your house."

"Then I'm getting a restraining order against you."

"Do that and I am pressing assault charges on your psycho neighbor."

"What?" I screw up my face. What the hell is he talking about now?

"I've got the photos of his little fist party on my face. I went to the hospital that night and made a full report of the incident. If he comes anywhere near you, I'm having him charged with aggravated assault."

*He wouldn't.*

"Go to hell, John. You're such a liar."

"You think I'm joking? Check the law. A pediatrician can't hold a medical license if they have a criminal record."

Reason two million why I hate this man. I begin to feel the hot surge of adrenaline as it rushes through my body.

"Don't call me again."

"We're going out on Saturday night."

"I won't be blackmailed into anything. If you have a bone to pick with Blake Grayson, you take it up with him."

He stays silent.

"But we both know you won't because you're a fucking coward, and we both know that Blake will beat you to a pulp again and rightly so." I hang up the phone and throw it into my bag.

Fuck.

I think on it for a moment. I have to tell Blake so that he knows what the idiot is threatening.

I dig my phone back out and dial Blake's number.

"You've called Blake Grayson. I can't come to the phone right now. Please leave me a message, and I'll get back to you as soon as I can."

"Hi, Blake, it's me. I think we've got a problem; can you call me when you get this, please?" I hang up and sit and stare at the wall for a while as my mind races at a million miles per minute. I can hear the other teachers all chattering happily in the background.

He wouldn't do that to Blake . . . would he?

Yes. He would.

My phone rings, and the name *Blake* lights up the screen. I scramble to answer it.

"Hello."

"Hey, Bec, what's up?"

"Um." Oh man, how do I put this? "So . . . John just threatened that if you come near me, he's going to have you charged with assault."

"Why were you speaking to John?" he fires back.

I screw up my face. Seriously? That's the only thing he heard in that sentence? "He called, and I told him not to call me again, so then he got nasty and threatened that if you come near me, he's going to have you charged with assault."

"Of course he did," he replies casually. "Don't worry, I've already covered my bases."

I frown. "I don't understand."

"Henley and I went down to the police station the day after it happened and made a formal complaint about him."

"You did?"

"I'm not stupid. I knew it was coming."

"How?"

"Not hard to work out. The man's a fuckwit."

"This is true." I twist my lips as I think.

"Did you tell him we're together?" he asks.

I hesitate before I answer. Wait a minute . . . "*Are* we together?"

"Yes. We're together," he snaps.

"Oh . . ." I think on this for a moment. "Are we not having a conversation about this?"

"This *is* the conversation."

"Oh." I smile. Why is his caveman act exciting to me? "How very presumptuous of you."

"Not presumptuous, just stating the facts. Tell him."

"No, because then he's going to file a complaint."

"He can do whatever he wants. I have it on record with a witness that he came over and caused a disturbance, and I was simply defending myself."

Relief fills me. This won't turn into a huge mess after all. "Oh, I love you." My eyes widen. I did not just say that. "I mean . . . not love, love, I just . . ." Oh my god . . . help. "You know, relieved. For you *and* Henley. I love you *and* Henley, like friends . . . you know?" I'm spluttering and tripping over my words.

"Relax." He chuckles. "I know what you mean."

I close my eyes as my face flushes with embarrassment. I just told him I love him, and we haven't even slept together yet.

I'm officially the world's biggest loser. I close my eyes and pinch the bridge of my nose.

"What do you feel like for dinner?" he asks to change the subject.

*A muzzle.*

"I don't mind, whatever you feel like," I whisper, embarrassed.

"I'm not sure you would want to eat what I feel like eating," he says. His voice has that playful, naughty edge, and it brings a smile to my face.

"Behave yourself, Dr. Grayson."

"Make me."

"I'm going now." I smirk.

"Goodbye, Miss Dalton." He hangs on the line, and I smile harder.

"This time tomorrow, we will be on our way to Cancún," I tell him.

"That's if you survive tonight."

I laugh out loud. "I really am going now, you deviant. Goodbye." I hang up and feel my armpits begin to heat as an excited flush falls over me.

How is he so hot?

I get a feeling that maybe *he* won't survive.

Lazarus's eyes roam over my naked flesh as I
lie on the table.

The firelight dances across his skin . . .

My cock twinges, and I hold my iPad closer . . .

Fuck me . . .

This story is hot.

"Good afternoon, Dr. Grayson," a voice says from the door.

I fumble to quickly shut down my iPad and glance up.
"Good afternoon, Judy." I smile.

"What are you up to in your office all alone?"

*Vampire porn . . . go away!*

"Reading some research notes," I lie.

"Anything interesting?"

"Not really." I fake a smile . . . seriously, fuck off right now.

"Catch you later."

I look left and right and open the file back up.

He steps closer, and I can see the huge erection tenting his pants. His arousal overtakes
the room with an energy all its own.

The candles flicker as he approaches, and we
stare at each other as the air crackles between
us. Without a word, his hand slowly goes
around my throat.

I swallow the lump in my throat as my cock thumps . . . fuck.

*Ring, ring . . .* My phone pulls me out of the moment.

"Blake Grayson," I snap.

"Did you read it yet?" Antony whispers.

"I'm trying to now, but everybody keeps interrupting me," I whisper.

"Seriously, it's so fucking hot I can't stand it."

"Yeah . . . I'm getting the gist." I wipe the perspiration from my brow.

"We need to find out who wrote this as a matter of urgency because I'm left on a cliffhanger."

"What do you mean?" I frown.

"The whole story isn't there. It finishes just when it gets good."

I scroll down. "What?"

"There's only six chapters, and then there's this weird iCloud link that's supposed to be to the rest of the story, but it goes to nowhere."

"What kind of setup is this?" I whisper angrily. "We find this stupid flash drive with all these half-finished stories on it, and it sends us down this stupid fucking Kindle hole, and now we don't get the end of the stories?"

"I know, bullshit."

"Listen, get into that iCloud and find the rest of this shit."

"I can't. I tried already."

"Get Henley on it."

"He tried too."

"Then go to a computer geek person, and get them to do it," I whisper.

The door bursts open. "Dr. Grayson, you're needed in room twelve," Judy tells me.

"Coming."

She disappears out the door. "Got to go," I tell Antony.

"Did you get to the part where he eats her out yet?"

"What?" I whisper. "With his fangs?"

"With his nine-inch tongue."

My eyes widen.

"Seriously . . . fuck. Ing. Hell."

"Get that fucking link open." I hang up, then stand up to get back to work.

Jeez . . . I need a cold shower.


*Rebecca*


I sit on the couch and peer through the curtains as I act casual, and by acting casual I mean I'm dressed in normal everyday house clothes as if this is just a normal day and Blake is coming over for a normal dinner. I'm not mentioning the hours-long primping session I had upstairs all afternoon. My hair is done, my makeup natural; I'm shaved and waxed to within an inch of my life, and my vacation spray tan has been well and truly activated.

Suitcase is packed, and my ducks are all in a row . . . at least, I hope they are.

I'm ready . . . well, as ready as I'll ever be.

I see headlights pull into the cul-de-sac, and my heart skips a beat. Blake's home.

My heart begins to thump in my chest . . . *Blake's home.*

Ahhhhhh.

Fucking Blake's home.

Suddenly I'm freaking out. I jump from the couch and run upstairs and look at myself in the mirror. "This is fine," I tell the nervous girl in the mirror. "You've got this." I turn and look at my behind in the mirror. "But do you really?" I reply to her.

I hear the front door open. "Hey," he calls from downstairs as he walks in.

*Shit.*

How do I get myself into these situations?

"I got Italian," he calls, and I hear him walk into the kitchen as he begins to unpack the food. "Where are you?"

I put my head into my hands and take a long, steadying breath.

I want this. More than anything I want this, and I know that I need to push through the nerves and get on with it. I drop my shoulders to prepare myself.

*Go.*

I walk downstairs to find Blake in the kitchen, pouring two glasses of wine. He's wearing a charcoal suit and a light-blue shirt. His hair is messed up, with a bit of a curl to it. He's the epitome of suit porn in all its glory.

"Hi." I smile nervously from the door.

His eyes rise to meet mine. "Hi." He gives me a slow, sexy smile as he steps toward me. He takes me into his arms and kisses me. "Hi." He smiles again.

"Hi," I breathe.

"You look lovely." His hands drop to my behind as his dark eyes roam up and down my body. "Like . . . really lovely."

"Blake, I'm wearing a tracksuit; you are very easily pleased." I try to act casual.

Ha . . . bingo.

The outfit is working. I looked in the shops for three hours for a not-trying hot tracksuit.

Seems that I nailed it.

He kisses me softly, his lips lingering over mine. "I've been looking forward to seeing you all day."

"How come?" I play dumb.

"Because then I get to eat pasta," he lies.

"Oh, you're here for the carbs?"

He gives me the best come-fuck-me look of all time. "I'm here for the meat."

302

A shiver runs down my spine as the air crackles between us.

"So I'm meat now?" I smirk.

"Among other things." His hungry eyes roam up and down my body as if imagining something.

I know exactly what he's imagining, because I'm imagining it too.

He kisses me again, this time with suction, and my feet nearly lift from the floor. "Did you put your piercing back in?" I smile against his lips.

He unzips his suit pants and pulls his boxers down. "You better check." He kisses me again as I slide my hand into his pants and feel his hard, engorged length.

*Oh . . .*

I slide down his shaft and feel the metal of the bar and then his tip. My hand slides through the pre-ejaculate that's beading on his end.

Fuck.

My body begins to thump with arousal.

I cup his balls as our kiss deepens, and then I wrap my hand around him and stroke him hard.

He slams me up against the fridge, and the contents rattle.

Suddenly we're desperate, kissing like animals. His hands are roaming all over my body as I jerk his cock with force. I glance over and catch sight of us in the mirror. He is still fully dressed in his suit as I ravage him.

It drives me further over the point of no return.

"Shower," he moans into my mouth. "A shower."

"The dinner . . . ," I pant back.

"Can wait." He takes my hand and pulls me up the stairs, and I would love to tell you that I am fully in control right now.

But I'm not.

My body is on a one-way ticket to Grand Central Station, and if the wind blows, I might just come.

With his eyes locked on mine, he grabs the bottom of my shirt and lifts it over my head, then puts his hands beneath the waistband of my pants and slides them down, and I step out of them. He throws them to the side, and I find myself standing before him in nothing but my underwear. Blake is still fully dressed in his suit. He circles me as if inspecting his meal; his dark eyes burn my skin as they roam up and down. "I've imagined seeing you naked again," he breathes.

The sound of my nervous heartbeat echoes through my ears.

"You have?" I whisper.

"Many times." He puts his finger under my chin and lifts my face so that his dark eyes meet mine. "But nothing could prepare me for how awestruck I would be."

I swallow the lump of fear in my throat. "I think you've got it the wrong way around," I whisper. "It's me who's awestruck."

He turns me away from him, and my heart hammers as he undoes my bra.

Every one of my senses is on fire.

His lips dust the side of my neck as his hands cup my breasts from behind. Not the gentle touch I was expecting. His hands knead my breasts aggressively, and it sends a shockwave through my system. Goose bumps scatter all over.

He sure knows his way around a woman's body. He puts his lips to my ear. "How does that feel?"

My breath quivers in excitement. "Good," I murmur.

His teeth graze my neck, and my eyes nearly roll back in my head. "How do you feel?" he whispers before biting me again.

I try to focus enough to form a coherent sentence.

"I'm nervous, I'm excited, I'm petrified . . . but in this moment, I am yours."

His hands still, and I close my eyes. *Why did I say that?*

"You've always been mine," he breathes into my ear. "From the first moment I met you, I knew we would end up here." He kisses down my neck to my shoulder.

I frown in confusion as I stare at the wall. "I was married when you met me."

I feel him smile against my skin. "Only so that he could bring you to me."

Goose bumps scatter again, and I turn toward him. "You wanted me when I was married?"

"I've wanted you every day since I met you . . . maybe even before that."

My eyes hold his.

"And if things didn't go to plan and he didn't mess it up . . ." He slides my panties down my legs. "I planned on stealing you from him."

*What?*

"You would have taken me from him?" I frown.

"In a heartbeat." He takes my face in his hands. "You were never really his." He kisses me softly.

"What makes you say that?" I whisper against his lips.

"Because you were always promised to me." Our kiss deepens. "You only married him so that you could find me." He takes my face in his two hands as we kiss, and my eyes flutter closed. "I've been waiting for you," he murmurs against my lips.

I feel my heart free-fall from my chest.

*Oh . . .*

Why does that feel like the most romantic thing I've ever heard?

I screw up my face against his as emotion overwhelms me. Dear god, how am I so attached to him in just one week?

This is a disaster.

I planned on being strong and tough and the woman in control. A few pretty words, and he has me believing we are soulmates.

"Stop talking, and start fucking," I snap as I act unaffected.

"Yes ma'am." He chuckles and takes my hand. I catch sight of us in the mirror. He's still fully dressed in his suit, and I'm completely naked.

Which is ironic . . . actually, it's symbolic, because he's completely in control while I'm just a lovesick fool.

We walk into my bedroom, and he kisses me once again. His tongue curls around mine with an intensity that I've never felt before. With every flutter of his tongue, I feel it between my legs.

"I need you," I breathe as I begin to lose control.

"I know." He pushes me back to the bed, lays me down, props me up on pillows, spreads my legs. Then, with his dark eyes fixed on mine, he slowly undoes his tie and slides it off.

I hold my breath as he unbuttons his shirt. His tanned skin and stomach ripples come into view, and I sit up onto my knees, wanting to touch him. "Come here."

He walks over to the edge of the bed, and I bend and kiss his stomach as he takes the shirt off over his shoulders. My hands roam over his skin as he kicks off his shoes and peels his socks off.

Suddenly I'm frantic. I need him naked, and I need it now.

I pull down his suit pants, and his cock springs free. It's hard, with thick veins coursing down the length of it. The piercing bar catches the light, and precome is dripping from the end. I'm shocked to silence.

*How is this man so physically perfect?*

I bend and kiss him there, and his hand goes tenderly to the back of my head. "Watch your teeth."

"Huh?" I glance up at him.

"Don't chip your teeth." His eyes dance with darkness.

Forget the stupid teeth, I'm about to rip out my tonsils.

I take him into my mouth and slide his girthy length down my throat as I stroke him.

He pants as he begins to lose control.

I take him deeper and deeper, and it's such a contradiction, new sensations all around. The metal among soft, velvety skin that covers a rock-hard erection.

His hands fist my hair, and he pushes himself deeper down my throat.

My body is dripping with excitement, and I smile around him. He likes it.

*I love it.*

"Enough," he growls as he bends and throws me back onto the bed. He spreads my legs and holds me open with his fingers and bends to lick me there.

I nearly jump from the mattress.

"Fuck," he moans into me. "You're so fucking wet." He sucks me deeper, and I nearly turn inside out. "You taste so good." His eyes are shut, and he's completely lost in the moment. His stubble burns me as he thrashes his head from side to side.

My feet lift into the air as I desperately battle to hold on to control, but I can't.

I'm hovering somewhere between heaven and ecstasy; he slides three fingers into me, and without warning, my body contracts into a tidal wave of an orgasm.

I cry out, shudder, and convulse as he holds me down and sucks it out of me.

His hooded eyes half close as he inhales every inch of me.

Perspiration dusts my skin as my sanity leaves the building. I've never had an orgasm like that before.

Blake Grayson doesn't go down on a woman for her pleasure; it's for his.

Primal mating, taken to feed his needs.

I pant hard as I lie back, and he gets up and goes to his suit.

"No condom," I say.

His eyes meet mine in question.

"I'm trusting you with my heart, so you're trusting me not to get pregnant."

We stare at each other for a beat, and I know that now is his time to freak out.

So be it . . . this is on him.

He can't tell me that I was always meant to be his and have no consequence.

You talk the talk, now walk the walk.

"It's okay, Blake," I murmur. "You know you can trust me."

His brow furrows, and then after a beat, he seems to come to an internal decision and crawls over me and spreads my legs with his knees.

*This is it.*

His lips take mine with reverence, and he kisses me softly as his cock nudges at my entrance. Having him so close like this is new and exciting. It feels so natural that I wonder how we haven't done this a million times before.

I can feel the cool tips of the piercing through the lips of my sex, and I hold my breath at the foreign sensation.

*Ohhhhhh . . .*

He pushes forward, and I feel the stretch as my body tries to resist him.

"It's okay," he whispers. "Let me in." He pushes forward again, and a burn stings my senses.

"Ahh." I wince.

"It's okay," he breathes again. "Relax, baby." He pushes forward with force, and I feel the tip of the piercing as it slides all the way home.

Deep inside of me.

"Oh," I moan. He's big. The girth of his cock is wide and leaves no room for doubt. My body ripples around him as she tries to deal with his size.

I frown as I look up at the ceiling over his shoulder. Is he really this big, or am I just really inexperienced right now?

He surges forward again, and the burn stings hard. He's here, and he's taking over my body, whether I like it or not.

I don't like it; I love it.

"Ahhh," I whimper.

"That's it." He smiles into my neck. "Let me hear you." He pumps me hard and knocks the air out of my lungs. "I want to hear you fucking moan."

My eyes roll back in my head, and just like he requested, my body lets out a deep, guttural moan. Once again, I feel him smile into my neck, and I find myself smiling too.

The man's a deviant.

He surges in deep, and I feel his piercing as it slides all the way in and drags all the way out. It's the weirdest sensation. It adds a whole new layer to the experience, or maybe it's just because it's Blake, and he's . . . well, from what I can see, he's the master of fucking.

The Fuck Master 100.

"I should make a model of your cock, complete with the piercing, and call it the Fuck Master 100 vibrator," I whisper up at him.

He breaks into a breathtaking smile as he pumps me. "This cock's just for you."

"I'm serious. We would make bank with this dick."

"If you can still talk, I'm not doing it right," he whispers darkly as he brings my legs up to around his chest. "How's this." He pumps me hard, and the bed creaks as it nearly breaks. He knocks every single piece of air out of my lungs, the sanity from my brain. "Try talking now."

I stare up at him in awe. My mouth hangs open in shock at the all-consuming sensation.

He's big and deep. His strong hands hold my legs back with force . . . and fucking hell, *is this what sex is supposed to be like?*

I feel insignificant to his power. This isn't an even game. I'm like a weak little petal being used for his pleasure. He's moving me how he wants me, taking me deep and uninhibited.

It's so hot that I can't stand it.

We get into a rhythm; my feet are up around his ears, and all I can feel is that damn piercing tickling my G-spot. Showing me exactly what it's there for. It's so . . .

Good lord, dick piercings should be mandatory for all men. I'm addicted.

"I . . ." My eyes flutter closed. "I can't . . . ohhhh," I moan.

"Hold it," he demands. "We haven't even fucking started."

His thick cock hits the right spot again and again, and I can't . . . "Ahhh." My toes curl, and I cry out as an orgasm tears through me. He fucks me through it with abandon.

Hard and thick.

The sound of our skin slapping together echoes around the room and . . . *fuck.*

Perspiration dusts my skin as he uses me.

His body is taking what it needs from mine, and I've never done this before.

This isn't sex.

This is an experience that every woman should have at least once in her life.

"Ohhh," he moans as his grip on my ankles gets harder, his pumps deeper, rougher. "That's it," he whispers. "Milk me," he whispers. "Give it to me."

I clench as hard as I can, and his eyes roll back in his head. He surges forward and holds himself deep. I feel the telling jerk of his cock as he comes deep inside my body.

The husky moan that leaves his body is a heavenly sound, and I smile up at the ceiling as angels sing in the distance.

I want to bottle this feeling, put a bookmark in time to come back to.

He falls down onto me, panting hard into the crook of my neck, and I hold him close.

We're both struggling for air, and intimacy is swimming between us.

I get a lump in my throat as I cling to him like my life depends on it.

I don't know what that was . . . but I'm officially ruined.


*Blake*


**I lie in the darkness and stare at the sleeping woman beside me.**

**Reeling from the events of tonight.**

**A vision runs through my mind of the two of us rolling around in the sheets.**

**The sound of her moans, the feeling in me . . . I've never . . . I swallow the lump in my throat as I try to process what the hell is going on here.**

**I knew we'd be good together mentally, but physically—I had no idea the level of connection we would reach. I mean,**

I'd heard people talk about it . . . but I always thought it was impossible.

Implausible, even utterly ridiculous.

And yet I lie here completely confused, because for the first time in my life, I'm sure.

Not just sure, I'm sold. I'm positive. This is a done deal . . . and as terrifying as this is, there's not a single doubt in my mind.

*Rebecca's the one.*

# Chapter 19

"So . . ." Antony raises his eyebrows. "How was it?"

"It was . . ." I smile dreamily. There are no words that accurately describe it.

We're at the mall. I need to pick up a few things, and then we're grabbing a quick lunch before I go away. The boys want a debrief of last night.

"So . . . ," Henley prompts me again.

"It was . . ." I put my hands in my pockets. "Incredible. She is . . ." I smile into the distance like a lovestruck schoolboy. "Seriously fucking wow."

"Look at you being all pathetic-like." Ant smiles as he slaps me on the back. "Good for you."

Henley gives me a halfhearted smile. "That's great, man."

"What's that look?" I ask as we get to the toiletries section.

"What look?" he asks.

"Yeah, I noticed that look too," Antony chimes in. "What's the problem?"

"I don't have a problem," Henley grumbles. "What are we looking for here?"

"I need a new toiletries bag." My eyes roam over the section. "I don't see a toiletries bag, but I do see something I need." I pick up a basket and walk over and take a bottle of lubricant off the shelf and throw it in.

"What's this for?" Antony digs it out of the basket and holds it in his hands as he looks it over.

"Overusage." I hold the basket out for him. "Put it back."

He inspects the bottle. "I never get why it's called lubricant and not lubricunt."

"That's a very good point." I smirk. "You should do a start-up."

"I'd buy it," Henley replies as he picks up some talcum powder and looks at it for a beat longer than normal.

"What?"

"This is the one Dad used."

I snatch it off him and throw it in my basket. "I'm buying it for you."

"I don't have sweaty balls."

"I beg to differ." I look around the store. "Where the hell are the toiletries bags?"

"Why do you need a new toiletries bag? Don't you have a ton of them, like everyone else?"

"I want a new one." I keep looking around. "I'm doing everything new from here on out." I pick up some deodorant and throw it into my basket. We look around some more.

"What time do you leave?"

"Flight's at three." I smile. "I can hardly wait to get there."

Antony smiles. "I like you like this."

"Calm down, Romeo." Henley sighs, unimpressed. "It's been one night."

"One perfect night," I correct him.

"I think he's been with enough women to know if something feels right," Antony replies. "The entire romantic world isn't doom and gloom, you know, Hen?" He throws his hands up. "What are you talking about, anyway? Look at you and Juliet. I mean, if you found someone to love your grumpy ass as much as she does, that proves there is definitely hope for the two of us. And now . . . with the baby coming." He squeezes Henley's traps and shakes his shoulders. "Big Daddy."

Henley rolls his eyes. "I'm just saying, take it slow."

"You go as fast as you need to." Antony elbows me with a smirk. "Don't listen to the grinch."

"I'm not, don't worry." I pick up some shampoo and throw it into my basket.

"Okay, what else do you need?" Antony asks as he looks around.

"I need to learn how to be romantic."

"Impossible." Henley looks at me deadpan.

"It's not impossible."

"Look it up in the dictionary, then."

"It's in the dictionary?" I frown as we walk between the shelves.

"Yes." He keeps walking in front. "It's in between the words *stupid* and *gullible*."


*Rebecca*

I bend down to zip my suitcase, and I feel a throb deep inside. My body is tender this morning, suffering the consequences of our rough night.

Images of Blake on top of me come floating through my mind. My legs were up around his shoulders, his cock so deep that I felt every single inch that he gave me.

*The look on his face as he came.*

I smirk to myself; I can still feel that damn piercing, and good lord . . . *it was good.* Who am I kidding: it wasn't good.

It was fucking phenomenal.

And now I get him all to myself for an entire week. I smile as I keep zipping up my suitcase.

Things couldn't be going any better.

Before he left this morning, he thought I was asleep. I could feel him looking me over as he lay beside me. He pulled the blankets up over me and tucked me in before softly kissing my forehead and whispering for me to have a good day.

*My heart.*

I knew we'd get along because of how strong our friendship is, but the physical side of us has blown me away. I never dreamed it would be this good or that he would be so tuned in to what my body needs.

To be honest, I don't know if it's because I haven't been with someone for so long or because I've just never had this level of connection before.

It feels different.

Like a storybook kind of swoony, the feelings I've been searching for.

*Have a good day.* I hear his whispered words again as they play in my head, and I glance at my watch.

Two hours until I get to see him.


The Porsche pulls up out front, and from my place at the window, I bounce up and down. I race back into the kitchen and check myself out in the reflection of the oven.

*Knock, knock.*

"Come in," I call.

The door opens, and there he stands, all six foot three of heavenly man. He gives me a slow, sexy smile. "There she is."

"Hi." I beam.

"Hi." He steps forward and takes me into his arms. His lips gently take mine. "Are you ready for Cancún?"

"I am." I smile as his lips drop to my neck. His hands go to my behind, and he drags me onto him. "Stop doing that, or we are going to miss our plane," I murmur as he gets rougher with his neck kissing.

"I'm just getting you ready for the plane."

I giggle as I try to pull out of his arms. "I don't need to be turned on for a plane ride, Blake."

"I need my girl turned on all the time."

My eyes meet his.

*His girl.*

A thrill of excitement rushes through me. I really need to get a handle on this fangirling; it's getting out of hand.

"My bags are here." I grab my suitcase, and he takes it off me. "Anything else?"

"Nope." I grab my handbag and follow him out the door. "Did you water your plants?" I ask as we walk to his car.

"Yes, Mom, did you?" He smirks as he puts my suitcase in the trunk.

"Yes, Dad."

We smile stupidly at each other, as if this is the best thing that ever happened to us.

*Maybe it is.*

We get into the car, and he grabs my hand and puts it on his thick quad muscle as he drives. He chats away, and every now and then, he mindlessly picks up my hand and kisses my fingertips while I try my hardest to act cool.

*Is this really happening?*

*This is already the best vacation of my life.*


"This is the captain speaking. We are preparing for landing. I trust you've had a pleasant trip, and thank you for flying with us today."

I smile over at my travel partner, and he gives me a sexy wink. Blake and I have drunk way too much champagne, and we've laughed and flirted for the entire six-hour flight.

"I still can't believe we flew business class," I lean over and whisper.

"I can't believe you've only ever flown coach." He widens his eyes.

I sit back in my seat as my mind returns to my marriage and the way things were. We never flew business; we never went to fancy restaurants or took exotic vacations. And it's not like we didn't have money; John was a top-paid surgeon with a giant family trust fund. We just never did anything that would spend unnecessary money, and at the time, I thought it was because we were being wise and saving for a rainy day. Now I know better—we were just saving for John's mistresses' bank account. The one he used to wine and dine his side pieces.

I've since found out that all those conference trips he went on were actually a cover for taking them on exotic holidays, and I'd bet my life they flew business. They went to the fancy restaurants that we weren't allowed to go to because it was stupid to spend that much on dinner.

Looking back on all his betrayal, knowing that he treated them with more respect and took them to better places than me was the information that hurt me the most.

He was happy to spend money on a random chick and yet was a tight-ass with the one woman who was desperately in love with him.

The person he was supposed to love the most—his wife.

Blake reaches over and takes my hand in his, pulling me out of the sad memory, and I smile over at him. "Where are we staying?" I ask.

"Somewhere fabulous."

The car pulls into a grand driveway, and I peer through the front window. The gardens are immaculate, and flaming torches light up the sweeping driveway. Men in white suits stand around the huge fancy doors of the sandstone building.

"My god," I whisper. "What is this place?"

"I hope it lives up to its reputation." Blake looks around and shrugs. "So far, so good."

The car comes to a stop, and the doorman opens my car door. "Good evening." He smiles.

"Thank you." I smile as I climb out, and a flurry of men begin to unload our luggage from the car.

"This way to reception," another man tells Blake.

"Thank you." He takes my hand and leads me through the foyer. My eyes are wide. "I've never seen anything so beautiful."

"I have." Blake gives me a soft smile as he cups my face.

Butterflies dance in my stomach. He's so dreamy.

We walk up to the desk. "Hello, we are checking in, please. The name is Blake Grayson."

"Hello, Mr. Grayson." The man smiles at both of us as he types on his computer. "My name is Allan, and I'll be looking after you today. Yes, here we are. We have you staying in the penthouse for six nights?"

"That's right." Blake nods.

*The penthouse.*

I bite my bottom lip to hide my smile, and Blake puts his arm around me and kisses my temple.

"I'll be back in one moment, sir; I just have to collect your keys from the back," Allan says.

"Sure." Blake kisses my temple again.

"You are so affectionate in public," I whisper, half-embarrassed.

"Why wouldn't I be? I'm proud of my girl." His hand slides down my arm, and he holds my hand up as his eyes drop down my body. "I mean . . . look at her."

*Oh . . .*

Allan returns with the keys. "This way. Mr. Grayson. I'll show you to your room."

"Thank you."

We follow him along the corridor and out through a fancy garden with a water feature and down a secluded path. "You have a private infinity pool with your own twenty-four-hour butler." The sound of the ocean is getting louder and louder the closer we get. It must be right on the water.

I hunch my shoulders up in excitement, and Blake's eyes dance with delight.

We get to the end of a pathway and go up some stairs. He unlocks the door, and my mouth falls open. Floor-to-ceiling glass overlooks the ocean; the furniture is all in creams, and the furnishings are luxurious.

"Wow," I gasp.

"The pool is out here." He leads us out onto the deck. "There's a spa, and the phone inside is for your butler. Call him anytime, twenty-four hours; he is at your service."

I look around as my mouth falls open. "This is stunning," I whisper in awe.

"You like it?" Blake rocks up onto his toes, as if proud of himself.

"I love it." He takes me into his arms and kisses me.

"Is there anything else I can help you with, sir?" Allan says.

Blake's lips stay locked on mine, and he waves his arm at Allan. Allan smiles and leaves us alone.

I stare up at my beautiful man. "You're spoiling me," I whisper.

He takes my face in his hands. "Get used to it."


"You nearly ready, Bec?" Blake calls.

"Just a minute." I hold the curling iron as I finish up my hair. It's taken longer than I expected. I had to curl it; with the humidity, it's taken on a mind of its own. Frizzy doesn't come close to what I'm dealing with here. I glance at myself in the mirror. I'm wearing a strapless, fitted coral dress and sky-high stilettoes. I wanted to be in the Cancún frame of mind and wear something colorful and happy.

I keep holding the iron as I try to curl the last piece. "Rebecca," Blake calls. "We're going to be late, babe."

"Coming," I call as I pull my fingers through my hair to try and calm it down.

Blake comes into view. He's wearing a black dinner suit and a crisp white shirt with a black bow tie. His sandy hair has a messed-up curl to it, and his jaw looks like it could cut glass.

I don't know if I've ever seen any man look so gorgeous.

He leans on the doorframe as his eyes roam up and down my body. "Wow . . . ," he murmurs, almost to himself.

My stomach flutters at his reaction. "Do I look okay?"

He gives me a slow, sexy smile and walks around me, as if sizing up his next meal. Without saying a word, he drops to his knees in front of me. He slides his hands up my thighs, pulling my dress up along with it. "You look . . ." He nuzzles my sex through my lace G-string. "Edible." He pulls my panties to the side and kisses me there. His eyes close in reverence, and he lifts one of my legs up over his shoulder as his kiss deepens. His tongue rolls through my lips, and I grip his shoulders to keep my balance.

I catch sight of us in the mirror, and my hands tousle through his hair.

*Oh . . .*

Fuck.

"You're so fucking beautiful, I can't stand it," he whispers into me; his teeth graze my clitoris, and I shudder.

"I'm going to come if you don't stop doing that," I murmur as I hold his head to me.

*Don't stop.*

His thick tongue strengthens its assault, and I shudder again. "Blake," I murmur.

"Yeah, baby?" He looks up at me from his knees. His lips are glistening with my arousal, and his big brown eyes are dark and dangerous. "You want me to stop?"

I swallow the lump in my throat as I stare down at him.

"What do you want, Rebecca?"

"I . . ."

"Tell me what you want," he demands in a whisper.

"I want to come."

"On my face?" His eyebrow rises in that sexy way it does. "In my mouth."

"Yes." I nod.

He gives me a slow, sexy smile. "Good girl." He licks me so deep that my toes curl. "I like it when you ask for what you want." He latches on and sucks me hard.

*Oh . . .*

My footing falters, and I sway on my one stiletto.

How is he so good at this?

He smiles into me as he flutters his tongue, and I see stars as I throw my head back. He does it again and again until I can't stand it anymore, and I plunge into the abyss.

The strongest orgasm I have ever had hits me hard, and I cry out. The sound of my scream echoes on the tiles around us.

He sucks me through it, then stands and bends me over the basin and pulls my dress up higher.

Somewhere in the arousal fog, I hear his pants unzip, and then I feel him slide his cock deep into my body. "I need you." He lifts one of my legs and puts it onto the basin beside us. We stare at each other in the mirror. His knees are bent as he fucks me hard. Fast and furious, as if we are fighting against the clock, as if we shouldn't be doing this.

My breasts bounce in my dress with every thrust, and this wasn't in the plan.

He turns my head and kisses me deeply as his hips fuck me at a piston pace. I can feel him swelling, getting harder and harder.

*This feeling between us . . .*

"Oh . . . ," he moans. "Fuuuuuck." He holds himself deep, and I feel the telling jerk of his cock as his hands grip my hip bones at an almost painful strength.

Our kiss turns tender, and our eyes are closed as we get lost in the moment.

It's unhurried and sacred.

A sweet moment between us, his hard body still deep inside mine, but the beast inside has been temporarily tamed.

"We're going to be late," I whisper against his lips.

"Do I look like I care?" He smiles.

"We have to shower." I pull out of his grip and step back.

"We don't have time."

"I am *not* meeting your mother smelling like sex, Blake."

He chuckles. "It's the priest you need to worry about."

"Blake." I laugh. "Stop."

"You're totally going to catch on fire in the church."

"Coming from you, that's a joke."

"Yes, it is, coming from me." He lifts my dress over my head. "Make sure you tell him that." I stand before him in my white lace underwear. His eyes drop down my body, and then when they rise to meet my eyes, they are blazing with arousal again. "Tell that priest how creamy and wet you are." He licks his lips. "Tell him how good you taste." He puts his hand around my throat and pushes me up against the wall.

The dominance of the act sends my hormones into overdrive. Adrenaline screams through my bloodstream as we stare at each other.

*Dear lord.*

Forgive me, Father, for I have sinned.


The car pulls up at the church, and I look around at the gathering crowd. Everyone is dressed to the nines, and people are laughing and chatting as they see each other. Lots of greetings between long-lost family and friends.

I'm not feeling so brave now.

"Just here," Blake instructs the driver. The driver pulls over and parks the car. Blake climbs out and then holds his hand out to help me. I give him a nervous smile.

"What?" He frowns.

"Do you know everyone here?" I ask as I climb out of the car.

"No idea." He looks across the road at the church and all the people. "Not everyone." He takes my hand in his. "Ready to meet my family?"

I swallow the lump in my throat and nod. "As ready as I'll ever be."

We walk across the road, and as we get closer, people turn to watch us.

"Oh my god," someone pretends to whisper. "Blake brought a date."

"Subtle." Blake winces. "My cousins are a nightmare with no idea how to whisper."

I get the giggles; all families are the same.

"My apologies in advance. We can leave as soon as the speeches finish." He frowns as he pulls me through the crowd.

"It's fine." I smile. It really is fine. The fact that his family is just like mine is somehow comforting.

"Hello." He nods to people as he leads me along. "Hello, Aunt Patty." He kisses her cheek. "This is Rebecca."

"Hello." I smile.

"Well . . ." Aunt Patty looks me up and down. "Aren't you just adorable."

"I love your dress," I tell her.

"Thank you. I have been dieting for a whole year to fit into it." She puts her hands on her hips. "I've been going to WeightWatchers on Tuesday mornings at the basketball center. It costs a bomb, but I really do think it's worth it because I couldn't do it by myself. Frank tells me I could save my money, but what does he know?" She gives me an overexaggerated wink.

Blake's brow creases as he stares at her, and I bite my lip to hide my smile.

"Catch you later, Aunty Patty," he tells her as he leads me through the crowd some more. "My family are abominable oversharers," he says over his shoulder. "Please forget everything you see or hear here."

"Oh," someone cries. "My shoes are giving me blisters already." I glance over to see a young girl, perhaps fourteen, all dressed up in a pretty dress with high heels. She's holding one of her shoes in her hand. "Does anyone have a Band-Aid?" she calls.

People begin scrambling through their purses, and my heart swells.

"Classy," he mutters dryly. "Hello, Belinda." He kisses the young girl. "This is Rebecca."

"Hello." She smiles as she holds her shoe. "You don't happen to have a Band-Aid, do you?"

Blake plays along and pretends to pat his pockets down. "I'm afraid not."

She turns to her mother. "I told you I shouldn't wear these stupid shoes."

"Blake!" her mother screeches as she looks him up and down. "My darling, you look so handsome."

"Hi, Aunt Thelma." He kisses her cheek. "This is Rebecca, my girlfriend."

*Girlfriend.*

"Ohhh." Her eyes widen to the size of saucers. "You're official now?" She pulls me into a bear hug. "Oh, welcome to the family, you sweet child. It will be your wedding next—don't let him get away. Will you, dear?"

Blake pinches the bridge of his nose, and I bubble up a giggle at his mortification.

Blake Grayson, the suave and sophisticated playboy, has an embarrassing family, and quite honestly, it's the best thing I've ever seen.

"What am I going to do about these stupid shoes?" the young girl interrupts. "Does anyone even care about the pain I'm in?"

"Not really, dear," her mother replies as she keeps her eyes on me.

"Where's Mom and Dad?" Blake asks as he looks around.

"Not sure," she says as she looks around too. "Your sister Catherine has a problem with her SPANX."

Blake frowns. "What kind of problem?"

"I don't know," she huffs. "Her dress is sticking to them and riding up or something. Your father went to find some hand cream from the corner shop."

"Good grief." Blake rolls his eyes. "What next?"

"Oh," I interrupt. "Blake, you should call your dad to pick up some Band-Aids for Belinda while he's there."

"Good point." He takes out his phone and dials the number.

"Oh . . . you're smart too." Thelma smiles all-knowingly. "I can see why he's so smitten."

I force a smile. Remembering Band-Aids for a child who can hardly walk isn't what I'd call smart . . . but I'll take it anyway.

Two hands snake around my waist from behind, and Blake laughs over my shoulder when he sees who they belong to. "Hi, Mom."

I turn to see a woman. She's short and curvy, with the most beautiful smile. Her hair is sandy brown, and she has Blake's eyes. "Rebecca?" She smiles.

"Yes."

She kisses my cheek, and she has the most gentle energy. I instantly feel at ease. "This is my mom, Rosemary." Blake hugs her.

"Hello." I smile. "I can see the family resemblance."

"You are divine." She holds my two arms. "I'm half in love with you already."

"Calm down, Mom." Blake widens his eyes, and I get the giggles.

"Oh, I've missed you, darling. I haven't seen you for weeks." She turns and hugs him again.

"I know, I'm sorry," he replies. "I've been working long hours."

*Taking photos of my feet.*

Guilt fills me. I need to stop being so demanding of his time.

Blake looks around. "Where are the girls?"

"Over here." His mom takes his hand and leads us through the crowd. "This way."

"What about my foot?" Belinda demands as she hobbles along behind us with her shoe in her hand. "Nobody cares about my feet."

"You got that right," Blake whispers under his breath.

Rosemary crosses her eyes.

I get the giggles again, and something tells me that Belinda is the drama queen of the family. We walk around to the side and see three girls standing together. "Here they are." Rosemary smiles.

Blake kisses and hugs each one. "Rebecca, these are my sisters, Catherine, Aubrey, and Emery."

"Hello." They all smile and shake my hand one by one.

"It's so lovely to meet you." Blake hugs each one, and they all begin to chatter.

I'm shocked. These girls aren't what I expected at all. Blake is so handsome and suave that I just assumed his family would be the same way. I expected glamour models and judgment and feeling inadequate.

They're a million times better than anything I ever imagined.

Pretty, curvy, and warm. Catherine is tall, and Emery is short. Aubrey is about my height. They look like normal girls; they feel welcoming and happy.

"It's so lovely to meet you," Catherine says as she takes my hand in hers. "We've been waiting for what seems like forever."

From the corner of my eye, I see Blake doing a tone-it-down signal with his hand behind my back.

"There you are," a man's voice says from behind. We all turn to see an older man approaching us. He's tall and handsome, with salt-and-pepper hair: Blake's twin.

"Your dad?" I smile.

"How'd you guess?" Rosemary smiles. "Twins, huh?"

"My god, you're so alike." I laugh.

"In personality too." Rosemary smiles as her eyes linger on her husband. "Luckiest girl in the world, I am."

"I got you some cream," he says as he hands the bag over to Catherine.

"Thank you," she says. "Hopefully this works."

His eyes come to me. "You must be Rebecca?"

"I am."

He holds his hand out to shake mine. "I'm Blake. It's lovely to meet you."

"Blake too?" I ask in surprise.

"They couldn't think of another name." My Blake rolls his eyes.

I smile. A weird sense of serendipity falls over me, and a few things click into place.

Blake Grayson Sr. is handsome and suave and everything that I imagine Blake's father would be. And yet he loves a normal woman and has normal daughters. He's normal; it's only his outside that seems different.

Is that the same for my Blake?

Have I been reading him wrong all along?

Aubrey links her arm through mine. "Let's go inside."

"Okay." I smile.

Emery links her arm through my other arm. "Off we go."

"What about me?" Blake calls from behind us.

"You get to see Rebecca every day, Blake. Tonight it's our turn."


"And then I dated an artist," Aubrey continues. "But he was all into creating and earthly experiences, and that's great, you know? But when he's too broke to buy a cup of coffee, and your entire relationship is based around what restaurant he won't go to because it's too expensive, what's the frigging point?" She sips her champagne. "We couldn't even go to McDonald's without him whining about the price."

"Ugh, that doesn't sound fun." I wince. I glance up into Blake's stare. He's sitting back in his chair with a glass of red wine in his hand as he watches me chat with his sisters. He's wearing his black dinner suit, his hair has a bit of a curl to it, and he's giving me the best come-fuck-me look of all time.

I smile shyly as I sip my champagne, knowing exactly what he's thinking about. I turn back to Aubrey to try and pretend to listen to what she's telling me. But who can concentrate when Blake Grayson is looking at you like the devil himself?

*He's so naughty.*

You know those moments in life where you pinch yourself because things are going so well?

I'm in the middle of one right now.

Blake's family is perfect—absolutely and utterly perfect.

His mom is friendly, his sisters are divine, and his father, well . . . let's just say he's a silver fox.

The man is ridiculously hot.

And kind and gentle and everything that I admire in a person.

His aunts and uncles and cousins, well, they're all a little kooky, but I think that's standard with extended families, isn't it?

Not weird kooky, just embarrassing kooky, and I have to say I find it all the more endearing.

"Oh my god, then she went out with a firefighter," Emery chimes in. "And he used to come over to Mom and Dad's without a shirt on."

"No." I laugh. "Surely not."

"It's true." Rosemary nods before breaking into a smirk. "I mean, it wasn't all bad. He was very easy on the eyes."

"Mom!" everyone cries, and I laugh. Oh, I love this woman.

Blake stands and comes around to my chair. "Dancing?"

"We're talking, Blake," Aubrey snaps.

"I would like to spend five minutes with my girl, if that's okay with you," he fires back. "Get your own date."

*His girl.*

I smile and put my hand in his, and he leads me to the dance floor and takes me into his arms. The string quartet is playing, and the music is floating through the room. "My beautiful witch." He smiles down at me.

"What?" I frown.

"Well, everyone you meet seems to be bewitched."

I smile up at my handsome date. "There's only one person I want to bewitch."

His eyes hold mine, and the air crackles between us.

"And who is that?" He plays along.

"Well . . . he's tall and handsome and kind and smart."

He smiles over the crowd on the dance floor. "Keep going. This is doing wonders for my confidence."

"And when he looks at me, I get all the goose bumps."

He leans in close and puts his mouth to my ear. "And how's his dick?"

I giggle in surprise. "I have no idea."

He pulls back to look at my face, puzzled.

"I'm talking about Blake Grayson Sr."

"My father?" he gasps as he pokes me in the ribs, and I laugh out loud. "You wound me."

"I'm joking." I laugh. "I'm joking."

He jerks me closer with his hand as a pretend punishment.

"How's his dick?" I repeat his question.

He smiles mischievously. "Yes."

"Incredible . . . I never knew sex could be so good." I smile up at my handsome date. "You are giving me quite the education."

His eyes darken as he stares at me. "Then we should go home and pound that pussy."

I burst out laughing. "So romantic, Dr. Grayson."

He spins me out and pulls me back in as I laugh out loud. "You have no idea." He pulls me closer, and his lips meet mine. We kiss tenderly, and he smiles down at me.

"Thanks for coming with me." His eyes roam over the crowded dance floor. "I know weddings are . . ."

"Fun." I beam up at him.

"Interesting." He kisses me again. "Let's sneak out of here."

I look around. "It's not over yet, though. How do we sneak out of here?"

"You go to the bathroom, and I'll go and tell my family that I have a headache."

"Right." I frown as I listen.

"You come back from the bathroom, and I'll ask you if we can leave."

"Ahh, so your family can't blame me." I tap my temple. "Smart."

"My family won't blame you, but I don't want you to hear me tell them we are going home to pound pussy."

I bubble up a giggle. "Please don't."

With one last lingering kiss, he releases me, and I make my way out of the ballroom and into the foyer to the ladies' bathroom. I push through the heavy doors and look at my flushed face in the mirror. A surprised smile covers my face.

I look carefree and happy. I haven't seen myself look this way for so long.

I float into the stall and sit down on the toilet. I hear the door bang as someone else walks in.

"Hey, did you see Blake on the dance floor just now with his date?"

My ears prick up. *Are they talking about us?*

"Who is she?" another woman asks.

"Oh my god, it's so juicy," the first woman replies. "She was married to his friend, and he stole her from him."

My eyes widen. Fuck. They are talking about us.

"What?" the second girl gasps. "So they had an affair?"

"Probably." The first girl snorts. "You know Blake—he always wants what he can't have."

I listen intently.

"He looks pretty smitten to me," the second girl replies, and I hear the toilet flush.

"Ha, give it time," she replies. "As if a washed-up divorcée could ever hold him. What idiot would throw away a marriage for a player?"

My heart sinks as I hear the tap turn on.

"Hey, it's Blake Grayson. I would throw away everything for just one night with him."

She laughs. "As would the entire female population." I hear the paper towel dispenser turn on. "Your time will come; he'll be single again in three months."

"I'm totally making my move on him at Ally's wedding."

"Definitely." I hear the door open. "Maybe I should call him before . . ."

"You should . . ."

The voices float into the distance as they leave.

Wow.

My breath quivers as I try to hold it together, and hot, caustic tears well in my eyes as I stare at the back of the door.

*As if a washed-up divorcée could ever hold him.*

I angrily swipe the tears from my eyes.

She's right.

What the fuck am I doing?

# Chapter 20

I stare out the window of the cab as the nightlife of Cancún flies by. Blake is holding my hand on his lap and happily chatting away.

*As if a washed-up divorcée could ever hold him.*

He picks up my hand and kisses my fingertips, and I drag my eyes to meet his. He smiles softly. I swallow the lump in my throat, fake a smile, and go back to staring out the window. My heart is racing. I feel hot and clammy, and a million emotions are rushing through me at top speed.

Suddenly I'm claustrophobic, and I just want to go home.

I want to run as far away from him and this place as I possibly can.

And I know that it was just some random girl from the bathroom whose opinion means nothing. I shouldn't care at all what she thinks, but let's be honest, she was only saying what everyone else is thinking.

"So tomorrow after we have breakfast with my family, we should hire a car and go sightseeing," Blake says.

I nod.

"Is there anything you particularly want to see while we're here?"

*As if a washed-up divorcée could ever hold him.*

My stomach churns.

"Not really," I murmur.

"You okay, babe?" He rubs my shoulder. "You've gone quiet."

*Don't be a drama queen.*

"Just . . ." I frown. "Not feeling well."

"What's wrong?" he asks softly.

"My stomach is churning," I lie. "Maybe the spicey entrée."

He chuckles and puts his mouth to my ear. "Maybe all that spicy dick you've been eating."

I smile sadly. Only he could make me smile when I'm feeling so crappy. "Most probably."

What's wrong with me?

Can't I just live in the moment for one fucking minute?

The lump in my throat begins to hurt, and tears threaten. I turn toward the window to shield my face from him.

It was a random girl who doesn't even know us . . . Why the hell has it upset me so much?

*Because deep down, I know it's true.*

The car pulls up at our hotel, and we climb out. Blake takes my hand in his, and we walk through reception. I notice the two girls at reception check him out, and I glance over at him. Tall, handsome, and dressed in a black dinner suit with an undone bow tie, he really does stand out. It's no wonder he garners so much attention. I don't blame them; I'd check him out too.

He's totally oblivious, and as we get into the elevator, he puts his arm around me and pulls me close. "I'll make you a cup of tea when we get to our room." He kisses my temple again. "Tea fixes everything."

*I wish.*

"Okay." I force a smile, and once again, tears threaten.

Ugh . . .

*What the hell is wrong with me?*

We get to our room, and Blake heads straight to the kitchen. I'm not actually lying.

I don't feel well.

My stomach is churning so hard that it's actually making me sick.

"Now, where would I be if I were a kettle?" Blake talks to himself as he opens and closes all the cupboards.

"I'm going to take a rain check," I tell him. "You have your tea, and take your time. I just need to shower and go to bed."

"You okay?" He frowns down at me as he pulls me into his arms.

"Yeah." I kiss him softly. "I'm sorry."

"Don't be."

"Take your time."

"Is that code for you want to be sick in private?" He smirks.

"Yes," I murmur.

"Got you." He releases me out of his arms. "You go be sick in private." He turns me away from him. "Call me if you need me." He taps my behind. "I'm right here for you."

"Okay." I march up the stairs as my caustic tears break the dam, and I rush into the bedroom, close the door, and lean up against it.

Just one week.

It's taken him exactly one week to break down my walls and for me to have deep feelings for him. I get a vision of us laughing and cuddling . . . making love.

I can't go through a betrayal again; I won't survive it.

The thought rolls my stomach, and I dry retch and run to the bathroom. I open the lid on the toilet and fall to my knees in front of it.

In silence, alone, poisoned by insecurity, I throw up again and again.


The bed dips as Blake climbs out of it, and I drag my eyes open.

I think I've slept all of an hour.

"Hey." I rub my eyes.

"Hey." Blake smiles as he sits on the bed beside me. "How are you feeling?"

"I'm okay."

He brushes the hair back from my face. "You don't have to come to breakfast with my family if you don't want."

"No. I want to." I sit up onto my elbows and look around the room. "What time did you come to bed? I didn't hear you come in."

That's an appalling lie. I pretended to be asleep when he came to bed, and only once I was lying safely in his arms could I finally relax.

What does that say about me? Pretending to be asleep to avoid him but only being able to relax once he's wrapped around me.

I'm an actual psychopath.

I can feel myself being one, and yet I have no control over my thought processes.

"What time do we have to be there?" I ask.

"Half hour."

"Okay, I'll get ready."

He goes to kiss me, and I pull out of his grip and stand. "Can you make me a cup of tea, babe?" I ask.

"Okay." His eyes hold mine, as if knowing something is wrong. "What?"

He raises an eyebrow. "What, what?"

"Tea?"

"You got it." He stands and walks out of the room, and I close my eyes and internally kick myself.

He should run while he can.


"So . . ." Rosemary smiles into her coffee. "What are you two going to do all week?"

"The question is what aren't we going to do." Blake winks across the table at me.

His sisters all laugh, and his dad nudges me with his elbow with a chuckle.

I force a smile.

The morning has been happy and jovial.

Blake's family are beautiful people, and yet I've sat here all through breakfast feeling like an outsider. I mean, what's the point of getting attached to them?

Just more people to lose.

They chat and laugh, and I stare into space a million miles away.

Coming here was a mistake.

Falling for Blake was the monumental mistake of all mistakes.

Now the worst possible scenario is going to come into play.

I'm going to lose him as a friend, which is something that I never, ever wanted to do.

It's only early days. Hopefully we can . . . be civil about this and retain our friendship.

I imagine a life without him in it, and my heart constricts.

So dumb, Rebecca.

"Okay, well, we should get going," his father says. "Our plane isn't going to wait for us."

We all stand, and everyone says their goodbyes. Rosemary pulls me into her arms. "Have the best week, darling."

"I will." I hug her a little bit tighter.

*It was nice nearly knowing you.*

"Have a safe flight home." I smile. I hug his sisters and then his father, and as they walk off into the distance, I'm left alone with Blake. I glance up, and he raises an unimpressed eyebrow.

"What?"

Huh?

"Are you still unwell?"

"I'm fine."

"Were you ever unwell?"

"What does that mean?" I fire back.

"Just that I know you, and I know that something is bothering you, and I would like to know what it is."

"Stop being so dramatic." I roll my eyes.

"So let me get this straight—you're telling me that there is nothing wrong with you?"

"Open your ears." I'm getting annoyed now.

"What the fuck was that, then?" he mutters under his breath.

"What do you mean?" I frown.

"You said two words through a two-hour breakfast and faked about two hundred smiles."

"I'm just . . ." I stop myself before I say something I'm going to regret.

"You just what?" He raises his eyebrow in question. "Spit it out."

I'm taken aback by his aggression; I haven't seen this side of him before.

"I'm sorry. I wasn't aware I had to"—I raise my fingers to air quote—"entertain."

His eyes hold mine before he turns and storms off.

*What?*

I march after him. "What are you doing?"

"Going back to the hotel." He walks ahead, and I nearly run to catch up with him.

"You're angry because I didn't talk through breakfast?" I scoff.

He keeps walking.

"Because damn it, if I had known, I would have juggled the salt and pepper shakers to be more interesting."

He rolls his eyes and keeps walking.

"Will you slow down," I snap as I run to keep up.

"Get your own cab back to the hotel."

"What?" I stop on the spot. "Why?"

"I don't share cabs with liars."

"Are you serious?" I'm infuriated.

I'm the one who's angry here, fucker . . . there are no prizes for second.

"How am I a liar?" I snap.

"Oh please." He rolls his eyes. "Do *not* insult my intelligence, Rebecca. Something is bothering you. Do not tell me otherwise." He holds his arm up for a cab, and I stand awkwardly beside him.

I can feel the animosity radiating out of him. Huh . . . Who knew?

Blake Grayson is feisty.

Not sure I like this side one little bit.

"Be careful, Blake."

In slow motion, his head turns toward me, and his eyes widen. "Did you really just say that?"

I wither a little.

Okay, maybe too far.

A cab pulls up, and he gets in and goes to shut the door behind him.

*Is he fucking serious?*

"I'm coming," I snap. He begrudgingly slides over, and I climb in behind him and slam the door shut. He glares out the window as we drive in silence. Why the hell is he so angry? I wasn't rude to his family . . . shit, was I?

Ugh, maybe I was.

Damn it, I thought I was hiding it well.

We ride in silence, and finally the car pulls to a stop at our hotel. He climbs out and turns to take my hand while I climb out, and then he drops it like a hot potato and turns and marches inside.

I fume all over again.

341

I follow him down the corridor and stand to the side while he opens the door, and then I storm past him into the room. I throw my bag down onto the table. "I don't know what your problem is."

He slams the door shut. "You're my fucking problem."

"Me?" I point to my chest. "*I'm* the problem?"

"I'm going to ask you one more time and one more time only. And if you dare fucking lie to me, I'll drive you to the airport right now." He puts his hands on his hips. "What *is* the matter with you, Rebecca?"

"Firstly . . ." I put my hands on my hips too. "Don't you dare threaten to take me to the airport. I have no idea who you think you are, but you do not get to speak to me like this. I'll drive myself to the fucking airport, thank you."

We glare at each other, animosity bouncing between us.

"You didn't answer my question," he growls.

"You want the truth?" I throw up my hands in defeat. "Fine. I don't think we should have started seeing each other."

"And why is that?"

"I just . . ." I pause as I try to articulate myself properly. "I liked how things were, and I think we're better off that way."

His eyes hold mine.

"I adore you, Blake, and I just think . . . we're better off as friends."

"So . . . what?" He purses his lips. "You don't like me?"

"Not like that."

He smirks and picks up my handbag and passes it to me. "That's the first and last time you'll lie to me. Get out."

My mouth falls open in shock. "What?"

"Get. Out," he growls. "I don't know much about anything, but I do know that you are lying, and if you haven't got the guts to tell me what your fucking problem is, then there's no point."

Anger wins. "You want to know my problem?" I spit. "I'll tell you what my fucking problem is. I went to the bathroom last night and heard two women talking about how there's no way in hell that a washed-up divorcée could ever hold you and that it's only a matter of time before you dump me."

He puts his weight onto his back foot, physically taken aback.

"And it got me thinking about our situation and how they are completely right. It *is* only a matter of time before you break up with me, and I'm not prepared to get my heart broken, so I'm saving you the trouble."

"You fucking coward." He sneers.

"What?" I explode.

"The only person who is in danger of getting their heart broken around here is me."

"You?" I cry. "How the hell are you in danger of anything?"

"See, here's where you and I are different. You're scared of falling in love with me."

"And you're not scared of that?" I cry.

"I'm *already* in love with you!" he yells so loud that the paint nearly peels off the walls. "And the fact that you don't know that is a fucking red flag."

"You want to talk about red flags!" I yell back, infuriated. "You telling me that you love me for the first time like that is a major red flag." I march into the bedroom.

"Where are you going?" he calls after me. "This conversation isn't over."

"Home. Yes it is."

"Henley is right about you," he calls.

Huh?

I march back out to the living area. "What the hell does that mean?"

"Never mind." He sighs as he drags his hand down his face.

343

"No. I want to know." I put my hand on my hips. "What does dear old Henley have to say about me?"

"He thinks that I'm the rebound guy and that you're going to break my heart."

My mouth falls open in horror. "Coming from him, that's an actual joke."

"That's exactly why it's coming from him. He knows this stuff; he's lived it. He keeps telling me that hurt people hurt people."

"Maybe hurt people are so scared of being hurt that they would rather be alone." My voice cracks, betraying my hurt.

His demeanor softens. "I'm not going to hurt you, Bec."

His silhouette blurs.

"Babe . . ." He pulls me into his arms and holds me tight. "I'm not going to hurt you."

"What if you do?" I whisper through the lump in my throat.

"What if you hurt me?"

The tears break the dam. "How could I ever hurt you?"

"By believing what other people say about me in a bathroom."

I screw up my face in shame. "It's just . . ."

"I know." He holds me tight. "It's going to be okay," he says softly.

I pull back to look into his eyes. "Is it?"

"I promise."

"This scares me, Blake."

"Me too."

"I shouldn't be this attached to you this soon," I whisper.

He kisses me softly. "Well, it's only fair when I am." Our kiss deepens, and I know that our first fight is over.

"That wasn't exactly the most romantic declaration of love." I frown up at him.

He winces. "Let's forget I said that, okay?" His lips drop to my neck.

"No." I smile as his teeth graze my skin. "I'm going to bring that up forever."

His eyes twinkle with a certain something. "*Forever* has a nice ring to it."

My heart swells. "It does."

Our kiss deepens, and an urgency takes over. Our teeth clash, and I make myself step back from him. "Can we . . . not do this."

Panting, he frowns in confusion. "What?"

"You're blinding me with all the orgasms."

"But what a way to go blind." He smiles mischievously.

"I'm serious. No sex today."

His shoulders slump.

"Well, at least not now." I put my arms around his waist and look up into his big, beautiful eyes. "Maybe later."

He breaks into a breathtaking smile.

"If you behave yourself," I add.

He kisses me.

"And don't give me any more red flags," I say to add further salt to the wound.

"Careful, Rebecca." He smirks. "You won't like me when I'm angry."

"Yeah, I just worked that out," I mutter dryly. "Where are you taking me sightseeing today?"


The sun is shining, and the laughter hasn't stopped.

I cling to Blake's broad back as I hold on. We're sightseeing on a motorbike, and it's day three of our vacation. My hair is flapping around in my helmet, and my lips are windburned. We've swum and lain in the sun, danced until our feet are sore, and lived every moment as if it was our last.

A new sense of what my life could be is falling into place, and boy . . . does the future feel bright.

I see a row of shops that I want to look through, and I tap Blake on the back with a pull-over signal. He parks the bike, and we amble through the quaint little street.

Cancún is so interesting. There's so much to see and do, and every day something shocks me.

"Do you want an ice cream?" I ask Blake.

"Sure."

I go to the counter and put down the ice creams.

"That will be one hundred pesos, please." The shop attendant smiles.

I count out my money, and as I pass it over to her, I notice the most beautiful ring. "Oh my gosh, your ring!"

"It's beautiful, isn't it." The woman smiles as she looks over at her husband. "It's a yellow diamond."

I wished for a yellow diamond engagement ring once upon a time, but I never got it, of course. That dream is long gone now that I'm never marrying again.

"Oh my gosh, yellow diamonds are so rare," I gasp as I hold her hand to get a closer look.

"Because they are so beautiful." She beams.

"How long have you been married?" I ask.

"Forty-two years this year." The husband smiles. "That ring cost me one year's wages, but it was worth every cent. It's brought me nothing but luck."

"You're a lucky man." Blake smiles.

"Goodbye." I smile. Blake takes my hand in his, and we continue our ambling down the street. I can hear music playing in the distance as I tear open my ice cream and lick the paper.

"That bloke must be loaded," Blake mutters as he thinks out loud. "Did you see the size of that ring? What would that be, like a ten-carat diamond?"

"How do you know about carats in diamonds?"

"I'm actually a specialist. Do you know how long Antony, Hen, and I looked for Juliet's engagement ring?"

I lick my ice cream and smile as I get an image of the three of them searching high and low for Juliet's ring. "Well, you did a good job, because Juliet's ring is perfection."

"As are you." He smiles as he throws his arm around me. "As are you."



The sun's rays beam down on us as we lie on our towels. We are at the beach, and Blake is reapplying his sunscreen.

"Who do you miss the most from home?" I ask.

"Hmm, probably Antony."

"Antony?" I smile into the sun. "Why Antony?"

He shrugs. "Well, Henley is all happily married now with a baby on the way. It's been just me and Ant for a while."

"You're not best friends with Hen anymore because he got married?"

"Of course I am; it's just different. His best friend is Juliet now. She's the one he can't wait to see."

"I love that." I smile sadly. "Is Ant seeing anyone?"

"He's sworn off women."

"Why?" I smile.

"Reckons he doesn't have time for bullshit."

I giggle. "Maybe if all they are giving him is bullshit, he is with the wrong women."

"Right." He smirks as he keeps applying his sunscreen. "Who do you miss from home the most?"

I think for a moment. "Honestly, I think Barry."

"Barry?" He frowns.

"Yeah, I loved having that little menace live with me, and I had a very good reason to walk every day."

"You should get your own dog."

"Yeah, maybe."

"I mean, now that you know you aren't going to have to move houses."

"True." I smile into the sun. "It does feel good knowing that." His phone dings a message as it lies on his towel.

"Someone messaged you," I say with my eyes closed.

"Can you see who it is?" he replies as he rubs in his sunscreen. "My code is 1209."

I open one eye and peer over at him. "You're telling me your phone code?"

"Yeah, why not?" He squirts more sunscreen into his hand. "I've got nothing to hide. Why, do you?"

"No." I shrug and type the code into his phone, and it opens up the message.

### Jade.
### I haven't heard from you in months.
### Can we catch up this weekend?

"Hmm," I reply, unimpressed.

"Who is it from?"

"Jade. She wants to catch up this weekend."

He curls his lip. "Block her number."

"What?" I frown.

"Actually, this is a good plan. Go through my phone now and block all the girls' numbers. I don't want them messaging me anymore."

I stare at him for a beat. "You don't need to do that."

"I don't want women from my past being able to text me."

"It's fine, Blake."

"It's not. All it's going to do is upset you and make us fight, and I don't want that. And besides, I don't want to talk to them anyway." He lies down onto his back and closes his eyes. "Start at *A*. Let's do this now and get it out of the way."

I stare at him for a beat. I can't believe he'd actually do this for me.

"All right." I scroll through his contacts back to *A*. "Angela?" I say.

"Block."

"Abby Brunette."

"Block."

I frown. "Why is her name Abby Brunette?"

"Because I know a few Abbys."

I roll my eyes. Of course he does.

"Block all Abbys," he adds.

"All right." I smile as I hit "Block Number." I have to admit that this really is very satisfying. "Anna."

"Anna is from work; she can stay."

My eyes flick up over the phone. "How old is Anna?"

"She's about sixty and a lesbian. You can relax."

"Okay, she can stay . . . I guess." I smile, grateful that he understands me better than I do.

"For the record, I'm blocking your contacts after this," he tells me.

"Fine." I sigh as I act perturbed. I have all of five numbers. Block away.


The hotel restaurant is packed to the rafters, and we walk in hand in hand.

There's music playing, cocktails are flowing, and laughter can be heard echoing through the resort.

It's late. After we got home from the beach this afternoon, we took a nap and slept longer than intended. We've already missed our restaurant booking across town.

"Hope they can fit us in, or else it's bananas for dinner," Blake mutters under his breath.

I smile. We bought a huge-ass bunch of bananas at the market yesterday. "I'm actually happy with eating bananas," I tell him.

"I noticed." He subtly elbows me in the ribs.

"Can I help you?" the waiter interrupts us.

"Yes, is there any possibility of a table for two?"

"Did you have a booking?"

"Ahh . . ." Blake looks around, as if contemplating lying. "Unfortunately not."

I smirk, and he gives me the side-eye.

"I'm sorry. We don't have anything available tonight."

"Right." Blake nods.

"Actually, let me check on something." He takes off across the restaurant.

"I'm fine eating bananas," I tell him.

"I'm not. I need some protein."

"I've got all the meat you need," I whisper.

His eyes stay fixed on the waiter across the room, and he smiles. "This is true."

"And the benefit of it is that you can eat while naked."

"That's an excellent point."

"Actually"—I smile as I try to up the ante—"I'd enjoy watching you go down on a banana."

"You're ruining it," he mutters dryly. "Too far."

I get the giggles, and he does too. The waiter comes back. "We do have a shared bench table at the bar available, sir. You can eat your meal there."

"That could work." Blake's eyes come to me, and I nod. "Okay."

"Great, this way."

We follow him through the restaurant and take a seat at two of the high-top bar's corner seats. There is another couple sitting at the other side of the corner. They are around our age, and I saw them at the pool earlier.

"Hello." Blake smiles as he sits down.

"Hello." The man smiles. He has an accent.

"Australian?" Blake asks him as he pulls out my stool for me.

"Close, New Zealand." The man smiles. He gestures to the woman sitting next to him. "This is Hannah, my wife, and I'm Peter."

Blake shakes his hand. "I'm Blake, and this is my girlfriend, Rebecca."

"Hello." I give a shy wave. I'm always hopeless in these types of interactions. Thankfully Blake is the friendliest person on earth.

"You guys having a good time?" Blake asks them.

"Yes, we love it," Peter replies.

"What will it be?" the bartender asks from across the bar.

Blake gestures to me. "I'll have a classic margarita, shaken and salted, please."

"Make that two." Blake holds up two fingers.

"Actually, make that four," Peter chimes in. "They sound good."

Blake picks up my hand and puts it on his thigh. His thick quad muscle is hard beneath my hand, and I smile.

Blake's love language is touch.

He wants to be touching me all the time. Even in bed when we're sleeping, his hand is on my behind or his foot is resting against mine. Never does he sit beside me and not touch me in some shape or form. Not that I'm complaining. I'm slowly learning that my love language is touch too.

"So, what brings you to Cancún?" Hannah asks.

Blake gestures to me. "We went to a family wedding," I reply.

She glances down at my hand. "You guys aren't married?"

"No."

"How long have you been together?" Peter asks.

"Well, that depends on who you ask," Blake replies.

Peter and Hannah laugh, and I frown over at him. "Huh?"

Our drinks arrive, and we all hold them up to tap. "Cheers."

"What does that mean?" Peter replies as he sips his drink.

"Well . . ." Blake shrugs. "I've been dating Rebecca for about four months, and she's been dating me for two weeks."

"What?" Hannah laughs. "Please explain."

"Yes, Blake." I laugh too. "Explain this to me as well."

"Well . . ." Blake's eyes dance with mischief as he sips his drink. "Bec and I have been friends for years, and I decided about four months ago that she was the girl for me, so I stopped seeing other women and began sleeping on her couch at every opportunity."

I smile as my eyes linger on his handsome face.

"She, however, took her time and didn't make a move until two weeks ago."

"What happened two weeks ago?" Peter smiles into his margarita.

"She followed me into the shower and seduced me."

I snort my drink up my nose in surprise, and the table erupts into laughter.

"I did not!" I cry.

"Oh please, admit it." Blake rolls his eyes. "You did too."

"This is a cute meet-cute." Hannah smiles. "He dated you for months longer than you dated him. Classic."

I can't believe he told them that. I tighten my grip on his thigh, and he puts his hand over mine and throws me a sexy wink as he blows a kiss.

"How did you two meet?" Blake asks them.

They begin to go into a long-winded story, but my mind lingers on what Blake said.

He stopped seeing other women . . .

For me.

I smile as I sip my margarita. All these little pieces of the Blake Grayson puzzle keep falling into place, and I have to tell you.

This man is a masterpiece.


My heart races as Blake's body stays buried deep in mine. We are lying on our sides, and he's curled up behind me.

The soothing sound of the ocean filters through the room, and the sun is just peeking through the curtains.

"This vacation is like a dream," I whisper sleepily.

We laugh all day and make love all night.

"Hmm." I feel him smile as he kisses a trail down my face and over my jaw. We cannot get enough of each other. He slowly pulls out and holds me close.

"I don't want to go home tomorrow."

"Hmm." He lifts my top leg and rests it over his body. His fingers slowly slide through my dripping, swollen sex. "I love feeling me in you."

I smile into my pillow. "That's because you're sick and perverted."

He nips my ear and slides his fingers into me. It's not in a sexual way; it's in an intimate way. He likes the feeling of my body filled with his. His fingers slide through my wet flesh, and he kisses my neck. "Seriously . . . how are you so fucking hot?"

I smile with my eyes closed; god knows what a mess I must look like. One thing I'm completely sure of is that Blake likes me however I come. Not once have I been self-conscious around him, which in itself is a victory, seeing how perfect he is.

"Our last day," I whisper sleepily.

"Hmm." He scoops his fingers out of me and begins to smear his semen through my lips and down to my back entrance, and he slowly rubs it in.

*Oh . . .*

My stomach flutters at the feeling of him touching me there. He's done it a few times, and each time, I like it more.

Not something I ever thought I'd say or feel.

His teeth graze my earlobe as he continues to rub his finger back and forth over me. "You like that, baby?"

I close my eyes at the sensation, too embarrassed to admit that I do.

His lips drop to my neck, and he slowly slides the tip of his finger in. My eyes roll back in my head.

*Fuck . . .*

The room is silent, and yet all I can hear is the deafening sound of the beat of my heart.

This shouldn't feel good . . .

His finger slowly works me; in and out he slides. Just the tip at first and then deeper, more sensation than I could ever imagine. An unexpected closeness swimming between us.

This feels intimate and special, not what I imagined at all.

I can feel his erection growing against my behind, and his breath quivers with arousal. "I need you here," he breathes into my ear as his finger slides in deep.

"I . . ." My eyes roll back in my head. "I have . . ." His finger gets stronger, and my leg lifts by itself to give him better access. *Fuck, that feels good.*

"I've never done it before," I whisper.

He stills.

I close my eyes in shame. I'm so inexperienced compared to him that it's just embarrassing.

He turns my head and kisses me. It's deep and erotic. "Can we . . ." His lips take mine with reverence, and damn it, I want this.

I want to be closer to him. I want to give him everything that I am.

I nod, and he smiles against my lips. He reaches over to the bedside table, and I hear the click of the lid on the lube and feel him fussing around.

"What are you doing?" I ask.

"Taking my piercing out."

*Oh* . . . fuck, this is actually happening. My arousal begins to dissipate as fear takes me over.

His lips drop to my neck again, and he rubs his fingers together to warm the lube up before smearing it over me. His fingers suddenly glide over my skin with ease. "That's it."

He repositions my body so that I'm lying on my side. "You okay like that?" he whispers. "I need you to stay relaxed, just like this, okay?"

I nod, although I'm not really sure I can.

To the sound of the ocean crashing on the shore, he takes his time. Together we lie here in our very own cocoon, just the two of us in a perfect intimacy bubble.

For a long time, we lie just like this. His finger works me. His slow, tender kiss makes me forget that I am a mere mortal. Because this feels heavenly.

Being here with him, giving this to him . . . my body shudders, and fuck, I'm going to come. "I need you now," I breathe against his lips.

"Shhh," he whispers. "Little bit more." He adds another finger and then another, and I feel the stretch. "Breathe," he reminds me.

*Fuck . . .*

My eyes roll back in my head at the sensation.

I lie here totally at his mercy, and I think that's what's turning me on so much. He has full control over me.

He nudges my entrance and turns my head and kisses me as he slides in.

His body meets resistance, and a sharp sting hits me.

"Owww," I whimper into his mouth.

"It's okay." He kisses me again over my shoulder. "Relax, baby, let me in." His hand is on my hip bone as he guides my body onto his, holding me in place for him to take me. He surges forward again, and pain sears through my senses. "I don't think . . ."

"Shhh." He pushes in harder as he pulls my body back onto his, and we break through the barrier, and he slides all the way home.

My vision nearly blacks out at the sensation, and I feel him smile against my cheek.

"I love you," he whispers.

*Oh . . .*

My eyes well with tears, and I put my hand up to his face. "I love you," I murmur as I turn to kiss him.

Our kiss is tender and intimate. A celebration of us.

So much love is in this room, and I never knew it could be like this.

My life mistakes all flash before me, and now I know the reason for everything.

We belong together. Everything I've been through was so that I could be here, doing this with him.

For the first time in my life, I feel complete.

The headlights light up the houses as we pull onto Kingston Lane.

Only six days ago we left, and yet here I am returning, feeling like a completely different person. Something happened in Cancún.

I left an insecure divorcée. I've returned as a woman who is blissfully in love.

When Blake and I . . . I smirk as I remember how hot it was, taking that extra step in our intimacy . . . my remaining walls came down.

I cannot deny it any longer. I am irrevocably and hopelessly in love with Blake Grayson.

He's strong yet gentle, sweet yet sarcastic. Intelligent and funny. Sexy and . . . my heart swells.

Who am I kidding. *He's everything.*

"We sleeping at my house or yours?" Blake's eyes flick over to me. There isn't a question that we aren't spending the night together.

"Well, we have to put your car away in the garage, so I guess at yours." I shrug.

He smiles wistfully, and I have to wonder if he's having the same inner thoughts that I am.

*How did we get here?*

Gratitude washes over me for this beautiful man, and I lean over and kiss his face as he drives. I cover him in baby kisses all over, and he laughs as he tries to swat me away. "Stop it, or I'm dropping you at home." He acts grumpy.

"Sure you are."

**Blake**

I read through the file and glance back up at the small boy sitting in the hospital bed. "You are getting stronger every day."

He frowns. "Where does it say that?"

I take the file to him and point to a line. "Right here, see?" He's only four, and I know he can't read yet. "Callum Rogers is getting better every day and is a fantastic patient. We're very impressed with how he helps the nurses and takes his medicine." I pretend to read the words out loud as I throw a wink to his mother. I run my finger along the line as if I am reading some more. "It also says here that you are brave, an excellent listener, and deserve two desserts today."

"It says that?" Callum bites his lip, trying to hide his goofy smile.

"It does." I nod. "You are doing so well, Callum; we are all very proud of you."

Mom smiles and rubs his arm. "Great job, baby."

Callum has tetanus from a scratch he got a few weeks ago. It was touch and go for a while, and he's been in the hospital for a few weeks, but thankfully he's now on the mend.

From my peripheral vision, I catch sight of someone standing just outside the door waiting for me. "I'll be back later this afternoon," I tell Callum and his mother. "Hopefully it will be home time soon." I close the file and put it back on the shelf. I make my way out into the corridor to see a woman standing there.

"Dr. Grayson?"

"Yes."

She puts her hand out to shake mine. "I'm Sam Holland."

"Oh." My eyes widen. *Shit, I thought she was a man.* "Dr. Holland, nice to finally put a face to the name."

Dr. Holland is the head of the pediatrics board and is revered among her colleagues. How didn't I know she was a woman? . . . An attractive one too.

"Yes, you too." She smiles. "I've been wanting to catch up with you before I return to New York."

"You have?"

"Yes, it seems you're hard to catch."

"Well, between here and my practice, I'm run off my feet twenty-four seven." I smile. "My apologies."

"That's why I'm here. I have an offer for you."

"You do?"

"Can we . . ." She looks around guiltily. "Talk somewhere in private?"

"Sure." I gesture down the corridor. "Come into my office." She follows me down the hall. We walk into my office, and I close the door behind us. "Take a seat. How can I help you?"

"I think we both know why I'm here," she says as she takes a seat.

"You've lost me."

"I'd like to offer you a position."

I frown. "What kind of position?"

"I want you to be the new medical director of Morgan Stanley Children's Hospital in New York."

I blink. *What?*

"Your reputation precedes you, Dr. Grayson."

"I . . ." I shrug with a smile. "Dr. Holland, I'm honored, but I don't believe I'm qualified for the position."

"That's not true."

"To lead an entire children's hospital?" I frown.

"I want you to streamline and implement your clinical policies and procedures. We need a leader who excels in patient care. Yes, it's true we have more-qualified applicants on paper, but it's your bedside manner with patients and parents alike and your desire to buck current trends in care that sets you apart. You've been nominated by the heads of your department, and it's not just them that think this is the role for you. Many do. I've had several recommendations."

I open my mouth to reply, and she cuts me off. "Just think about it." She passes me her card. "Albert Costantino is retiring, and we want fresh, new blood from a doctor who's hungry to deliver the best possible care."

"I'm flattered." I smile. "Although I must decline. I couldn't possibly leave my practice here. I've worked way too hard to walk away from it now."

"Disappointing. This would be a life-changing role for your career." She shrugs with a smile. "I do understand, though." She shakes my hand. "Call me if anything changes." Her hand holds mine for a beat longer as her eyes hold mine. "It's so nice to finally meet you."

"You too."

*Hmm . . .*

With one last look, she gets up and leaves my office and closes the door behind her. I stare at it for a beat.

*Did that just happen?*

I make my way to my car with a spring in my step. Although I have no intention of taking it, the offer is a huge ego boost. I work so hard to build strong relationships with my patients and their parents, so to have it acknowledged like that feels like I've won the lottery.

I smile as I pull out of the parking lot. Who am I kidding? I've already won the lottery. The most beautiful woman in the world is in love with me.

*Ring, ring . . . ring, ring . . .*

My phone echoes through the car.

"Blake Grayson."

"Hi, baby."

I smile when I hear the familiar voice and turn the corner. "Hi, Mom."

"What are you up to?"

"Just on my way home."

"Ah, that's right, the Christmas concert is tonight. I wish we could come."

"Yeah." I smile as I drive. "If it wasn't sold out, you could have."

"Your first Christmas concert," she gushes. "The first of many."

"I've been picking glitter out of my hair for a week," I tell her. "You have no idea how many props we've painted over the last few weeks."

"These Christmas concerts are a big deal." She laughs. "Look at you."

"Look at me what?"

"Being the perfect boyfriend. You've transitioned into this part of your life so incredibly well. I'm so proud of you, love." I can hear the pride in her voice, and it makes me smile. "Rebecca is a lucky girl to have you."

"I'm the lucky one, Mom."

"Are you sure about Christmas Day?" she asks. "There's a heap of us."

"Yes. Rebecca wants to do it at our house."

"You're living together now?"

"I guess." I shrug. "We sleep between our two houses and are never apart."

"How long have you been together now?"

"Three . . ." I frown as I think. "Four months."

"Time flies when you're having fun."

"It sure does."

I drive onto Kingston Lane and see everyone on our golfing green, glasses of wine in hand and chattering away.

I smile. Seriously, best street ever.

I drive into my garage and park my car. Rebecca is already at the school, and I've got an hour to kill before I have to leave. I grab a beer from my fridge and walk out front.

"Hey."

"Hi," they all call. Juliet and Chloe are sitting on the chairs, and Antony and Henley are putting balls into the hole. Winston and Carol are in the road talking about her garden.

"How was your day?" Chloe asks.

"Good, and yours?" I sip my beer and notice the collar sticking out of her sweater.

Pink with red hearts.

Huh?

"What's that top?" I ask.

"My pajamas." Chloe smiles. "I wasn't planning on drinking wine tonight. I came over to pick up something, and next thing I'm here."

*What?*

"You got matching pants to those?" I try to act casual.

"Yeah, but I can't find them anywhere." She looks down at herself and dusts a piece of lint from her sweater.

*What the actual fuck?*

Henley glances over, and his eyes widen as he puts the dots together.

I hear my heartbeat in my ears as I drag my hand down my face.

I know where Chloe's pajama pants are.

They were under my bed.

# Chapter 21

*Rebecca*

The children stand on the stage, the audience gathers in the auditorium, and Christmas lingers in the air.

The children run their Christmas concert. They sing and they dance, and the world is a better place for it.

I glance out into the audience, and there he is, my greatest cheerleader. Sitting in the front row. Smiling as if his own children are on the stage.

Blake Grayson is another level of perfect.

He's been painting backdrops and hanging art and doing coffee runs for me and my colleagues when we worked all through our weekends to prepare for tonight.

He put up the tree in my classroom and helped me decorate it with the children's art.

It's our first Christmas together, and this year . . . everything is magical.

The concert was a raging success, and I walk out to find Blake standing in my classroom with a big bouquet of flowers.

"Oh, I love you." I laugh as I run to him.

"You were great." He smiles, but it doesn't touch his eyes. "Incredible, amazing even."

He's got a weird expression on his face.

"You didn't like it?" I smile.

"I loved it."

"What is that look for, then?" I tease.

"What look?" He pulls me in close and kisses my temple. "There is no look."

I kiss him as I take the flowers from him. "Thank you for being so wonderful."

"Not as wonderful as you would like to think." He widens his eyes. "Let's go home."

I collect my things, and we walk out into the parking lot hand in hand. While I'm jabbering on about everything, he's staying unusually silent.

"What's wrong?" I ask. "You're quiet tonight."

"Just tired."

"Been ruling the world all day, have you?"

"Not so much," he mutters under his breath as we get to my car. "I'll see you at home."

I get into my car and smile all the way home as I reminisce about the Christmas concert.

Everything went perfectly. We put so much work into it, and to have it turn out like that is a dream come true.

We make our way home, and Blake drives into his garage to park his car.

I make my way inside and begin filling up my vase with water for my flowers, and Blake comes bursting through the front door like he's being chased.

"What's wrong?" I frown.

"Why . . . why . . . why would anything be wrong?" His eyes are crazy, and his hands are on his hips.

"No reason." I frown as I keep filling my vase.

He's walking around with his hands on his hips as I fuss about in the kitchen. "You want a grilled cheese sandwich?" I call.

"Please."

I glance out and he's pacing back and forth. His eyes are crazy, and he's muttering to himself.

What *is* he doing?

He must have had a really bad day. I can't begin to imagine what it's like to be a doctor.

We eat our grilled cheese and have a cup of tea in silence. He has hardly said two words all night.

He must have had a really stressful day.

"I'm going to have a shower, babe." I make my way up the stairs.

"Uh-huh."

As I walk up the stairs, I see him spring from the couch and begin pacing again while dragging his hands through his hair.

He is acting *very* weird tonight.

I get into the shower and under the hot water, and I smile as relaxation mode is activated. There's nothing on earth better than a hot shower.

The door bursts open.

I jump, startled, and turn to see Blake standing before me. "I think I accidentally slept with Chloe," he blurts out.

"What?" I frown.

"After Carol's, I found pajamas under my spare room bed, and we all got blacked out, remember, and I don't remember a thing, remember?"

"There's a lot of *remembers* in that sentence."

"And I didn't know whose pajamas they were, and today I saw that Chloe has those pajamas, and I think . . ." He drags his hands through his hair as if this is the end of the world. "I think I might have slept with her."

He screws up his face as he waits for my reaction.

I roll my eyes. "You idiot."

"I know," he gasps.

"Those were *my* pajama pants."

"What?"

"We hooked up that night, you fool."

"*What?*" he gasps, wide eyed. "Are you sure?"

"Positive."

"Why didn't you tell me?"

"Because I was embarrassed that you didn't remember!"

"Did we fuck?" he squeaks.

"No." I roll my eyes again. "We fooled around, and you were so blackout drunk that we both fell asleep."

His eyes search mine. "So you're Nooky Nights?"

"Who?"

"The flash drive I found in my pocket. It's yours?"

"What are you talking about?" I screw up my face.

"Did you write it?"

"Write what?"

"The two-cocked green alien stories?"

"Blake. What the hell?" I hold up my hands. "Speak English!"

"I found a flash drive in the pocket of my jeans the next morning after Carol's, and it's a backup for someone who writes raunchy shit."

"What kind of raunchy shit?"

"Like two-cocked, tit-sucking hucows."

"What?" I scoff. "Have you gone insane? I never wrote any two-cocked stories. Is that why you wanted to borrow my books?"

"Yeah." He thinks for a moment. "So it was *you* who gave me the giant-ass hickey that I had to hide from you for weeks?"

"Guilty for that one." I smile. "Didn't think I had it in me, did you?"

"You old dog." Fully dressed, he steps in under the water and takes me in his arms. "Thank god for that. I thought I fucked it. Sleeping with your girl's best friend cannot be good."

I giggle. "Well, in truth . . . I didn't actually remember for a few weeks."

"What?"

"But then I checked the security camera and saw us kissing on my front porch, and it all came back to me."

"What?" His eyes widen. "Was I good in bed?" he whispers.

"You fell asleep, so I'd say not."

"Ugh . . . we shall never speak of that night again."

I giggle. "You idiot."

His lips drop to my neck. "Now . . . let's get to business. I'm sober tonight."


"Put my favorite song on again," I call as I fuss in the kitchen.

Blake hits play on Spotify, and "Carol of the Bells" rings out. His house is a Christmas wonderland.

We've gone all out decorating.

The tree is twinkling, and the fairy lights are strung up above.

I wanted to host his family this year on Christmas Day, and I've been cooking all week in preparation.

For some reason, this year family has a stronger meaning.

Blake's family has welcomed me with open arms, and I want them to know how much I appreciate them and their son.

He passes me a glass of eggnog, with a kiss on the cheek from behind. He's wearing navy pajama pants and a Santa hat.

His stomach muscles are rippled, and I never saw a Santa look so hot.

"I have a surprise for you."

"You do?" I smile as I turn toward him. "Please tell me that I get to do Santa tonight?"

"That's a given." He shrugs. "Come with me." He takes my hand and leads me through the house and opens the front door.

A large basket with a red bow sits there. "What's that?"

"I don't know." He smiles like a Cheshire cat as he picks up the basket and walks inside.

"What did you buy me?" I smile. "I thought we weren't doing gifts until tomorrow."

"This is for both of us." He puts the basket down next to the tree and sits down beside it. "Open it."

I smile and pull the ribbon and lift off the lid, and my eyes widen as I gasp. "Oh . . . a puppy."

A beautiful little golden retriever looks up at me.

"Oh my god." I gasp as I pull it out. "You bought me a puppy?" I whisper. I hold it up. "A little girl puppy?" I squeak. "Blake . . . ," I whisper.

"What are you going to call her?"

"Oh." I look at her beautiful little face. "What shall we call her?" I whisper in awe.

His eyes twinkle with love. "Whatever you want, baby."

"Daisy?" I hold her up. "Do you like the name Daisy?" I ask her.

She replies with a big lick to my face, and I laugh out loud. "Oh, I love you." I reach over and kiss him as she wiggles in my arms to break free. "Thank you."

"Do you like her?" he asks.

"I love her, and I love you."

# Chapter 22

*Rebecca*
*Seven months later*

*Ring, ring . . . ring, ring . . .*

"Hello," Blake grumbles from beside me in bed.

I squint at the clock. "What time is it?"

3:00 a.m.

"That's great, man." Blake smiles. "Can I do anything?" He listens for a moment. "Just stay fucking calm, okay? Juliet needs you to be calm."

I sit up. "Is Juliet in labor?" I mouth.

He nods with a smile.

"Ahhhh." I jump out of bed, run to the bathroom to get my robe on, and race downstairs to get my phone. I accidentally left it charging.

I see three messages in my group chat with the girls. The first message is from Juliet.

**It's happening.**
**Contractions are five minutes apart.**
**My water just broke.**

**See you on the other side.**

**xoxo**

Chloe replies.

**Ahhhh, I'm so excited.**
**Good luck baby.**

I quickly reply.

**You're going to be such a great mom.**
**It's your baby's birthday.**
**Ahhhhhh!**

I wait for the reply. It doesn't come.

I take the stairs two at a time and run into the bedroom to find Blake lying down peacefully with his eyes closed. "What are you doing?" I stammer.

"What does it look like? I'm going back to sleep."

"How can you sleep at a time like this?" I gasp.

"I close my eyes." He snuggles in to get comfortable.

"Shouldn't we do something?"

"Yes, come to think of it." He flicks back the blankets. "We should have sex."

"Oh my god, how can you think of sex at a time like this?" I splutter.

"Because tonight we are celebrating vaginas. Let's go." He smiles sleepily and pulls me down on top of him.

"But Juliet . . ."

"Is fine." His teeth go to my neck, and he smiles against my skin. "Now, where were we?"

371

Blake and I sit at the table and sip our coffee in silence. It's 8:00 a.m., and the night has felt never ending.

We haven't slept a wink and haven't heard from Henley and Juliet either.

"What if something's wrong?" I frown.

"Nothing's wrong." He takes my hand over the table. "These things take time."

My heart is racing, and I have that sick nervous feeling in my stomach. "Poor Juliet . . . this is too long."

Blake's phone rings. "Hello." He smiles. "Okay, hang on." He hits the speaker button.

"Hi, guys," Henley's voice says.

"Hi." I screw up my face. "The anticipation is killing me."

"We have a little girl."

"Ahhhh," Blake and I gasp.

"Everything go okay?" Blake asks.

"Textbook. Juliet was incredible," Henley replies proudly.

"Do we have a name yet?" Blake asks.

"Hannah Juliet James," he says. "She's so . . . perfect."

My eyes well with tears, and even Blake is overcome.

"Tiny. Five pounds, nine ounces."

"Oh, congratulations." I smile.

"I've got to go, but I'll see you both later?"

"Yeah, we'll be in tonight," Blake replies. "Well done, guys."

We hang up the phone and hug in joy.

Hannah Juliet James . . . I'm in love already.


I stare at my reflection as I brush my teeth. My hair is up in a messy topknot. I have a towel wrapped around me, and I've just gotten out of the shower. My body throbs from the pounding it's just received, and I glance over at the perpetrator.

Blake has his eyes closed as he washes his hair, and my eyes drop down his body that only moments ago was deep inside mine.

He's so perfect that I can't stand it.

I wouldn't change a thing from my past because it's brought me to where I am now, to who I'm with now.

There isn't a doubt in my mind that Blake is the love of my life, and if I'm being honest, I can let you in on something that I never thought I would feel: I'm glad my marriage crumbled.

Because it brought me to him.

And even when I was happy with John, it was never like this.

The love we have is like a fairy tale.

Blake is besotted with me. Our time together has been the best months of my life.

We laugh, we make sweet love and fuck like strangers, but more than that, we adore each other. Our love is based on friendship and a deep understanding.

This life with this man is where I'm meant to be.

Blake hops out of the shower and dries himself with a towel. He comes up behind me, pushes my hair to the side of my neck, and kisses me. "Round two." He smirks up against my skin.

"Are you kidding?" I mumble around my toothbrush. "We were just hard at it for forty minutes in the shower. You cannot want more."

But I know that he will. The man's insatiable.

"Behave yourself and go to bed."

"Or what?" His eyes glow with mischief.

"Or you are grounded."

"In my bedroom?" He gives me the look, the one that he does so well. *Fuck me,* it says, *and do it hard.*

I point to the bed as I keep brushing my teeth. He ambles into the bedroom, and I smile to myself in the mirror. Being the object of Blake's affection will never grow old.

I'm the luckiest girl in the world.

A million thoughts and no direction.

Tomorrow I've got the vet appointment, and then I'll drop by the market and get some groceries. I want to try that new recipe this weekend. I mean, I might do it with chicken instead of beef. Yeah, I think I'll do that.

And then I want to do some meal prepping. Do I have enough containers? I don't want to use plastic anymore. I'm moving to glass. I'll put those on the grocery list too.

*Ugh, why am I thinking of all this random bullshit?*

I stare up at the ceiling in the dark. I shouldn't have had that afternoon nap today. It's 3:00 a.m., and I've been wide awake for two hours. Blake is fast asleep beside me. His gentle breathing is a calming sound. Who knew that someone breathing beside you could be comforting?

I roll onto my side and face the wall with my back to him and hear his phone as it vibrates on his side table. I roll over and frown into the darkness.

Who would be texting him at this hour?

I lie back down and close my eyes. What if something's wrong? It could be an emergency.

I get up and walk around to his side of the table and pick up his phone. I walk out into the hallway with it so that I don't wake him up. I go to swipe it on and put in his code, and it rejects it. I put his code in again.

**Wrong passcode.**

Huh?

I screw up my face in question and put the passcode in again.

**Wrong passcode.**

That's weird.
I try it again.

**Wrong passcode.**

He's changed his passcode on his phone. Why would he do that? Hmm.

I make my way downstairs and flick the kettle on as my mind begins to go over the last few weeks. Come to think about it, he *has* been working late a lot recently . . . my stomach rolls as an all-too-familiar feeling falls over me.

Blake's hiding something.

Two weeks is a long time to feel sick in the stomach.

It's a long time to feel scared every time he picks up his phone; it's even longer to have thoughts so dark in your head that you wonder why you even bother.

At first I thought it was in my head, and maybe it is. I hope to god it is.

But Blake's phone is still locked, which can only mean one thing: he's messaging someone he doesn't want me to know about.

I'll never be that woman who demands to know everything. I'm not jealous; I'm sad, because I thought maybe I'd just gotten a bad egg with the first one.

But maybe it's me. Maybe I'm the one that's not enough.

I stir the spaghetti Bolognese that I'm making as my mind races off on another tangent. It's like I've become this superdetective again, analyzing everything that comes out of his mouth.

I want to believe that nothing is happening. I want this just to be a scar from my past relationship. But the reality is that things aren't adding up.

And I hate feeling like this and being insecure.

I would rather be single.

I don't want to ask him why he changed his passcode because then it will only give him a chance to lie to me, and I know as soon as he does that, our relationship is over.

*Buzz, buzz, buzz, buzz.* My phone vibrates on the bench, and I pick it up.

"Hi, babe," Blake's happy voice sounds down the phone.

"Hi." My heart goes into my throat. *Don't say it; please don't say it.*

"I've got to work late tonight. The children's ward is swamped. I'll be late."

"Okay." I force the words out.

"Don't wait up, okay?"

My eyes well with tears. "Sure."

"You okay?"

"Yep. Good night," I whisper through the lump in my throat.

"I love you," he says.

I hang up before he has a chance to hear my tears or feel my heartbreak through the phone.

*It's happening again.*

My stomach rolls, and I heave and run for the bathroom. I fall to my knees and throw up violently into the toilet as the tears run down my face.

Dear god, it's happening again.


I sip my coffee and stare across the table at my friends as I contemplate telling them my deepest fear.

It doesn't feel like that long ago that we were having this exact same conversation about another man in my life, and I'm embarrassed that I'm the only one who seems to bring these conversations to the table.

Chloe and Juliet chat away happily, but I feel like I'm hovering way above, watching their perfect lives unfold. Oliver and Chloe have just moved in together, and Henley and Juliet are in bliss with their bundle of joy.

And me . . . it seems as though I'm just about to go back to square one.

Juliet looks over and frowns. "Are you okay, Bec? You're very quiet today."

I force a smile. "Just got a lot on my mind, that's all."

"Like what?" Chloe asks.

"I think Blake is seeing somebody else on the side." I sip my coffee casually, as if this is not the end of the world for me.

The girls' faces fall. "What do you mean?" Juliet whispers. "What's happened?"

"Lots of things, and yet . . ." I shrug. "Nothing at all."

"Well?" Chloe prompts. "Details."

"Let's see, where do I start?" I roll my eyes in a dramatic fashion. "He's changed the passcode on his phone. He's working late all the time, and suddenly he's talking softly on the phone in another room." I sip my coffee again. "It is what it is, I guess."

"What did he say when you asked about it?" Juliet asks.

"I haven't brought it up. I mean, what's the point? He'll only lie."

"No. I don't believe it," Juliet snaps. "Blake is so in love with you that it's pathetic. I'm sure there's a logical reason."

"I agree," Chloe says. "It's not what you think."

"I wish I had your optimism." I sigh. "Unfortunately for me, I have been here before, and I know the signs."

"But this is Blake." Juliet takes my hand over the table. "He wouldn't do this to you."

"John was a good man too." I sigh sadly with a shrug. "Maybe it's me? Maybe I'm just not enough to hold a man."

"Don't be ridiculous," Chloe snaps.

"I really don't think this is what you think it is. You need to talk to him," Juliet says. "Maybe he's just working late more for extra cash."

"Maybe." I sip my coffee. "When this all started with John, I ignored every gut instinct about it and was constantly defending him to myself. I can't do it this time. My gut tells me that something is off, and I have to trust it."

"How long has this been going on?" Juliet frowns.

"A few weeks."

"Why haven't you said something to us?"

"I haven't seen you alone without the boys, and besides, in the beginning I just thought that maybe this was just my problem and in my head. But as the days tick over, I know that there really is something going on."

"What are you going to do?" Chloe asks.

"I don't know." I shrug. "I guess I'll just wait for confirmation of some sort. He'll catch himself out. They always do. I knew long before I caught John, but I just had to wait for the proof."

"How *did* you know that John was having an affair? Like, what was the main thing that made you think that he would do that?"

I think for a minute. "It was the hiding of the phone, the whispered conversations, working late all the time, and then the work trips away. But I guess the biggest clue was when he completely changed his entire personality."

"Like how?"

"John was tight, never spent a cent on us, and then out of the blue, he started booking romantic weekends away for me and him."

"What do you mean?" Juliet frowns. "How is that a clue? I'm confused."

"He began to book these elaborate weekends away. Random off-the-grid places, and he would spoil me, make me feel like I was a princess . . . actually, he made me feel like I was his queen."

Juliet frowns again. "But I don't understand. Why would him booking a weekend for the two of you make you think that he was cheating with someone else?"

"Guilt. Don't you see? It wasn't who he was. For so long, he wouldn't spend a cent on me, and then suddenly he started with the over-the-top grand gestures of love."

The girls stare at me as they listen intently.

"John loved me, there was no doubt in my mind that he loved me, but he felt guilty. I had been with him for years, and I knew him better than he knew himself. All of a sudden, his behaviors changed: bringing me flowers. Overwhelming me with affection." I take a long, shaky breath as the dark memory lingers. "It was as if every time he slept with another woman, he knew it was wrong, and he had to make it up to me."

"Fucker," Chloe whispers.

"I knew him. I had known him for years, and the man that I married wasn't the same anymore. He had become more attentive than he'd ever been. I guess that's what made it even more painful, because even though I had that bad feeling in my gut, I felt as though I was being ungrateful and that he was just making it up to me for working all the extra hours."

"What a nightmare," Juliet whispers. "I'm so sorry you had to go through that."

"Thankfully I'm not married this time." I shrug with a sad smile. "And I have my house. I'll be fine, whatever happens."

"You will." Juliet squeezes my hand. "But I honestly don't believe that Blake would do this to you."

"You really need to talk to him," Chloe tells me.

"So that what . . . he can lie to me?" I give a subtle shake of my head in disgust. "I'd rather him not know that I'm onto him so that I can at least catch him out."


I stand at the window and watch Antony and Henley putt the golf ball into the hole. It's late, nearly 9:00 p.m.

I can't hear what they're saying, but they're talking with Winston, and it seems to be a very in-depth conversation. I wonder, What *are* they talking about?

Blake is lying on the couch watching the game, and his phone vibrates on the coffee table. "Hello," he answers. He stands and walks into the kitchen with his phone as he begins talking. I walk to the door to try and listen, but he's talking in a hushed voice, so I go back to the window and keep watching the boys play golf.

I contemplate what I should say. What could I ask that would get me a straight answer?

Would he lie about who he's talking to?

Blake walks back out into the living room and lies back down on the couch.

"Who was that you were talking to?" I ask innocently.

He holds the remote up to the television and flicks the game back on. "Antony."

My eyes linger on Antony out on the street, and my heart sinks with an overwhelming sadness.

I wanted the proof, and now I have it. Confirmation in black and white.

*That hurt more than I thought it would.*

"I'm going to bed," I say softly.

"I'll be up soon, babe," he says as he keeps watching the television.

"Don't rush, I'm tired." I walk past him, and he holds out his hand.

"Hey, where's my kiss good night?"

I turn back to see him lying there on the couch, and I get a vision of me picking up the lampshade and beating him with it. Hurting him half as much as he's hurting me.

I hate him.

But more than that, I hate myself for loving him, for believing he was different.

*Men are all the same.*

"I'll see you upstairs," I say softly.

"No kiss?" He frowns.

I don't feel strong enough to have this argument today. I wonder, will I ever be strong enough to have this argument?

*Tomorrow . . . I'll be stronger tomorrow.*

I quickly peck him on the cheek. "Good night."

"I love you." He smiles.

*Sure you do.*

I walk upstairs like a zombie, get into the shower . . . and like the pathetic, jilted woman I am, I sob in silence.


Daisy pulls me along as she rushes to get to Juliet and Barry as they wait on the curb outside their house. "Morning." Juliet smiles.

"Morning." I bend and pat Barry. "How's my little man this morning?" I ask him. I bend and peer into the stroller at the cuteness overload. "Good morning, sweetness." I smile.

"Are we doing the short walk or the long walk today?" Juliet asks.

"Long. I have some extra energy."

We start walking, and I just have to tell her. It's eating a hole inside of me. "So last night, I got proof."

"Of what?" Juliet stops walking and stands on the spot.

"Blake was watching television, and his phone rang, and when he answered it, he went into the kitchen and was talking in a whispered voice."

"Right," she says, listening.

"I couldn't hear what he was saying, but when he got back, I asked him who was on the phone, and he said Antony."

"Okay." She frowns. "Hang on, I'm lost. Why is that a bad thing?"

"The whole time he was on the phone in the kitchen, I was watching Antony talk to Winston and Henley as they were putting on the green."

Her face falls.

"Antony wasn't on the phone at all."

"Why would he say he was on the phone with Antony if he wasn't on the phone with Antony?"

My eyes hold hers.

"Babe," she whispers as she pulls me into a hug. "I can't believe this. What did you say to him?"

"Nothing, I went to bed." We continue walking.

"What?" She screws up her face. "Why didn't you say anything to him?"

"I couldn't . . ." I shrug, embarrassed. "I'm just going to get through the next two weeks of lessons, and then I'm going to have it out with him and end it."

"Why are you waiting two weeks?"

"Because I have two weeks of summer school left, and I want to not have to go to work and be happy in front of children with a broken heart."

*And the masochist in me doesn't want to say goodbye.*

"I can't believe he lied. He blatantly lied."

"I know." We walk in silence for a while.

"Are you okay?"

"It's weird, you know. I just . . ." I pause as I try and get the wording right in my head. "It kind of feels like I'm dead inside."

"Like how?"

"Like I'm heartbroken and devastated . . . but not surprised."

"Well . . . I'm fucking surprised," Juliet snaps. "Not just surprised, I'm absolutely infuriated."

"Let's face it. I have a type, and I should have known better. Two more weeks and I'm going to end it, and then I'll go and stay with my parents for a couple of weeks, and by the time I get back, I'll be stronger. This entire thing is a magnified nightmare because I have to live across the road from him. It's not like I can never see him again. It needs to be amicable."

"I can't believe he lied. I'm honestly so shocked. I wonder, does Henley know?"

"Don't say anything to Henley," I say. "Promise me."

"I wouldn't, but I can't believe it still. I'm just so shocked."

"Jules, why would he lie if he had nothing to hide? Why would he lie?"

"You're right. I know you're right." She puts her arm around me. "Fucking asshole."

We walk in silence for a little bit longer. "So, two weeks, huh? How are you going to hold it together for two weeks?"

"I'll be fine." I smile sadly. "I'm going to be very busy so that I don't have to see him, and then I might go away for the weekend with Daisy."

"Maybe we could come too?" She smiles hopefully.

"Thanks, but I just kind of want to get away from everything and read a book with a glass of wine."

"You're going to be okay, Bec." She links her arm through mine. "Whatever happens, you will be okay."

"I know."

"Okay, class, let's pack up our pencils and get ready for this afternoon. The bell is just about to ring."

The class gets to packing up their equipment. It's Friday afternoon, and thank god for that. It's been a long week. "Remember, Monday morning we've got the farm animals coming in to meet us. Don't be late because I hear there are baby sheep."

The class chatters with excitement.

"Dr. Grayson," someone yells. "Dr. Grayson is here."

I glance out the window to see Blake with Daisy on a leash. He's still dressed in his suit, so he must have come straight from work. What the hell is he doing here?

I walk out the front door of the classroom. "What's going on?" I call out to him.

He smiles and waves, then walks over to me. "Daisy and I are here to sweep you away for the weekend."

*What?*

"I don't want to go away this weekend."

"You will when you get there." He smiles.

Damn it, this is the last thing I feel like doing.

All I know is that if I'm trapped away with him for the whole weekend, we are going to fight. It's already on the tip of my tongue.

"I've got some more things to do. I'll just be a minute." I bend down and pat Daisy as she jumps around on the leash. Great, now he brings my fur baby into it too.

"Okay, we'll be waiting." He gives me a playful wink.

Ugh . . .

I go back into my classroom and wait as my class packs up their things, and I glance out the window at him standing there in his suit with my dog.

A sense of déjà vu comes over me.

*The exotic weekend away.*

Exactly like I predicted, exactly like I've lived before.

384

Indigestion burns my chest as the stress takes a physical hold.

My heart begins to seep into the bottom of my shoe, and I know that I can't do this anymore. I have to talk to him today. As much as I've been dreading doing it and hoping that it wasn't going to come to this because he was going to prove me wrong, I can't hold it in anymore. I can't act like I'm not dying inside.

Because I am.

Every single second that he lies to me, it's like a knife through my heart.

I thought Blake was my forever man, my one true love.

"Once you have packed everything away, can you all come and sit on the mat as we wait for the bell, please?" I call to my class.

They run around and hurriedly pack everything away, then dive for the mat. They sit with their legs crossed and their backs straight.

I smile as I look around. Oh, to be so young and innocent and so excited to sit on the mat before you get to go home.

I wish my life was so simple.

"Good afternoon, class." I smile.

"Good afternoon, Miss Dalton," they reply in their singsong voices.

The bell rings, and they leave the classroom. I take my time to try and prepare myself.

Blake waits patiently outside with Daisy, and I feel like I'm walking to the gallows. I'm probably about to hear something that I don't want to and then be forced to talk about my worst nightmares.

Finally, when I can't delay anymore, I grab my bag and walk out.

Daisy dances around, excited to see me, and Blake smiles softly and gives me a kiss on the cheek. "Took your time," he teases.

"Well, if I had been given some notice, I would've been prepared."

"Well, if I had given you notice, it wouldn't be a surprise, would it?"

"I don't have anything packed."

"I packed a bag for you."

"I just really don't want to go away this weekend."

Blake smiles. "That is until you get there. Trust me, this weekend is going to be the bomb."

"Blake." I sigh.

He throws his arm around my shoulder as we begin to walk to the car.

"Why do you want to go away, anyway? We've got so much to do at home."

"Because I want to take my girl away for a special weekend and show her how much she means to me."

My eyes search his.

I think I've heard that exact sentence before. Another dagger goes through my heart, and emotion overwhelms me.

I drop my head to hide my face from him as we walk to the car. Daisy is dancing and bouncing around and thankfully distracting from my sadness.

Blake loads her into the car, and I get into the passenger seat. "Oh, so this is why you wanted to take my car today, so Daisy could come?"

"Yes, unfortunately Daisy in a two-seater Porsche doesn't work that well."

"So I'm not getting new tires?"

"Not today." He smirks as he gets into the driver's seat and pulls out of the parking lot.

"Where are we going?" I ask as we drive along.

"It's a surprise."

"How long does it take to get there?"

"About ninety minutes."

I turn my attention to stare out the window. Maybe this is a good thing. Maybe this is a blessing in disguise so I won't have to have a sad memory in my house.

*Another sad memory in my house.*

Who am I kidding? My house is a fucking nightmare for memories.

Blake chats happily about everything and anything, while I stare into space and mentally prepare myself.

This is it, the beginning of the end.

"Rebecca," Blake says forcefully.

I glance over at him. "I'm sorry, what?"

"Have you been listening?" He frowns.

"Oh, I'm . . ." I drag my hand down my face. "Not really."

"Are you okay?" He reaches over and takes my hand in his and puts it on his thigh. "You've been quiet the whole trip."

"Just got a lot on my mind."

"Like what?"

I can't hold it in any longer. The poison is starting to seep into my bloodstream. "Have you got anything to tell me, Blake?"

"Like what?" His eyes glance between me and the road.

"Please just be honest with me. I thought we were friends above anything else."

He frowns. "What's that supposed to mean?"

"I know."

"You know what?"

"Please don't drag this out. A messy breakup is the last thing I want. Be an adult about this."

"What are you talking about?" He screws up his face. "Why the hell would we be breaking up?"

"You are seeing other people on the side."

"What?" he explodes as his eyes nearly bulge from his head. "What are *you* talking about?"

"Do not raise your voice at me," I spit.

"Why the hell would you think I've been seeing other people?"

"Oh, let me count the ways," I say sarcastically. "You've changed the passcode on your phone, you're working late all the time, and now you're fucking lying to me."

"I have never lied to you. *Not once,*" he yells, infuriated.

"Oh no," I scoff. "What a fucking joke. You've definitely lied to me."

"When?"

"When you told me that you were on the phone with Antony while I was actually watching Antony out the window the whole time. You were on the phone with somebody else."

He falters, and I know that he knows that I've got him.

"I can explain that."

"Please do."

He puts his blinker on and pulls into a driveway.

"What are you doing?" I snap.

"We're here," he growls.

We start driving up a hill on a sweeping driveway. "I don't want to be here anymore. Can we just go home, please?"

"No." His jaw ticks as he grips the steering wheel with white-knuckle force. "So let me get this straight—you think I've been cheating on you for . . . how long?"

"A couple of weeks."

"And you never thought to bring this up with me fucking once?" he explodes.

"Why would I? You'll only deny it."

"Do you know me at all?" he spits. "What the fuck are we even doing here?"

"My point exactly. Can we turn around and go home?" I scream.

We come to a clearing, and there's an old wood cabin. He pulls the car up in an overdramatic fashion before turning to me. "So let me get this straight—in your mind, I have been cheating on you?"

"You haven't denied it."

"No, no. Let's go back to your mind here. Let's discuss what *you* think I'm doing."

"You've changed your passcode on your phone, you're lying to me, and you're working late all the time. I think we should call time on our relationship."

His eyes hold mine. "So you want to end our relationship. Is that what you're saying?"

"It's for the best."

His eyebrows flick up. "Wow."

*He's such a fucking smart-ass.*

"What does *wow* mean?"

"Nothing." He gets out of the car and slams the door.

I roll my eyes. This is exactly why I didn't say anything earlier. I knew this was going to turn into a huge, big fight, and now I'm stuck out here in the middle of nowhere with him.

He opens the door of the log cabin while I get out of the car. "Come on, Daisy." I lead her into the house, and as I look around, my heart drops.

The cabin is filled with roses and a huge sign.

**WILL YOU MARRY ME?**

*Oh no.*

My eyes flick to Blake. "What are you doing?"

"Asking myself the same question," he growls.

"Blake."

"You want to know why my fucking phone's code has been changed? It's because I was planning a weekend away to propose to the person who I thought was the love of my life. I've been talking to a diamond trader from Mexico to buy her dream fucking ring." He throws a ring box at me from out of his pocket. "Now I find out that she wants to break up with me and that she doesn't know me at all."

Fuck.

"I . . . I mean . . . what . . ." I'm tongue tied and have no idea what to say as my eyes flick around at the grand gesture.

"So you would happily walk away from me without asking me a question?" His eyes search mine.

"Blake . . . why would you want to get married?" I whisper.

He screws up his face as if I'm crazy. "Because I love you," he bellows.

"We don't need to get married to be happy."

"I want to get married, Rebecca. I love you, and up until ten seconds ago, I thought that you loved me."

"I'm not getting married again, Blake. I'm sorry, I just can't do that," I stammer. "It's . . . it's just a piece of paper. It means nothing."

He puts his weight onto his back foot, as if I've just dealt him a physical blow.

"We've never even talked about getting married. Why would . . . why would you think that I want to get married?" I'm talking fast and spluttering, trying to get my words out.

"I want a family, Rebecca."

"We can have a baby. We don't have to be married to have a baby."

"We have bigger fucking issues than a baby right now,' screams. "You just ended it with me because you thought I v lying. *You* are the one who told me I was ready to settle down. Y assured me that I could be that person, and like the Rebecca disci ple I am, I believed you. I have done everything in my power to be the man that you deserve. And now I find out that everything you have said to me is a complete lie. You actually thought I was sleep- ing with other women? *You're* supposed to be my best friend, and now I find out that you have no idea who I fucking even am?" He seemingly remembers something. "If anything, you've been lying to me all along!"

"I have never lied to you."

"You knew that we were together after Carol's, and you didn't say a single fucking word. I was freaking out that I had been with someone else, and you didn't once think to let me in on your secret?"

"With my history, I just . . ."

"You know what?" He throws up his hands. "You don't deserve me."

My face falls as my greatest fear leaves his lips.

"If marriage is just a piece of paper to you, then you really should go back to your husband, because that's exactly what it was to him. And I deserve fucking better than this secondhand love that you're dishing out."

His words cut me like a knife. "I just . . ."

"You just fucking blew it with me; that's what you just did."

"Blake, don't be angry. I want you to think about this from my side. We're happy; we're content. We don't need to be married."

His eyes hold mine for a beat. "You're wrong. Let's be real, Rebecca. You're wrong."

"What's that supposed to mean?"

"*I* was happy. *I* was content. You're still thinking about your ex-husband." His eyes fill with tears. "I went through all the trouble to get a yellow diamond from Cancún. I've been working extra hours to help pay for it," he whispers. "I wanted you to wear your dream ring." He angrily wipes his eyes. "But it turns out, it was never your dream. It was only mine."

*Oh . . .*

"Blake," I whisper.

"You let his love taint mine," he murmurs.

I screw up my face in tears.

"And I'll never forgive you for it." He turns and walks to the door.

"No, Blake, don't go," I stammer as I run after him. I grab his arm to try and stop him from leaving. "Stay. We need to talk about this."

"There's nothing to talk about. You've said all I need to hear." He pushes past me out through the door.

"Blake, talk to me. Stop," I call.

He's visibly upset as he gets into the car, and I stand in front of it to try and stop him from leaving. "Blake. Calm down. I don't want you driving like this."

"Get the fuck out of my way!" he screams as his anger takes him over the edge. He begins to drive, pushing me backward. He's going to run me over, he's so angry.

"Blake, don't." I bang on his side window as he drives past me, but he doesn't stop and he doesn't look back as the car careens back down the driveway. The tears roll down my face as I watch it disappear into the distance.

Fuck.

*What have I done?*

# Chapter 23

I drag my hand down my face and look around the deserted mountain.

I couldn't have messed that up harder if I tried.

What was he thinking?

We are nowhere near ready to get married . . . *are we?*

This is a discussion that you have. You don't just assume that someone wants to get married, for fuck's sake.

I wait for a while, hoping that he'll come back, and then eventually I go inside and catch sight of the ring box on the floor. I pick it up and open it. It's a beautiful yellow cushion-shaped diamond. Exactly like the one that we saw on that woman in Cancún.

*He remembered.*

The vision of the ring blurs as the caustic tears fill my eyes.

Guilt fills me, and I grab my bag and take out my phone. I dial his number and wait for him to answer. He doesn't.

"Blake, turn around and come back, please. We need to talk about this. We need to be together right now."

I wait on the line, as if willing him to pick up the phone.

"Please come back."

I hang up and begin to pace. This is a literal nightmare. I can't even go after him. I don't have a car, and I have no fucking idea where I am.

Oh my god.

He'll come back; he wouldn't leave me here.

He'll come back when he cools down.

The scent of the roses is strong through the cabin. I open the fridge to see chocolate-coated strawberries and a bottle of champagne and two crystal flutes. I look around the cabin to see it covered in Blake's love, and my heart hurts.

*I don't deserve him.*

The lump in my throat is so big it's nearly cutting off my air, and I wish it would because I deserve to suffocate in this guilt.

He hasn't been lying. He was trying to surprise me, and all I've done is be a selfish cow.

I dial his number again with renewed purpose. "Blake. Please pick up. I need you to come back," I whisper through panic. "I'm sorry. I need you to come back. Please forgive me. I did not handle that well, and I need you to come back."

I hang up and begin to pace.

*Please come back, baby. Please come back . . .*

Thirty-five phone calls and two hours later, I hear a car pull into the gravel driveway.

*He's here.*

I run to the front door and open it, and my face drops when I see Juliet and Henley.

"Where's Blake?"

I look around for his car. Is he coming too?

Juliet gets out of the car, and her face falls when she sees my tearstained cheeks.

"Blake called us to come and get you," she says softly.

My heart drops. "He's not coming back?"

"No, Bec," she says sadly.

I screw up my face in tears, and she pulls me into her arms. I cry into her hug.

"I didn't know," I cry. "He didn't tell me."

Henley walks past us into the house. He doesn't say anything to me, and he doesn't have to. It's obvious he's pissed.

I can feel his thermonuclear anger radiating out of him.

Juliet pulls me into the house and gasps as she looks around at the roses and the Marry Me sign. Her face screws up in tears too. "Poor Blake," she whispers.

"Let's go," Henley snaps as he looks around. "This place is fucking depressing."

Juliet picks up the ring box from the table and opens it up. Her mouth drops open. "Oh my god," she whispers.

I go to take the ring off her, and Henley snatches it out of my hands. "I'll keep this safe."

My eyes search his.

"I believe you said no," he snaps as he puts the ring in his pocket.

My heart dies a little. He told Henley I said no . . .

*I did say no . . .*

"Do you want to take anything?" Juliet looks around at the roses. "What do we do here? Shall we take them all, or . . . ?"

"No point," Henley snaps as he walks past us out the door and gets into the car.

"Don't mind him," Juliet whispers as she puts her arm around me. "He'll calm down."

I put my head into my hands. "I was just taken by shock, you know, and . . . I just handled things so bad, and . . ."

"I know." She tries to comfort me.

"And I thought he was cheating, and I just was so mad and horrible, and I just didn't know, you know? And I just . . ." Snot is running down my face, and I'm near hysterical.

"I know, baby."

"And Blake won't answer his phone, and I tried to get him to come back. Where is he? Is he okay?"

"I don't know. He called Henley to come and collect you."

"Can we go find him?"

"Let's just get you and Daisy home, shall we?" She puts her arm around me.

"But what about all the roses?" I stammer as I look around.

"We can come back tomorrow; I don't know, let's just go home. Maybe Blake is at home."

"Where's the baby?"

"Chloe and Antony are minding her."

*Oh god, everybody knows.*

I follow her out to the car. Daisy and I get in the back seat, and Henley pulls out onto the road.

The drive home is made in silence as I mentally go through our fight and stare at the scenery through tears.

*If marriage is just a piece of paper to you, then you really should go back to your husband, because that's exactly all it was to him.*

I close my eyes in horror.

*I deserve better than this secondhand love that you're dishing out.*

I imagine Blake going to all the trouble to find my engagement ring and working extra hours to pay for it, and all the while I was at home imagining terrible things about him.

What the hell is wrong with me?

I stare at the scenery through tears.

*You let his love taint mine . . . and I'll never forgive you.*

I'll never forgive myself.

I sit at the dining table and stare into space as Chloe paces back and forward in the kitchen. "I don't understand where he'd go."

"Try him again," Juliet says.

With shaky fingers, I dial Blake's number. It's 10:00 p.m., and no one's heard from him. Henley and Antony are out looking for him, and this is turning into an absolute fucking nightmare.

That's if it wasn't already.

**You've reached Blake Grayson.**
**Leave a message.**

I close my eyes. Answering machine again. I've lost count of how many messages I've left tonight.

"Blake, it's me. Can you call me back, please? We are all worried sick. I love you." Dejected, I hang up the phone.

Chloe keeps pacing, and Juliet walks into the kitchen and puts the kettle on.

The house is silent and sad, and I get the feeling that everybody hates me. Damn it, I hate myself for what I did to him.

My behavior has been inexcusable, but in my defense, I had no idea his head was even in this space.

"He'll be fine," Juliet says. "He's just cooling off somewhere. As soon as he calms down, he'll come home."

I twist my fingers together on my lap and nod.

I wish I was so sure.

I have this sick, sinking feeling in my stomach telling me that this isn't going to be all right.

Juliet's phone rings, and we all jump. "Hello," she answers. She listens for a minute. "Oh, thank god." She puts a hand over the phone. "He's fine. The boys found him."

"Where is he?" I stammer.

"Where is he?" she asks. She listens for a beat. "He's at a hotel. He's fine, don't worry."

"Thank god." I put my head into my hands as relief overcomes me.

"Okay, great." Juliet listens. "Yeah, good idea; you stay there with him. Okay, love you. See you in the morning." She hangs up the phone. "Henley and Antony are going to stay with him tonight. They'll be home in the morning."

I smile sadly. Not the outcome I wanted . . . but thank heavens he isn't alone.

Juliet sits down on the couch beside me. "I told you he'd be fine."

I nod.

"It's been a big day, and you've been crying for hours. Why don't you just go and have a shower and head to bed?"

"Yeah, I might. You guys go home. Hannah needs to go to bed."

"You don't want us to stay?"

"No. Honestly, as soon as my head hits the pillow, I'm going to be asleep. I'm emotionally exhausted."

Juliet rubs my shoulders as she gives me a sad smile.

"Thanks for today, guys. You are the best friends." I walk them both to the front door. "Can you call me, Jules, if you hear anything from Henley?"

"Of course I will."

"Are you sure you don't want me to stay with you?" Chloe asks.

"No, I'm fine. Thanks anyway."

I watch them walk down the street, and I close the door behind them and lock it.

The house is suddenly eerily quiet, and I'm left alone with my conscience.

It's lonely here.

I drag myself up the stairs and have a hot shower. For a long time I stand under the hot water and stare at the tiles on the wall. I have this weird sinking feeling. For weeks I felt that our relationship was going to end, and I've been dreading it.

But never in a million years did I think it would be at my hands.

The worst part is that I didn't even tell him about the contract I signed with John yet. I'm still legally married to another man, and now that all this has transpired . . .

I put my head into my hands in shame.

Fuck . . . what a mess.

Eventually, I'm so exhausted that I can't even stand up in the shower, and I drag myself out and get into my pajamas.

The house is quiet and empty and sad.

Tomorrow I'm going to make this better if it kills me.


*Ring, ring. Ring, ring.*

My phone ringing on the side table wakes me from my sleep, and I scramble to answer it. I tossed and turned all night and finally fell into an exhausted coma around 6:00 this morning. "Hello," I answer.

"Hi, Bec, it's Jules."

"What's wrong?"

"Nothing. I just wanted you to know that the boys have decided to stay away for the weekend."

I frown as I listen. "Is Blake all right?"

"I don't know. I just tried to talk him into coming home, but . . ." Her voice trails off.

"What?"

"He doesn't want to see you."

My heart constricts.

"We need to talk," I stammer. "I need to see him."

"I know, but I think you just need to let him cool down for a while."

I close my eyes in horror. The longer he cools down, the less chance we have of getting over this. "We need to see each other to talk this through."

"He doesn't want to see you."

My eyes well with tears.

"Look, just take the weekend. Get yourself together. They'll be home Sunday night, that's only tomorrow, and then you can talk to him when he's fresh and you both had time to cool down."

"I have cooled down."

"Yeah, well, he hasn't, and it's not all about you."

*Ouch . . .*

"I know that." I sigh softly.

"Do you want to go and grab a coffee or something?" she asks hopefully.

"No. I'm just going to go back to bed. I've not slept all night," I lie. As if I could sleep right now. I'm just about to jump out of my skin with worry.

"Okay, go back to bed, baby. It's going to be fine."

"Juliet," I whisper.

"Yes."

"Do you think I was in the wrong?"

She stays silent on the other end of the phone, and I close my eyes once again.

*That's a yes.*

"It's not for me to decide who's in the wrong. I love you both," she eventually replies. "Go to sleep. I'll call you later."

"Okay, thanks for everything." I hang up the phone and flop back onto the bed.

Ugh . . . the day is not starting well.

I sit curled up on the window seat in my front room, rolling my fingers as I wait.

It's Sunday afternoon, and I haven't heard a word from Blake.

The rain has come down in buckets, and with every splash of water on the earth comes an overriding sense of doom.

He'll be home soon, and hopefully we can talk. The ball of nervous energy in my stomach has me sick.

I go over my speech again in my head and hold the letter in my hand.

I couldn't work out the words to say, so I've written him a long letter, hoping to try and explain everything that's been in my head for the last few weeks.

Seeing it all written down in black and white hasn't eased my stress; if anything, it's escalated.

Because now I know how fucked up I really am.

My car comes around the corner, and I jump to my feet and run out the front door. It pulls into my driveway, and as it gets closer, my smile fades.

Antony's driving it.

I walk out into the rain as he gets out of the driver's seat. "Where's Blake?"

He hesitates as his eyes dart around. "He wanted to stay at the hotel for a few more days."

"He's not coming home?" My voice cracks, betraying my hurt.

"No. He wanted a few more days."

"Where is he?"

"I'm not telling you."

"We need to speak, Antony. It's urgent. I've been worried out of my head."

"Trust me, I think it's best you just stay away from him."

"Is he all right?"

"He's fine."

The rain begins to really come down.

"What does that mean?" I call over the rain.

"It means he's fine," he snaps in frustration. "I'm sorry, but if you expect me to have sympathy for *you*, Rebecca, I just don't. You've broken his fucking heart."

I step back from him and nod my head. The rain is heavy and loud.

Henley pulls onto the street and drives into his driveway. The garage door slowly goes up, and he drives in. No wave, no hello.

Just a whole lot of disappointment.

"I've got to get going," Antony calls. "Go in out of the rain and try and get some rest."

"Can you tell me where he is? Please?"

"He's safe. That's all you need to know."

"Does he hate me?" My eyes search his.

He exhales sadly. "Bec . . . I don't know what's going on, but . . . just give him some time, okay?"

My eyes well with tears. "Okay, thanks for bringing my car back."

Without another word, he sprints across the lawn and into his house, and I sit down on the front steps and watch the rain come down.

Sopping wet and with nowhere to go, I pray for a miracle.

I stand behind the pole in the parking lot. I never saw myself as much of a stalker, but he's giving me no choice.

It's Thursday, and Blake hasn't come home.

He won't answer my calls, he doesn't reply to my texts, and quite frankly, I'm going out of my mind.

I'm waiting at the hospital for him to arrive at work in the parking lot by his car space. It's 7:00 a.m., and if this is the only way that I can speak to him, then so be it.

Late Sunday night, I saw Blake's Porsche leave his house with Antony and Henley inside. They obviously took him work clothes and his car, and it seems that I'm the street pariah.

They are both openly angry with me, and I guess I would be, too, if someone did this to my friend.

But to not even want to talk about it? I'm getting kind of pissed. He's acting like a two-year-old.

I see his car come through the boom gates, and I clutch my handbag. I wait for it to pull into his parking spot, and then I scooch down and run around to the passenger side. I open the door and dive in and close the door behind me. His face falls when he sees me.

"Hi, Blake."

"What are you doing here?"

"I need to see you."

"I don't want to see you."

"Can we talk?"

"There's nothing to say." He stares out through the front window.

"Blake."

He keeps his vision straight ahead.

"Can you look at me?"

He drags his eyes to meet mine. "What do you want?"

"I want to explain a few things."

"It's fine, Rebecca. I know how you feel. You don't need to explain anything."

"But you don't know how I feel. I was just so shocked, and there's some things that you don't understand about my situation that just complicate everything, and I'm scared to tell you."

403

"Like what?"

I pick up my bag by the strap and accidentally tip it over. Everything goes flying onto the floor. I scurry down to pick up the contents, and Blake bends and picks up a lipstick and hairbrush and passes them over.

I give him the folded-up piece of paper, and he takes it off me. "What's this?"

"Open it."

He unfolds the piece of paper and his eyes scan over it. He frowns. "I don't understand."

My heart is beating hard and fast. "In order to keep my house, John made me sign a contract to enforce that I couldn't divorce him for five years."

His eyes rise to meet mine before returning to the piece of paper. "You signed this?"

Panic sets in.

"It was the only way I could secure my house, Blake. You have to understand, this has nothing to do with me and you. This is about him blackmailing me."

He drags his hand through his hair and lets out a low, long sigh. "Why didn't you tell me this before?"

"Because I didn't want to fight about it."

"Because you didn't want to fight about it, or because you knew it was the wrong thing to do?"

"I didn't think you'd want to get married, Blake. Especially this soon."

"Why the fuck would you think that?" he barks.

The venom in his voice makes me tear up. "Can you please not be angry?"

"Not be angry?" he cries. "Why do you think you signed this contract, Rebecca?"

"To keep my house," I splutter.

"Not even by a long shot."

"What do you mean?"

"I know you. I know you better than anyone, maybe even more than you know yourself. You signed this contract because you still want to be married to him."

"What? No!" I scoff. "That's ridiculous, and you know it."

"Is it?"

"Yes. It is."

"A house is not worth selling yourself for, Rebecca . . . unless you have an ulterior motive to stay married to somebody."

"You don't understand what it's like to have nowhere to live," I cry. "You cannot judge me for wanting to keep my house. You have no idea what it's like!"

"It's a fucking house," he growls as he punches the steering wheel. I jump in fright. "Do not insult my intelligence by telling me you won't divorce him to keep a pile of bricks and mortar."

"You honestly don't get this?"

"What . . . the lie?"

"I'm not lying, Blake."

"You don't even know that you're lying. That's the joke of it all."

"You don't know what you're talking about. I'm telling the truth."

"You want the truth, Rebecca? I'll give you the truth. You are stuck back in time with your ex-husband. You still have the wounds that he gave you; you wear them like a badge of fucking honor. You are still comparing everybody to him, and as long as you are living in the past . . . we will never have a future." He bends and picks up a bunch of papers that fell out of my bag off the floor and passes them over to me. "Just go." He sighs as he bends to pick up another piece of paper. He holds it in his hands for a minute. I glance over to what he's reading . . .

*Oh my fucking god.*

I try to snatch it from him, and he holds it out of my reach and begins to read it out loud.

> *Fifteen years ago today, we went on our first date.*
> *Every happy memory I ever had is with you.*
> *Of you.*

"Stop reading," I cry. "This is stupid . . . this . . . I don't . . . this is old, it's . . . I don't know why it's in my bag, it's just . . ."

It's the card that came with the roses John sent me all those months ago. I didn't even realize it was still in my bag.

Fuck. *Fuck.*

He keeps reading.

> *You were my first love.*
> *My only love, my last love.*
> *Forever your husband,*
> *John*

His gaze rises out the window, and he gives a smug smile and passes the card back to me. "Go home to your husband, Rebecca."

"It's not what you think. This is months old. I didn't even keep the flowers," I stammer in a panic.

"But you didn't tell me about them either."

"I didn't want to upset you."

"There's only one deceitful person in this car, and we both know that it's not me."

"Blake, please, we have to work through this because I cannot live without you."

"I cannot live *with* you," he whispers.

My eyes well with tears. "What are you saying?"

"I'm saying goodbye."

*No . . .*

My face screws up. "Don't say that. I just panicked, and you scared me, and I don't know why I acted the way I did."

"You don't. But I do," he says calmly.

My eyes search his.

"You're never going to leave him, Rebecca, and you don't even realize it."

"That's not true. I love you."

"On some level . . . but not enough."

"Blake."

"Get out of my car."

"Blake, please." I grab for him. "I take it back. Everything I said, I take it back; I don't know why it came out like it did. Forgive me."

"I can't."

"You can't, or you *won't?*"

"I've taken a job in New York."

"What?" My face falls. "What do you mean?"

"Just what I said. I've taken a job in New York."

"Why?"

"I don't want to see you every day. I don't want to look at you and know what I almost had. I don't want to look at you and have my fucking heart broken again and again knowing that you still love him."

His silhouette blurs.

"We never had a chance, Rebecca. You're still married to him," he spits through tears. "You'll always be his battle-scarred wife."

*Oh . . .*

That cut deep.

If he hit me with an axe, it would be less painful.

I sob out loud, and he gets out of the car and slams the door before walking across the parking lot.

Panic sets in. *He's leaving me.*

"No. Blake. Don't go," I whisper.

My heart hammers in my chest, and unable to control the hurt as it screams through my veins, I sob. "Please don't go."

# Chapter 24

The cone of silence.

I've been here before. The voices are muffled; the thoughts are magnified.

But it's the regrets that are overwhelming.

I sit in my dark living room, no television, no lights. Just me and my shiny conscience, my constant dark friend.

Blake left three days ago for New York. Sneaked out under the veil of darkness and didn't even say goodbye to our friends on the street.

*Tick.*

*Tick.*

*Tick.*

The sound of my clock in the distance echoes, chipping at the bones holding me together. The more time that passes without him, the stronger he gets without me.

I'm having some kind of existential crisis.

Old wounds have opened back up, and the infection is beginning to fester, poisoning the life out of me breath by breath.

There are so many questions that he raised, and deep down I'm also wondering about the answers.

Why did I sign that contract when I knew it was wrong?

Why did I keep that flower card?

Why would I even want a house that reminds me of John and of our life together?

And more than that, why was the first man I slept with a dear friend?

Was I ready for love, or was I simply seeking comfort in the arms of another?

Physical contact and a safe place to fall.

I was in a dark place when my marriage broke up, but that place seems like a children's picnic ground compared to where I am now.

I picture my beautiful Blake all alone in New York, and my heart breaks.

He deserved so much better than what I offered.

I haven't tried to call him again; I need to get myself together.

I'm no good to anybody like this, least of all to someone I care so deeply for.

I'm quite the expert now.

I should write a book of heartbreak: *Memoirs of the Battle-Scarred Wife.*


I walk into the restaurant with my head held high.

Gone is the worried woman who was afraid of her own shadow.

Today . . . I'm here for blood.

I see John sitting at the table, and I walk over.

"Hi." He smiles all sexy-like. He stands to kiss my cheek, and I push him back into his chair.

"Don't touch me."

He frowns up at me. For the first time, he seems confused as I sit down.

"How are you?"

"I'm great." I pull out the contract from my bag and tear it in two.

"What are you doing?" He frowns.

"Divorcing you."

"You can't."

"I filed this morning."

"I'll take the house."

I look him straight in the eye. "Nothing on earth is worth being tied to a loser like you."

His face falls.

"This is your first and last warning, John. Stay the fuck away from me, or I'll have a restraining order put on you."

He sits back in annoyance. "You don't mean that."

"Try me."

His eyes hold mine. "You're not thinking straight."

I smile. The audacity of this pitiful man.

*So pathetically weak.*

"For the first time in my life, I'm seeing things with crystal-clear clarity. You are the biggest regret of my life, and I'm embarrassed to even know you."

His face falls.

"I hope you rot in hell." I stand.

"Rebecca," he stammers, as if sensing that I'm completely done. "I love you."

"Goodbye, John."

I walk out of the restaurant and smile as I hit the fresh air.

That felt good.

## Blake

The sirens echo in the distance. Has there ever been a more iconic New York sound?

I look around my new apartment. So different from home.

411

With such short notice, I had to take whatever furnished apartment that I could find. Thankfully I could organize another doctor to stand in for me back home and take care of things. It wasn't urgent that I come here immediately—I don't start at the new hospital for two weeks—but I just had to get out of Kingston Lane.

I couldn't be there anymore.

Even the thought of one more day was unbearable.

My heart is heavy and painful in my chest, and with the way that I feel right now, I'm not sure if I'll ever recover.

Or if I even want to.

Because if I lose this feeling, then there will be nothing left of us. She'll just become someone that I used to know.

Another slot in the memory bank that will weaken over time.

I sip my red wine and slowly turn the glass by the stem to look over the rich color.

It's been eight days since I last saw Rebecca, and like a man starved for air, I can feel myself dying without her love.

*Marriage is just a piece of paper.*

The biggest disappointment was learning that I didn't even know her.

Not really, anyway.

I may have gotten around in my former life, but deep down I wanted the happily ever after . . . with someone who . . .

Maybe this is my punishment for being so insensitive to all the women I dated over the years.

Karma.

I swallow the lump in my throat, and it hurts all the way down.

I close my eyes and take a long, steadying breath; I need to stop wallowing in this self-pity.

It isn't healthy to be acting like this.

Tomorrow, I'm going to go back to the gym. I'm going to eat healthy. My eyes linger on the deep-plum liquid in my glass. I'm going to stop fucking drinking all the time.

I'll be okay.

I take a big gulp of my wine and slosh it around in my mouth, and like the masochist that I am, I hit play on Spotify. I've been listening to this song on repeat, again and again.

I tell myself it's to make me feel better, but the reality is that I want to keep being sad. Because sad is all I have left of her, and I'll hang on to anything that I can.

The thought of never having her in my arms again is . . . I close my eyes and see Rebecca's beautiful smile.

"Lovely" by Billie Eilish echoes through the speakers.

The familiar tone of the piano brings with it a comforting sense of melancholy.

*Isn't she lovely . . .*

Yes . . . yes, she was.

*Three weeks later*

No conversation, no love . . . no contact.

I sit in the back of a yellow cab on my way to work and stare out the window.

At least when she continually called me in that first week, it appeared that she cared.

Did I mean that little to her that she gave up so easy? . . . She didn't even fight it.

Or for me . . .

Her silence is the confirmation that my deepest fear was true. She still loves him. She'll *always* love him.

I get a vision of the two of us rolling around in the sheets, and my stomach drops.

Nothing more than the rebound guy.

I blow out a deep, deflated breath. I feel like fucking shit.

I've never been so low.

The boys arrive tonight, and I can't wait to see them. A weekend on the town with my two best friends is exactly what I need.

"That will be twenty-two dollars," the bored cabdriver tells me. I glance up. I didn't even realize that the car stopped. I dig out my cash and pay him. "Thank you." I get out of the cab and slam the door.

Fuck this.

I miss my Porsche.


"Hey." Henley pulls me into a hug. "I missed your ugly face."

I laugh and hug him back. "Wish I could say the same." I turn to Antony and hug him next.

"I'm taking you home with us," he tells me. "This fucking sucks."

I smile into his shoulder, grateful for his friendship and missing everything about it.

"How was the flight?" I ask.

"Long."

"I had a fucking baby sitting next to me," Antony grumbles. "Bastard cried for the entire six hours. I nearly stuck my sock in its mouth."

"Why do you hate kids so much?" Henley rolls his eyes.

"I just do." He curls his lip. "I'm not having any; it's already decided. Screw that shit."

I laugh. "You hungry?"

"Yeah, where we going?"

"Out."


"Can I get you any dessert?" the waitress asks.

I hold my hands up. "I'm good."

Henley cuts me off as he opens the menu. "No, you're not. He will have the . . ." He peruses the choices. "Tiramisu."

"Sounds good. Make that two," Ant chimes in.

The waitress leaves us alone, and my eyes go to Henley. "What's with ordering my food tonight? I've never eaten so much."

"You've lost weight."

"What?" I glance down at myself. "No, I haven't."

"Ant, has he lost weight?" Henley asks.

"Yeah."

"You think?" I pat my stomach.

"Ten pounds at least."

"Come off it," I scoff.

"Have you been eating?" he asks.

"Yes," I lie.

My appetite has died, along with my heart.

"I've taken up running." Not a lie. I actually have been running.

"Where do you run?"

"Around Central Park each morning."

"So . . . how's New York?"

"It's . . ." I shrug. "Okay."

"Just come home, man," Antony says. "You belong at home with us."

"Now, now." Henley holds his hand up. "He hasn't even settled in yet. Give it time."

My eyes hold his. The thing with Henley is, it's what he doesn't say that has meaning. His messages are delivered in between the sentences.

"How's everything at home?"

"By everything . . . you mean Rebecca?" Henley asks.

I sip my beer and shrug. "I guess."

"She's . . ." His eyes flick to Antony. "How's Rebecca?"

"She's not doing great," Antony replies. "Lost a lot of weight and . . ." His voice trails off.

My heart sinks. "Are you checking in on her?"

"She's fine," Henley snaps. "The girls are taking care of her."

I nod as my mind goes into overdrive. "Has she . . ."

"Has she said anything?" He finishes my sentence.

I nod.

"She told Juliet that you deserve better." His eyes hold mine as he gives me a silent message.

"Any sign of John?"

"I'll kick his ass if he steps foot on our street," Antony huffs.

"Has she been going out?" I ask.

"No." Henley sips his beer. "Didn't even go to work for a couple of weeks."

"She didn't?"

"No." He shrugs. "Apparently she's started seeing a therapist."

*Oh . . .*

"You did the right thing by coming here," Henley says matter-of-factly.

"Why do you say that?"

"Rebecca's got a lot of baggage."

I nod as a sinking feeling creeps back in.

"I still think that one day, you two will end up together." Antony sighs.

"We won't." I shake my head. "She had her chance."

"I don't believe this is all her fault," Henley fires back.

"So it's mine?" I point to my chest.

"Not at all. The timing's not right, that's all."

"The timing is never going to be right for us." I sip my beer. "She made sure of that, and why the fuck are you defending her all of a sudden?"

"Because she's suffering, and I feel sorry for her . . . but I did warn you."

"When did you warn me?" I scoff.

"All along I told you that she wasn't ready. Remember, hurt people hurt people."

"What was that bullshit, anyway?" I roll my eyes. "Why didn't you just speak English and spell it out for me? It would have saved me a whole lot of heartbreak. It goes like this: *Listen, Blake, Rebecca is still in love with her ex, so you should steer fucking clear of her at all costs.*"

"Believe me, I tried," Henley fires back.

"She is not in love with John," Antony snaps, disgusted. "Are you crazy?"

"All I know is that she's not in love with me."

"You know that's not true," Henley says. "She's just sorting through some shit."

"I don't care, anyway." I shrug. "I'm getting back on the dating scene. Rebecca who?"

Henley winks and clinks his beer with mine. "Attaboy."

## Rebecca

I lie on the couch and scroll through my phone. My finger hovers over the name.

*Blake.*

It's been seventeen weeks since I spoke to my best friend. And I want to tell him all about the things I'm doing to try and get better.

All the silent tears that fall.

Can he feel my love from here?

I go to yoga and meditation and therapy, and I'm keeping a journal, and Daisy and I walk twice a day . . . and . . .

I miss him.

More than I've ever missed anything.

I have this deep ache in my heart that won't go away, and I fear that I've ruined my life forever. For how can I ever feel whole again if I don't have him by my side?

But then the coin flips, and I feel insecurity creep in, and I know that I can't go back to that place.

Not now, not ever.

So I'll stay in my lonely bubble for one.

It's safe here.

My finger hovers over his name . . . What if I messaged him just to say hi?

Would he answer?

I throw my phone onto the floor to rid myself of temptation and let out a deep, deflated breath as I hold up the remote to the television.

Netflix, my constant companion.

The light shines through the window, and I squint as I try to get my bearings.

Hazy images of last night dance through my mind, and I look over at the bedside table to see two wineglasses, one with the red lipstick still on it.

*Fuck.*

My stomach turns, and I pick up my phone and scroll through my numbers. My finger lingers over the name *Rebecca*.

I have to hear her voice . . .

Just once.

I can't stand it one day longer.

If I can just hear her voice . . . then . . .

I stare at her name, and I desperately want to press it.

Could I . . .

*No.*

I get up in a rush and tear the sheets off the bed in disgust. I march to the laundry room and throw everything in the washer and fill it with disinfectant.

Every time is the same.

I get into the shower, and I soap up and scrub my skin with vigor until it's red and raw. I scrub and scrub and scrub.

I feel dirty, so fucking dirty.

The necessary evil is about to fucking kill me.

Why does everything feel so wrong now?

Trapped in purgatory with no way out, I slide down the tiles and sit on the floor.

The hot water falls over me like a dark blanket.

Physically in New York, emotionally back on Kingston Lane.

Mentally fucked wherever I go.

"Yeah, and then at halftime, they got the goal." I push through the door of the bar; it's Friday night, and I'm having drinks with some colleagues from work.

New York has grown on me; work is amazing, and I've made some great friends.

Things are better . . . *I* am better.

"So what, the ref was at fault?" Andrew asks.

"Absolutely." I roll my eyes. "And then to top it all off, he missed the shot." We wait at the concierge area. "Hello, table for four, please," I tell the waiter.

"That will be a few minutes. You can take a seat at the bar while you wait, if you like."

"Sure thing." We make our way through as we keep discussing the game in great detail and take a seat at the huge, horseshoe-shaped bar.

"Four Heinekens, please," Stuart tells the bartender.

We keep chatting and get our beers, and eventually the waiter comes over. "Your table is ready, sir."

"Thanks." I stand, and as I go to turn, I see a familiar face at the opposite side of the room. Wearing a tight red dress with her hair down and curled, she's sitting at the bar.

*Rebecca.*

She smiles softly, and before I can stop myself, I'm walking over to her.

"Hi, Blake." She smiles up at me.

"Hi." I frown.

"You look good." She smiles as her eyes drop down to my toes and back up to my face.

She seems different and yet so familiar.

I stare at her like I've just seen a ghost. "What . . . what . . ." I glance over to my friends and then back at her. "What are you doing here?"

"Looking for you."

# Chapter 25

*Rebecca*

A frown flashes across his brow. "Why?"

"I . . ." My heart is hammering in my chest. "I wanted to talk to you."

"About?" He raises an impatient eyebrow.

I smirk. God . . . he's still so gorgeous. "Everything and nothing."

"I'm very busy, Rebecca. You can't just turn up here and . . . ," he says sternly. "I'm out with friends."

"I know." I look around as I try to regain my composure. I wasn't counting on seeing him in the flesh throwing me this much. "Have you got ten minutes to spare to speak to an *old* friend?"

His eyes flick to the men he was just with.

"Ten minutes." I hold my two hands up in surrender. "Not a minute over, I promise."

He exhales, as if I'm the biggest inconvenience. "Fine, just a minute." He walks over to his friends, who are now sitting at a table, and says something before returning to me. I gesture to the stool beside me. "Take a seat."

He pulls up a chair and sits down. We stare at each other, and it's still there.

The stars, the sky, and the moon. Electricity bounces between us.

And now I know that it's real, because I've been with other people, and this wasn't there with them.

He's wearing a gray suit and a cream shirt. His hair has a bit of a curl to it, but it's his beautiful face that I've dearly missed.

"What do you want to see me about?" he asks.

"I . . ."

*Fuck.*

"I wanted to tell you that my divorce has gone through."

His eyes hold mine.

"And I'm selling the house."

He stays silent. I know he hasn't heard this from anyone else, because I purposely haven't told a soul. I wanted him to hear it from me and me only.

"And . . . that you were right."

A frown flashes across his face. "About what?"

"Everything."

He nods softly, as if acknowledging my failures.

"I . . ." I shrug.

"Go on," he prompts me.

"At the time we were together, I wasn't emotionally in the right place for our relationship, and you have every right to hate me."

His eyes drop to my lips and then dart back up to my eyes. "I don't hate you, Rebecca."

"I deserve it; it's okay." I shrug.

The bartender interrupts us. "What will it be?"

"I'll have a margarita," I say. I turn to Blake. "Do you have time for one drink?"

His eyes hold mine.

"As a friend, nothing more."

"Sure, make that two."

We fall into an uncomfortable silence.

"I want to apologize for what happened between us," I tell him.

His eyes hold mine.

"I said some terrible things that I didn't mean, and . . ." I shrug. "I know why you left."

He stays silent, as if processing every word I'm saying.

"I've spent the last year healing my demons."

"Demons." He smirks sarcastically. "Is *that* what we're calling them now?"

"Look. You don't need to be a dick. I came to apologize and to tell you that you are free to move home. I'm leaving the street, and you won't have to see me again."

"Good."

"Good," I reply.

Ugh . . . still a smart-ass.

"Are you seeing anyone?" I ask.

"Yeah," he replies flatly.

"Here you are." The waiter puts the two margaritas down in front of us.

"Thanks."

"Are you seeing anyone?" he replies as he picks up his cocktail.

"Yeah," I lie.

Animosity bounces between us.

"Who?" he asks.

"No one special."

He nods and clinks his glass with mine. We take a sip as we stare at each other.

"You look good." I smile. "New York suits you."

"Thanks." He sips his drink. "I'd tell you that you look good, but you already know that. Did you wear my favorite dress on purpose?"

I smile. "Maybe."

"What are you doing here?" he asks.

"I miss you."

"And you think, what . . . you can just swan in here a year later in a red dress and click your fingers and everything is going to be okay?"

"No."

"What *did* you think?"

"I wanted to tell you about my divorce face to face."

"Why?"

"I needed to see if it was still there between us."

"And is it?"

"You tell me."

The air crackles between us like a sonic boom.

"Would you like to go on a date with me sometime?" I ask.

His eyes hold mine. "What kind of date?"

*Huh?*

He wasn't supposed to say that. I've practiced this conversation a million times over in my head, and he never said that.

"What kind of dates are there?"

"Well, if you came here to fuck me . . ." His eyes dance with defiance. "I wouldn't say no. But if you came here to ask me to go on a real date, I would say not a chance in hell."

Ouch . . .

I nod as I swallow the lump in my throat. "Right."

*Short-term pain for long-term gain.*

"Then . . . looks like it's no date."

His eyes hold mine.

"I can fuck anybody, Blake. I didn't need to come all the way to New York to do that."

"Sweet."

"Looks like it."

He downs the rest of his drink. "I'll see you later, then."

"I'm at the Hilton, room 706."

"And you are telling me this . . . because?" He raises an eyebrow.

"No reason." I shrug. "Just in case you change your mind."

"Do you fuck on first dates now?"

"That's for me to know and you to find out."

His eyes hold mine. "How many men have you slept with?"

"None that matter."

"Very amusing, Rebecca, but stop wasting my time."

"Okay."

"Happy divorce. Good luck in the new house."

"Not the way I wanted to celebrate it . . . but whatever."

"Not my problem." He stands. "Go find another first date to fuck." He walks off back to his friends as I stare after him.

Damn it.

That was not the way that was supposed to go down.

Shit . . .


I lie in the dark and glance at the clock: 2:00 a.m. I roll over and punch my pillow.

He's not coming.

I don't know what I was thinking. Of course he's not fucking coming.

He was right. Did I actually think I could show up and he would run into my arms with a declaration of love?

Oh god, I'm so cringey.

Why would I give him my hotel room number? What do I think this is, a James Bond movie or something?

Get it together, Rebecca.

If you want Blake back, you need to work smarter, not harder.

And I do . . . god, I do.

I've worked so hard to get to where I am now.

I'm ready for love . . . but I only want it with Blake. He's the only one that matters.

I toss and turn and punch the pillow again.


I sit in the coffee shop and stare out onto the busy street. New York has an energy like no other place on earth. The smells, the sights, the sounds of the sirens in the distance. And where is everybody rushing to all the time?

Is everyone really this late?

I sip my coffee as I sit in the window that faces onto the street, and although things didn't turn out how I wanted them to this weekend, I do have a sense of achievement.

I got to tell Blake that I divorced John. I got to tell him that I'm selling my house. He didn't hear it secondhand from anybody; it came from my lips, and you have no idea how hard it was to keep that secret from the girls. The problem is, when your friends are married to their friends, things get out.

I glance at my watch. It's 5:00 p.m., and my flight is at 8:00.

My bags are with the concierge at the hotel, and I've been lingering around all day waiting for my flight tonight.

I specifically took the late flight in case things went well, and . . . let's just say I was hoping to spend the day with Blake.

I wasn't that lucky.

I finish the last of my coffee and make my way back to the hotel.

"Hello, I would like to check out and collect my bags, please," I tell the girl at reception.

"Of course, what was the name?"

"Rebecca Dalton."

She types into her computer. "Here it is."

I slide the key across the counter to her.

"Thank you," she replies as she takes it. "Do you have the second key?"

"No, there was only one key."

She frowns as she reads something. "It says here that your husband picked up another key at three this morning?"

What?

*He came.*

"Oh, I . . ."

I'm lost for words. "I see, I'm . . . he's already left for work this morning. I thought that he had my key. Sorry, just charge me for the extra key, please."

"Of course." She smiles.

I begin to hear my heartbeat in my ears. He came and then left without seeing me.

There's hope.

She rattles on with some kind of conversation, but my mind is far from here.

*What do I do?*

He wanted to see me, but something stopped him.

"Thank you. Here's your bag." She slides my suitcase around the desk.

I stare at it, unsure what my next move is, so excited and panicked that I can't comprehend what to think. "Thank you."

I scurry over to the couch in the lobby and take out my phone and call Juliet.

"Hey, babe," she answers. "How's your mom's house?"

"So . . ." I close my eyes, unable to believe what I'm just about to tell her. "Promise me this conversation is going to stay between you and I."

"What do you mean?"

"What I'm about to tell you . . . you cannot tell Henley, promise me."

"Of course. What's wrong?"

"Promise me."

"I promise."

"I'm in New York. I came to see Blake."

"What?" she whispers. "What happened?"

"I bumped into him last night."

"How did you bump into him?"

"Not so much bumping . . . more like stalking. I followed him from work to a bar in a cab."

"Rebecca," she whispers. "What the fuck are you doing?"

"I don't actually know. Anyway, listen. Last night didn't go as planned, and I just found out that he came to my hotel looking for me at three this morning, and I need you to tell me his address."

"What?" she gasps. "Three a.m.?"

"Do you have his address?"

"I mean, it's written down somewhere, but who knows where. And besides, how do I find it without asking Henley where it is?"

"Look. I just need you to find it out for me and call me back, because I'm going to go over there, and he can't know I'm coming because he won't be there if I am."

"Oh my god."

"You have to promise not to tell Henley."

"All right." She thinks aloud. "Maybe it's . . . give me a bit to try and find it. I'll call you back in ten minutes."

"Okay." I keep sitting on the foyer couch with my heart in my throat, and a message pings on my phone.

**I need you to distract Henley. Can you call him and tell him that your alarm has gone off so he can go over to your house and check things out?**

I text back.

**Great idea.**

I scroll through my numbers until I get to Henley's name, and I dial his number.

"Hey, Bec," he answers.

"Hen, hi, I'm so sorry to bother you. I'm at my parents' this weekend, and my security alarm just picked up something in my house. Can you go over and check on everything for me, please?"

"What did it say?"

I screw up my face as I try to think of the most believable lie that I can. "Just that movement has been detected or something. I'm not sure what it is. I know that Chloe has Daisy, so it's not Daisy. Maybe just go over and walk around outside for me, if you could?" I shrug as I try to sound serious. "Perhaps take Antony in case there's something untoward going on."

"Yeah, sure thing, no worries. It's probably just a bird or something. I'll call you in ten."

"Thanks."

He hangs up, and my heart beats ferociously. I just hope that Juliet can pull off a miracle.

I wait.

I wait.

And I wait.

Finally a text bounces back.

**I'm not sure if this is the right address, but it was in Henley's contacts.**

Hope blooms in my chest.

**Thanks, wish me luck.**

**Good luck baby.**
**Love you**
**X**

Forty minutes later, I find myself standing at the front of Blake's building.

He has a doorman.

Shit . . . of course he has a fucking doorman.

What do I do?

Do I just buzz and ask for him to let me up?

I really didn't want him to know I was coming. I just wanted to knock on his door and surprise him.

If he doesn't know that I'm coming, then he can't tell me not to.

I walk in through the grand foyer and look around. "Can I help you?" the doorman asks.

"I'm just waiting for a friend." I smile.

He nods and goes back to whatever he's doing at his desk while I take a seat on the fancy leather lounge.

*What the hell do I do now?*

On his desk I can see a set of keys with a swipe card attached to it. That's the card I need to get upstairs.

I look left and I look right. How do I get it?

Would he take a bribe?

Shit.

This is a disaster.

A car pulls up into the parking bay outside the building, and as the cabdriver is getting the person's suitcase out of the trunk, the suitcase bursts open. Books and things go flying everywhere. The doorman runs out through the front doors to help, and my eyes flick to the keys on his desk.

It's now or never.

I stand and walk straight to the desk and pick up the keys and go to the elevator.

If I'm going to hell, I may as well get arrested while I'm at it too.

I push the button as I look over my shoulder. "Come on."

I push it again and again. "Hurry up. Hurry up."

My eyes flick out front to the commotion of the broken bag as people scramble to pick everything up.

The elevator doors finally open, and I dive in and hit the close button. I swipe the card and hit level 7. It lights up.

*Success.*

My heart is hammering hard in my chest, and I cannot believe I just stole the fucking keys. Maybe I am a Bond girl after all.

The doors open, and I stride down the corridor with purpose. Then I knock hard on his door.

No answer.

I knock hard again. *Knock, knock, knock.*

Silence.

Damn it, he's not even home.

The door opens in a rush, and there he stands. The beautiful Blake Grayson in all his glory. He's wearing gray track pants and a white shirt, and his hair is a disheveled, beautiful mess.

He frowns when he sees me. "Rebecca."

"Hi, Blake."

He glances up the hallway. "What are you doing here?"

"Can I come in?"

His eyes hold mine for an extended beat before he moves to the side, granting me access to walk past him into his apartment.

My eyes roam around his apartment. It's dated but nice, nothing like his extravagant house at home.

"I'll ask you again, Rebecca, what are you doing here?"

"You came to my hotel last night."

A frown flashes across his face.

"But you didn't come to my room. Why?"

"I thought better of it."

"Why?"

"I didn't want to see you."

"But that doesn't make sense. Why did you come if you didn't want to see me?"

His fists are clenched at his sides. "It doesn't matter now."

"It matters to me, Blake. Why did you come to my hotel?"

"To get closure."

"On us?"

"What else would I be getting closure on, Rebecca?"

We stare at each other, and it's the weirdest thing. He's so familiar, but at the same time, he feels like a stranger.

So much water has passed under the bridge between us that I'm not sure the raft is even still afloat.

"Blake." The nerves in my stomach are pumping so hard that I can hardly form a sentence. "I came to New York because I love you. And I want to beg for a second chance."

"Bec, don't."

My eyes search his. "Is there any chance for us at all?"

"No."

"Not even one percent? Because one percent would be great."

"I care for you, Rebecca; I'll always care for you."

"But you don't love me anymore?" I whisper.

"Life isn't as black and white as you would wish sometimes."

"Blake, I was broken when we were together, and I didn't know it at the time. I was insecure and blaming myself for so many things

433

that had gone wrong in my life. It wasn't until you left me that I realized just how dysfunctional I was."

His eyes hold mine.

"I love you, and I know that you probably don't even need me anymore or think about me anymore or . . . I just want you to know that . . . you are my grand love," I whisper. "You were the person that I was supposed to spend my life with. And I know that I've ruined it, but I just think you should know that."

He exhales softly. "Bec," he whispers.

"You want closure?"

"I need closure."

"Then kiss me goodbye."

His eyes search mine.

"Please, Blake, kiss me goodbye just once. You want closure, so then we need to say goodbye to each other, because the way we ended before was just so sudden and so traumatic."

He nods softly. "It was."

I step toward him, and he stands his ground.

"All stories have a kiss goodbye, Blake."

He cups my face with his hand, and he looks so sad as I stare up at him. "Kiss me and make it better," I murmur.

"It's only going to make it worse."

"I'll worry about that tomorrow."

In slow motion, he bends, and his lips softly take mine. My eyes close at the intimacy of his touch. We kiss again, and this time, his tongue slowly slides through my lips.

*Oh.*

I've missed this. I've missed everything about this.

Our kiss deepens further; it becomes desperate. So much pain between us, and yet this kiss is a beacon of light in a very dark sea.

"Bec," he murmurs against my lips, "you need to go."

"I can't. Don't you see? We need this. Even if we aren't going to be together anymore, we need to finish this. Don't we owe it to ourselves to have one last time?"

He stares at me, and my eyes fill with tears. "I know you don't feel the same about me as I feel about you," I whisper. "I don't deserve for you to. But everything in my soul is telling me that you need this as much as I do."

"I do," he whispers.

Our kiss turns desperate as his hands grab my behind and grind me onto his hardened cock. He falls back onto the couch and pulls me over the top of him, my legs straddled over his.

We kiss as if our lives depend on it, hungry and desperate.

A reminder of all that we've missed.

He grabs the hem of my dress and pulls it up over my head and throws it to the side. Suddenly I'm in my underwear with my legs spread around his and his hard cock nudging up against my sex.

*Yes.*

I take his T-shirt over his head, and I'm blessed with the sight of his broad, muscular body.

Oh lord . . . how I've missed this.

I slide his tracksuit pants down, and his huge cock springs free. It's engorged, with a thick vein running down the length of it.

I've never seen anything more beautiful.

My eyes linger on his manhood, half in disbelief.

You really don't know what you've got until it's gone.

I fall to the floor and take him into my mouth; the taste of his salty pre-ejaculate is like honey on my lips. He inhales sharply as his hands tangle in my hair.

I take him deep down my throat. I need him closer.

So much to make up for.

His breathing is ragged, and he shudders as if close. "Get up here," he growls. "Get the fuck up here on my cock." He grabs my

435

arms and pulls me up to my position on his lap, my legs spread back around his. Holding his base, he swipes the tip of his cock through my dripping-wet flesh.

*Oh.*

We stare at each other, arousal and thick want bouncing between us.

"Get on it," he mouths darkly.

I slide down, but he's too big; my body meets resistance. He rocks me from side to side to try and loosen me up.

"Oh god," I moan. "I've missed this beautiful cock of yours."

He smiles darkly, and with his two hands on my hip bones, he slams me down hard, forcing my body to take him all.

I cry out at the possession as his body overtakes every single inch of mine.

My body ripples around his as we stare at each other.

"I love you," I whisper.

"Don't." His eyes flutter shut, as if he's trying to block me out.

"It's true."

Something snaps inside of him, something dark and sinister.

The next thing I know, I'm bent over on my hands and knees on the couch. He slides in deep, unforgiving, forcing me forward until my face crushes into the couch.

Then he's riding me hard, thick, fast pumps, and I can't even breathe as the air is knocked out of my lungs.

Good lord, nobody fucks like Blake Grayson.

*Nobody.*

He lifts one of my legs as he takes me deeper, harder, and faster, and I see all the stars as I scream for mercy.

"Blake," I whimper.

"This is what you came for, isn't it?" He continues to give me the beating that my body's been craving. Our skin slaps together, and he lets out a deep, guttural moan that turns me inside out.

I clutch the lounge as he pumps me one . . . two . . . three times, and my vision blacks out as I come hard and fast.

I cry out as I lose all control.

He holds himself deep, and I feel the telling jerk of his cock as he empties deep inside me.

We pant, gasping for air.

I feel a soft, tender kiss on the back of my shoulder blade. It reminds me of so many happy memories, and I smile into the couch cushion.

"I missed my plane," I pant.

"Who said I'm finished with you?"


Is there a better place on earth than lying with your head on Blake Grayson's chest?

No.

No, there is not.

We are naked, our bodies tangled together under the blankets. His lips are pressed against my temple.

It's late, and I've lost count of how many times we've made love tonight.

We fucked a few times, but then in the shower it changed. It was like I wore him down, and the longer I was in his arms, the more tender he became.

His fingers run aimlessly through my hair, and I know that he's as deep in thought as I am.

"God, I missed you," I murmur softly.

He kisses my temple but doesn't reply.

"Do you like living in New York?"

"Surprisingly, yes." I feel him smile against my skin.

"What do you like about it?" I ask.

"The anonymity."

I smile. "Somehow I don't think you could be anonymous anywhere you go, Blake."

It feels like old times between us, the tenderness, the love. The perfect fitting together of our bodies.

He was right. All that time, long ago, he was right—I was always meant to be his. And he was always meant to be mine.

"Good night, Blake," I whisper into the darkness.

"Good night, Bec."

For the first time in what feels like forever, wrapped safely in his arms, I drift into a restful sleep.

The scent of cologne wakes me, and I roll over to see Blake fully dressed in his suit. I sit up onto my elbows and look around groggily. "What time is it?" I murmur.

"Time for you to get up." He adjusts his cuff links. "I've booked you on a flight this morning at eleven."

"Oh." I frown. I fiddle with the blankets as I think out loud. "Maybe I could stay for a few extra days?"

His eyes meet mine in the mirror. "No, I think you should get going."

"Blake, I could move here. I mean, I know it's not perfect for Daisy, but I could walk her three times a day, and maybe I could do some online tutoring from home, and . . . ?"

He comes in, sits on the side of the bed, and tucks a piece of my hair behind my ear.

"Bec, you need to go home."

"But when will I see you again?"

"Remember what this was . . ."

I cut him off. "I don't want closure. I want this to be a new beginning."

"Bec, I . . ."

438

"If I could take back that day, Blake, I would give anything to be able to do that. You and me, we're too perfect together."

"Rebecca." He sighs.

"I ruined our relationship because I wasn't past my hurt, and now you're going to do the same thing."

His eyes hold mine.

"You love me. I know you love me."

"I do."

"Then what's the problem?"

"I'm not where you left me. I've moved on."

My eyes search his. "You've met someone else?"

"Yes."

My heart free-falls from my chest.

"Who is she?"

"She's my boss."

I sit up, outraged. "So you slept with me last night knowing that you are with somebody else?"

"I slept with you last night to get the closure we both needed. Just like we discussed we were going to do. Do not fucking turn this back on me. You knew exactly what you were getting."

I jump out of bed in outrage. "You have a girlfriend?"

He goes back to adjusting his cuff links. "That's what I said, isn't it?"

I feel sick to my stomach.

"You cheated on her . . . with me?"

"Spare me the angelic act." He rolls his eyes as if I'm a major inconvenience. "Don't act like you didn't love every fucking second of it."

I open my mouth to say something, and he cuts me off.

"If I had told you last night, it wouldn't have mattered one iota . . . you were here for one thing and one thing only . . . and you got it."

*What?*

"Who even are you?" I whisper.

His cold eyes meet mine. "I'm exactly who you always thought I was." He holds his hands out in a dramatic fashion. "The player who cheats." He gives me a sarcastic smile. "Be careful what you wish for, Rebecca."

*Touché.*

His silhouette blurs.

"Fuck you," I whisper.

"You already did that . . . now go home." He walks out of the room, and moments later, I hear the door close behind him.

I drop my head into my hands. *Fuck.*

# Chapter 26

I read the email Blake has forwarded to me, and I walk to the front desk at the airport.

"Hi, I'd like to check in, please. The name is Rebecca Dalton." I pass over my identification.

She types into her computer. "Do you have any luggage to check in?"

"Just my carry-on."

She prints out the ticket and passes it over, void of emotion. "You may go to the members' lounge to wait for your check-in. Have a nice flight."

"Thanks." I glance at my ticket as I walk away from the desk.

Business class.

Of course he bought me business class. Typical Blake.

Ugh . . . the man is infuriating.

I stomp through the airport.

*I'm not where you left me. I've moved on.*

My stomach twists as the memory of his words cuts like a knife.

*I'm exactly who you always thought I was. The player who cheats. Be careful what you wish for, Rebecca.*

I feel sick to my stomach.

His boss, no less.

She's a doctor, so obviously a brainiac, probably gorgeous, and she gets to see him every day, so . . .

I drag my hand down my face in disgust.

Honestly, I just want to crawl under a rock and hide.

He wanted closure, but all it has done for me is open up a wound in my heart. A deep gash that I now know will never fucking heal.

Only now I can add the title Seedy Side Chick to my résumé.

I go through check-in and find my way to the members' lounge and take a seat at the bar.

"What will it be?" the bartender asks me.

I look over the choices. Screw it, it's five o'clock somewhere. "A glass of champagne, please."

"Ten in the morning." He smiles as he wipes the counter. "Are we celebrating or commiserating?"

"Commiserating."

He gives me a knowing smile. "Rough weekend?"

*In more ways than one.*

"You have no idea."


### Blake

**I sit in the hospital cafeteria and stare into space.**

**It's been a rough three days.**

**Pushing Rebecca away has been the hardest thing I've ever had to do.**

**I keep going over our night together in my head.**

**The perfect storm.**

**I know it shouldn't have happened, and yet I couldn't stop myself from touching her one last time.**

***She came to me.***

442

But I lied to her . . .

*She gave me no choice.*

I mean, it wasn't completely untrue. I have been talking to Sam, although I haven't asked her out yet.

I get a vision of Rebecca and me rolling around under the sheets, and my heart somersaults in my chest.

No.

I can't go back there. I need to move on.

Rebecca had her chance with me, and she blew it. I'm nobody's punching bag.

Least of all somebody who is supposed to love me.

"Hey there, you," a familiar voice says from behind me. I look up to see Sam.

"Hey, you joining me for lunch?"

"Okay." She smiles.

Sam is beautiful and intelligent and funny. We get along like a house on fire and have been hanging out for weeks.

*It's time to move on.*

My eyes hold hers as I come to an internal decision. "Would you like to go out on the weekend?" I ask her.

"We go out every weekend," she replies as she looks over the menu.

"I mean on a date."

Her eyes rise to meet mine. "A date?"

"That's what I said."

She smiles softly as electricity bounces between us. "I thought you'd never ask."

*That makes two of us.*

"So, Saturday night?"

"I can't wait." She smiles sexily.

"Me too."

Laughter echoes through the cul-de-sac as the boys sink a ball into the hole.

I rock on the swinging chair on the front porch.

"I'm going to miss this street," I say sadly.

Chloe's lying on the ground with the cushion under her head. She's on her phone. And Juliet is sitting beside me.

"Wait a minute," Chloe says. "I think I found something." She frowns as she concentrates. "Is her name Sam Holland?"

"I don't know. He just said she was his boss." I shrug.

"You know what I don't understand?" Juliet frowns. "If he's really in a relationship with this woman, then why did he sleep with you?"

"He said he wanted closure."

"But did he get it . . . is the question," Juliet huffs. "And I want to know, does this Sam Holland bitch know what her stupid boyfriend is doing?"

"She's a doctor; she's not stupid. And it wasn't his fault. I went to him, and looking back, I basically threw myself into his arms. So what kind of woman does that make me?"

"Someone who's in love with him." Chloe rolls her eyes. "Don't you let yourself feel like crap over this. He should have told you before he got his dick out that he had a girlfriend."

I pinch the bridge of my nose in disgust. "I'm just grossed out by the whole thing."

"You know what? Screw him. You're better than this bullshit," Juliet huffs. "I'm off him. Who does he think he is, you know? You reacted bad to a wedding proposal, so what?"

I look over at her deadpan, and she smirks. "Well, okay, I get it, but honestly, don't get your cock out if you're seeing someone else, that's all I'm saying."

"Maybe they have an open relationship?" Chloe says. "Give me some more details. I'm going deep on this bitch."

Juliet googles her name. "Okay, it says here that Sam Holland is a specialist pediatrician who is the head of the American Pediatric Board."

"What does she look like?" I ask.

She holds her phone over, and I see a beautiful blonde with shoulder-length hair. She's around our age and has that successful air about her.

"Ugh." I roll my eyes. "Yeah, that would be her. She's his taste for sure."

"Found her," Chloe snaps. She begins to scroll through her pictures on Instagram. "I don't see any pictures of Blake on here . . . they can't be too serious."

"Good."

"Oh no . . . here's one."

"Show me." I snatch the phone off her.

There's a picture that she's taken at a dinner table in a restaurant somewhere. The photo is supposed to be of the meal, but Blake is strategically sitting behind it, holding his knife and fork with a sexy smile. "When was this posted?" I think out loud.

"Three weeks ago."

"Is that the first pic posted of them together?"

Chloe takes the phone back off me and keeps scrolling. "Think so. Oh wait . . . Is this his arm in this picture?" She holds the phone out again, and this time, she's taking a selfie, and there's a hand in the picture. I'd know those sexy veins in the back of that hand anywhere. "Yep, that's Blake's hand." I pass the phone back in disgust.

"Okay, so this photo was posted six weeks ago."

"He can't be too in love with her."

My face falls. "You think he's in love with her?"

"Don't know." She shrugs.

"He did say he's not where I left him. He's moved on."

"Maybe you should do the same," Chloe huffs. "Screw him."

"I'm trying. Trust me, I'm fucking trying."

"How is going to New York and sleeping with him moving on?" Juliet mutters dryly.

"Look, I just needed him to know that I'm selling the house, and I'm moving out of the street, and he can come back anytime he wants to."

"That's fair, I guess."

"And maybe we will never get back together . . . we'll actually probably never get back together. But at least he knows what I wanted to say. I kind of feel like both he and I needed that night. I don't regret it."

"Even though you're a home-wrecker?" Chloe smirks up at me.

"If I was a home-wrecker, I would message that stupid doctor woman on Instagram and tell her."

"That is a very good point."

We sit in silence for a while, and there's a chill in the air as the season changes. I can smell someone barbecuing on the grill, and the sound of laughter is prevalent.

Change is coming.

My life here will soon be a memory, and although I'm excited to start this new chapter of my life, I'm devastated to be leaving it behind.

I've always felt protected on this street. Kingston Lane has been my home. Whether that had anything to do with Blake and his undying friendship, or Carol and her gossip, or Winston and his bad jokes, even Barry . . . I'll never understand.

My new house is not far from here, about six blocks. I couldn't afford to stay in this area, but I'm close enough that I can still walk here if I want to, and I guess for now, that will have to do. My long-term goal is to get back to this side of the suburbs one day.

Who knows: if this move doesn't go well, and I don't stay in touch with my friends here, I may even end up moving home to be closer to family.

I considered it for this move, but . . . the thought of breaking all ties was just too much to bear.

"Oh . . . get off it," Chloe spits. "Look at her in a fucking bikini. Come off it, poser."

She holds the phone up, and I take it off her and study the picture. Sam Holland the genius supermodel is wearing a white bikini and water-skiing behind a boat. "She can water ski?" I scoff. "Is there anything this bitch can't do?" She's tanned, with abs and quads and biceps, totally toned. "How can you be this gorgeous and be a fucking doctor?" I scoff in disgust.

Juliet takes the phone off me and studies the picture too.

"Jeez, she's buff," she whispers.

I imagine Blake and her rolling around in the sheets, and I just want to throw up.

I pass the phone back in disgust. "Don't show me anything else. I don't want to see it. Screw Blake Grayson; I'm done with him."

She keeps scrolling while I sip my wine. "Oh crap, she used to go out with that hot politician."

I snatch the phone back off her. "Who?"


I put the last of the dinner plates into the box and tape it up.

I've been packing up my house and keeping myself busy, trying to forget all about a certain person who we shall not name.

Three weeks until the move.

You know, it's the strangest thing—when I was trying to fix myself, I always had it in my head that once I got better and found who I was again, Blake and I would have a chance.

But now to know that I was too late . . . by a few weeks.

If I'd gone two months earlier, would he have been single? Would he have considered my offer?

So many what-ifs, and not one damn answer.

Some days, I win. I have my ducks in a row, and I'm looking forward to the move, and Daisy and I walk for miles.

Some days, I can't get out of bed for my hatred of the entire male species.

To make matters worse, the dating pool at my age is not a pool at all. It's more like a muddy puddle. There's no plenty of fish in the sea, just mangy, three-eyed tadpoles.

I slump down onto the kitchen stool and take out my phone and scroll through to Blake's Instagram. No new posts.

He hasn't posted for two years. I really wish that he would, because damn it, I'm dying not knowing what's going on in New York.

So, of course, my next move is to do something completely toxic and unproductive: I scroll to his girlfriend's page to see if she's putting up any more posts of my beloved.

She hasn't. No posts in the five weeks since I left there.

I wonder, did he tell her about our night together?

I doubt he would have.

When I was in my fix-myself era, I went on a few dates with people and did the deed a few times, more because I felt like I needed to than because I wanted to.

And honestly, sex without Blake really isn't that great.

*At all.*

Just like he promised, that damn piercing of his has ruined me for all other men.

Maybe having a life partner isn't in my future. Maybe I'll be an animal mom instead of a human mom.

That's okay. Nobody could love me more than my little Daisy does.

My mind flicks back to the night that Blake gave her to me in the basket, on the most magical Christmas Eve of my life.

I smile sadly at the memory.

You know what? I was blessed, because at least I got to know what it felt like to be loved by a man like him, even if only for a short period of time.

I'll be okay, whatever happens, and screw him—I'm not looking them up anymore.

They can move to the moon to start up a new hospital for aliens, for all I care.

I tape up another box and get back to work. Why the hell do I have so much kitchen crap?

*Knock, knock.*

Henley appears. "Hey, Bec."

"Hi, is Jules home?"

"No, she'll be back soon; she's gone to get some milk. Do you want to wait for her? She'll only be a minute."

"Yeah, okay. I'll just sit here." I sit down on the front step, and he sits down beside me.

It's funny between us now. Ever since that weekend where Blake and I . . . well, the log cabin incident, Henley has kept me at arm's length, and I know why.

I get it.

If I'm being honest, I respect it. He's Blake's friend.

"Nearly packed?" he says.

"Yeah, just winding up the last of it now. It's such a big job to pack up a house."

"I dread moving. Not that I ever will, I hope."

I smile as I look out over the street.

We sit in silence for a while, and I just can't hold it in. I have to ask. "How's Blake?"

"He's good."

"I'm happy for him." I smile sadly. "I want him to be happy."

"Yeah, well . . ." He frowns. "I have a sneaking suspicion that he'll be back for you."

I frown. "What makes you say that?"

He smiles wistfully as he looks out over the street. "Blake has been in love with you from the moment he laid eyes on you, Rebecca."

I get a lump in my throat.

"Not because he didn't know what other women were like. He had plenty of women chasing him."

I smile as I look at the ground. Isn't that the truth?

"The thing is with Blake, he was so in love with you that . . . he was too blinded by his own feelings to gauge where you were at."

*What?*

My eyes search his.

"You know, when you're besotted with someone for so long and you haven't been in a serious relationship before, I imagine that it's easy to do. He backed you into a corner where you felt the only way out was rejection. He rushed you into something you weren't ready for."

Oh . . .

"Our demise wasn't his fault; it was mine," I whisper.

"He needed to get some perspective."

"What do you mean?"

450

"I'm just saying, you two were always going to break up. You were just out of a relationship, and this was his first real one. Not to mention he was head over heels in love with you in an almost—"

I cut him off. "Well, I've lost him now. So I guess it doesn't matter."

"He'll be back for you. Mark my words."

"How do you know?"

"Because I know Blake, and you weren't a flash in the pan for him. You were his grand love, and I know in my heart that one day he *will* come back."

"Well, he might be too late by then." I act tough. My eyes click over to him. "Wait, why? Did he say anything?"

Henley gives me a broad smile. "No."

I nod and stay silent. "Does he ever ask about me?"

"Not really."

I twist my fingers together on my lap, not sure if I even want an answer to this question. "Does he love his new girlfriend?"

"He doesn't talk about her to me."

"But you know of her?"

"Yeah, I know of her."

"Did he tell you that I went to New York to see him?"

"Yes."

"What did he say?"

"He just asked me to watch over you when you got back to make sure you're okay."

An unexpected lump forms in my throat. *That's my Blake, always thoughtful.*

"I might just wait for Juliet at home." I stand.

"You okay?"

"Depends what day you ask me." I smile.

"Do you need help with the move?"

"No, I'm all packed, and the truck comes on Saturday."

"Are you sad to be leaving?"

"Yes and no."

"What do you mean?"

"Well . . . for so long, all I wanted to do was hold on to my house. Now all it reminds me of is that it cost me Blake, so . . ." *Stop talking.* I shrug, embarrassed. "Anyway, I'm going to get going. I'm just rambling."

"Goodbye."

"Bye."


Moving day is never fun, but this one is especially hard.

How do you say goodbye to friends that you thought you would know for life? The moving truck is full of my furniture, and one by one, my friends and neighbors turn up on my front lawn to say goodbye.

I'll see them again, of course, when I come to visit Juliet, but the reality is that things will change.

I will become the outsider who is just visiting.

I've cried all the tears that I can cry, and honestly, I just want to be rid of this house and the bad memories it holds.

Funny thing is that it's not even bad memories of my marriage anymore. This is the house that cost me Blake. The love of my life.

And no matter how many times I can try and tell myself that it's fine, it isn't fine. It will never be fine.

I click Daisy's lead on, and we walk out front. "You all ready to go?" Henley asks.

"Yep." I smile and pull him into a hug. "Thank you for everything."

I hug Antony and Ethel and Winston. I get to Carol, and she starts crying.

"I'll see you all the time, Carol." I hug her tight. "It's fine."

"I know, I know." She sniffs. "I just never wanted you to move. You're such a beautiful girl, and I'm going to miss you, too, Daisy."

I walk to my car and take one last look around Kingston Lane. Such a wonderful little street with such beautiful people in it.

Not the happily ever after I was hoping for, but maybe the fresh new start that I need.

I open the door, and Daisy climbs in the back. I get into my car.

And as my friends wave goodbye, I drive out of Kingston Lane with tears in my eyes.

"It's just me and you now, Daisy. It's just me and you . . ."

It's winter. The air is crisp, and frost glints in the corners of the window.

I have the most beautiful bay window in the front living room with a big window seat with cushions. My house is freshly painted, and I'm suddenly into nesting.

It's weird—I've been in this house now for eight weeks, and it's the happiest I've been in a long time.

I feel free.

No longer held hostage to the bricks and mortar that I feared losing so much.

No more stupid foot photos.

The future is bright, and the world is my oyster.

Things have changed a lot. Liam, Juliet's brother, has moved into her old house, and a new family with teenage kids has moved into mine.

The cul-de-sac will be different now with all the new people, and it wouldn't have been the same even if I'd stayed.

My timer on my oven dings, and I walk into the kitchen. Then Daisy starts to bark at the window.

"What is it, Daisy Doo?" I call to her.

I hear the front step creak, and I walk to the front door and stop on the spot when I see who it is.

"Blake."

"Hi, Bec." His eyes search mine.

"Hi." My heart somersaults in my chest. "Are you . . ." I put my hand on my chest to try and calm myself. "Visiting?"

"No."

"No?"

"I moved back . . . last week."

"Last week?"

"Oh." I nod as I search for something to say. "But your job . . ."

"I've returned to my practice here."

"Right." I nod in an overexaggerated way.

The air swirls between us, but with what, I'm just not sure.

"And your girlfriend?"

"We broke up."

"Why?"

"Because she wasn't you."

My eyebrows shoot up in surprise. "That's a good reason."

"She didn't seem to think so."

*Ha!*

I bite my bottom lip to hide my smile.

"What are you doing here?" I ask.

"I . . ." He pauses as his eyes search mine. "I needed to see you."

"Yeah, well . . . I don't associate with men who cheat, so . . ." I shrug.

"I wasn't with her when you came to New York."

My eyes hold his as I listen.

"I only told you that because I knew it would make you leave."

*Asshole.*

"Right . . ." I pause as I try to articulate my thoughts. "I was a mess before we broke up, and I've owned that, but the way you handled our breakup was just as bad. To not even talk to me until I hijacked you in your car at work was pathetic."

"Agreed."

"And immature, not to mention selfish."

He twists his lips. "The evidence does suggest that."

An awkward silence falls between us.

"Maybe . . ." He shrugs. "Maybe . . . I needed to do some work on myself too."

"Maybe?" I raise my eyebrow in disgust.

"Probably." He gives a subtle shake of his head. "Definitely."

"I'll ask you again, Blake. *What* are you doing here?"

"I want a second chance."

"Why?"

"Because a life without you isn't one that I want." His eyes search mine.

I get a lump in my throat as I feel my defenses drop.

"Will you make me lasagna?" he whispers.

*Oh . . .*

"For how long?"

He smiles softly. "Forever sounds pretty good."

"Well, forever is a bit presumptuous." I shrug. "We didn't even go on a first date yet."

"Rebecca." Amusement flashes across his face. "Do you want to go on a date with me?"

"Where to?" I hold my hand up and pretend to look at my fingernails.

His amusement breaks into a smirk. "To a restaurant."

"I'll have to think about it. I'm pretty busy."

"Get into the house before I smack your ass." He points into the house, and I laugh out loud and turn and run.

He chases me down and crash tackles me to the floor and holds my hands up above my head. His lips take mine in a soft kiss. "Hi." He smiles down at me.

"Hi." I smile back.

Who am I kidding?

*Forever does sound pretty good.*

# Epilogue

*Twelve months later*

The dinner table erupts into laughter, and I smile as I watch the game.

Carol, Taryn, and Chloe are on the couch talking to Juliet, and Winston is playing cards with Antony, Blake, and Henley. I'm bouncing Hannah on my lap; she looks up at me with her big blue eyes and tries to grab my necklace. "Hey." I smile.

"Hey," she coos right back.

The cutest little baby girl that you ever did see.

"You are *one hundred* percent cheating," Henley tells Antony.

"I am not," he scoffs. "You're just a sore loser."

Blake smirks as he looks at his cards, and I get the feeling that he's the one who's cheating.

Some things never change, and yet some things do. Life is different for me now.

I live with Blake in his house. Our life is filled with love and laughter, and I guess, as the saying goes, time does heal all wounds.

I'm laughing my way through life with my best friend.

"Could you be any cluckier, Bec?" Juliet teases.

"Not really." I bounce Hannah as I hold her little hands in mine.

Blake's eyes are glued to his hand of cards. He's deep in concentration.

"Give the woman a baby, Grayson," Henley mutters.

"I want to be married before I have a baby," I announce.

Blake chews on a toothpick, his eyes not rising for even a second. "You're as subtle as a Mack truck, Rebecca."

Everyone chuckles. It's become a joke between us now. I want to get married, and Blake won't hear a word of it.

"He's going to ask me any day," I tease.

"No way," he mutters as he pulls a card out of his hand and throws it down onto the table.

"Way." I widen my eyes. "Henley, I want my ring back out of your safe."

"Not happening, Dalton," Blake says as he collects the cards. He scoops them up into his hand. "I've still got PTSD from last time."

Everyone laughs.

"Keep going, and I'm going to have to ask you," I warn him.

"Good," he fires back. "I can't wait to say no."

I smile. He acts so tough . . . but deep down, we all know the truth.

Everyone chuckles and goes back to their conversations.

*Maybe I actually should ask him?*

Hmm . . .


### Blake

**The chatter from the golfing green fills the street, and as I walk over to them, I check the mailbox. I shuffle through the mail as I stand on the driveway and get to one and stop still.**

Nooky Nights
Kingston Lane


What?

I tear the letter open at double speed. "The fuck is this?"
I haven't thought about Nooky Nights for months.


Dear Nooky Nights,

Thank you for your recent inquiry.

We adored your story about Lazarus and
Freya and were swept away with your writing.

We would love to offer you a publishing
contract. However, our emails to you keep
bouncing back.

Please contact us as soon as possible, as we
don't have another means to contact you apart
from this mailing address.

Sincerely,

Dark and Dangerous Publishing House


"What the hell?" I march over to the boys. "Look at this."
I hold the letter out, and Henley takes it from me and begins
to read.

"The fuck . . ."

"What is it?" Ant asks.

"Hey there, cutie." I touch the end of Hannah's cute little
button nose. She's in a sling on Henley's chest. Her favorite
pastime is playing golf with us.

"Shit." Henley passes the letter to Antony, and he begins
to read.

Antony's mouth falls open, and he looks up at us. "I told
you that story was fucking good."

"What good is it, though, if it doesn't ever get published? Someone on Kingston Lane is sitting on a gold mine, and they don't even know it."

"We have to find who wrote it."

"But how?"

"Well . . . we know it's definitely not Rebecca," I reply.

"True."

I glance over and see Carol talking to Winston on her front steps. "How come those two are so friendly lately?"

"Fuck knows," Henley mutters. Hannah starts to fuss. "I have to go in."

"But what about Nooky?" I call after him.

He holds his hands up. "Fuck knows."

"Stop cursing. Hannah can hear you," I call. "She's going to learn the word *fuck*."

He gives me the bird as he disappears inside.

"Hmm." Ant reads the letter again. "I reckon just ask everyone."

"But then their secret will be out. Whoever wrote it wants it to be kept private."

He holds his hands up. "I don't know, man."

"Blake," Rebecca calls.

I glance up to see Bec standing on our front steps. "Dinner's ready. Got to go."

"See you." Ant keeps putting the ball.

I walk back into the house to see everything in darkness and a trail of candles leading from the front door.

"Huh?" I frown. "Bec?"

"In here."

I walk into the kitchen and see a mass of candles on the table and little dishes of lasagna.

"What the . . ." I frown.

It's then that I see the lasagnas are in letter tins.

## MARRY ME

I spin around to see Rebecca on one knee. "Blake Grayson."
I smirk.

"Will you do me the honor of becoming my husband?"

"What do you mean?" I tease.

"Will you marry me?" She smiles up at me, all hopeful.

"What kind of marriage—"

"Blake," she snaps, cutting me off, "don't push your luck."

I drop to my knees in front of her. "You took your damn time, woman." I smirk.

She smiles. "Is that a yes?"

"That's an abso-fucking-lutely." I kiss her softly as I take her face in my hands. Our lips linger over each other's as we bask in the moment.

"Oh . . . just a minute." I get up as I remember something. "Stay there."

"What?" She frowns as she stays kneeling.

I take the stairs two at a time and run into the spare room and reach under the bed. I feel and feel . . . Where is the fucking thing?

Got it.

I run back downstairs and open the ring box. Her yellow diamond rings sits proudly on display.

"Oh," she gasps. "You told me you returned this."

I take her hand and slide it onto her finger. "I never gave up on my dream of marrying you."

Her eyes well with tears. "I love you, Blake Grayson."

"I can tell by the marry-me lasagna." I smile against her lips.

**"The way to a man's heart is through his stomach, right?"
I chuckle. "We're a match made in heaven already."**

*Rebecca*

"I now pronounce you husband and wife." The priest smiles. "You may kiss your bride."

Blake takes my face in his hands and kisses me as our friends and family all cheer.

We did it.

Husband and wife. We made it.

He takes my hand, and we make our way out of the church as everyone throws confetti.

We laugh and smile, take photos and bask in the glory.

*We made it.*

"Speech," everyone calls.

Blake holds his hands up and stands, and I smile as I look up at him.

We had a traditional wedding, and now we're at the reception. He looks so handsome in his black dinner suit.

This is the happiest I've ever seen him.

He picks up the microphone. "Hello." He gives a sexy smile to the crowd, and everyone laughs, unsure what to expect.

This man is so exuberant.

"Hello," he says loudly.

"Hello," everyone calls back.

He looks out over the beautiful event room at our closest friends and family. "Thank you for coming today. It means a lot to us to have such beautiful people in our lives."

I smile up at him as I listen.

"Now . . . many of you are here because you think I fell in love with Rebecca Dalton."

"Aren't you?" Henley mutters, and Antony chuckles.

"But that's not actually how it happened."

I frown, and the crowd laughs out loud.

Oh hell . . .

*What is he going to say?*

I smile nervously as everyone laughs hysterically. I never know what's going to come out of Blake's mouth at any given time.

"You see, the word *falling* indicates that it was an accident." His eyes find mine. "I didn't accidentally fall in love with Rebecca. I knew the sound of her heartbeat, craved the feel of her touch." He gives me a slow, sexy smile. "I purposefully walked into love with open arms, an open heart, and a dream to make her mine."

The crowd swoons.

"Praying to god that one day, she would hopefully learn to love me back."

His silhouette blurs.

"We didn't take it the easy way." His eyebrows flick up as if he's unimpressed.

Everyone laughs again.

"But I wouldn't change a thing, because it brought us to where we are today." He bends and kisses me softly. "Even though she's a giant crybaby."

Everyone breaks into laughter again as I chuckle through my tears and swat him away.

*He's completely right.*

"So, I would like to propose a toast to my beautiful wife, Rebecca Grayson." The crowd cheers once more. "I love you, and

I'm going to spend the rest of my life making you happy." He raises his glass in the air. "To my Rebecca."

"To your Rebecca," the crowd cheers.

### Paris

The final destination of our wonderful six-week honeymoon around Europe.

We've been to the most beautiful places and seen the most incredible things. Tomorrow we fly home, and I start work on Monday.

We are at the Eiffel Tower, ambling along the promenade and eating ice cream.

Blake digs his phone out of his pocket and frowns when he looks at the screen. "Why is Antony awake and calling me at this time?"

I shrug. "Probably can't sleep."

"Hey," he answers. His face falls, and he stops on the spot. "Calm down. I can't understand you."

*What's happened?*

"What?" His eyes widen before he closes them and drags his hand through his hair. "Oh my god."

"What?" I mouth. "What happened?"

"I'm so sorry," he says as his eyes cloud over. "Yeah." He listens. "Okay." He closes his eyes. "Okay, when do you go?" He listens again. "Hang on."

He covers the phone with his hand. "Antony's brother and his wife have been killed in a car accident in Thailand while on vacation."

"Oh no," I whisper.

"Their three kids are with the hotel babysitters, and Ant has to go and collect them. He needs help."

"Go meet him in Thailand. Of course," I stammer.

He picks the phone back up. "Okay, I'll be on the first flight. Text me the hotel." He listens again. "Ant . . . it's going to be okay." He listens again. "I promise you, it's going to be okay. I'll see you and Henley soon."

He hangs up, and his eyes come to meet mine.

"Those poor little babies," I whisper.

"Three little ones under four."

"Oh no."

"It gets worse." He drags his two hands through his hair. "Much worse."

"How can it get any worse than that?" I gasp in horror.

"Being a lawyer, Antony did his brother's will two years ago."

"And?"

"Her parents have passed, and she's an only child. Antony's parents are in Italy and very elderly. Antony's the last . . ." His voice trails off.

"I don't understand."

"They left the kids to him."

My eyes widen as I put the puzzle together.

*Dear god.*

I can't wait to return to Kingston Lane in 2025.
Thank you so much for reading, everyone.
You have made my dreams come true.

All my love,
Tee xoxo

# ACKNOWLEDGEMENTS

There are not enough words to express my gratitude for this life that I get to live.

To be able to write books for a living is a dream come true. But not just any books—I get to write exactly what I want, the stories that I love.

To my wonderful team: Kellie, Christine, Alina, Keeley, Abbey and Rachel, Lindsey and Sammia.

Thank you for everything that you do for me.

You are so talented and so appreciated.

You keep me sane.

To my fabulous beta readers, you make me so much better.

My beautiful mum, who reads everything I write and gives me never-ending support. I love you, Mum. Thank you—xo.

My beloved husband and three beautiful kids, thanks for putting up with my workaholic ways.

And to you, the best, most supportive reader family in the entire world.

Thank you for everything. You have changed my life.

All my love, Tee xoxo

READ ON FOR AN EXCERPT OF
*THE BONUS.*

# The Bonus

*Grace*

My name is Grace Porter, and I am the personal assistant to Gabriel Ferrara, CEO of Ferrara Industries in New York.

And it's the perfect job: great pay, beautiful office, everything I ever dreamed of, if not for one small detail.

I am utterly and hopelessly in love with my boss.

Every day, it starts the same. At precisely 8:20 a.m., I make my way into his office. By this time, he's already run on his treadmill, had an infrared sauna, and showered. We run through his day while he dresses.

Watching Gabriel put on his suit each morning is the highlight of my day. Who am I kidding—it's the highlight of my fucking life.

I pick up my notes and knock softly.

"Come in," his strong voice calls.

I tentatively open the door to see him standing at his coffee machine, white towel around his waist. Tanned muscles, broad back, and dominance for miles, the lethal trifecta. "Morning, Gracie."

"Good morning, Gabriel," I reply. My eyes drink him in while he has his back to me. It's the only time I can stare uninterrupted.

He turns and passes me my cup and saucer. "Your coffee, madam."

"Thank you." I tentatively take a sip. Warm and delicious. Even his coffee is smooth. He goes back to making his coffee while I take a seat at his desk. I open his computer and log in to his schedule.

My eyes flick over the screen to his sculpted back. Damn it.

Why is he so delicious? How could any female work in these conditions and not be completely besotted with him?

And then he opens his mouth . . . and I remember why.

"Did you sleep at all last night? You look like shit."

"Thanks," I mutter as I refocus on his day.

"I didn't sleep much either. Actually, can you remind me later to send flowers?"

I bite the side of my cheek.

*Fucker.*

Not only do I have to watch him date every beautiful woman in the world, I have to send them fucking flowers too.

"Of course," I reply as I act unaffected.

I'm positive that I could win an Academy Award for acting as casual as I do.

"What have we got today?" he asks as he disappears into his large closet. From my peripheral vision, I see the white towel drop as he puts his briefs on.

*Focus.*

I exhale as the screen jumbles. He's busy.

Even reading his schedule is exhausting. "Board meeting at nine."

"Let's run through that agenda." He walks out of the closet in black briefs, his suit and shirt on hangers.

"You are talking about the flow-on effect from the defamation case against Noble Industries," I reply.

"Yes, that's right. Did we get that information?"

"Bryce sent it to your email, and it's saved in your Noble Industry file."

"Thank you." He pulls on his white shirt and slowly does up the buttons. "And do I have the graph?"

"Uh-huh." I bite my bottom lip as I try to focus on the screen. Something about him standing there in his briefs doing up a white shirt . . . it scrambles my brain.

Every.

Single.

Morning.

"Okay, so what then?" he asks.

"You have a meeting with Roger at ten fifteen." My eyes flick up to him. "Why do you have a meeting with Roger?"

"I'm letting him go." He pulls up his navy suit pants and zips up.

"What?"

He shrugs. "He's not performing."

"You can't fire Roger; he's going through a lot right now. His wife left him."

"Probably wasn't performing in bed either," he mutters dryly as he puts his gold cuff links on. "Wouldn't surprise me."

"Now is not the time. Can you just give him a warning, please?"

"It's amusing that you think you have a say in this matter." He pulls his suit coat on. "Next appointment?"

"You have a phone conference with Holly. You are closing on the land for the shopping mall at three p.m. today, and she needs to run through a few details."

"Uh-huh."

"At eleven, you have a walk-through of the finance department to see the new refurbishment of their office."

He screws up his face in disgust. "Why?"

"Because you do," I snap in frustration. "You paid for it. The least you can do is be excited."

"You're getting a bit lippy this morning, Grace," he snaps. "Don't piss me off before nine."

He walks back into his wardrobe, and the scent of his aftershave wafts through the office.

Fuck it . . . Why does he spray that when I'm in his office?

It's morally wrong.

I keep reading through his schedule. "You have lunch at twelve thirty with . . ." I frown, and my eyes rise to meet his. "Veronica."

"Uh-huh," he says casually. "Drink your coffee so I can collect your cup."

I sip my coffee as I plot his death.

*Is it Veronica Rothchild?*

That's a new name. I don't know a Veronica other than Veronica Rothchild, the supermodel, and I know that they met two weeks ago at a charity event.

I'm happy with his regular women because I know that he sees them just as that . . . regulars. But every time he meets someone new, I panic a little. This could be the woman who he finally falls in love with.

As well as acting, another job I excel at is undercover detective. I know who he is sleeping with before he does.

"Well, you don't have long for lunch. You have to be back at the office at one thirty for a very important meeting." I focus on the screen.

"Cancel it."

"Impossible." I keep typing and try to change the subject. "Who am I sending flowers to today?"

"Hmm." He purses his lips as he thinks. "Melissa."

"The card reading?" I act uninterested.

"You were incredible last night."

I clench my teeth so hard, I nearly break my jaw. "Is that it?"

"Um." He walks over to the window and looks down over New York. "Come away with me this weekend."

My eyes linger on his back as sadness sets in.

I can't do this anymore.

Every time I send one of his girls flowers or gifts, I die a little inside.

I'm twenty-nine years old, and for seven years, I have hung off Gabriel Ferrara's every word, waiting for him to notice me.

Waiting for even a speck of his attention, for him to admit his undying love and sweep me off his feet.

But it's never going to happen, is it?

He doesn't see me like that. He is *never* going to see me like that.

I run through the rest of his day on autopilot, my mind off in another place, and I know that while he is away with Melissa this weekend, I will be at home wishing the time away until Monday so that I can see him again. So that I can be a personal assistant to his full and exciting life.

*Pathetic.*

"What are you waiting for?" he snaps.

I glance up. Huh? Was he talking?

"I beg your pardon?" I ask.

He gestures toward his door. "Leave. I have work to do."

"Oh . . . right." I stand, embarrassed, and walk toward the door.

"Gracie," he calls, and I turn back to him.

"Yes."

"Don't wear that perfume again."

I frown in confusion.

"I don't like it."

I bite my lip to hold my tongue and make my way out of his office. I take a seat at my desk, deflated.

*He doesn't like my perfume.*

Well, fuck him!

I do, asshole, and I'm going to slather it all over myself tomorrow until he throws up.

I might even spray it in his eyes for added effect.

One by one, the office fills up, and then like clockwork, right at nine, his office door opens, and he marches out like the king of the people.

Gabriel Ferrara in all his bossy glory.

"Maria," he barks.

"Yes, sir," she stammers.

"Why isn't the advertising report in my email?"

"I . . . I . . ."

"You what?"

"I haven't finished it yet. I thought you didn't need it until tomorrow."

"You thought wrong." He strides through the office and stops in front of Allen's desk. His eyes roam over it. "Why does your desk look like a fucking dumpster fire, Allen?"

"Ahhh." Allen begins to nervously collect the coffee cups and stacked papers. "Sorry, Mr. Ferrara. I'll clean it now."

Gabriel glances up, and his eyes meet mine. He strides back to my desk. "Miss Porter." He calls me Miss Porter in front of everyone. I'm only ever Gracie in private.

"Cancel my one-thirty appointment," he demands.

He wants to extend his lunch date with fucking Veronica.

"Impossible, Mr. Ferrara. I told you that already. Please listen," I fire back.

You have *one* hour with her, motherfucker.

*That's it.*

"Then you can go in my place, because I won't be at the meeting." He marches back into his office and slams the door.

The staff all lets out a collective sigh of relief that the tyrant is gone. I tap my pen on the desk while my blood boils.

Asshole.


The sun shines down on me as I sit in the park. My lunch break is the best part of my day. I love the fresh air, watching the dogs play off leash and the birds fly around. I never realized how much I love nature until I hardly saw any. As beautiful as New York is, it's the city of concrete.

When I moved here seven years ago, I was going to work for twelve months, get some experience with a big firm, and then move back to the suburbs somewhere.

Being infatuated with my jerk of a boss was never in the plan.

A dog runs up to me, and I bend and pat him. He's big and brown. "Hey there, cutie." I smile as I pat him.

His owner walks up. He's in running gear and all sweaty. "He likes you."

"I like him." I smile.

"Do you have a dog?" the guy asks.

"No, I wish." I keep ruffling the dog's ears. "What's his name?"

"Bernard."

I giggle. "Hello, Bernard."

"You should get a dog," the guy tells me.

"I will one day, when I buy a house in the suburbs." I smile.

"One day?" He frowns.

"When I get my act together." I smile.

Code for when I get over *him*.

"You should do it now," the guy says.

I shrug.

"What are you waiting for? Life is now. Decide what you want and take it."

I smile sadly. "I wish."

"Don't wish for it. Do it. If you want a house in the suburbs, save and buy one. You never regret the things that you do, only the things that you don't." He throws the ball, and Bernard takes off after it. "Catch you later."

"Bye." I frown after him as he runs off.

*You never regret the things that you do, only the things that you don't.*

Hmm . . .

8:20 a.m., and I inhale deeply to calm the beast within.

I'm furious.

Like a cornered animal waiting to strike.

Mr. Ferrara didn't come back from lunch yesterday. He messaged me to say he was taking the rest of the day off and to cancel all appointments.

Must have been some lunch date. He's never done that before.

This is it; she's the one. It's finally happening, and I have no one to blame but myself.

Stupid fucking fuckface.

I hate him. I hate everything about him.

I collect my diary and pen and knock tentatively on his door. "Come in," his deep voice purrs.

I open the door, and with one look at him, I melt into a puddle of patheticness. He's just gotten out of the shower; the towel is around his waist. Water is beading all over his skin, and his black hair is hanging in curls. "Good morning, my Gracie." He smiles.

My eyes drop to his big red lips, and I want to stab my eyes out with my pencil.

Anything to stop me from seeing this perfection.

"Good morning, Gabriel," I reply. "Last time I looked, I was not your Gracie."

He lets out a deep chuckle. "You will always be my Gracie." He walks to the coffee machine and begins making us coffee. "What's on the agenda today, boss?" He smiles.

I stare at him as a clusterfuck of emotion runs through me.

*Did you fuck her?*

Of course you did. I slump into my chair at his desk.

I open his computer and see him bend and pick something up from the floor. "What's this?" he asks.

"What?"

He opens a booklet. "It's a pamphlet on Sardinia."

"Oh, it must have fallen out of my notebook."

His eyes rise to meet mine. "Why do you have this?"

"Because I never want to go there. Why do you think?" I roll my eyes as I click through to his schedule.

"You want to go to Italy?" he asks, as if surprised.

"Of course I want to go to Italy," I scoff. "Everyone wants to go to Italy."

He sits down on the corner of his desk. "I'll take you one day."

I twist my lips, annoyed. I hate you . . . remember?

Get with the program.

"What, you don't believe me?" he asks.

I exhale heavily. "Will you just get dressed?"

He holds his hands out, as if surrendering. "You don't like me in a towel?"

"No. I don't, actually," I lie.

*I love you in a towel.*

"It's off-putting having to watch you get dressed every day, and frankly, very annoying. I don't make you watch me get dressed."

"Ahh . . ." He laughs. "Wouldn't that be something. Gracie Porter getting dressed in my office."

I glare at him as I point to the coffee machine. "Make my coffee, Gabriel. You have a very busy day, seeing as you didn't come back from lunch yesterday." I widen my eyes to try and stop myself from throwing a tantrum on the floor.

He smiles, amused, and begins to make our coffee.

Calm, calm . . . keep fucking calm.

"At nine thirty, you have a teleconference with London." I begin to read through his day. From my peripheral vision, I see his towel drop in his closet. I glance up to see his bare bottom, and I die a little inside.

*I really can't do this anymore.*

I love him, completely and utterly love him, and I'm just . . . I don't count to him at all.

The schedule on the screen blurs as my eyes fill with tears.

Focus.

I continue to read out his day as he dresses in his power suit and puts his aftershave on . . . and, shock of the century, I didn't wear the perfume he hates.

"And that's your day." I smile as I close his schedule. I stand and make my way to the door.

"Gracie," he calls.

"Yes." I turn back.

"Can you book me a hotel for the weekend? Somewhere hot and heavy."

I stare at him, my heart breaking in my chest.

*Ouch . . .*

"Of course, sir," I reply through the lump in my throat.

He gives me a sexy wink. "What would I ever do without you?"

*Fall in love.*

I fake a smile and walk out to my desk and slump in my chair.

That's it.

This is the sign.

I've got to get out of here.

As much as I love Gabriel Ferrara, I can't do this to myself anymore. I'm getting older, my biological clock is ticking, and I won't even date anyone because I'm so blinded by my fatal attraction to my boss. Nobody stands a chance while I work with him.

I need to start thinking with my head and do what I know is right for me.

Make a future without him.

My heart constricts at the thought of not seeing him every day. How could I bear it?

But then, it could be worse. Staying here, watching him fall in love and marry, start a family with someone else is a torture I cannot deal with.

It's time to rip off the Band-Aid. I need a fresh start.

I open Google and type into the search bar.

### Properties for sale in Greenville, Maine

I went to Greenville for a wedding a few years ago, and I just fell in love with it, and for some reason, it's always been in the back of my mind that one day I'm going to move there.

Maybe one day is now.

I scroll through the pages. Wow, it's cheap. You can buy a three-bedroom home on a quarter of an acre for a fraction of the price of New York.

I scroll through the towns and options with my mind going into overdrive.

I could get a dog of my own.

I smile, and for the first time in a long time, hope blooms in my chest.

I'm going to do it.

Gabriel's office door opens, and we all jump to attention. I quickly close my real estate screen. He marches through the office. "Geoffrey," he snaps. "This isn't a fucking marathon. Hurry up."

"Yes, Mr. Ferrara," Geoffrey stammers.

Without another word, Gabriel walks to the elevator and gets in. I stare at the doors as they close.

You're right, Gabriel; it isn't a fucking marathon.

I'm going for a sprint.


### Six months later


I print out the letter and carefully fold it. With my heart in my throat, I slide it into the envelope.

Today's the day.

I bought a house on a lake in Greenville and am moving out of state.

It's my last week working at Ferrara Industries.

*My last week with him.*

I'm about to resign; I'll only have to work the four days until Christmas. I've already booked my owed four weeks' vacation for January, and that will count toward my one month's notice that I must give.

I'm trying to make this as seamless as possible, and in a perfect world, everything would run smoothly, but I know Gabriel is going to make my life a living hell once I tell him. I've already trained Greg to cover my position while I'm away, and I'm hoping that he will get to keep my job in the New Year. And yes, it's true. I know what you're thinking, and to answer your question, yes.

Yes, I did. I trained Greg. Did you really think I was going to hand Gabriel over to another female PA to watch him get dressed every morning?

I'm moving on . . . not stupid.

Right, this is it.

I let out a deep breath and knock tentatively on the door.

"Come in," his deep voice calls.

I push the door open, and there he stands wearing white briefs, his suit and shirt in his hand. I could just cry. I would give anything to see him get dressed at the end of my bed, even just once.

*Focus.*

"Good morning, Gracie," he says as he takes his suit pants from the hanger. "You look lovely today."

*So do you.*

"Morning." I smile. My heart is racing, and I just know this isn't going to go down well.

"Before I forget, can you drop down to Tiffany's and pick up a gift for me today?"

Huh?

Actually . . . good . . . a reminder of why I'm doing this. Thank you, universe. I needed this.

Hit me straight in the face with it.

"Sure thing. What am I getting?" I ask.

He pulls his shirt around his shoulders. "I don't know. Earrings, necklace . . . some bullshit."

I roll my eyes and take out my notepad. "Um . . . What are we talking? Gold, silver . . . platinum?"

He twists his lips. "Gold."

"What's the budget?"

"I don't know, you pick."

I exhale as I write it down. "Diamonds?"

"Fuck no." He fakes a shiver, as if disgusted.

I glance up. "Why fuck no?"

"I'll only ever buy a diamond for someone I love."

"You should probably buy yourself a few, then," I mutter, deadpan.

He smirks as he buttons up his shirt. "I *am* the diamond."

I roll my eyes. No shit, Sherlock. A diamond python. Looks pretty . . . but if left unattended, will suffocate you to death.

"Okay . . . if you say so." I roll my eyes.

*Thump, thump, thump* goes my heart. I can't wait until the end of our meeting; I need to tell him now. I pull out the envelope and hold it out to him. "I've got something for you."

He turns, and his eyes fall to the envelope and then rise up to me.

"What's this?"

I swallow the lump in my throat. "It's my resignation."

His face falls. "What?"

"I . . ."

"No."

"Gabriel . . . I'm not asking for your permission. I *am* leaving."

He snatches the envelope from my hand and tears it in half, then throws it in the trash bin. "You will do no such thing."

*Here we go.*

He marches to the door and opens it in a rush. "Go back to your desk and get to work."

"No."

"Do. As. I. Say," he growls.

"No."

"Do not tell me no!" He's about to go into cardiac arrest. "You work for me, not the other way around."

"You're in your underpants, you know?" I gesture down at his body. "The whole office could walk in and see you."

"I fucking know that!" he screams, but he must realize that I'm right and slams the door shut again. He marches over to his suit as it lies on the chair.

"And where do you think you're going to work, huh?" He picks up his pants, and being so angry, he struggles to put them on. "Do you think you are going to work with a competitor? Because I call fucking bullshit."

"I'm taking some time off for me." I cross my arms as I watch his tantrum unfold.

He flicks his pants angrily in front of him. "You can't afford to take time off."

"Yes, I can."

"Well, you can get this harebrained idea out of your head right fucking now, Grace," he yells. He pulls his pants up so fast that his leg gets caught, and he nearly falls over. "Fuck off!" he cries in frustration.

I roll my lips to hide my smile.

"Get out!" he screams. The veins in his forehead are bulging, and he's going red.

I let out a deep exhale. "There is no need to be this dramatic, Gabriel."

"I tore up your letter. It doesn't count. Take the day off and come to your senses."

"That's not happening. I've already emailed my resignation to HR and will be finishing up on December twenty-second."

"What?" he explodes. "That's four days away."

"I know."

"Get out!" he screams as he loses all control.

"Fine." I walk out, and he slams the door behind me. It echoes through the whole of New York.

Jeez.

I sit for a moment.

*Bang.*

I jump when I hear something hit the back of his door; I think it was his pen holder.

Ugh . . . He's always so over the top.

*Bzzzzz.*

I push the button to answer my intercom. "Yes, Mr. Ferrara."

"Get to work!"

I smirk. Man . . . I need caffeine. It's way too early for all this drama.

I make my way to the kitchen, and I hear the elevator ding.

Gabriel comes flying out of the office like a hornet.

"There is a gas leak on this floor. Go away," he yells to Geoffrey.

"What?" poor Geoffrey stammers, wide eyed. "Should I call someone?"

"I already have. Work from level two today," he barks. "Tell everyone else from this floor to work from there too. Put a note in the elevator."

I pinch the bridge of my nose . . . Seriously?

This is going to be the day from hell.

I walk back out into the office with my cup of coffee.

"We need to work from level two today," Geoffrey tells me. "There's a gas leak."

"Oh, okay." I act oblivious. "I'll grab my things."

Gabriel narrows his eyes and points to his office. "A word, Miss Porter," he sneers.

Geoffrey looks between us in confusion.

"It's okay, Geoffrey. You go on without me. Mr. Ferrara has been sniffing too much gas. He's having a meltdown."

Geoffrey's eyes widen as he looks between us. "Oh no. Should I call an ambulance?"

"Go to level two, Geoffrey!" Gabriel screams.

Geoffrey scrambles to get his things and half runs to the elevator.

I sit down and open my computer. Gabriel paces back and forth in front of my desk. His hands are on his hips, and his eyes are crazy.

"Fine, twenty percent pay raise; that's it," he snaps.

I stay silent.

He continues to pace. "Hardball, huh . . . twenty-five percent, and that's it."

I begin to type as I act uninterested. "No thanks."

"What do you mean, *no thanks*?" he barks.

"It's not about the money."

"Everything is about money," he fires back.

I roll my eyes and go back to my computer.

"Fifty percent pay raise, and that's totally fucking it."

I keep typing. "No."

"Double your wages, and do not fucking talk to me again. This is daylight robbery!" he screams. "You are trying to fuck me up the ass, and I won't have it."

I was expecting a tantrum, but this is the living end. I shake my head in disgust. "Can you even hear yourself right now? The last thing I want to do is fuck you up the ass."

He puts his hands on his hips and begins to pace again. His mind is racing.

I continue pretending to type, and I do have to admit, watching him grovel is doing wonders for my confidence.

"Fine, don't go to Tiffany's today; it doesn't matter. I won't get her the gift."

Huh?

I look up from my computer. *Does he know?*

"Why would you say that?"

"That's it, isn't it?" he says.

"We are not having this conversation, Gabriel," I snap.

"Yes. We. Fucking. Are."

"I'm leaving because I bought myself a house."

He takes a step back, completely shocked. "You bought a house?"

I nod. "In Greenville."

"Where's that?"

"Maine."

"Why the *fuck* would you buy a house in Maine?" He screws up his face in horror.

"Because . . . it's time."

"For what?" he bellows. "To turn fucking Amish?"

"I want a family home with a garden and a dog, maybe even a family. Renting a tiny apartment in New York is never going to get me there."

He blinks as he processes my words.

"I need to get out of New York, Gabriel."

"New York is your home."

"New York is *your* home. I've been here for eight years, and I . . ." I shrug, not wanting to elaborate on my loneliness. "I haven't met anyone, and it's time for me to pull up my big girl panties and move on."

He pauses for a moment, as if processing my words.

"You're leaving me?" he whispers.

"I have to."

His eyes search mine.

"I'm sorry."

His jaw clenches, and then without another word, he marches back into his office and slams the door. It echoes as the walls shake.

Hot tears burn my eyes.

*You were supposed to beg me to stay.*

It's 6:00 p.m., and everyone has cleared out for the day. Gabriel hasn't left his office all day, not even for lunch.

I've been hoping to have a quick word on his way out, but there's still no sign of him.

The office is deathly silent, and I quietly knock on his door.

"Yes," he calls.

I open it and peep in. "I'm going to head off soon."

He doesn't look up from his computer. "Okay."

I wait for him to look up at me . . . he doesn't.

"Close the door on your way out," he replies flatly as he picks up a pen and starts signing some documents.

Great. Now that the tantrum is over, he's going to give me the silent treatment. "Are you not talking to me?" I ask.

"I have nothing to say." He keeps writing.

"Gabriel . . ."

He lets out an overexaggerated sigh as he glances up. "What is it?"

"I don't want this to end badly."

"It's already ended. You can finish now. No need to come back and work this week. I've signed the last of your leave documents. You are free to go."

I get a lump in my throat as I stare at him . . . That's it?

*He really doesn't care.*

He keeps his head down as he writes, seemingly totally unaffected.

I will not cry in front of this selfish bastard. It's all about him . . . it's always been about him.

I quietly close his office door and walk to my desk. I take my bag from the drawer, and with one last long look around the office, I feel my heart break.

Maybe he's right. Maybe I *am* doing the wrong thing. Who's to say I'm going to like Greenville, anyway?

*No.*

This is what he wants. If I give up on my dream now, I'm only cheating myself.

No pain, no gain.


The thing about being a glutton for punishment is this . . .

Nothing.

Turns out that I'm a total ho for gluttony punishment, and there is no excuse for my needy behavior. After tossing and turning all night, there's only one thing I know.

I am *not* a quitter.

Just as I said I would, I will work until the end of the week, and then I'm going to the Christmas party looking shit hot, and then I'm walking out on my terms. He cannot finish me up on a whim.

Who the fuck does he think he is, anyway?

Right at 8:20 a.m., I knock on his door.

"Yes," he barks.

I smirk. He's annoyed that I came back. Well . . . prepare to be angered, fucker. I open the door in a rush and step back as my eyes widen in horror.

He's making coffee in his briefs. Black, sexy Calvin Klein ones.

Lingerie for men.

He turns toward me, giving me a full frontal. "What are you doing here?"

I open my mouth to say something, but no words come out.

"Ahhh." My eyes bulge from their sockets. "What are you doing . . ." I put my hands up toward his body. I'm flabbergasted as my eyes drop to the bulge in his briefs. "Doing that," I gasp.

"I'm making fucking coffee. What does it look like?"

Something snaps in my brain. "It looks like you're being a poser, that's what it looks like. This isn't a Calvin Klein runway show, you know."

"Nobody has a gun to your head to look." He angrily tips the coffee into his cup. "I think you like what you see, that's what I think."

"Oh . . . you think that!" I yell, infuriated that he's onto me. "I think you're . . . hideous."

"Hideous?" he screams, infuriated. "*You're* hideous."

Something about my boss standing there in his underpants yelling that I'm hideous tickles my fancy, and I burst out laughing.

"Nothing is funny about this," he fumes. "Look away while I dress."

"Oh please, I've seen it all now," I scoff. "Stop acting frigid. We both know you're not." I sit down and open his computer.

"Apparently I'm too hideous to look at," he mutters as he disappears into his closet.

I smirk as I open his schedule.

*Not really.*


I take one last long look in the mirror.

This is it.

My last time at Ferrara Industries, the Christmas party at the office.

Most people stayed back straight from work, but I wanted to duck home and shower, try and pull a miracle together and make myself irresistible.

I'm wearing a red wrap dress, and I feel self-conscious as fuck.

I never wear red; I have red hair, and that's enough. Well, it's not really red; it's a deep auburn, but you get the gist. It's down and full, my makeup a little sexier than usual.

The dress has a V-neck that shows a peek of cleavage and a tie around the waist. It feels happy and Christmassy. I wanted to wear something different—he's never seen me in something like this before, so I wanted it to be a wow . . . not sure if it actually is, but that's the plan.

I am waxed, fake tanned, and moisturized to within an inch of my life. Who knew it took so much work to look hot? I really need to step up my self-care routine when I get on the dating scene in Greenville.

I smile to myself. *The dating scene in Greenville.*

That's the first time I've let myself consider the possibilities of dating in my new life.

Apart from the leaving-Gabriel part, I'm really beginning to get excited. I've been saving for years, and with the cost of the house being cheaper than I thought, I have enough money to buy myself new furniture and do up the house exactly how I want it.

I even booked myself a trip to Hawaii.

Who even am I?

Right. I collect my coat and bag. Let's do this.


Carols ring out as the band onstage does their thing.

The ground floor of Ferrara Industries has been transformed into a magical wonderland. The Christmas decorations are over the top, and waiters are walking around with silver trays of eggnog and champagne.

People are wearing bright dresses and Christmas outfits; laughter rings out as people chatter, and the mood is jovial and jolly. I'm glad I wore my red dress now; I feel better knowing that everyone else is dressed up too.

It was the last day of work today, and everyone is pumped for the holidays and celebrating together.

I walk in and, feeling self-conscious, flag down the first waiter I see. "I'll have one of those, please."

He smiles as I take a glass of champagne. "Thank you." I smile.

I wonder, Could I take two?

No, don't be an animal.

"Grace," I hear someone call. I turn to see Geoffrey and some of the others from our floor.

"Hi." I make my way over.

"Wow, you look gorgeous." Geoffrey smiles as he looks me up and down. "Like, really, really good."

"She does, doesn't she," says Paul.

"Who knew you were so hot, Porter."

I smile as I take a sip of my champagne.

*Awkward . . .*

Fuck it.

Don't tell me this dress is going to bait the wrong one. I try to act casual as I look around. "Where is everyone?"

And by everyone, I mean your boss.

"The girls are at the cocktail bar, and accounting is dancing. Marlene from level three flashed her tits onstage."

I giggle as I scan the room, and then I stop still as my eyes meet Gabriel's.

He's wearing a dark-gray suit, a white shirt, a Santa hat, and my heart on the bottom of his shoe. He gives me a slow, sexy smile and raises his glass.

I smile and raise my glass right back.

He goes back to talking to the people he's standing with, and I watch him, waiting for him to glance back over at me.

He doesn't.

My heart free-falls from my chest at his totally unaffected demeanor. It's not going to happen . . . is it?

I don't know who I was kidding.

"Tell us about your new house." Geoffrey smiles excitedly. "I can't believe you're actually doing this."

"Me neither," chimes in Paul.

I smile, grateful to the people who actually do give a crap about what I'm doing.

I drain my glass; I need to forget about my asshole boss and just enjoy the night.


It's 11:30 p.m., and Gabriel left hours ago. He didn't even say goodbye.

Wow.

More than wow. *Fucking* wow.

What a prick!

I'm going to get going. My eyes linger on the elevator, and I just . . . I want to see my office one last time. I don't know why, but I do. I take the elevator to the top floor and make my way to my desk.

I look out over the view. It's so different at night up here. The lights of New York light up the entire skyline.

Unlike the busy and bustling daytime.

It's peaceful.

Serene.

I sit at my desk and look around.

So, this is what closure feels like. The end of one era and the beginning of another. I swivel on my chair, feeling proud of myself.

I did it. I made a plan and stuck to it. Did exactly what I needed to do.

I'm moving on.

I sit for a long time as I process everything that has happened over the last eight years. The dressing schedule sessions, the fights and tantrums. The sarcastic snark. The laughter, the crush.

Oh . . . the crush. I crushed hard, but in my defense, I am only human.

I walk to his office and open the door; it's darkened, lit only by a lamp and his bathroom light. I look over his desk and smile sadly. It's hard to believe I'll never see him sitting here again. I run my hand over his desk, the back of his chair, the keyboard that houses his fingers all day.

His presence is so strong in here, I can almost feel him.

"Couldn't even say goodbye," I mutter to myself as I cross my arms and look out over the view.

"Goodbye," a deep voice says.

I spin to see Gabriel sitting in the darkened corner of the room.

He's got an amber drink in his hand, his elbows resting on his thighs as he watches me.

"Gabriel," I gasp. "I . . . didn't see you."

He stands and puts his drink down; his eyes are dark and dangerous, and he walks over to me and stands so that his face is an inch away from mine.

The air leaves my lungs as I feel the heat from his body.

"I didn't give you your Christmas bonus yet," he murmurs.

## *The Bonus* is available to read now.

# ABOUT THE AUTHOR

A psychologist in her former life, T L Swan is now seriously addicted to the thrill of writing and can't imagine a time when she wasn't. She resides in Sydney, Australia, where she is living out her own happily ever after with her husband and their three children.

# Follow the Author on Amazon

If you enjoyed this book, follow T L Swan on Amazon to be notified when the author releases a new book!
To do this, please follow these instructions:

### Desktop:

1) Search for the author's name on Amazon or in the Amazon App.
2) Click on the author's name to arrive on their Amazon page.
3) Click the "Follow" button.

### Mobile and Tablet:

1) Search for the author's name on Amazon or in the Amazon App.
2) Click on one of the author's books.
3) Click on the author's name to arrive on their Amazon page.
4) Click the "Follow" button.

### Kindle eReader and Kindle App:

If you enjoyed this book on a Kindle eReader or in the Kindle App, you will find the author "Follow" button after the last page.